... ...nna is one of Ireland's favourite authors and a regular number one bestseller. She is the winner of the prestigious International Reading Association Award and is a regular contributor on radio and TV. She lives in Blackrock, Dublin, with her husband and family.

For more information on Marita Conlon-McKenna and her books, see her website at www.maritaconlonmckenna.com

By Marita Conlon-McKenna

THE MAGDALEN
PROMISED LAND
MIRACLE WOMAN
THE STONE HOUSE
THE HAT SHOP ON THE CORNER
THE MATCHMAKER
MOTHER OF THE BRIDE
A TASTE FOR LOVE
THREE WOMEN

The Rose Garden

Marita McKenna

TRANSWORLD IRELAND

TRANSWORLD IRELAND
An imprint of The Random House Group Limited
20 Vauxhall Bridge Road, London SW1V 2SA
www.transworldbooks.co.uk

THE ROSE GARDEN
A TRANSWORLD IRELAND BOOK: 9781848272088

First published in 2013
by Transworld Ireland,
a division of Transworld Publishers
Transworld Ireland paperback edition published 2014
Transworld Ireland paperback edition reissued 2014

**Bracknell Forest
Borough Council**

5430000033397 0	
Askews & Holts	2014

Addresses for Random House Group Ltd companies outside the UK
can be found at: www.randomhouse.co.uk
The Random House Group Ltd Reg. No. 954009

The Random House Group Limited supports the Forest Stewardship
Council® (FSC®), the leading international forest-certification
organisation. Our books carrying the FSC label are printed on
FSC®-certified paper. FSC is the only forest-certification scheme supported
by the leading environmental organisations, including Greenpeace.
Our paper procurement policy can be found at
www.randomhouse.co.uk/environment

Typeset in 11/14.5pt Sabon by Falcon Oast Graphic Art Ltd.
Printed and bound by CPI Group (UK) Ltd, Croydon, CR0 4YY.

2 4 6 8 10 9 7 5 3 1

For my father, Patrick J. Conlon –
a man who loved his rose garden.

'To be happy for an hour, have a glass of wine. To be happy for a day, read a book. To be happy for a week, take a wife. To be happy for ever, make a garden.'
– *Proverb*

Prologue

Molly Hennessy stood in the garden of Mossbawn House taking in the view.

She loved this old house, standing amidst acres of land made up of gardens and woods and grassy fields only fifteen miles from Kilkenny. As she looked out over the garden, with its large herbaceous borders, lavender walk and lawn, the pond with its wooden bridge, the distant oakwoods and the kitchen garden with her badly neglected vegetable patch, she felt such a strong emotion. She didn't know how she could ever bear to leave it.

But already the garden was falling into disarray, with weeds and brambles creeping where they shouldn't be. The neat hedges and paths were now straggly and untidy, the borders overgrown and messy, the lawn and grass far too long.

She was doing her best to maintain the place, but she knew in her heart it wasn't enough. The size of the garden and grounds of the old country house was proving far too much for her. It was a near impossible task for a woman on her own to manage.

She and David had fallen in love with the place from almost the minute they had seen it – Mossbawn House, a faded photo in an auctioneer's window. Coming to view the neglected old Georgian house with its large hall, dusty drawing room and library, its run-down orangery with panes of broken or cracked glass, they had both instantly decided that this was the place they wanted to live. David had been determined to make it their home. They had sunk every penny they had into buying it, taking out a massive mortgage, but David considered it a very good investment and they'd been full of all sorts of plans for the old house, both of them excited about it becoming a perfect family home.

Mossbawn House had welcomed them, and over the years it had filled with family and friends, parties and gatherings. Work on the house was ongoing: over the years they had fixed the roof, then the windows, replaced ancient plumbing and installed gas heating, lovingly restored old plasterwork and woodwork, and eventually even restored the old orangery, so that Mossbawn was once again a beautiful home. There was still work to do, but they were proud of what they had achieved. Restoring the house was more than a project – it was a labour of love and they were both looking forward to spending the rest of their days there together.

That was the plan – well, the dream. But David's death a few months ago had utterly changed everything. Devastated, Molly tried to cope with his loss, struggling to keep herself going, let alone the old house.

The girls too were distraught at the sudden loss of their beloved dad. They were both in college, Grace in Dublin and Emma at Galway University. They tried to come home at weekends to help and be supportive, but more and more Molly was left rattling around the place on her own.

When David was alive everything had seemed perfect. He had loved the garden and the house and ensured that everything was kept running smoothly. Year after year they had enjoyed family life in this beautiful place, but now Molly was unsure of the future.

Keeping the old house was an expensive business. The bank had contacted her again and again; she had tried to ignore them, but knew that she could no longer put off meeting with them. Without David's income to help with the constant bills she had no idea how she was going to survive ... Her family and friends were advising her to be sensible: sell up, downsize and move to a smaller home in Kilfinn, or move back to the city. Perhaps they were right, but she couldn't imagine leaving Mossbawn behind and trying to make a fresh start.

She had absolutely no idea how she was ever going to keep this beautiful old house, but looking around her at the garden and grounds Molly was determined somehow to hold on to Mossbawn, the home she and David loved so much.

Chapter One

Molly spread some honey on a slice of brown bread as she listened to the radio. More doom and gloom on the morning news. Was it any wonder that the people were downhearted?

Having breakfast like this, sitting alone in the kitchen, was something she still found hard to get used to. She missed having David to talk to. Now the only one to listen to her was her little Jack Russell, Daisy.

She was up early this morning, as she was driving to Dublin for a meeting with the bank, something she was absolutely dreading. Her neighbour, Rena, had offered to take Daisy and she would drop her off there en route.

Later, leaving Kilfinn and heading up on to the motorway, Molly had to admit she was looking forward to a few days in Dublin, with the chance to see her twenty-year-old daughter Grace and to catch up with a few of her old friends. Roz had insisted that she stay with her in Donnybrook.

Over the past few days she had gone through all her bank statements and accounts, with everything spread out on the big dining-room table as she tried to make some sense of the debits and credits and establish the exact financial position she was in. Following David's death their remaining mortgage had been cleared by their mortgage protection insurance policy, and another life insurance policy had also kicked in, but Molly was still struggling to pay off the various other loans they had taken out to do essential repairs on Mossbawn.

Going over it and over it again, she realized that, except for the life insurance payout, she had absolutely no income of her own. They had virtually no savings and she'd no idea what the pension portfolio the bank had recommended for when David retired was worth now. They had barely made a dent in some of the loans they had taken out for running repairs and renovations, but David hadn't worried about it as he had taken the view that he was generating an income and they were looking after their home. Like every other legal firm, Coleman Quinn, where David had worked as a partner, had seen its business affected by the downturn. Although David had always maintained that they were financially secure, now, without his earnings, Molly had no idea how she would survive. She was dreading her midday meeting with the bank manager. Her brother-in-law Bill, an accountant, had offered to come with her to the meeting, but she had declined and arranged to see him afterwards when she could go through things with him.

As she neared Dublin, she began mentally to run through possible questions that she had for the bank. It had started to rain and the traffic was terrible as she wound her way through the city streets towards the bank's head office. Molly prayed that she would find a car park. She felt flustered enough about meeting the bank manager without the ordeal of not being able to park.

'It's good to see you, Molly,' said Dermot Brennan, the manager, welcoming her to his third-floor office. 'I'm so sorry about David. It must be very hard for you and your daughters.'

Molly nodded, not trusting herself to speak. David's death had been so sudden. A strong, fit man like David having a massive brain aneurysm and never even regaining consciousness . . . it still shocked her.

Dermot ordered coffee for them both and she was glad – caffeine was just what she needed. Dermot had been looking after their accounts for years. Sitting across from him, she could see that he looked tense, as if he was going to be the bearer of bad news. Molly braced herself as he began to produce facts and figures, and she listened in dismay at the decline in value of David's pension fund.

'Should I use it to pay off the loans?'

'You could withdraw some of the funds, but it's probably better to stick it out and hope for an increase in values, an upturn in the market,' he advised. 'Either way it is a bit of a gamble.'

Molly had always hated gambling; it was something she and David would never contemplate. David had been sensible, paying into a proper pension fund recommended by the bank and now where had it got them?

'What should I do?'

'Obviously the fact that the mortgage on Mossbawn has been cleared is of immense value, but it's the other outstanding loans that worry us. The bank is concerned about how these loans will be serviced given your current circumstances.'

'I have no idea,' she admitted honestly. 'I've got the life insurance policy money but that's about all. David's pension, from what you are telling me, is worth nothing by all accounts and I'm not working.'

'The important thing for the bank is that you find some way to clear these loans or reduce them to a manageable scale. Would you consider using the insurance money you received for David's death?'

Molly didn't believe what he was saying. That insurance money was all she had.

'Or perhaps you'd prefer to free up some of your assets?'

'What assets?'

'Well, there is the house itself, of course, now that it is "mortgage free",' he said calmly. 'Perhaps you should consider selling Mossbawn, though unfortunately property prices are low at present.'

'Sell the house? It's my home, the girls' home . . .'

'Then perhaps there may be some antiques or heirlooms or the like?'

Molly had to stop herself from laughing aloud at the thought of some valuable undiscovered heirloom! If there were anything of value they would have sold it by now.

'I need to think about this,' she said, trying not to give in to the panicky feeling that made her feel like she couldn't get a breath.

'Of course,' he said, 'of course.'

'I'm meeting my brother-in-law Bill later. He's an accountant. I'll talk to him about it.'

'I know how difficult this must be for you, Molly,' Dermot said apologetically. 'But the crash in the market and drop in bank shares is something none of us could ever have expected.'

She didn't know what to say to him. She had no intention of letting him off the hook.

'My own pension is only a fraction of what it should be,' he admitted, 'and I'm due to retire next year so it is a worry, a big worry.'

'Perhaps you will have to sell your home?' she offered testily.

At least he had the good grace to look discomfited.

'Molly, we need to work things out in the most financially beneficial way for you and the bank in order to ensure a way for you to clear or pay down these loans and the overdraft.'

'David was putting money into his pension here in the bank month after month under the impression that he was building up a nice nest egg for when we were older and he'd retired,' she said angrily.

'Nest eggs are few and far between these days.'

'I have to think about all this, talk to the girls, get Bill's advice . . .'

'Of course, but I shall expect to hear back from you within the next few weeks,' he reminded her firmly, standing up from his desk. 'Then we can clarify the new loan-repayment schedule.'

Walking away from the bank, Molly was shaking. Her world was falling apart and she had no idea what to do. She just longed to be out of the city and back home in Mossbawn, far from all this stress and pressure.

Chapter Two

Walking to the nearby Merrion Hotel, Molly's mind was in turmoil. As she entered the old Georgian building opposite Leinster House she was relieved to see that Bill O'Reilly, her brother-in-law, was already sitting in the hotel's comfortable drawing room perusing the *Financial Times*.

He got to his feet the minute he saw her approach. Bill, as handsome and strong as ever, was sporting a tan and was more relaxed than she had seen him in a long time. A bit greyer, but still dressed immaculately in a good shirt and smart blazer.

'How are you, Molly dear?' he asked as they hugged each other.

'Upset,' she admitted.

She could see concern flit across his broad face as she sat in the plush, gold-striped velvet armchair across from his.

'I've just come from meeting the bank manager,' she confided, 'and basically they want me to consolidate the loans and pay them back immediately. He even suggested that I sell Mossbawn!'

'Oh dear,' said Bill. 'I suppose it was to be expected, given the situation.'

'I have no idea what to do . . . what David would have wanted . . .'

'First let's order something – you must be exhausted,' he coaxed.

'A double brandy, that's what I need,' she joked.

'Not to be recommended this time of the day,' he smiled, 'but what about the warm chicken salad, or soup, or the smoked salmon?'

Molly studied the menu quickly and opted for the chicken salad.

Bill sat back, listening as she began to tell him about her earlier meeting. Being an accountant, he had a sound business brain and she knew that she could trust him to have her best interest at heart. He was a good man, the man her sister Ruth had fallen in love with and married. When David had died last year, Bill was the first on the phone to her, not just to commiserate but to help organize things. He'd been wonderful, as he was the one person who knew and understood exactly how she was feeling – for he had lost Ruth a few years ago.

Her sister and Bill had been such a great couple, with three great kids. She and David had always loved when they came to visit them at Mossbawn and the two families had got together at weekends and holidays. She missed those days – and still missed Ruth terribly. Losing her older sister to cancer twelve years ago had been such a blow. Bill and their three children, Liz, Kim and Mike, had been left utterly devastated.

'Molly, at least you are lucky that you own Mossbawn outright and have no outstanding mortgage on the place,' Bill said, serious. 'Mortgages – that's what's crippling most people.'

'But there are debts,' she admitted. 'There are the loans for the money we spent on the house. David had always planned to pay them back bit by bit over the years.'

'Loans can be restructured,' he murmured firmly.

'But David's pension is practically worth nothing,' she said angrily.

'Some of my clients have lost almost everything,' Bill admitted, 'and even Carole's taken a huge hit with her pension.'

Molly blushed. She had avoided asking him about his wife up to now. She still found it so hard to accept that Bill was remarried; that despite his love for Ruth he had managed to find himself another wife.

'How is Carole?'

'She's fine,' he smiled. 'She's good for me! We play golf, travel, go to the theatre . . . We've managed to downsize and de-clutter our lives.'

'So I've heard.'

'The girls been complaining again?' he joked.

She smiled. She was in regular contact with her two nieces, who kept her up to date with the various goings-on of their new stepmother and her influence over their father.

'I am lucky to have found Carole,' he said slowly. 'You know I wasn't very good at being on my own.'

'I hate it,' she said vehemently. 'I just hate being on my own . . . I'm not used to it!'

'Molly, I understand, believe me,' he said gently. 'I know how much you miss David.'

'Every day,' she whispered. 'But at times like this . . .'

'Listen, why don't you give me a copy of all the relevant accounts and statements and interest payments and bank stuff and I'll see what I can do?'

She watched as he flicked through her folder, extracting exactly what he needed.

'I think the bank just want me to sell Mossbawn,' she sighed.

'Well, that would certainly solve their problems,' he quipped, 'but you must only consider selling the house if it is what you really want to do.'

'I can't even think at the moment,' she admitted. 'Half the time my brain feels like slush. But the house is big – it's too big to manage on my own without him.'

'Molly, don't rush into any decisions. Let me look at the figures first,' he said calmly, 'before you do anything.'

'Sure,' she said, relieved that Bill was there to advise her.

Over coffee they put business matters aside, chatting about their kids and their latest antics, as Bill showed her photos of his grandchildren on his phone. Finishing up, he insisted on paying for their lunch.

'I'll be in touch with you if I need anything else,' he promised, standing up. 'We should probably aim to talk once I've had a chance to go through everything.'

'Bill, that would be great.'

'Why don't you come and have dinner or lunch with Carole and me the next time you're in Dublin?' he offered.

'Thanks, Bill.' Molly knew in her heart that having lunch with the woman who had replaced her sister was something she could never do.

Walking out to the street they said goodbye and headed in opposite directions. Realizing that the time on the meter had nearly expired, Molly had to rush back to where she had parked her car, hoping that she hadn't been clamped.

Chapter Three

They say things come in threes . . .

First Kim had lost her job . . . then her boyfriend . . . and now she was losing her home. Her life was a *disaster*!

Standing among the jumble of boxes and bags and suitcases scattered around her feet on the floor as she packed up and got ready to leave the apartment, Kim O'Reilly realized that this was all she possessed. Shoes, handbags and clothes, all with the right fancy labels but nothing worth a fraction of what she had paid for it . . . Her life was a mess, everything collapsing around her, and there was absolutely nothing she could do about it.

She was moving out of the apartment she'd shared with Gareth, her boyfriend, for the past year and a half. She'd been happy, looking forward to the future, to getting engaged and married like some of their friends. But then Gareth had suddenly ended it. Maybe she was stupid or dumb, but Kim certainly hadn't seen it coming . . . hadn't expected their relationship to break up the way it did with both of them angry and hating each other. Now she felt so alone and hurt, and she couldn't imagine her life without him.

In the kitchen, she checked the pristine shelves of expensive glasses and plates and dinnerware. They'd bought most of this stuff together, imagining a lifetime of dinner and supper parties and shared meals. In fairness, Gareth had paid for most of it, so he should keep it. She grabbed her two favourite mugs – one with a dog on it and the other a souvenir of New York; her rainbow-coloured pasta bowl and plate set; and her Cheeky Pigs apron – Gareth would never use that anyway. She took two paintings of Evie's that hung in the dining area down off the wall. No way she would let Gareth have them!

Sniffing back her tears, she continued to pack. A part of her was waiting . . . hoping for the impossible, a phone call or a text message from Gareth telling her to stay, that they would sort it out, try to work things out . . . but there was nothing, just utter silence – a miserable reminder of the end of their fractured relationship and her need to move out and try to begin again. How she was ever going to do that was utterly beyond her, but staying here on her own and trying to pay the massive rent was not an option.

In the bathroom she collected her shower cap and

toothbrush, all the face oils and creams and scrubs that littered her side of the bathroom cabinet. The pile was growing and back in the bedroom she shoved them into her smaller weekend case. Pulling her bundle of glossy *Style* and *Celeb* magazines from the bedside locker, she marched back into the kitchen and junked them in the fancy silver recycling bin.

Looking around her, she seemed to have managed to remove all traces of her having shared Gareth's life here for those nineteen months. The apartment had returned to the way it was before she had moved in with him. This was so shit. She had nothing . . .

It took three trips in the lift, laden down with all her bags and boxes and two suitcases, to get all her stuff squashed into her car. Heading back up to the fourth floor for the last time, Kim stood for a few minutes, overwhelmed, taking in the ceiling-to-ground glass windows of the living room which overlooked Dublin's former docklands. With the cream leather couches and expensive circular dining table and coordinating display unit, it was all so perfect. The kitchen, the massive bedroom, even the silver-and-grey bathroom – too perfect . . . She didn't fit into it, this place, this life with Gareth Allen. She wasn't perfect enough.

Taking her keys from the ring, she put them on the table and, closing the door, began to walk as fast as she could, wanting to get the hell out of there before she broke down again. Moving out was the end – the end to her life with Gareth.

* * *

26

Driving out of the city towards Stepaside, Kim tried to stay calm and focus on her driving – the last thing she needed was to be in a car accident. Her sister Liz had insisted that she come and stay with her and Joe until she got back on her feet.

Okay, her friends Alex and Evie had also offered to put her up for a few days, but sleeping on a couch or a futon in their already cramped apartments for the foreseeable future didn't seem a good idea. Besides, Alex's girlfriend Vicky hated her and Evie's tiny flat at the top of a Georgian building was so cluttered with Evie's art paraphernalia that she doubted she would fit!

Kim braced herself for that barrage of questions she would face once her sister got her hands on her. Liz had offered to help her pack up and move, but she had just wanted to do it on her own. But at least going to stay at Liz's she didn't have to pretend or put on a brave face. Liz knew exactly how utterly shit her life was at this present moment.

Finding herself unemployed, homeless and single at almost twenty-nine was a nightmare. Eight months ago she'd lost her job in the Irish Bank Group. Kim had been one of over two hundred staff members called up to the big HR department in the sky to be given a spiel about the company's need to cut costs in the current economic climate and rationalize by closing departments and branches. She'd worked there since college and had never particularly liked her job, but had enjoyed the salary and benefits that came with working in a busy banking team. Confident of her ability to find a new job, she had signed up immediately with about twelve recruitment firms, but months later still found herself unemployed and considered almost unemployable.

'The world is full of bankers,' one of the recruiters had told her, suggesting she return to college or retrain for some other type of career, or emigrate.

Gareth had been really supportive at first: encouraging when she went for interviews, helping her to re-draft her CV over and over again, but as time went on and no job offers came, his attitude to her began to alter. Her finances were tight and she struggled to pay her share of the rent and expenses, and as her savings dwindled and her cash dried up things had somehow changed. Maybe Gareth had lost respect for her, found her less interesting, less attractive. She had no idea.

It was disheartening sending out CV after CV and getting so little response, but she tried to stay positive, keep in touch with people, tried to make contacts and chase up jobs. Gareth worked long, crazy hours. His job in aircraft-leasing was stressful enough, but her seeming lack of career focus irritated him.

She signed up for a diploma in website design, a course her friend Evie had told her about. It was tough and very technical, but she was really enjoying it. Then one night a week she was doing a digital photography class – something she really liked; and she had taken up running, as it was much cheaper than being a member of a gym. At home she made great efforts to keep the apartment looking well and to cook healthy organic meals, but Gareth barely noticed what she put in front of him, protesting he was on a high-protein diet or not hungry. He stayed late at the office and often did not return home until she was in bed. Instead of coming together as a couple, they had bit by bit grown apart.

Then last Saturday, after they'd had breakfast, he sat down seriously and said, coldly and calmly, that it wasn't working out, and that he believed it was time for them to call an end to a relationship that clearly wasn't going anywhere. Stunned, Kim had begged him to give them a second chance, that once she'd found a job things would go back to the way they were before, but Gareth had made it clear that this decision was final and what he was doing was for the best for the two of them.

'You'll see that, Kim, believe me you will.'

Being a gentleman, he had offered to move out and let her continue to live in the apartment, but knowing the state of her finances Kim had realized that there was utterly no way she could afford to stay on and rent such an expensive place. So Gareth had gone to stay with his best mate, Cormac, for a few days while she packed up and got ready to move out.

Liz lived in one of the many estates built in the foothills of the Dublin Mountains. Kim edged her car up past the massive Dundrum Shopping Centre, trying to force herself to concentrate as she changed lanes and headed on to the busy Sandyford Road. She cursed as she almost missed the turn off the Stepaside Road, but somehow she managed to swing the car into Holly Park. A minute later, as she pulled up, she spotted her sister's silver family car, then her three-year-old niece Ava waving madly at her from the window.

Liz ran out the front door to meet her. Kim sat frozen solid in the car, unable to move as heavy tears slid down her face. It was as if a huge dam had burst inside her. Wordlessly, Liz opened the passenger door and, lifting two big plastic bags on to her lap, sat in beside her.

'It's okay, Kim – everything is going to be okay, I promise.'

Kim clung to her sister as Liz hugged her and told her that she was safe now . . .

Chapter Four

Kim managed to stop crying, dry her snotty nose and blot off her smudged mascara before she went inside. Ava and Finn, her little niece and nephew, flung themselves at her like two puppies, as her brother-in-law Joe welcomed her and offered to carry two or three of her bags upstairs.

'The dinner is just about ready,' said Liz, lifting Finn into his highchair.

Three quarters of a bottle of Sauvignon Blanc later, and after a plate of Liz's renowned spicy chicken Madras with poppadums and all the trimmings, Kim had to admit she felt somewhat better . . . certainly less alone.

'I'll never see Gareth or talk to him again!' she declared, feeling utterly desolate as they sat around the kitchen table.

'Highly unlikely. We're living in Dublin,' Joe reminded her, 'not London or New York.'

'But it's so awful. I'll never wake up in his arms or sleep with him again.'

'I should hope bloody not!' added Liz furiously. 'Gareth doesn't deserve a girlfriend like you. He's a cold-hearted shit to treat you the way he has done, Kim. You have to realize that! A decent guy wouldn't care if you are broke or unemployed. He'd have stood by you and loved you for just being you, warts and all!'

Kim said nothing. What Liz was saying was true. She would have loved Gareth and stuck by him no matter what his career situation was. It wouldn't have changed anything.

Joe, clearing the table and packing the dishwasher, insisted on opening another bottle of wine before scooping baby Finn up to take him upstairs to change his nappy and put him to bed.

'Let me give him a kiss,' Kim pleaded. Her little nephew was the cutest baby ever with his blond curly hair and brown eyes – a real mix of his mum and dad.

'Be careful – he stinks!' laughed Liz as she handed him back to Joe.

'I'm not going to bed yet,' insisted Ava stubbornly, stomping around the kitchen in her Batman suit and rabbit slippers.

Forty minutes later both kids were in bed and Joe had discreetly disappeared off to watch a football match on Sky Sports. Kim and Liz sat at the kitchen table, talking and polishing off the remains of the chocolate-chip cookies Liz had made.

'Do you want coffee?'

'No, thanks – I'll stick with the wine. It might help me sleep.'

Kim had barely slept for the past week. She felt exhausted, battered and bruised all over. It was like she had been in a car crash but with no car involved.

'Heart sore!' said Liz wisely, giving her a hug.

Liz had put her in the small bedroom at the front of the house where sixteen-month-old Finn normally slept.

'I've moved his cot and the changer into Ava's room to give you a bit of space.'

The room was bright and sunny, but how she would fit all her stuff and clothes into such a tiny space was beyond her.

'Joe says he'll put some of your bags in the garage.'

Liz had made up the single bed and put a bunch of flowers and some books and magazines on the chest of drawers, and done her best to transform the blue-and-white pirate-themed bedroom into a place for Kim.

'Liz, I really appreciate you and Joe letting me come and stay here.'

'Shush – we're family. What else would we do?'

Kim knew how lucky she was to get on with her older sister. There was only five years between them, yet Liz had always seemed far more grown up. A straight-A student, she had studied engineering and now worked for Microsoft. She had always had a proper job. While on her J-1 Visa to San Diego, Liz had fallen madly in love with Joe, a tall, long-haired student from Belfast who made her laugh. They got married and now Liz had two wonderful kids, a career, a home and family of her own. She always did everything perfectly! Kim tried not to be jealous of her sister, but sometimes she couldn't help herself . . .

'My life is such a disaster,' she admitted, taking a slow sip of wine. 'I don't even know where to start.'

'Forget Gareth, forget that bloody bank . . . forget the past,' said Liz hotly. 'You deserve far better than Gareth. He was never good enough for you, Joe and I both thought so.'

'But I thought you liked him!'

'I did. He's an okay guy, but he's not really good husband or father material.'

'But you never said anything.'

'You were living with him. You loved him!'

Appalled, Kim remembered all the family meals and dinners and events she'd brought Gareth to, imagining him as a part of the family. She'd presumed they all liked him, but how wrong she had been!

'What are you going to do?'

'I don't know. Almost three years together – it's a long time. I'm used to having him around, to us being together. I hate being on my own, Liz . . . I hate it!'

'I know, but sometimes things happen for a reason.'

'If you say this is for the best, Liz, I'll bloody strangle you!' she gulped.

'Fate plays tricks on us,' her sister insisted.

'Do you know how many weddings I went to in the past year?' Kim sighed, topping up her glass. 'Nine. Nine bloody weddings! Call me crazy, but I just presumed that one of these days it would be my turn – Gareth and me being the ones walking up the aisle.'

'I know,' sympathized Liz. 'I thought that I'd be your bridesmaid and maybe Ava would be a little flower girl.'

'I never, ever thought about us breaking up, and me ending up alone and single again. It's so shit!' Kim found herself crying again, overwhelmed with a sense of fear and panic.

'I know it's shit,' said her sister, hugging her. 'I know you're scared, but you've got me and Joe and the kids, Dad and Carole, and of course Mike.'

'Mike's in Canada and Dad—'

'You have told them?'

'Not yet.'

'Kim, they're family!'

'Carole's not! She's Dad's new wife, that's all.'

'She's part of the family now – you know she is.'

Kim still found it so hard to accept that her dad had remarried four years ago, Carole Lennon totally changing his life . . .

She wished she could have run back to the comfort of her old bedroom in Ingleside, their home on Waltham Road, but Carole had got their dad to sell the house they had grown up in and move to a small townhouse in Milltown. Number twenty-five was now owned by a young dentist and his family.

'I'll talk to Dad tomorrow,' she promised. 'Sometimes I just wish that Mum was still—'

'I know,' Liz said, wrapping her in her arms. 'I know . . .'

It was almost 1 a.m. before they finally went to bed, the two of them talking back and forward for hours about her break-up with Gareth.

'I have to go to bed,' pleaded Liz, yawning. 'Finn wakes up between six thirty and seven for his bottle and I have to get some sleep before I go to work tomorrow or I'll be like a zombie.'

Collapsing drunkenly into the small, narrow bed in her room, Kim prayed that the pirate room would not shift or spin or make her feel dizzy as she fell into a deep, heavy, exhausted sleep.

Chapter Five

Pulling the duvet over her head, Kim tried to ignore the noises from the bedroom next door. She glanced at her phone. It was barely 7 a.m. and already both kids were wide awake. She could hear 'Old Macdonald Had a Farm' blaring somewhere and the shower going.

Ava shyly opened the door to peek in at her.

'Ssssh, let's leave Kim alone – she needs to sleep,' whispered Liz, grabbing her daughter's hand and taking her downstairs to have breakfast.

Turning over, Kim closed her eyes and tried to pretend that she was asleep in her own bed and that Gareth was busy making some Nespresso coffee for them in the kitchen. When she woke four hours later, the house was quiet, absolutely deadly silent, with everyone gone. She felt awful, dehydrated and hungover as hell as she went to the bathroom and then downstairs.

Liz and Joe had both gone to work and the kids were at the crèche where they were minded. The remnants of breakfast lay scattered on the kitchen table and, as she made some toast, she automatically began to clear up the mess. She checked her phone and emails to see if there were any messages from Gareth . . . but nothing. The silence was oppressive, so she flicked on the TV in the far corner as she sat down to eat. She spent the next hour watching *Cash in the Attic* as she drank mug after mug of coffee and got through almost half a sliced pan toasted and covered with chocolate spread.

Then, after a long shower, she got dressed. She pulled on her jeans, a long-sleeved T-shirt and sleeveless zip-up navy jacket. She looked wrecked, circles under her eyes, a huge spot on her chin – brought on by sheer stress – and her brown hair all split ends, as she couldn't afford to get it cut for another few weeks. She was almost out of perfume and stole a little of Liz's Acqua di Giò.

Getting out her laptop she began to trawl through the online jobs section of the *Irish Times* and also the job and career sites she had registered with.

Nothing. Today absolutely zilch . . .

Sipping her coffee, she looked out at the houses and could see that most of the driveways were now empty, family cars gone, windows shut. The kids in the road were all gone to school or crèche. The place was like a morgue, except for a young Filipino nanny who was laughing and talking on a cell phone while pushing a baby in a buggy towards the house at the bottom of the road. She'd go crazy living in a place like this. She didn't know how Liz stuck it.

Making another mug of coffee, she went and sat in front of the TV, torn between an old episode of *House* or *Come Dine with Me*, where the guests were almost coming to blows across the dinner table.

Evie phoned her and spent half an hour patiently listening to her talking about Gareth. The two of them arranged to meet up next week for lunch.

'My treat,' insisted her friend, who knew she was absolutely skint.

Then Liz called.

'Have you talked to Dad yet?'

'Can't you tell him?' Kim begged. 'Please.'

'No deal – you have to tell him yourself!'

Since there was utterly no point trying to have a long conversation with her dad on the phone, she texted him to tell him she was calling over to see him.

Her father's silver Audi was parked on the neat, cobble-lock driveway at the front of the townhouse. He opened the door almost the minute she rang the bell. She'd seen him only two weeks ago, when he'd treated her to lunch and tried to encourage her to consider going back and doing a postgraduate degree in university. The fact that so many postgraduates were still struggling didn't seem to register with him.

'Hello, Kim – what a lovely surprise!'

At sixty-three years of age Bill O'Reilly was still a very handsome man, tall and grey-haired, wearing navy trousers and a classic white shirt with pale-blue cashmere jumper.

Kim still found it hard to adjust to him being in this house instead of the home where she had grown up. Looking around the neat, bright living room that overlooked the small patio garden, she was glad that at least a few pieces of furniture from their old home, Ingleside, had survived the move: the mahogany sideboard, the pretty glass-fronted bookshelf and her father's comfy high-backed armchair and matching footstool. There had been two of them side by side in the old house, but Carole had refused to keep the other. Liz had taken it and had it somewhere up in her attic, as it was too bulky for her modern sitting room.

'Everything okay?' he asked.

He probably assumed she was short of funds and looking for money.

'I need to talk to you, Dad.' She tried to control the wobble in her voice.

'Sounds serious. I'll make us a cup of coffee. Carole's off playing golf – she won't be back for a while.'

Kim followed him into the white-and-sage-green galley kitchen. Everything was so tidy and organized. Liz maintained that Carole was a neat freak and that's why she objected to coming to her house, because of the kids' mess everywhere. 'She nearly sat on one of Finn's rotten nappies the last time she came for lunch with Dad. Joe had left it on the couch. She thinks that we are both right slobs!'

'There's some carrot cake here – will you have a slice?' offered her father.

Curled up across from him in the sitting room, nibbling the cake, Kim found herself telling her dad all about the ins and outs of her break-up with Gareth.

'I'm sorry to hear that it's over between you,' he sighed, 'but hearing of his behaviour towards you, just because you found yourself temporarily unemployed, disappoints me. He should have been supportive not just financially but emotionally until you got back on your feet again.'

'Dad, he was financially supportive,' she found herself defending Gareth. 'But it was just the whole job thing . . . I felt he looked down on me, and it made me feel useless.'

'I'm sure Gareth didn't mean to hurt you like that – but a good relationship always needs balance, especially when one hits rough waters. You need to be there for each other; not just in good times but in bad . . . That, I suppose, is the true mark of the people we are,' her dad said firmly.

Kim tried to compose herself, remembering her dad's strength and courage and love during the last year of her mum's life. He had done everything in his power to help when her mum was diagnosed with an aggressive form of breast cancer. They had tried everything, searched for new and alternative treatments, seen different doctors, but in the end it had made no difference and her mum had died, leaving all of them devastated.

'Gareth may have many fine points – no doubt that's

41

why you fell in love with him in the first place – but he is not good enough for you, Kim! Not good enough at all. You deserve someone much better – a much better man.'

'Dad, I still love him,' she countered. 'Please don't tell me to go and meet someone else! You have no idea what the guys out there are like! I'm nearly thirty . . . and I thought we were going to end up together. I really did.'

'I'm sorry, Kim. I didn't mean to be insensitive,' he apologized. 'I know how much well-intentioned words often hurt. Telling somebody when they lose the one they love that they will meet someone else is bloody awful – an insult, and certainly not what they want to hear.'

'Dad!' Kim flung herself into his arms and hugged him. One of the things she loved most about her dad was that he never changed. He still smelled of the same soap and aftershave, and wore the same clothes and shoes, and held her the same way he had done ever since she could remember.

'Where are you staying? You are welcome to move in here with us if you need to.'

She thought of their spare room. There was a single bed, but the room was turned into a study with a computer and printer, and all her father and Carole's books and papers and files neatly displayed on one wall.

'It's okay – I'm staying with Liz for the moment.'

'I could talk to Carole,' he offered. 'She'd under-stand.'

'Honestly, it's fine, Dad.'

42

Kim knew that moving in with Carole and her father was certainly not an option. Carole was very good to her father and had given him a new lease of life. She got on well with everyone in the family, but had made it clear when she married him that she was marrying Bill and not his children. Carole had no intention of trying to step into the late Ruth O'Reilly's shoes.

'Dad, it's fine, honest. It's nice being with Liz and the kids, but I've got to find a place of my own.'

'If you are short of funds for a deposit or whatever, let me know.'

An hour later Carole returned from golf.

'What a surprise!' she smiled, joining them in her pink Pringle jumper and golfing gear.

'Kim came over to tell me about her and Gareth breaking up,' explained Bill. 'It's all rather awkward.'

'Oh,' said Carole, glancing nervously at her.

'I've told Kim she can stay with us if she needs to,' he continued.

She could see the look on Carole's face, torn between being polite and supportive but not wanting to be involved.

'Dad, Carole, it's fine,' she interjected. 'I'm staying at Liz's until I get a new place.'

'Well, that's okay, then.' Kim could see relief etched across the older woman's face. 'I know how close sisters can be.'

'Well, she'll stay for dinner with us at least,' her dad continued. 'I think there's some chicken in the fridge.'

'Liz is expecting me.' She'd no intention of having dinner here and hearing Carole lecture her about her poor life choices. 'She's making a big dish of lasagne.'

'Another night, then,' he promised.

As he walked her out to the doorstep, it amazed her how her father had somehow managed to adjust to life without her mother. He seemed happy despite everything. Living here in his small house with a woman who was so different from her mum, it was unbelievable.

'I know how awful you must be feeling, Kim, but things will get better – I promise,' he reassured her as she got into her car.

'Dad, to be honest, right now it feels like they couldn't get any worse . . .'

Chapter Six

Roz Gilmore welcomed Molly warmly to her red-brick terraced home on Victoria Road.

'You sit down and I'll get us a drink. What will it be – a sherry, a G & T, or maybe a glass of wine?'

'I could do with a glass of wine – a big one!' Molly laughed, flopping down in the massive armchair in the sitting room as Roz disappeared off to the kitchen.

Looking around she could see that nothing had changed here over the years. Everything was practically the same as when they were kids and had gone to school together. Roz was still living in her parents' house in Donnybrook; she had never married and had ended up looking after her elderly mother, Betty, for years. A lecturer in Celtic Studies, Roz worked at Trinity College. There had been a romance with a visiting Scottish lecturer many years ago, but Roz had stubbornly refused to give up the security of her job and to leave her aging parent to move to Edinburgh with him. Molly suspected she often regretted it, but Roz never said anything and just got on with living alone, busying herself with her research and lectures and obsession with the mythology and stories of ancient Ireland and its people.

'How did your meetings go?' asked Roz, arriving back with two glasses of wine.

Molly told her briefly about what had happened with the bank manager.

'The bankers have a nerve. They've destroyed the country with their behaviour,' Roz said angrily. 'The whole thing is a disgrace and the awful thing is that those involved have all got hefty bonuses and handsome early-retirement payments, rewarding them for bringing the country to its knees!'

Molly nodded, totally agreeing but making a mental note to avoid talk of the economy or banks over dinner later as they caught up with each other's news.

Two glasses of wine later, Roz insisted that Molly go up and have a quick nap before they went out. Molly, grateful to have a chance to put her feet up and rest, fell asleep almost instantly in the neat guest bed-room, with its Laura Ashley décor, overlooking the street.

That night they tried out Le Bon Poisson, a fancy new fish restaurant in the heart of the city.

'I knew that you'd like this place,' beamed Roz. 'It's

always busy, which is a good sign, and Patsy and John are always talking about it.'

Molly smiled. Roz's younger sister Patsy and her husband John always seemed to come up in conversation and she knew that Roz loved to keep up with them and try the places they visited and ate in, or see the plays they saw. Good old sibling rivalry. Thank heaven she and Ruth had never been like that. As sisters they had been very close and always mutually supportive. When she had lost Ruth she had not only lost her only sister but her best friend.

Over dinner they chatted about mutual friends and politics and the pluses and minuses of living alone.

'It's just so hard, I don't know how I am ever going to get used to it,' Molly admitted.

'Maybe that bank man is right, that you should consider the house-selling and moving,' suggested Roz. 'Mossbawn must be far too big now with only you and Daisy rattling around it. Just think how easy life would be if you moved back up to Dublin!'

'Roz, I love Mossbawn and I love living in the country,' she retaliated stoutly. 'Besides, you're a fine one to talk about moving and you've lived in the same house and place all your life!'

'I know,' laughed Roz, embarrassed. 'I'm hardly the one to be giving advice to anyone. It's just that if you were back living here in Dublin you'd be here while Grace is in college, and near Ruth's girls, and you still have friends here – and think of all the restaurants and cinemas and shows, and lots of interesting lectures and things to do here in Dublin. I always keep myself almost fully occupied.'

'So do I!' Molly laughed. 'Keeping up the house and the garden at home is a full-time job, believe me. I like the odd trip coming to Dublin or to London, but I honestly don't know if I could ever settle back here again.'

After two cappuccinos they paid the bill and headed back home.

Sitting in the kitchen, Molly found herself confiding in Roz over her worries about the future.

'I just never pictured this – my life without David,' she said, getting tearful.

'You are so lucky to have had such a good husband,' Roz told her. 'He was a lovely guy.'

'I know.' Molly sniffed. 'I was so lucky, but it's so lonely now . . .'

'You get used to being lonely,' her friend said encouragingly. 'You'll fill your life with other things . . . keep busy . . . It's what I do.'

'Oh Roz, I'm sorry – I didn't think.'

'Come on, let's have a nice brandy before we go to sleep,' Roz offered. 'I've organized for us to meet Helen and Anna for lunch in the National Gallery tomorrow. They've that new Walter Osborne exhibition on.'

'Well, I couldn't miss that!' Molly teased, slowly sipping the warming brandy.

Chapter Seven

Lunch in the gallery with the girls was fun. She and Roz and Helen and Anna had all known each for years and the girls had been so supportive of her since David's death.

'We're thinking of going to Italy next spring for a few days. Why don't you come too?' asked Anna, who had gone through a messy divorce about six years ago. 'There's so much to do and see, with galleries and places to visit.'

'Plus lots of nice meals and vino! It will be a laugh,' promised Helen.

'Let me think about it,' she smiled, suspecting this lunch was a bit of a ready-up. She hadn't been on holiday without David for years, but if she were to go away, this sounded exactly the type of holiday she would like – no couples, just the girls.

'It would do you good!' said Roz firmly.

After lunch she had mooched around Grafton Street and bought a new dress for herself.

'No black!' Roz had urged, passing her a soft, oyster-coloured shift dress from the rail in Pamela Scott's. She had tried it on and was surprised how well it fitted. She must have dropped a dress size without even trying.

'But where would I wear it?' she worried.

'In Italy!' laughed Roz, persuading her to buy it.

Afterwards Roz had disappeared off to give a lecture to some Japanese exchange students. 'It will be all questions about fairies and leprechauns, no matter what I tell them!' she sighed. 'Listen, I'll see you at home later, okay?'

Molly wandered around town, taking in the shops and the crowds, the buskers playing on Grafton Street. She loved Dublin; it was such a great city, full of music and heart.

As the shops started to close for the night she walked towards O'Connell Bridge and up along the busy quays towards Doyle's, the restaurant where she was meeting Grace. She went up a few steps and was shown to a table beside the window, where the waitress brought her a jug of water and the menu. She had just started to read it when Grace arrived in a flurry of long legs in skinny jeans, a fitted suede jacket and a tumble of golden-red hair, the exact same colour as her dad's.

'Hi Mum,' she said, hugging her tightly. 'You look great! What have you been doing all day?'

'Lunch with a few of the girls and a bit of shopping – I even bought a dress.'

Grace peeked in the bag.

'And I love your new jacket!' Molly exclaimed.

'Vintage – only eighteen euro in the market near Christchurch,' smiled her daughter proudly.

'How are things?'

'Great, Mum, everything is great,' said Grace, flopping down across from her. 'College is fine, the house is fine, though our landlady is a bit of a weirdo. She's always coming in to check on things.'

'That's not right.'

'I know, but the house is so handy. I can cycle or get a bus to college and our road is full of student houses so there are great parties . . . So we're all planning to rent it again next year.'

'And what about while you're away during the summer?' pressed Molly.

'I'm only away backpacking for six weeks, but Sophie and Niamh will still be there and when we get back they'll be going to Greece. So it will all work out, don't worry!'

Molly did worry – about rent money and about her daughter heading off around Europe with a gang of friends, planning on sleeping on trains, beaches and in the odd hostel as they backpacked around Holland, Germany, France, Italy and Croatia.

The waitress came and took their orders, both of them opting for the dish of the day – cannelloni with a salad.

'Is everything okay at home?' quizzed Grace.

She had debated telling Grace about her meeting yesterday, but there was no point in worrying her younger daughter.

'Fine, and Rena's minding Daisy while I'm away, so hopefully she's behaving.'

'I really miss her.'

'Well, come home and see her then,' she urged.

'Mum, I've two massive projects to hand in in the next week or two! Then Sophie and I are going to the *Star Wars* Ball in two weeks . . . Maybe after that I'll try to get home for a weekend.'

'A *Star Wars* Ball!'

'The computer science geeks have organized it, but it should be fun. I'm wearing that silvery dress and Karl, one of the guys in my class, is loaning me a light sabre.'

As they ate, Molly listened as Grace told her all about her friends, her classes, her lectures and her housemates. Her daughter's life was packed to the brim, as any twenty-year-old's should be.

Molly smiled as Grace devoured a big slice of chocolate fudge cake for dessert.

'Are you staying in town tomorrow, Mum? Maybe we could meet up again!'

'Sorry, but I plan to head back home mid-morning,' she explained. 'I'm trying to get Jimmy Fallon to come and fix the leak in the bathroom, so I need to be there . . . You know what that man is like, and I don't like leaving Mossbawn empty . . .'

'Mum, I'll try to get down home soon,' promised

Grace. 'It's just that with the exams the work is piling on.'

'Of course, pet . . . don't worry, and remember to send me some photos of that ball!'

Paying the bill, the two of them headed back towards O'Connell Bridge and Molly insisted that they share a taxi home. Hugging Grace tightly when they reached Ranelagh, Molly watched her daughter disappear into a narrow road of similar-looking red-brick houses, then she gave the driver Roz's address.

Chapter Eight

It was good to be back in Mossbawn, enveloped in the familiar routine of the old house.

Rena had stayed for coffee when she had brought the dog back; Molly thanked her as Daisy raced off immediately on an inspection tour of the garden.

'She's no trouble,' laughed Rena. 'She got on fine with George once she didn't try to eat from his dog bowl. Anyways, I hope you enjoyed yourself.'

'Thanks, Rena, it was great. I got to see Grace and Roz and a few of my friends and did a bit of shopping. But to tell the truth it's a great relief to get back home,' she confessed. 'I missed the place.'

'I'm the exact same! A few days on holidays or staying with my sister in Cork and I'm ready to come back home again,' confided Rena. 'Jack complains I've lost my adventurous streak, but I'm not sure if I ever really had one!'

'But you and Jack have been all over the place!' exclaimed Molly; her neighbours were renowned for their travels all over the world.

'I know, but once you've seen one rainforest, sat on one deserted tropical island and visited one more temple, you find yourself wanting to be back sitting pretty here in Kilfinn.'

Molly burst out laughing.

'You can't beat it,' Rena added, laughing too. 'It's not just the place, it's the people too.'

Molly had to admit there was a lot of truth to what her neighbour was saying. Living here in Kilfinn she was part of a community where everyone looked out for everyone else. When David had died she had been inundated with help and support, and had been shown a genuine kindness by all those around her. It was something that she would never forget.

Later, when Rena was gone, Molly decided to get stuck in doing a bit of much-needed work in the garden. Pulling on her wellington boots and her light fleece jacket, she decided it was high time she began to tackle some of the heavy, overgrown sections in the large herbaceous borders. There was no room for anything and she urgently needed to strip out some of the plants and trim others back so there was space for the spires of growing delphiniums, lupins and tall fox-gloves. This work preparing the beds for the summer should have been done months ago, but she had barely noticed what was going on around her, let alone here in the garden. She had neglected it like everything else and now it was gone mad ... Arming herself with her secateurs and clippers, spade and fork, she set out across the lawn.

Working with plants and flowers was probably one of the most rewarding things a person could do after raising children, thought Molly. As she worked, cutting and clipping back, digging up and making space for light and air and room to grow, she got totally involved in what she was doing. She worked for a few hours, took a quick break for coffee and a sandwich, then headed back out again. A day like this with no rain or showers was a gardener's delight and meant that she could get a good run at the job. Though she was tired, she had no intention of stopping until she had one whole section of the large bed done. A few more days like this and she could achieve so much.

Molly found that time and worry seemed to disappear when you had a trowel or clippers in your hand, as your full concentration was needed for the job. Perhaps that was why she enjoyed gardening so much. Nothing else mattered when a plant or shrub demanded your attention. While it was back-breaking and aching and exhausting splitting, lifting and digging out plants, filling the wheelbarrow time and time again and wheeling it off to the compost heap, she found it relaxing in a way far more beneficial than any pills a doctor could prescribe.

As she was finishing up she wheeled the barrow, filled with some heavy stones and a rock she had decided to move, back towards the old walled garden enclosure. She looked around as she emptied the barrow. This was a place she should do something to. The previous owner had used it as a hidden area for storage and David had followed suit, dumping debris or rubble from the garden, and also storing paving slabs, roof tiles and bricks, keeping them safely along with old garden pots and roof slates, as it was out of the way and enclosed by lovely tall brick walls. It was overgrown now with dandelions and weeds, but Molly stopped, surprised to see a rambling rose clambering up the south wall, cheekily reaching the top.

The old rose bush struggled between a mound of stones and gravel, part of it dead and wizened, and without thinking she took out her secateurs and gave it a prune, stripping out the dead branches to let the new growth flourish. Then she pushed the stones away from it.

Among the clutter there was a broken garden bench and some old deckchairs, and a rusted wrought-iron sewing table. David hated getting rid of things – he always had plans for them; but with David gone this was just a dumping ground and it needed to be cleared.

In times past this must have been a proper garden, with its rusty old gate and broken pathways and wizened bits of box hedge. It had been David's spot, so she had hardly bothered with it; but now, sitting on a low piece of wall, she could see its appeal. The brick was still warm to touch, sheltered, a perfect place to sit hidden away from everybody.

She could see wild roses and stumps of shrub roses and the skeletons of a few climbers scattered about like old soldiers in a battle. It must have been some kind of rose garden a long time ago. There were still some traces of beds and paths. Poor, poor garden! she thought as she walked around, searching to see if there were any signs of growth or budding that showed a plant might still have a chance of survival.

She spent the next hour in the garden, overcome by a strange sense of wanting to do something here. Could she fix it? Repair it some way? The soil was compacted from all the rubble and gravel and stuff dumped everywhere, difficult to work with, but surely it was possible to replenish and enrich and fertilize it? As she walked around she began to imagine this old garden as it must have been a hundred years ago – a secret garden . . . a rose-filled bower . . . a place of peace and quiet and secret thoughts – and she was excited by the notion of trying to restore it . . . return it to its former glory . . . replant it . . .

It was late when she realized the time, the air cool as the sun began to go down – a large bundle of roof slates moved and some ground cleared already . . .

Inside, she switched on the radio and caught the tail end of the news and the weather forecast for tomorrow, which was dry with sunny spells.

'Perfect!' she shouted aloud as she began to prepare some pasta for herself. Pasta in a cheesy sauce – the single diner's friend!

Soon she was curled up barefoot on the kitchen couch, eating, browsing a garden catalogue, searching the rose section with a notepad on her lap as she jotted down names and varieties, doodling a rough outline of a new garden.

The original house and garden plans were kept in a leather folder in David's study in the old library. Surely the walled garden would be somewhere in those? Somewhere there were also photos and some drawings and designs that she should root out, see if she could discover what the original garden looked like.

She was trawling through the old books and files, trying to find what she needed, when Emma phoned. They talked to each other every second day. She loved to hear stories of Emma's student life in Galway, which lately seemed more and more to involve her daughter's new boyfriend, Jake.

She found herself telling Emma about the old garden. 'It's in such a terrible state!'

'Mum, it sounds like one of your projects!' warned her elder daughter.

'My projects?'

'Yeah, like when you re-did our two bedrooms and you sourced the original wallpaper designs and stencils, and when you and Dad got the new wooden bridge built over the pond when the old one broke, and remember you got them to get all the old pieces of wood from the old bridge and got a guy to copy and re-make a new version of it.'

'That was fun!' Molly admitted. 'It was based on a Japanese design.'

'See what I mean?' teased Emma.

'But don't you think it would be lovely to see it restored and for Mossbawn to have a rose garden again?'

Sitting up in bed later, with books and papers spread out everywhere, Molly studied the old sepia photo she'd found in a box in the library. She recognized the gate and a section of wall. There was something scribbled in faded pencil on the back: *'The Rose Garden'*.

An old man was in the picture, leant on a spade, in an overall and rolled-up shirtsleeves and boots, squinting into the sun . . . A gardener! She wished there were more photos of the garden so she could get some real idea of the way it was originally laid out. She yawned; she'd search again tomorrow, she promised herself as she laid everything carefully on the top of the silk-padded ottoman at the end of the bed. She usually hated night-time – being on her own, sleeping in their bed – but tonight she was so exhausted she just wanted to lie down, pull up the quilt and sleep. No dreams . . . no worries . . . just good old-fashioned sleep.

Chapter Nine

Kim sat in front of one of the senior executives in Javelin Jobs. Liz had suggested she give the recruitment firms another call and set up a few meetings: 'You met with most of them months ago. They have so many people on their books you need to jog their memories.'

'I'll be honest,' Brian Jennings said. 'Except for banking experience, what you're offering is very limited in terms of other employers. They are looking for a range of skill sets – technical ability, financial acumen, and exceptional experience in terms of client interface.'

'But I've worked in banking for six years. That must count for something,' she said doggedly. 'I was part of the Finance team.'

'A junior member,' he said softly.

'Since I left Irish Bank Group I've been improving my skills,' she said defensively. 'I'm doing a diploma course in website development and design, which I've almost finished, and I've also undertaken a digital photography course.'

'The more skills people have the better. Clients like to see someone who is stretching themselves, continually learning,' he praised her.

'That's what I am trying to do,' she said forcefully.

'But you need to show these new diplomas and certificates and things on your résumé.'

'Maybe there are jobs out there that I could go for, not necessarily in banking but maybe in digital marketing?'

He raised his eyebrow. 'Listen, Kim, we have something coming up in a few weeks in an insurance company. They have a strong online presence and are looking to recruit a few people. It's all at a very early stage, but if you would like to update your CV and re-send it to me, I will put your name forward.'

'Honestly? Oh thanks, Brian.'

'As I said, it's early days and there are no guarantees, but once I have the new CV I will send it on to them.'

Kim smiled. Job-wise, this was the first bit of encouragement she'd had in weeks. Okay, online insurance didn't sound very exciting, but if she got a job, any kind of job, it would be just brilliant.

As they were having a sandwich in O'Brien's, Kim told Evie about the possibility of a job, making it sound rather more exciting than it was.

'That's great, Kim! Fingers crossed that you'll ace the interview and land the job!'

'We'll see.' She shrugged.

'Imagine if you got it,' sighed Evie. 'That would show bloody Gareth how good you are!'

'I suppose it would be great!'

'Have you heard from him?' quizzed her friend.

'No,' she sighed. 'Nothing. I texted him a few times but he never texts me back . . .'

'Kim! Stop texting him!' pleaded Evie. 'You have got to accept Gareth's not on the scene, and that you need to try and get back out there.'

'I'm not ready for that,' she admitted. 'I still really miss him.'

'Okay, point taken, but what about just coming out with the girls on Saturday for something to eat and a few drinks? I'm meeting Lisa and Mel and Rhona – why don't you come along too?'

She had to agree it was tempting. Last Saturday she'd ended up babysitting for Liz and Joe, and it was shaping up to her babysitting again this Saturday if she was around.

'Yeah, maybe you're right. A night with just the girls would be great.'

Evie had insisted on paying for her sandwich, which was a relief as her wallet was pretty empty-looking. Standing at the cash machine an hour later she couldn't believe it! Shit, shit . . . shit – her money was dwindling away at an alarming rate. Thank heaven she was stay-ing with Liz and not paying rent and gas or electricity bills for the moment. She had to get a job – just had to . . .

Joe was busy organizing dinner when she got in, and she read a story with the kids as he sliced the vegetables. Liz was so lucky to have such a good husband. Gareth had been utterly hopeless at cooking.

Finn was starving and she offered to feed him as Joe made the chicken stir-fry.

'Liz is on her way.' He smiled as he handed her a clean bib.

Feeding Finn was a messy job, as every now and then he would plunge his hand into the bowl for a taste, or try to grab the spoon from her. He had a spare plastic spoon which he couldn't really manage.

'He'll soon be feeding himself,' joked Joe. 'He loves finger foods – you should see him demolish a few chips!'

Liz looked tired when she got in, throwing her bag and jacket in the hall, lifting Ava and Finn for a kiss before chasing upstairs to change.

Kim felt guilty as her sister reamed off what a busy day she'd had. She herself was a disgrace . . . but at least today she'd been to a recruitment agency and she found herself telling them about the insurance job.

'That's great, Kim,' smiled Liz. 'Any company would be lucky to have you work for them.'

'Well, let's see if I even get called for an interview!'

Sitting at the table talking as Ava told them about what she'd done in playgroup, it reminded her of when they were kids and her mum and dad would ask them about their day and school. Liz had made such a good home and life with Joe and the kids. Kim wondered if a home and family would ever happen for her. She tried to picture Gareth and somehow, in a weird way, it just didn't fit.

They were having coffee afterwards when Liz asked her about babysitting on Saturday.

'I'm sorry, but I said I'd go into town for a meal with Evie and the girls, but I could do Friday if you two want to go out.'

'Most definitely,' said Joe. 'A great escape – we'll head for a drink to the Step Inn.'

'Are you sure you don't mind?' asked Liz.

'Of course not . . . you've been so good to me. I don't mind doing a bit of babysitting and if you want I'll make dinner for us all tomorrow night.'

'I'll take you up on that!' Joe grinned.

Kim felt relieved that at least she could help out, even if she couldn't contribute very much financially. Her stay here was only meant to be short-term, but, having trawled a lot of rental sites on the internet, paying out rent in a house or apartment on her own was not a viable option while she was so broke and on the dole.

Later she helped bath the kids and put them to bed. Having the children sharing the one bedroom was hardly ideal, as she had almost to whisper so she didn't wake the sleeping Finn.

Downstairs she virtually collapsed in front of the TV. Joe and Liz were in the kitchen getting clothes and things sorted for the next day – parenthood was sure tough work.

By eleven o'clock everyone was in bed, the house quiet. She could hear Liz and Joe talking and laughing in bed together. Snuggled against her pillow, Kim found herself going back over all her old messages from Gareth. She wondered what he was doing and if he was missing her the way she missed him . . .

Chapter Ten

'You look *beuuutiful*,' pronounced Ava, who was watching her as she got ready for her night out with the girls.

Glancing at herself in the mirror, Kim was pleased with her efforts. Tight jeans, expensive Karen Millen top, and her classic fitted black jacket. A bit of eyeliner made her eyes look huge and she ran a slick of fresh lip gloss across her lips.

'And you look beautiful too,' she told her niece, who was in her pink rabbit pyjamas with her hair washed. '*Mmm* – and you smell really good too.'

'Where are you going?'

'I'm meeting some of my friends and we are going to have dinner and have some fun. I'm staying in my friend's tonight, so I'll see you tomorrow.'

Downstairs Liz and Joe had rented two DVDs and had a bottle of wine chilling.

'Once Ava is safe in bed, we are enjoying our Saturday,' teased Joe, kissing Liz.

Kim laughed – it didn't sound too bad to her.

'Enjoy your night!' called Liz.

Kim parked her car near Evie's apartment and left her overnight bag there. They each had a glass of wine as they set up the futon in the living room where she would sleep later. Evie's place was such a mess, she had no idea how her old schoolfriend managed living this way; there were canvases and paints and clutter everywhere.

'Did I tell you that I've got a spot in the artists' exhibition on Merrion Square for the next two weekends, selling my work?'

'Oh Evie, that's brilliant news!'

'Spots are like gold dust and I've been waiting months for this. It gives me a chance to show off my work and hopefully sell a few paintings.'

'If you need any help, I'm free,' offered Kim.

'Thanks – it would be nice to have a bit of company.'

Kim knew how much painting and art meant to her friend. So Evie had studied art and had really struggled after college to find a market for her big, strong canvases. She had done a teaching diploma and now worked three days a week as an art teacher in a city-centre school. The kids there loved her and she was always doing big art projects with them, but Evie really wanted to sell her own work and make a name for herself as an artist.

Kim loved her friend's paintings and was busy

creating a website for her that showcased her artwork and gave details of how to buy it and even commission pieces.

'Hey, we'd better hit the road. Ali and Mel and Lisa just texted to say they're already on the way into town,' urged Evie, and they made a run for the Luas tram.

Alfredo's on Wicklow Street was packed and Kim couldn't believe how lucky they were to get a big table near the window. She hadn't seen some of the girls since her break-up with Gareth.

'You okay?' asked Rhona, who was sitting beside her.

'Not really,' she admitted. 'It hurts like hell, but I've got to try and get used to it.'

'Gareth's such a wally! When he comes crawling back to you, promise me that you won't cave in and go back with him!'

'I don't think that's going to happen,' she sighed, grabbing a glass of the house white.

'It will – he'll realize that he had one of the nicest girl-friends on the planet and he let her go . . .'

'Thanks, Rhona,' said Kim, a lump in her throat.

'Don't underestimate yourself,' continued Rhona firmly. 'Women do it all the time.'

Kim nodded. Rhona had been in school with herself and Evie, and worked in one of the big law firms. Her husband, Will, was a lawyer too. They'd got married two years ago and had a baby boy of about five months.

'How's Baby Ollie?'

'He's thriving. Will and I might be exhausted, but he's

great! We're mad about him. It changes everything, but in a good way . . . But listen, no baby-talk tonight. I finished breastfeeding ten days ago and after fourteen months am finally able to drink again! I'd kill for another glass of wine.'

'Sure thing!' laughed Kim, topping her up.

They ordered two big plates of antipasti for the table and Kim went for the seafood risotto.

Mel was getting married in five months' time and entertained them with awful stories of the outrageous behaviour of her future mother-in-law, who wanted to invite fifty friends to the wedding.

'We keep telling her that it is going to be a smallish wedding, but she doesn't believe us. She thinks that we're made of money.'

'Set a limit and tell her she has twenty-five or thirty places, and that you don't care who makes up her thirty places but that there is no going over on that,' advised Rhona.

Kim loved the girls; most of them had been friends for so long and knew each other really well. Husbands and boyfriends didn't really come into it when they were together, which meant she wasn't over-conscious of being single again. Anyway, she knew the girls were all on her side no matter what happened.

The waiters kept them topped up with wine and she shared some dessert with Rhona. They were happy there, talking and swapping places and chatting, and as they ordered coffee the head waiter brought them each a flaming sambuca on the house.

It was long after midnight when they began to break up.

'Fingers crossed that Ollie is conked out,' muttered Rhona, getting into a cab with Lisa. 'If he wakes up Will is going to have to deal with him and give him his night feed – I'm far too tipsy to manage!'

'The night is still young,' slurred Ali. 'Why don't we hit a nightclub?'

Kim had absolutely no intention of going to a nightclub; she wasn't in the mood for dancing and shouting at people.

'Let's find a nice cosy bar where we can have another drink or two,' suggested Evie.

'Davy Byrne's,' said Ali, leading the way up towards Duke Street.

Town was busy and they stopped for a few minutes to listen to a young band performing U2 songs in front of a massive crowd on Grafton Street.

'Bono'd be proud!' laughed Kim.

The bar was busy, but Evie and Ali managed to find a booth near the back that they could all squeeze into.

Mel was being chatted up by some gorgeous Frenchman who seemed oblivious to the engagement ring sparkling on her finger.

'Maybe he's blind,' teased Evie.

Kim was so glad that she had made the effort to come out with her friends. She'd economize for the next week. Seeing the girls had made her feel like herself again – the old Kim who had existed before Gareth had come along. Sipping her wine, she relaxed as Evie and

Ali talked about going away to the sun in a few weeks' time for a girly break.

'If you want to come with us you're welcome,' laughed Ali. 'My dad and mum have a place near Marbella and I'll get it for a few days. We'll just have to pay our airfare and spending money.'

'I'll have to see if I can afford it . . .' she trailed off.

'Maybe you'll get that great job that you were telling me about,' Evie encouraged her.

'Maybe!' she said, embarrassed. She'd love to go on a break with the girls, do all the things they could afford to do, but at the moment she was stony broke.

It was almost 2 a.m. when they decided to call it a night and, grabbing her coat and handbag, Kim joined the throng of people on Dawson Street. There was no shortage of taxis on the busy street, with all its late-night bars and restaurants. As Evie and she headed towards the front of the rank, Kim stopped suddenly, realizing that Gareth was further up in the queue. He was laughing and talking with some guys, probably his mates Cormac and Shay.

Kim stopped. Should she say hello to him, or pretend she didn't see him? He was deep in conversation, unaware of her watching him.

'Gareth!' she shouted drunkenly. 'Gareth!' She started to move towards him.

Suddenly Kim realized that Gareth wasn't with a few of the guys, but had his arm loosely around the shoulder of a tall, skinny, dark-haired girl.

'No!' shouted Evie, grabbing her arms and dragging her back. 'Leave him!'

She watched as he got into a cab with the girl. Who the hell was she? Had he just met her in one of the bars?

'Was that Gareth?' asked Ali drunkenly as they got into a cab of their own.

'Shut up!' hissed Evie.

Kim stared out at the city lights, street after street, unable to think of anything but the fact that tonight Gareth was with someone else . . .

Chapter Eleven

Somehow Kim managed to hold it together until she and Evie had climbed up two flights of steep stairs of the tall Georgian building to her second-floor flat. The ancient lift was dodgy and Evie refused to put foot in it once darkness fell. Ten minutes earlier they had deposited a very drunken Ali safely to her door.

The minute they got in Kim began to cry. Evie made her sit down on the couch and have a pint of water.

'Gareth didn't even say hello to me!' she sobbed.

'Luckily he didn't see you!'

'He's met someone already!' she wailed. 'I can't believe it! Do you think he was seeing her while we were still living together?'

'I know Gareth's a bit of a shit, but I don't think he's the two-timing type,' said Evie. 'He's too old-fashioned and boring to be having an affair under your nose!

Odds are he just met that girl tonight, or maybe she's a work client or something.'

'Sure,' sobbed Kim, imagining the dark-haired girl arriving back at the apartment and being romanced by Gareth, who could be so bloody charming when he wanted.

'There's nothing you can do about it,' Evie said gently. 'Let it go.'

'I can't,' she wailed, 'I just can't!'

'Remember when Brian and I split up two years ago and I found out that he'd been seeing bloody Aoife behind my back for weeks? It nearly drove me mad. The fact that my boyfriend was going out with someone who I used to call a friend nearly drove me crazy.'

'But they broke up, didn't they?'

'Yes, but it was the betrayal and the broken trust that got me. Brian was bad, but Aoife was worse for going out with him. I haven't spoken to her since.'

'I shouldn't have gone out tonight. I should have stayed in and babysat for Liz.'

'You babysat for them last night,' Evie reminded her. 'Besides, just because you and Gareth aren't together doesn't mean you can't go out with the girls for a meal and a drink. Don't be so stupid, Kim!'

'But if I wasn't in town,' she hiccupped, 'I wouldn't have seen him!'

'You are hardly going to hide away. You know what Dublin's like – everyone knows everything about everyone!'

'I just wish that I had stayed home and hadn't seen him.'

'I know,' Evie consoled her. 'It's shit seeing your boyfriend with someone else.'

'It's so crap that he's not my boyfriend any more,' she said, feeling sadness overwhelm her. 'I just don't know how I'll ever get used to it.'

'You will,' said Evie loyally, getting up and bustling about the tiny kitchen area on one side of the large room. 'I'm making us toast and hot chocolate.'

'Sure.' Ever since she was about nine years old, Evie had always believed that hot chocolate was the best drink there was in a time of crisis and this was most definitely a crisis.

'I hate my life! I hate the way things are,' Kim confessed as she sat in front of the gas fire with her mug of hot chocolate. 'Everything is a disaster.'

'You have to start believing in yourself,' Evie insisted. 'Forget Gareth! Forget those stupid wanker bankers you used to work for! You've got to find something that you really want to do for yourself – something that makes you happy, like my painting, or Lisa and her running, and Mel and her mania for interior decorating. You've got brains to burn, Kim, but you just need to find the right thing to do in life – no more second bests! You have to change things.'

Drunk as they both were, Kim knew what Evie was saying was true. She was the only one who could change her life – the only one.

*   *   *

76

She had tossed and turned on the futon before finally giving in to sleep. When she woke it was lunchtime and Evie was in her pyjamas painting.

'Hey, I've got bacon and scrambled egg for brunch,' she said, standing over Kim.

'I'm not really hungry.'

'You hop in the shower and I'll get it ready,' Evie said, ignoring her protests. Fifteen minutes later Kim was beginning to feel human again as she sat on the couch in her jeans and sweatshirt eating.

'It was a great night,' murmured Evie, 'except for us seeing you know who!'

'Yeah.'

'Do you want to do something today?'

'Not really . . . well, unless you count sleeping . . .'

'Okay, I am going to paint, but you are welcome to hang out here.'

'What you said last night – it made me think.'

'I was probably far too wasted and said more than I should have,' said Evie apologetically.

'No, you were right. The only one who can change my life is me. Not a job, not a guy – the elephant in the room is me. I need to sort that out, find out what I want . . .'

'Oh Kim!' said Evie, throwing her arms around her. 'I just want you to be happy!'

'I know.'

Later, as she drove back to Liz's house, she wondered how the hell she was going to even begin to change things.

Chapter Twelve

Gina Sullivan stood at the counter looking out on the street. Rain again. God, did it ever stop raining? Heavy rain and showers kept customers away, and heaven knows Cassidy's Café could sure do with more of them.

Norah Cassidy had put up the day's lunch menu: vegetable soup, roast pork with apple sauce and potatoes, and ham salad up on the board; hardly the fare to tempt hungry diners. There were also fresh scones and Norah's famous apple tart, and Gina's own home-made brownies and cupcakes for those coming to have a coffee or tea and while away the time.

There were already two customers sitting at a table in the window, one eating a lemon drizzle cupcake. Gina had made it herself, getting up at six this morning to bake, and Paul, her husband, had dropped her off at work with her just-baked delivery for the café. Then he had gone off to deliver her order to Beech Hill, the old folks' home on the outskirts of Kilfinn, and another dozen of both cupcakes and brownies to Ramona's Coffee Shop in the nearby town of Castlecomer.

Twice a week Gina rose early to bake, amazed that something she loved to do was also proving a fairly regular source of income for the family. In fact it was her brownies and cupcakes that had first helped her to get to know Norah. She had come into the café with some free samples of her baking and Norah had tasted them and given her an order straight away. Three months later, when Sonya the girl who helped out in the café decided to head off to Australia with a few of her friends, Norah had asked Gina if she would be interested in coming in and helping. Gina couldn't believe her luck, and though her salary was nothing to write home about, it was a job, when she hadn't expected to find one and when she and Paul needed work.

That was two years ago, and it had been one of the best decisions ever. She loved working in the village café, meeting the regulars, hearing all that was going on in Kilfinn and having the chance to test out a dish of her own every now and then on the customers. Her boss, Norah Cassidy, was a good woman – old-fashioned and somewhat stuck in her ways, but a good cook. Okay, she tended to have the same dishes on the menu week in, week out, but the food was always good and, if possible, sourced locally. Gina tried to expand the menu range every now and then, with Norah sometimes grudgingly admitting that the customers liked something new.

Norah was working away in the kitchen, the smell of her warm tarts filling the café. She might not be the most adventurous of cooks, but she was a dab hand at pastry. People went mad for her apple tart and ice cream. It had been strange for Gina coming to work in a small village café after her job in a busy catering company, but Norah had been kind and generous to her and over time the older woman had come to rely on her.

The past few years had been tough, with Paul's job in construction just disappearing overnight, and then Grattan's Gourmet Foods, the busy caterers where she'd worked part-time for years, getting into financial difficulty and eventually shutting down. They had struggled on for months, not knowing what they should do, when fate had intervened and Paul's mother Sheila had offered them to come and live with her in Kilfinn.

Sheila Sullivan had fallen downstairs at home and broken her collarbone and wrist. However, the hospital discovered that she was suffering from heart failure and suggested that she move into a nursing home. But Sheila, an independent, feisty woman, made it very clear she was not budging and wanted to stay in her own home. Paul and Gina coming to live with her in Kilfinn was the obvious solution.

They had put their own three-bedroomed house in Dublin on the market, and to their relief had actually managed to sell it, finally able to clear their outstanding mortgage and pay off everything they owed. There had been no money left over – not even a euro – but it was a huge weight off their shoulders.

Saying goodbye to their neighbours in Firhouse had been hard. Also, their two boys had kicked up a huge fuss about leaving their school and their friends and moving to the middle of the country to live with their granny. But in time Conor and Aidan had both settled really well into the local village school and made new friends. Now they both played Gaelic football and were obsessed with their local team and the big gang of kids that they hung around with.

Paul, who had grown up in Kilfinn, was happy to come back to his home village and to have time with his mother in the last year and a half of her life. Gina had been the one who found the move away from Dublin, the city she loved, very difficult. However, as Sheila got weaker and frailer, unable to climb the stairs or even dress herself, Gina was there to help her, relieved that Sheila had enjoyed her final days surrounded by her family.

Last year, when Sheila's will was read and Paul's two brothers discovered that she had left him the family home on the outskirts of the village, there had been massive upset and a family row. Fortunately, eventually Jack and Leo had grudgingly accepted Sheila's wishes, conceding that over the years they had both visited Sheila only sporadically, as one brother lived in Manchester and the other in Dundalk, whereas Paul and Gina had always visited and taken care of her when she needed them.

Gina would be eternally grateful to her mother-in-law for her generosity and for ensuring that, no matter what happened, they need never again worry about having a roof over their heads.

She smiled when Johnny Lynch came into the café, dripping with rain, hung up his navy waterproof jacket and made a beeline for his favourite table in the corner. He'd retired about a year ago and came in almost every day for a pot of tea and a scone and to read the free newspaper that Norah provided for customers. Gina went over with the menu and the pretence that he might order something different.

''Tis an awful day,' he murmured. 'Sure what could be nicer than a pot of tea and a hot buttery scone?'

'Perfect,' Gina smiled and disappeared back to the counter to make the tea. Johnny would sit here for at least an hour, if not two, perusing the paper and talking to some of the customers he knew.

The café was a place for some of the older locals and various groups to congregate during the day, Norah providing a service that nobody else did in the small village. But lately things had begun to change, since Mulligan's pub at the end of the town had closed down. Larry Mulligan had decided to retire and had closed up the small traditional pub with its open hearth, Súgán chairs, stone floor and daily special of a traditional bowl of Mulligan's Stew, to the consternation of many of the locals who had sat there day in, day out, nursing pints and enjoying a bit of male camaraderie.

However, Johnny Armstrong and his wife, Bernadette, who ran the nearby Kilfinn Inn, had seized the opportunity to increase their business. They had always done teas and coffees and sandwiches and snacks, but now began to offer a simple pub lunch too. Norah, when she heard about it, had gone in next door to have lunch with her best friend to check out the competition.

'I had a nice bit of beef, and Una went for the roast chicken – a bit dry by my mind, and the gravy was one of those instant ones you mix from a tin. We both had the pavlova for dessert. It was good enough but not a patch on our lunch special,' Norah said firmly. 'But imagine, the TV was on all the time and there was music blaring. We could hardly hear ourselves think, let alone talk! Why would people go there?'

But people did go there, and Gina tried to persuade Norah to diversify from her traditional roast of the day, suggesting serving lasagnes, quiches, pasta bakes, chicken or seafood pies instead; but Norah didn't take well to change and insisted Cassidy's Café would continue the way it always had done from her mother and father's time to her own.

However, Gina persisted and did her best to broaden the menu once or twice a week at least, noticing that the day she served chicken and leek pie, with its crunchy cornflake topping, the place seemed busier than usual.

As the rain eased up they got a bit busier. Maeve McCarty came in to talk to her.

'Gina, I'm having a few girlfriends over for supper

next week,' she explained, 'and I wanted to ask you if you could make me a large lasagne for Saturday night. Your lasagne is the best ever!'

'Thanks for the compliment,' laughed Gina, agreeing instantly and writing down the order.

As the weather dried, the place seemed to fill up. Gina tried to make sure everyone managed to get a seat. The mid-morning coffees turned to lunches as a few members of the local bridge club took up the big table at the back after their bridge session in the parish hall and ordered a full lunch each.

Norah was in and out, talking to everyone. Gina had soon realized after starting to work there that the café was more than just a business for Norah: it was her life. She might be in her seventies now and a bit slower than she used to be, but Norah had started working there when she was a young girl helping her parents. She lived above the café and her life revolved around it. Marriage might have passed her by, but Norah was so caught up with the lives of her customers and local goings-on that she was never lonely.

Gina smiled as the Lennon sisters came in for lunch. They were sweethearts, both in their eighties, quite alike and living within a half-mile of each other. Rosemary, the elder, who had been a great friend of Sheila's, beckoned to her.

'Gina, dear, I'm having an awful problem with my kitchen tap – it's leaking all the time. Do you think that nice husband of yours might be able to come over again and fix it for me?'

'I'll ask him to call over to you tomorrow,' she promised.

Another benefit to working in the café was that she often got to hear about someone thinking about a new kitchen or putting in wardrobes, or considering doing a small extension long before anyone else, and Paul could put in a quote for doing the work. Gradually he was gaining a reputation for good work at a reasonable rate and was getting busier.

When Gina had first come to Kilfinn to live she had missed her family and friends back in Dublin so much. She'd been so homesick stuck in a village in the middle of nowhere that she didn't know how she could bear it. But now, with working in the café she felt so much a part of the community, a part of the village, that she didn't ever give moving back to Dublin a thought. She loved this place and harboured a secret dream to have a café like this or a little business of her own one day . . .

'Gina!' called Norah. 'There's a hot rhubarb tart and an apple tart to go out to the front of the shop. And you'll whip up some more cream to go with them, please!'

'Of course,' she smiled.

The sun was now streaming in the window and she watched as another couple came in searching for a table for two to have afternoon tea. The café might be small, but it was a little goldmine with its steady stream of customers all day.

Chapter Thirteen

Gina had made a creamy fish pie for the lunch menu and there was Norah's boiled ham with parsley sauce too. A few of the younger teachers from the school had come for lunch to celebrate one of their birthdays and she made a mental note to bring a large cupcake to the table with a candle on it once she had cleared away their plates.

Mary White, the public health nurse whose daughter Suzie was in class with Aidan, came in to have a bowl of soup with another nurse. Gina went over to take their order and have a chat.

Checking the tables, she noticed that an elderly couple in the corner hadn't got their mains yet and went into the kitchen to get them.

'Norah, I need two more hams, please!' she called, then suddenly realized that Norah was sitting on a chair trying to get her breath back, with a heavy oven tray lying on the ground.

'Are you okay?' Gina asked, concerned. Norah looked awful and when she tried to talk her speech seemed slurred.

'I was lifting the tray out of the oven . . .' she kept trying to say.

'It's all right, Norah,' Gina reassured her, going to get her a glass of water and making her put her feet up. 'Maybe we need to get a doctor?'

'No . . . n-noo.' Norah shook her head, but Gina realized that her face looked different, slightly lopsided.

'I'll be back in a minute,' she said, running out to get Mary, who was still outside at a table. The nurse came in and quickly began to examine the older woman.

'Norah, how are you feeling?'

Norah's speech was slow and definitely slurred.

'Can you raise your arm for me?' asked Mary calmly.

The effort was too much and Gina could see the fear in Norah's eyes.

'Listen, Norah, I think you need to go to hospital. It might be a slight stroke and the sooner the doctors see you the better.'

'Doctor JMMM,' Norah tried to say.

'I know you'd prefer Dr Jim, but today's Wednesday and it's his golf day,' Mary reminded her. 'There'll be no one in the practice. Listen, I could phone an ambulance but it could take at least thirty minutes or more to get one from Kilkenny to here, so I'm going to bring you in my car. It's faster.'

Norah protested about leaving the café, but Gina and Mary got her to see sense.

'The lunches are nearly over, Norah, and I'm well able to manage,' Gina reassured her. 'Honestly, the sooner you and Mary get on the road to the hospital the better.'

'Do you think you can stand and walk?' asked the nurse.

'Yes,' nodded Norah slowly.

'Gina, can you ask one of the men outside to come and give us a hand? My car is literally parked outside the door on the main street and I'll phone the hospital ahead so they'll expect us.'

Gina went out and saw that Brian Canning was sitting on his own reading the paper and finishing his lunch. He worked as a sales rep, and when she explained the situation he was delighted to help. Five minutes later, with Brian's help, they had calmly and quietly got Norah out through the café and into the car.

'You are going to be all right, Norah,' Gina promised, sensing the older woman's fear. 'Don't worry about the café – I'll look after everything here. Everything will be fine, I promise.'

After they had driven off, Gina knew that everyone was concerned about Norah. She made a big pot of coffee and one of tea and went around the café refilling cups and reassuring their customers that Norah was going to be okay and that in the café it was business as usual.

Chapter Fourteen

Gina had phoned the hospital to see how Norah was doing, and the next day after work went to visit her. She found Norah lying in a ward with five other patients. She was half asleep and the twist to her face on one side was quite noticeable. Mary had explained to her on the phone that Norah had been given immediate treatment for her stroke on arrival at the hospital's emergency department.

'It should help,' Mary explained, 'but the brain scans will show just how significant a stroke she's had. However, one has to take her age into account.'

Looking at Norah, who as she lay in the hospital bed suddenly seemed a frail, small woman with a shock of white hair, Gina pulled up a chair to sit down beside her. She had searched Norah's address book and phoned her nephew, Martin, and her cousin, Sadie, who lived in

Cork to tell them that Norah was in hospital. Poor Norah had hardly any family when it came down to it . . .

'I got you some nightdresses and a dressing gown and some things for hospital,' Gina said slowly as she bent down and put them neatly in the small locker beside her.

Norah had lived in the rooms above the café for most of her life and Gina had rarely gone beyond the front door of the place, let alone searching the woman's bedroom for things to take to her. Norah lived very simply and frugally, sleeping in an old double bed in one room with the other two smaller rooms used for all kinds of storage. There was a small galley kitchen and a neat sitting room with a gas fire and a TV. The room was also filled with cats not real ones, but china ones, toy ones, a bronze statue and a few cat photos. Norah obviously collected them. Cats clearly meant a lot to her, so it was strange that she didn't own one.

When Norah was more awake, one of the nurses helped Gina to sit her up in the bed.

'How are you?' Gina asked.

Norah spoke so slowly and with huge effort. She began to get agitated trying to ask about the café.

'The café is fine,' Gina said firmly. 'Everything went well today. The weather was pretty bad, so it was just a few regulars. They were all asking for you and said to get well soon.'

Norah nodded and her eyes welled with tears. Automatically, Gina reached for her hand.

'Norah, you're going to be fine,' she comforted her.

'You just have to take your time. Everything in work is okay, so please stop worrying. I did some new orders today – heaven knows I've watched you often enough to know what to do . . . So don't worry.'

Norah squeezed her hand.

'I've phoned Martin and Sadie. They both said they'd come here as soon as they can. I think Sadie's coming from Cork tomorrow.'

Norah patted her hand.

A nurse came over and it was clear that not only Norah's speech but also her swallowing had been affected by the stroke, as she couldn't even manage a simple sip of water and had some kind of thickened liquid to take.

Gina made smalltalk about the customers and when Norah dozed off again she slipped away.

'She's really bad, Paul. The poor thing, you should see the state she's in – she can hardly do anything,' she confided as they sat having coffee in the bright cream-painted kitchen that Paul had fitted a few months ago. The boys were in the other room, homework done, playing FIFA.

'Do you think that she'll be in hospital for long?' he asked, worried.

'It's hard to say. I don't know if she will get better or not. Mary says strokes are one of those things where it is almost impossible to say, but from what I can see Norah's has really affected her badly.'

'Do you think she'll have to retire or shut up shop?'

'I've no idea, but it doesn't look likely that she'll be back at work any day soon, so I'll just have to manage.'

'No better woman,' he laughed.

'I know that I can manage the café, but it's dealing with Norah's suppliers, like the wholesalers and the butcher, that's the problem. As you know, she always keeps herself to herself. I can use cash for payments, lodge money to her account. There is a bank lodgement book kept under the counter, but I don't have any access to withdraw from Norah's bank account. I have no idea about anything like that. I can probably get credit for a few weeks, but after that people will expect to be paid.'

'I have no idea what you should do. Maybe one of her family will be able to help,' he suggested.

'She only has that nephew, Martin, and his wife Cliona, who she sees about three times a year. Remember they wanted her to go to them last Christmas and she wouldn't go as she said they drive her mad with all their talk about their expensive holidays and restaurants they have tried? And her cousin Sadie is the same age as her and lost her husband a few years ago and can just about manage herself. I think that she has a daughter married and living in Kerry.'

'So not much help there?'

'I doubt it,' she sighed. 'But what happens if Norah doesn't come back and the café closes down?'

'Don't think that!'

'I'm being realistic, Paul. The woman is about seventy-five – she should have been retired years ago!

What happens if she doesn't come back to the café and it closes down? Where does that leave me?'

'We'll cross that bridge when we come to it,' he said soothingly.

Gina tried to control her anxiety. She and Paul were so different. He let things roll off him, not worry him, but she had shouldered a huge amount of the stress and burden over the years and knew that her income was very necessary for the family budget.

That night as she lay in bed she thought about the café – but under her ownership, with not only a change to the menu but perhaps also a change in the décor. She didn't mean to be disloyal to Norah, but she had to consider, if the opportunity were suddenly to come up to take over the café or rent the premises, should she do it?

Chapter Fifteen

For the first few days business in Cassidy's café was quiet. It was as if the people of Kilfinn and the locality, sensing Norah's absence, were reluctant to come into the café, but when Gina assured them that Norah was hoping to be back in attendance once she was able, the customers returned. Gina substituted some dishes and, chalking up the new daily specials, was encouraged by the way the customers liked them. Twice a week she called after work to see Norah, who was still in the hospital, and to update her on how the business was going. She lodged the money she took in to Norah's business account and brought along the business chequebook for Norah to sign cheques to three key suppliers, plus her own wages. She could see how much effort it took for Norah to manage even that and wondered how much longer this could all go on . . .

Martin Cassidy had come into the café twice, looked all around him and gone upstairs. Gina couldn't help herself, but she didn't trust him to look after Norah's interests. He'd asked to see the business accounts and she had refused, saying that only Norah could give permission for that. She could see him looking for them but she had the accounts ledger and lodgement book safely at home where she was trying to work out payments due. Sadie, Norah's cousin, had also come into the café. A nervous woman, she had sat down to a lunch of shepherd's pie over which she had fretted and worried about Norah.

'What is to become of her? I'm retired on a small widow's pension, so I'm not much help to poor Norah. Who is to look after her? If only she had married or had a family of her own . . .'

Gina had absolutely no idea what was going to happen, but as week after week went by it was clear that Norah was showing very little sign of recovery.

Gina had a few small catering jobs which, even though she was basically running the café single-handed, was something she had no intention of giving up. If the café were to close down and she were made redundant, it might be the only thing that she would have to fall back on.

She had normally worked only lunchtime on a Wednesday and three full days on Thursday, Friday and Saturday, but now she also opened up on a Tuesday and all day Wednesday. Monday was such a quiet day it wasn't worth opening. If she had had her way she would have opened on a Sunday, to catch people coming from mass, serve a family-friendly lunch, be open for afternoon tea and coffee and cakes when friends were off work and wanted to meet up – but Norah had resolutely refused to open on the Lord's Day, and it was Norah's café.

The staff nurse in the hospital had mentioned to her the last time she visited Norah that there was talk of transferring her to Beech Hill, Kilfinn's nursing home for the elderly. Gina supplied them with cupcakes, and the few times she had been in the place she had liked it. It was bright and airy and had been purpose-built, and it was all on one level and only a few minutes out of the town.

Norah had always been independent, but for now it seemed her independence was gone; she would be reliant on nurses and carers for the time being and the hospital's social worker had tried to explain to her the necessity of moving to a step-down facility. Norah had shaken her head, vehemently protesting about moving to an old people's home. Norah Cassidy, of Cassidy's Café, had never once in all her seventy-seven years of life considered herself old or even aging, so why she should be consigned to the place where all the old folks of the locality ended up was beyond her.

'But they'll take good care of you there. You'll get the speech and physiotherapy you need,' Gina assured her. 'From what I've seen when I do my delivery, it's lovely there. You'll have your own room and bathroom and television.'

'Just till I get better,' mumbled Norah loudly.

Aware that it was unlikely Norah would return to work in the café, Gina wondered how much longer the situation could continue.

At night she worked on her laptop, planning out various scenarios that involved her either taking over running the café, or otherwise renting it or buying it from Norah and creating a café of her own.

'What are you up to?' teased Paul as she sat on the couch beside him.

'You watch the news – I'm working out a new menu plan and also I have done a few mood boards of ideas for doing up the café if I took it over.'

'Gina, don't get ahead of yourself,' he warned. 'You don't know what's going to happen with Norah and that family of hers.'

'If Cassidy's closes down somebody else will take it over!' she remonstrated. 'I'm the one who's been working there for over two years and I know I could make a go of it – increase business, attract new customers – if I got the chance. Maybe we should go to the bank and find out about taking out a loan, Paul.'

'I'm not sure we should do that,' he worried. 'We are only getting back on our feet.'

'I know, but this is different. It's a business loan; we'd be paying a business rate. We own this house lock, stock and barrel, so no one can touch this place and it will not be part of the loan,' she insisted. 'Paul, do you realize, Norah having to retire might be my chance to have a business of our own?'

'I know that, love,' he said, hugging her.

'I was thinking we could do up the place,' she coaxed. 'You could do some of the work, maybe we could buy new chairs or paint the old ones and give it all a fresh look. It's got so dated. And we could get rid of that oilcloth on the tables, and have fresh flowers and colour and a different look and feel.'

'I think you should wait and see,' he said gently.

'I know, but maybe I should talk quietly to Billy Wright from the bank about getting a loan, sound it out with him.'

'We are hardly the bank's best customers!' he laughed.

'I know that,' she said, hugging him. 'It's just that I can see it – me running the place, getting it the way I want. This might be the right opportunity for us actually to have a business of our own.'

'I understand how you are feeling, Gina love, but it's Norah's place, you know that . . . it's still her café.'

Gina sighed. Maybe Paul was right – she was getting ahead of herself, letting her ideas run away with her. In time, Norah would realize that she could no longer work and a decision would be made with regard to the café. That was when Gina Sullivan would be ready either to take on running it or to try to persuade Norah to let her rent or purchase the premises.

Chapter Sixteen

On Sunday morning Kim and Evie were up early as they wanted to get a good pitch for displaying Evie's paintings in the popular weekend open-air art show held on Merrion Square. Town was still quiet as they unloaded the car and hung her paintings from the old park railings of Dublin's well-known Georgian square, bordered by Holles Street Hospital, the National Gallery and the Dáil.

All around them other artists came with their work, all jostling and vying for position. Everyone was keen to sell their work, but there was a great sense of artists' camaraderie as they admired and studied each other's pieces. A few regulars came over to welcome Evie to the Sunday on the square and wish her well. Space was at a premium so they created a second row of canvases on the lower level, standing them against the bottom of the railings.

'Where will we put this one?' Kim asked, holding up the massive canvas covered in brown, yellow and red swirls which Evie called *The Vikings*.

'There in the middle – it should attract attention!' Evie directed her.

On a narrow fold-up table they had Evie's cards and an info sheet about her work, as well as a box crammed with smaller prints and sketches of her work for people to buy and frame themselves.

'Are you selling all these?'

'Yes, they're all over the flat, so I might as well try and get some money for them. Besides, the flat is bursting and I needed to clear a bit of space. Honestly, the two of us are such hoarders!'

'I'm not a hoarder!' protested Kim, who objected to being compared to the messiest person she knew.

'Yes, you are! I've got all my art gear and drawings and canvases, and you've got all your fashion and clothes stuff.'

Kim reddened, thinking of the boxes and bags of clothes in her sister's house. Some had been consigned to the attic, but the rest still remained around the place. She'd nearly tripped over one of her bags getting ready this morning.

'What are you going to do with it all when you move out of Liz's to a new apartment or have to share with someone else?' teased Evie.

Kim hadn't a clue. In the old apartment with Gareth she'd taken up three quarters of the wardrobe space and had also commandeered most of the storage in the spare bedroom, turning it into a kind of personal dressing room.

'Well, if you must know I'm putting some of my stuff up on eBay and selling it. And I'm going to take a few things into Chloe's – that vintage place – and sell them there.'

'That's a great idea. Some of your stuff must be worth a fortune!'

'Obviously a lot less than what I paid for them, but still – money is money!' she admitted, the idea growing on her.

'I love the way they call second-hand stuff "vintage",' laughed Evie.

They were lucky the day was dry and bright, if a little breezy – perfect weather for walking and browsing, looking at the huge array of art on display. Evie's work was attracting lots of interest from passers-by and Evie was soon deep in conversation with a couple who had just bought a new house and wanted a big piece of art for their living room. They were torn between two canvases and Evie was holding back, as she didn't want to lose the sale.

'If you take one and you get it home and don't like it, there is no problem swapping it for the other,' she assured them, giving them her address. 'My studio is quite near here.'

As they paid for the painting, Kim couldn't believe it! This exhibition was a great opportunity for Evie to sell her work without gallery fees and commission. Kim sold three of Evie's prints and gave one of her cards to a man who wanted two paintings for his office. They were kept busy all day, with lots of people praising her friend's work and admiring it as well as buying.

Walking around the square, Kim couldn't get over the wide variety of art on display: everything from watercolours of flowers, portraits, Irish landscapes, Gothic etchings and cartoons to the bold canvases of artists like Evie which attracted huge attention. People flocked to see the paintings and have a ramble around this open-air art show, held so near to Ireland's National Gallery.

'They like to see the Old Masters in the gallery over there,' explained Evie, 'and then come across to the square and buy a piece of art they like and can afford from one of us, and hope that the artist will become famous some day and that they have been lucky enough to have an early work!'

By four thirty things had begun to slow down, except for a few tourists who enjoyed talking to the artists. Kim delighted in giving them the address for Evie's new website.

They packed up the paintings and headed back to the flat, where, both exhausted, they ordered a Chinese takeaway and flopped on the couch. Evie was absolutely thrilled with the money she had made from the sale of her work.

'It was well worth paying the money to get a licence to exhibit there,' she laughed as they read their fortune cookies.

* * *

Kim was pleased with Evie's website, which had been updated with photos from Sunday's art exhibition. It looked so cool and really had accomplished all she had hoped for, with lively Facebook and Twitter connections and Evie's art blog.

'I don't think I can improve it any more,' she admitted as she submitted it for one part of her final design project.

'It is really good – different and eye-catching with lots of content,' praised Piotr, one of her classmates, who was a computer genius but was always ready to give her a hand if she got stuck on something.

Kim was really going to miss her course and felt she had learned a huge amount over the past few months. The thing was, how to put her knowledge to good use. The class had been small, the students all different and from various walks of life, but they had gelled and got on well, encouraging each other and hanging out together . . . but what she was going to do after this she had no idea.

At home she spent her time on eBay watching to see if her items had sold, checking offers, sometimes relieved that there were none for her high black boots, or her Stella McCartney jacket, other times torn because someone was actually going to buy her Hermès handbag or her Simone Rocha white blouse.

Liz had also helped her to go through all her things and pick out a whole load of barely worn clothes and accessories and bring them in to sell in Chloe's Vintage Room, the vintage shop on the upstairs floor in the

Powerscourt Centre. Chloe Garnier had raved about some of the items that she was willing to sell.

'You need money in the bank,' Liz reminded her sternly, 'not clothes sitting in your wardrobe that you never wear!'

Kim was sad to say goodbye to some of the beautiful things that she had collected, but money in her account was far more important.

But now, with her course finishing, she was worried about what she should do. She envied her friends who had regular jobs and regular incomes. She knew that somehow her life had to change and little by little she was trying to do that . . .

Chapter Seventeen

Molly was busy clearing a section of the herb garden; the rosemary had gone woody and the lemon balm was running amok everywhere. Serious cutting back was needed and as she cut and trimmed she listened for a car pulling into the driveway.

Bill had phoned to say he'd gone through all the paperwork and suggested meeting up. Perhaps he sensed her reluctance about going to Dublin again so soon. 'If you want I could drive down to Mossbawn?' he offered. 'I haven't seen the place properly for years.'

'Bill, that would be perfect – and I'll make us both a lovely lunch,' she added, feeling guilty, as Bill had barely been in the house since his marriage to Carole. David had suggested a few times inviting the two of them to visit, but Molly just couldn't find it in her heart to entertain the woman who had replaced her sister. She knew it was stupid and pathetic, as Ruth herself had said to her often enough that she hoped that Bill would in time remarry, her sister being more open-hearted than she was.

Cutting some rosemary, she headed back across the lawn as Bill's car pulled up.

'Bill, it's so lovely to have you back here in Mossbawn,' she said, running to welcome him.

'And it's good to be back,' he said, looking around him.

'Will you have a coffee or something?' she offered. 'I've lunch in the oven, but it won't be ready for a while.'

'Sounds good, but Molly, I'd love to stretch my legs, have a walk around the place first. I haven't seen it for so long.'

Bill grabbed a sweater from the car. 'This place brings back so many happy memories of the four of us and all our kids,' he said as they walked. 'Do you remember the picnics?'

'The girls were obsessed with them!' she laughed. 'One year we even had a midnight summer picnic with candles and lanterns.'

'Any fish left in here?' he asked, peering into the murky water in the pond.

'I doubt it. I'm afraid the heron got what was left last year. I keep meaning to clean it up and re-stock it, but just haven't got round to it.'

Turning right, they headed towards the back field, the grass almost knee height, and back across the old paddock.

'What about the South Field?'

'The McHughs use it for their cows – at least it keeps the grass and weeds down – and I'm letting Pamela Reynolds use the Blackberry Field for her horses.' They stopped and looked at three mares, heads bowed, cropping the grass around them.

'You have so much space here, Molly,' Bill said admiringly.

'Too much space,' she admitted as they turned towards the oakwood that divided her property from the Reynolds'. 'Now come and I'll show you the garden.'

Bill was the perfect guest, admiring the large borders and flowerbeds as they passed.

'You must miss your garden?' she said without thinking.

'Sometimes,' he admitted, 'but I don't miss cutting that lawn. When I think of all the weekends I spent up and down with that bloody mower. The patio garden we've got now is easy to manage and I've got pots with strawberries and a few herbs growing.'

'Sounds tempting!' she laughed as she led him around by the side of the house.

'Hey! I see you still have the maze! It's got huge!'

'I know. When I think of all the kids that have played hide and seek over the years since it was first planted by the Moores . . . It's part of the history of the house,' she said proudly.

'Molly, how are you managing all this?' he quizzed as they walked on.

'To be honest . . . not very well,' she admitted. 'I get Paddy, the gardener, and his nephew Tommy in to help with the heavy work – I'd be lost without them.' Molly and David had inherited Paddy Flynn from the previous owner. He was a Trojan worker and as honest as they come. In his early seventies, he and his nephew were a great pair. 'But even still, there's so much to do . . .'

They turned into the rectangular walled kitchen garden, where the sun streamed down on them.

'There's me talking about my little patio garden, and look at all the things you have growing here: grapes, strawberries, raspberries and gooseberries!'

'We've lots of veggies too – onions, carrots, cabbage, broccoli, potatoes, lettuce, peas, runner beans, and tomatoes in the greenhouse and some peppers! Bill, take some lettuce and some beans and spring onions for you and Carole,' she insisted, pulling them and putting them in a basket.

As they walked back towards the house, Molly turned through the gate, stopping to show him where she was restoring the rose garden.

'You can still see some of those lovely old roses,' he said admiringly.

'I know. Even though they've been so badly treated they're trying to come back,' she smiled as they walked along the path to the house.

Molly set the kitchen table quickly and served rack of lamb with rosemary and baby potatoes.

'Wow, this was worth the journey,' laughed Bill

appreciatively as he began to eat. 'Honestly, Molly, how are you finding things?' he probed.

'Hard – bloody hard. I hate being on my own.' Tears welled in her eyes.

'It must be tough in a big house like this.'

'When David was alive, to be honest we mostly lived here in the kitchen and the sitting room and he had the study. The rest of the house we only used for entertaining or the weekends when the girls were around or we'd people staying.'

Bill said nothing, but she could tell what he was thinking as she made a pot of coffee.

'I've got some toffee squares. I made them this morning.'

'You remembered my sweet tooth,' he joked, helping himself to one. 'You and Ruth were always great bakers!'

As she poured the coffee he produced his briefcase and spread the paperwork on the table. Molly sighed. Normally David had taken care of all their finances. Now she would have to try to understand things.

'I've had a good chance to go through everything.'

'And what do you think?'

'The fact that there is no mortgage on Mossbawn is great,' he explained, 'but the repayments on the other loans you and David took out are quite hefty as they were for a shorter term. I would definitely advise clearing them if at all possible, as you don't want to find yourself struggling with the repayments.'

'Should I use the insurance money?'

'Some of it, because you're making very little interest on it but are paying high interest on the money you've borrowed. But I think you should draw down a part of David's pension and use it for the repayments.' He explained patiently, 'It would be more tax efficient to use it to pay off the loans and leave the rest of the pension untouched in the hope of seeing it grow. Then I'd advise putting the rest of the money into an easy-access savings account that suits you and makes it fairly easy to manage along with your normal current account.'

'Will I manage . . . be able to survive on the remaining insurance money?'

'Hopefully, though this is a house that probably costs a fortune to keep.'

'Bill, be honest – do you think I should sell the house?'

'I am not here to tell you what to do,' Bill said, raising his hands, 'but Mossbawn is a valuable property.'

'But I love this house,' she protested. 'David wouldn't have wanted me to sell.'

'No one wants to sell their home,' he said softly, 'but many of us have to.'

'Is that why you sold your house?'

'After Ruth died I found it lonely as hell without her. The house was full of memories. But then Liz got married, Mike moved to Canada and even Kim was off doing her own thing. To tell the truth, I'd been thinking of selling and downsizing for ages. When I met Carole I knew that she was never going to live there; she wanted us to have a new place and I wanted that too.'

Molly didn't know what to say.

'The only person who can decide about selling is you,' he said firmly. 'But the market is difficult at the moment, so even if you put Mossbawn up for sale there is no guarantee it would sell.'

'So basically the insurance money is my only income until the pension fund goes up?'

'Exactly, unless you make the house earn for you or find a job.'

'So what am I to say to the bank on Thursday?' she worried. 'I just want to get all this bloody loan stuff sorted.'

'If you want I'll come with you,' he offered.

'Bill, that would be wonderful,' she said, unable to disguise her relief.

'It's the least I can do,' he said. 'Molly, you have always been very good to me and the kids when we needed you.'

'How are they all?' she asked.

'Fine, I guess. Liz is busy with work and the kids. We don't get to see each other half as much as I'd like. Mike talks to me on Skype, so at least I get to see my Canadian grandson. And Kim — she's the one I worry about most. I don't know if you've heard that she's broken up with that boyfriend of hers.'

'Oh, poor Kim! How awful for her!'

'It's all a mess. She moved out of the apartment they were sharing. She's staying with Liz for the moment. But she still hasn't got a job, and I suspect deep inside doesn't really know what she wants to do.'

'But she's such a bright girl.'

'I know,' he sighed, 'but it's a worry.'

'Why don't I give her a call and arrange to see her?' she offered.

Kim, Ruth's youngest, was her goddaughter and always had been very different from her older brother and sister. Ruth's death had hit her the hardest and she still remembered how her niece had turned up on her doorstep, a skinny, pale, broken-hearted streak of misery who had ended up staying in Mossbawn for six weeks that summer, Molly taking her under her wing as if she were her own daughter.

'Thanks, I'd really appreciate it.' Bill sighed. 'The two of you have always been so close.'

'I'll phone her tonight,' she promised.

'Look, I'd better get going. Carole and I have a bridge game at the golf club this evening,' he said standing up and taking his briefcase. 'But I'll see you next Thursday.'

Molly thanked him profusely.

'It was really good to see the place again,' he said, hugging her before he got in the car and set off down the driveway.

Chapter Eighteen

Molly felt relief wash over her as she left the bank. Bill had been wonderful. Dermot hadn't expected her to bring him along with her today and her brother-in-law had been so professional in negotiating a deal on her behalf.

All their loans were cleared, every bit of money owed on the house settled. Okay, she mightn't have a huge amount of money left to live on after agreeing to use some of the insurance money to pay off what was due to the bank. Bill had also advised the bank that she was drawing down 25 per cent of David's pension and using that to pay off the rest. Molly decided to put a sum of money into an account for each of their daughters; it was something she knew that David would have wanted. The remainder was split between her current account and a savings account.

'I've been having nightmares about it all,' she admitted as they chatted outside afterwards, 'but thank heaven it's all sorted. I am so grateful to you, Bill.'

'It's what accountants do all the time,' he laughed. 'I'm glad I could help. Do you want to come for coffee or grab a sandwich?'

'Actually, I'm meeting Kim for lunch.'

'Molly, thanks. I appreciate it – but please don't mention my concerns to her.'

'I wouldn't dream of it,' she assured him. 'Besides, I love seeing my lovely goddaughter!'

Molly strolled up towards St Stephen's Green. She'd always loved the big city-centre park with its lake and bridge and walks. She'd time to kill before meeting Kim. Passing the windows of one of the country's biggest auctioneering firms, she found herself stopping to study the photos of various properties that were for sale: houses and apartments and duplexes and townhouses, and on one stand a number of large expensive city and country properties. Over in the other window there were country houses and estates, and even two castles displayed. She studied them. Beautiful old houses all for sale from one end of the country to the other, many of their owners deceased or struggling to maintain them . . . She gave a sigh. What option did people have?

What option did she have? She knew after meeting the bank that things were going to be tight. Dermot and Bill had both made that crystal clear.

She found herself pushing the polished glass door. If

she was even to consider selling Mossbawn House, she needed to find out what kind of value a firm like this would place on her home.

An hour later Molly found a small sunny outside table on the corner near Duke Street. A few seconds later Kim appeared in leggings and a bird-print dress.

'Hello, darling,' Molly said, getting up to hug her. 'It's lovely to see you.' Kim was so like her sister Ruth – tall, with the same blue eyes and tumble of dark hair. It was almost a sense of déjà vu, seeing her.

The waitress was hovering so, glancing at the menu, they ordered quickly.

'How are things?' Molly asked casually, putting the menu away.

'I don't know if you heard, but Gareth and I broke up.'

'Oh Kim, I'm so sorry.'

'So . . . I've no boyfriend! No job! No home!' Kim giggled, desperately. 'Things couldn't be worse really!'

'You poor pet!' Molly said gently. 'I know how much you cared for him.'

'I loved him, and stupidly I thought he loved me.'

Molly could see that her niece was fighting to control her emotions.

'I honestly don't know why things didn't work out between us,' she continued. 'Gareth's big into career and work and he hated that I wasn't working. But surely we should have got over that. Besides, I am trying to get a job.'

'Perhaps there is more to it than that, Kim love,' she suggested, noting the grey shadows under her niece's eyes and that she was far thinner than she had ever seen her before.

'I suppose. It's weird, because even though we were living together we were growing apart instead of being closer . . .'

'Nothing worse,' said Molly. 'Life is tough enough for us all without being lumbered with the wrong partner.'

'Everyone keeps saying I'll meet someone else,' Kim said, her eyes welling with tears.

'I wouldn't dare.'

'It's just that it doesn't really help, because I miss him so much.'

'I understand, Kim love. I miss my David every day, and it doesn't matter what good advice people give you about time healing, it's just so hard losing someone we love, no matter what the circumstances are.'

Molly really felt such sympathy for her young niece. Kim had always worn her heart on her sleeve, been impulsive and giving, and rather reckless, throwing herself into things without thinking, and now she had got hurt, badly hurt, by falling in love with someone who wasn't as passionate and caring as she was.

'How are your courses and classes going?' she asked, trying to change the subject as the waitress appeared with their plates of pasta and a salad.

'I had photography last night. I took photos of Dún Laoghaire Harbour at night with the yachts and boats and the sun going down, and they've turned out really well. I'm doing some portraits of Finn and Ava as a surprise for Liz. Do you want to see them?' She passed Molly her phone so she could see the photos of the children.

'They are gorgeous!' she said. The photos seemed to capture their spirit, the look in their eyes – their sense of mischief. 'These are beautiful.'

'Finn is so funny and a dream to photograph. They're both wild and keep Liz and Joe busy all the time!'

'Your mum would have loved them! Ruth would have been in her element, in the thick of it, helping Liz with babysitting, outings . . . She'd have been a wonderful grandmother.'

'I know Liz really misses her . . . We both do,' said Kim softly.

'Well, these photographs of the two of them look amazing.'

'I'll make you a copy. I've learned a lot about how to take photos,' she laughed, 'but I've only one class left. And my website-design course in Rathmines is finishing up too. I've been doing it for six months and it's been brilliant. I was struggling at first because it's so technical, but I absolutely love it! It was tough trying to get my head around so much jargon about programs and that, but it's fascinating seeing what you can actually do with technology.'

'I'm afraid I'm a bit of a dinosaur where these things are concerned,' Molly admitted.

'I hadn't a clue when I started, but our tutors really make you understand how things work.'

'When do you finish?'

'The end of the month, and I'm going to miss it and the group. There are only twelve of us. I'd love to try and get some work in that area. Do you remember my friend Evie – she's an artist?'

'Yes, is she the girl with all the different hair colours?'

'Yeah,' Kim giggled. 'I've designed a website to show off her paintings. They are brilliant and people can find out about her and buy some of her work online.'

'That sounds very interesting,' Molly said, relieved that at least Kim was keeping herself busy.

'But I don't know what I'm going to do when it finishes,' Kim conceded candidly. 'I was supposed to have an interview for a job, but apparently they have already filled the position internally and there's nothing else.'

'So what will you do?' asked Molly.

'That's just it! I don't know what I'm going to do. Things are a mess right now and I can't keep on staying with Liz and sponging on her and Joe.'

'I'm sure Liz doesn't mind.'

'I've taken Finn's room,' she admitted.

'Kim, why don't you come and stay with me in Mossbawn?' Molly found herself offering. 'I'm down in Kilfinn on my own and would love a bit of company.'

Kim had always loved coming to stay in the house ever since she was a little girl. Why, hadn't she run away to Mossbawn when she was barely twelve years old? Bought a train ticket on her own and taken the train to their station, walked up to the house and surprised herself and David? There'd been utter turmoil at home when Bill and Ruth had discovered that she was missing, but she'd stayed for three days with them before Molly had brought her back home to Ruth. And then of course she'd stayed with them again a few months after Ruth's death, rambling around the house and garden like a lost kitten, David and she doing everything they could to help her get through her grief.

'Are you sure?' Kim asked, a catch in her voice.

'Of course I'm sure. Emma is studying for her thesis thing in Galway and Grace after her exams is off back-packing around Europe, so I'm on my own.'

'I haven't been for ages, but it's funny,' Kim confided, her lip trembling, 'when Gareth and I broke up I just wanted to get in my car and drive to Mossbawn.'

'Why didn't you?' wondered Molly.

'I was too upset to drive – I'd probably have crashed the car. Anyway, I told myself to be grown up and stop running and face things.'

'Well, you'll come and stay now,' Molly coaxed. 'Daisy and I would love to have you.'

'Oh Auntie Molly, that would be lovely!' she said, leaping up and hugging her.

'Well, that's settled then,' Molly said firmly. 'You just let me know when you are coming, Kim, and I'll have the room aired for you and the bed made.'

'I'll come as soon as my course is over, if that's okay.'

'That sounds perfect.' She was really looking forward to Kim coming to stay with her in Mossbawn.

Chapter Nineteen

Kim surveyed the back seat of her car crammed with her clothes and luggage. Thank heaven Liz and Joe had agreed to store the rest of her stuff, or her aunt would think she was crazy!

'Drive carefully,' warned Liz, 'and give our love to Molly.'

'I wish that you were coming down for a visit too,' Kim coaxed, checking that her laptop was securely stored. 'Promise you'll try to come down!'

'Kim, you know how hard it is for me to get a night away from this crew,' Liz said, grabbing a struggling Finn into her arms. 'Joe would have a fit.'

Leaving the estate, Kim headed up to join the steady stream of cars flowing on to the M50. The traffic was light as she took the exit road for Cork and Kilkenny and put on the radio.

She had always loved going to Mossbawn. The big old house just outside Kilkenny, surrounded by trees and fields and woods, was like a magical kingdom that she had loved to explore, pretending she was a wood sprite or fairy or enchanted princess when she was a kid. They used to go and stay with Molly and David regularly – her dad and mum, with the three of them in the back seat, squashed with their luggage as they drove the winding country roads to Kilfinn village where her aunt and uncle lived. Molly had always made them feel welcome and there would be a massive dinner with a home-made tart or cake afterwards and ice cream.

Kim remembered wriggling in her chair, itching to run around and explore, to check that nothing had changed since their last visit . . . Mossbawn was somehow always the same.

She and Liz used to share a massive room with an old-fashioned four-poster bed. They loved it and would stay up late reading from the big bookshelf filled with dusty old books belonging to their aunt. Enid Blyton, E. Nesbit and Frances Hodgson Burnett were their favourites. Their brother Mike would sleep in the Captain's Bed – the room done out like a ship's cabin with mementoes of voyages from all around the world displayed on two shelves, the wall adorned with maps which Mike convinced them were secret treasure maps. Come rain or shine, there was always something to do – tennis, fishing in the river, riding, playing in the fields and hanging out in the village. Sometimes she wished that she lived there and would never

ever have to go back to Dublin and normal life!

One time she'd run away there. She had just moved into secondary school, finding herself in a new class in a new school and separated from her close friends. She was unhappier than she had ever been before. It was awful, and she remembered just wanting to escape to Mossbawn and the comfort of the old house. Apparently she had caused uproar with her disappearance, but she just remembered the adventure of it! Molly and Uncle David had made no fuss and treated her arrival off the Dublin train on her own like a routine visit.

The summer after her mum had died, when she was nearly seventeen, she had gone to stay at Mossbawn for six weeks. She remembered being sad and angry, lost and lonely, and just wanting to escape to the place she felt safe. Liz had gone to Bordeaux for four weeks to learn French and Mike had gone off backpacking around Europe with some friends. Kim spent most of that summer with her aunt and uncle, mooching around the house and garden, day-dreaming, reading, playing cards and hanging out with her younger cousins and their new puppy Daisy, listening to music, sunbathing on the terrace.

Her aunt was endlessly patient, showing Kim how to bake bread, make a cake, and in the garden teaching her how to plant things and divide plants and when to give them support, food, a stake, a watering, showing her just how much care and attention a garden needed. It seemed to Kim that her aunt was an artist and the garden was her painting. Her uncle had brought her out on the river in his boat, showed her how to catch a fish, and how to play threes tunes on his piano; he told jokes and played tricks on them all, and loved playing rounders as the sun went down . . .

When Uncle David had died last year she'd been devastated. He was one of the kindest men she had ever known and Kim had struggled to accept that she had lost someone else that she loved.

Since her uncle's death things hadn't been the same. Molly was mostly on her own . . . Kim felt guilty about it, but was really looking forward to staying there now.

As she drove she put on a CD and sang along with it. It was weird, but driving along she felt sort of happy – the first time in weeks.

Coming off the motorway, she relaxed as she drove through one small town after another until she came to Kilfinn. As she passed along the main street she spotted all the familiar shops: O'Donnell's Supervalu, Cassidy's Café, the Kilfinn Inn, Grogan's Pharmacy, Reynolds' Newsagents and the Post Office. She was surprised to see a For Sale sign up in Molloy's Drapery; the shop was an institution in Kilfinn, an emporium stocking everything from underwear to wellington boots, knitted jumpers and rain gear to tea towels and tablecloths and bed linen. Mulligan's Bar was also closed with a For Sale sign over the door. It was awful seeing shops shutting down, businesses closing. Dublin was full of them, but clearly even somewhere like Kilfinn was being affected.

At the end of the town she saw the familiar iron gates of Mossbawn House and turned up the driveway. Coming to a halt outside the large country house with its bay windows, red-painted door and stone dogs guarding the entrance, she suddenly felt home. As she opened the car door she heard Daisy barking and a few seconds later the little dog was out jumping around her feet as Molly came to greet her.

'Welcome, Kim pet. It's so good to see you.'

Molly looked tired and she guessed that her aunt had been busy cleaning for the past few days and getting things ready for her arrival.

'Did you have a good drive?' Molly asked, looking into the packed car. 'Let me give you a hand with some of your luggage.'

'No, it's okay, Molly; I'll take some stuff in now and get the rest later.'

As Kim walked through into the hall, Daisy ran around, tail wagging with excitement at seeing her.

The hall hadn't changed, with its black-and-white tiled floor and the old grandfather clock ticking away, and the table with a big vase of flowers from the garden sitting under the mirror. She loved this old house, even the way it smelled and sounded and its atmosphere of calm and acceptance.

'Come down to the kitchen and I'll make us some tea,' smiled her aunt, leading the way.

Kim had always felt at home in this kitchen, with its Aga cooker and massive Irish pine table, its scattering of comfy chairs, her aunt's display of antique blue-and-white china on the dresser and the pantry stocked with all kinds of things.

'Will you have a scone?'

Kim laughed. How well her aunt remembered that warm scones were her favourite thing in the world.

'I've a jar of bramble jelly here somewhere.'

Sitting down at the table, Kim let her aunt fuss over her like she used to when she was a child. It felt good to be back . . . safe.

'I've put you in the old bedroom. I know how much you and Liz loved it.'

'Thanks.'

'It's so good to have you here again, Kim,' her aunt confided. 'To tell the truth, I get lonely here without David.'

'Then I'm glad I came. I've always loved coming here.'

Kim carried most of her bags and gear upstairs to her bedroom, with its floral-patterned wallpaper and the pretty quilted bedspread and enormous bed. The carpet was rather threadbare, but the rest of the room was rich and warm-looking, with sunshine streaming in. Unzipping her case, she took out her boots and pulled them on, making a mental note to tidy up later as she headed down the large staircase and out through the front door, Daisy at her heels as she set out to explore the garden.

Chapter Twenty

Life in Mossbawn was so simple and uncomplicated compared to being in Dublin. Kim missed her friends, but chatted to them on Skype and Facebook most days. Molly put no pressure on her and let her do what she wanted, the two of them falling into an easy routine of walks, working in the garden and going to the village for food and newspapers, watching TV or listening to the radio in the evenings. Her aunt left her to her own devices a lot of the time, as Molly was engrossed in restoring the old walled rose garden and totally replanting it.

'It gives me something to do, and God knows I could do with that!'

In the village Kim popped into Cassidy's Café. It seemed strange, as Norah Cassidy was sick and in hospital, but Gina, the new manager, filled her in on how she was doing as she ordered a cappuccino and a cupcake. The cupcakes were on a pretty tiered cake stand and after much deliberation she opted for an iced lemon one. It was gorgeous, and she instantly sent a photo of it to Evie and the girls to drive them crazy!

Over a bottle of red wine after dinner one night Molly had confided that she was considering selling the house.

'You can see yourself that it's far too big for me now that David has gone. Maybe I should listen to everyone and sell it, and move to something smaller and get on with my life.'

'But you love this house and the garden!' Kim said, dismayed.

'I know, but things change as we get older. Nothing can stay the same and we have to change too, as you've already discovered, Kim! I've talked to an auctioneer and they are going to send someone down to see the place, give me a rough estimate of what it's worth and what the market for a house like this is at present.'

'Have you told Emma and Grace?'

'No, not yet. There's no point saying anything to them until I know a bit better what's happening about the house.'

Kim was shocked. She herself couldn't bear the thought of losing Mossbawn and having someone else live here, but she could see how lonely her aunt was and how much work and expense were involved in running the place.

* * *

While Molly worked like a Trojan most days in her rose garden or in the kitchen garden, Kim got out her expensive Olympus camera and began to shoot photographs around the house and grounds. The camera was almost like a fresh eye, taking in the old house, the stone, the curving pillars, the decorative window fan over the front door, the stairs and hall, and the old grandfather clock, the collection of boots near the door, the fireplace with logs blazing, the pantry, the old family portraits and photographs, her aunt's collection of crystal, the view of the lawn from the bedroom window, the wonderful free-standing bath, even the sturdy Aga.

Outside, Kim with her camera in hand captured the garden in the early-morning light, as the sun warmed the brick in the old stables and dew clung to the tall bushes of rosemary and lavender, the dainty pink leaves and buds of a new rose beginning to open, the mighty beech tree, a curious red squirrel, the robins and the rooks that flocked to the woods. She wanted to capture it all – before everything disappeared and changed . . . She wanted to keep it for ever.

It was as if the old house had put a spell on her, and going through the library room where her uncle used to work she was fascinated to discover documents and ledgers and a leather folder that held so much information about the history of the house and its previous owners. The more she read about Charles Moore, the original owner, and his wife, Constance, and their eight children, the more interested she became. Turning to the internet she searched through birth records and parish records and census forms to find out more about the past of Mossbawn House and its inhabitants.

The local graveyard yielded no clues, but Father Darragh told her that there was a much older graveyard that was no longer in use about two miles away on the other side of the village.

'I'm sure that might be where your Moore family are buried if they died in Kilfinn,' he explained as they walked up to it together.

The graveyard was overgrown, and most of the inscriptions on the headstones were worn away and covered in moss and lichen, but Kim persisted until she found a Constance, *dearest mother and wife*, who had died in 1877. The second name was almost illegible, but it looked like a Mo—. Another name had been added later – she could read 'husband' and only the initial C. She wondered, was that Charles? The year of death was 1904, which would have meant he had lived for many years after his beloved Constance and had died a very old man. She needed to find the death records or burial records to check them. Curious to discover more, she talked to Kilfinn's local librarian, Una Swann.

Una showed her many of the records and photographs and items related to the village. A family called Cavendish had lived in Mossbawn for a number of years when the house had gone out of the Moore family's hands. Then, around 1888, Charles's youngest son James Moore and his wife had managed to regain possession of the house and most of the grounds.

'The county library, which is much bigger, would have some of the famine records and land records from the time, Kim. Why don't you try there?' she suggested.

Kim's file and photos and records about Mossbawn's history seemed to grow and grow, and as she scanned in documents and photos and old letters she realized that she was creating almost an archive about the house. Curious to find out more, she often stayed up late, working on her laptop at night.

Molly too was fascinated by it and helped her as much as she could, both of them aware that if a suitable buyer was found for Mossbawn another owner's family history would be added.

'The house has always been bought by people when they had money and then sold by them when they needed it!' admitted Molly. 'Apparently a huge amount of the surrounding land had to be sold over the years to keep the house or owners going.'

'It's such a shame when you see how big the original grounds of the estate were on the map!'

'Kim, you really have got caught up in this,' teased Molly, glad to see her niece display such a passion for something.

Kim didn't know what she would do if or when Mossbawn was sold. It had always been such an important part of her childhood and she would miss it terribly. Taking photos and creating an archive about the house and its owners was something she felt compelled to do, just as Molly seemed obsessed with her garden.

Chapter Twenty-one

Kim was busy weeding in the vegetable garden when she saw the old jeep pulling a trailer drive up in front of the house. Molly had gone off with her friends for the afternoon, so, standing up, Kim brushed off the dirt from her hands and jeans and went to see who it was.

As she neared the trailer she got the smell. It was horrendous.

'Manure for Molly's roses,' laughed the driver, who seemed immune to the foul stench that filled the air.

Molly had mentioned trying to get some manure for feeding the roses from one of the nearby farms.

'Where do you want me to dump it?' asked the dark-haired guy, clearly amused by her reaction.

Kim hadn't a clue. Looking into the trailer, she could see there was a stinking huge pile of it.

'It's horse dung from our place,' he explained as she

got him to drive over to the area where Molly usually dumped rubbish from the garden.

'Hold on – let me phone Molly,' she said, walking a little away from him.

A few minutes later he had driven the trailer over to a spot closest to the outside wall of the rose garden. Kim stood back, watching as he opened the end of the trailer and tilted it so that the massive brown pile of manure began to fall on to the grass below; then he got out and, taking a pitchfork, emptied the rest from the trailer.

It was disgusting and she had to hold her nose against the stench.

'Best fertilizer ever!' he joked. 'It's got to be good for something.'

Kim found herself laughing at the bizarreness of the situation. Was she meant to pay him for it? Her aunt hadn't said anything about it.

'Molly said I am to fix up with you?' she offered.

'You're fine – Dad sent me over with it,' he nodded, watching her. 'I'm from Grangefield, the stud farm out the road. My mum, Judy, is in the book club with Molly.'

'I'm Kim, her niece,' she said, suddenly aware that her hands were filthy, her nails black, and she was wearing an old knitted jumper of Emma's that had a massive rip on the elbow, and she hadn't even a scrape of mascara or lip gloss on . . .

'Luke, Luke Ryan.' He smiled, staring at her intently with the most incredible grey-green eyes. 'I'm presuming you're from Dublin – am I right?'

'Yes, but I'm staying with Molly for a while. I've spent a lot of time over the years here since I was kid. I always love coming to Kilfinn.'

'Centre of the universe!' he joked. 'Are you not bored?'

'Not at all,' she said defiantly.

Looking at him, she had to admit that he was dead attractive. Even in shitty clothes he looked good . . .

'Do you want to come in for a coffee?' she asked, trying to be polite. Molly had ingrained in her the importance of neighbours when living in the country and how much people depended on each other when they were farming, and helped each other.

'No, you're fine, thanks. Anyway, I'm hardly dressed for it . . .' he gestured.

She watched as he closed up the trailer and, adjusting it, clambered back into the jeep.

'But maybe I'll take you up on that coffee another time,' he grinned as he started the engine and drove off.

Molly wasn't home till nearly six o'clock, and came out to the back field immediately to admire the manure.

'This is like pure gold for my roses,' she enthused. 'It's late in the year, I know, but the soil has been so impacted that this will help. Mulching and feeding and this horse dung will really encourage the plants that are there to grow. Judy and Tom are so good to send it over. Did one of the boys bring it?'

'Yes, Luke did.' Kim was curious about him.

'Oh, he's their middle son. Justin is on the stud farm

133

with Tom – he's the married one – and the youngest boy, Sam, is studying equine science. Luke's a teacher, and a very good one by all accounts.'

Kim would never have imagined him as a teacher, with that sturdy, strong build.

'They have a sister too, Melissa; she's a sweetheart. She lives in Dublin with her boyfriend.'

Kim had to laugh; Molly was a mine of information on everyone who lived not only in Kilfinn, but for miles around the locality.

'It's a bit too late today to start working, but we'll get up early tomorrow morning and start spreading the manure. I want to use most of it in the rose garden.'

Kim felt she must be gone mad as she found herself agreeing to help with the rotten mucky digging-in job . . .

'It was so nice of Luke to bring it over,' smiled Molly. 'I must phone Judy to thank them.'

Chapter Twenty-two

Gina was kept busy at the café all day and was also catering for a retirement party on Friday night being held down at the local GAA club. Her brother Dylan and his wife, Jenny, were down from Dublin to stay for the weekend with their new baby, Aisling. It was lovely to see them, as they had got married years ago and were now finally holding their precious little daughter, who had been born after a single programme of IVF last year.

'We're the lucky ones!' said Jenny, a very proud new mother.

Gina's boys had surprised her and were literally fighting over holding baby Aisling and playing with her. Dylan, enjoying fatherhood, was happier than she had ever seen him before.

They went for a forest walk and picnic, and on

Saturday night Paul barbecued for everyone. Sitting around chatting over a few beers, Gina confided her secret hopes about the café.

'Fingers crossed it all works out for you, sis!' wished Dylan.

When they packed up to return to Dublin on Sunday evening everyone was sad to see baby Aisling go.

'I wish that we had a little brother or sister,' said Conor.

'Me too,' said Aidan. 'I'd teach them how to play football.'

Were the men in her family gone mad! thought Gina; their lives were busy enough without a baby! When Paul snuggled her close in bed that night, she pushed him away, laughing.

'We have more than enough on our plate,' she giggled. 'With any luck, we might even be running the café in a few months, so there's certainly no time for babies in this house!'

'I'm happy with the boys,' he said proudly, 'and you. That's more than enough for me.'

'I'm glad to hear it!' she smiled, reaching forward and kissing him.

It was Monday, her day off, before she managed to go and see how Norah was settling in to Beech Hill Nursing Home. A young Filipino nurse showed her to Norah's room at the end of a long, narrow corridor.

Norah was sitting in a special chair at the window, looking out over the grounds. Her bedroom was lovely but impersonal. Norah looked pale and tired, and without thinking Gina grabbed a tissue and wiped away a bit of spittle from her chin.

'How are you, Norah?' she asked, sitting down opposite her.

'OKAY,' said Norah slowly, making an effort to try to get the words out. 'Want hoommmee.'

'Not yet. Marian and the nurses here will take great care of you, Norah, until you get well again,' she soothed.

'But wwwant to go hhhhome.'

Gina had suspected as much. She'd gone upstairs to Norah's place before she came over and collected a few of her small personal items: a bronze cat figurine and a soft black toy kitten, some family photographs, a bright patchwork throw and a plump cushion with an embroidered picture of a bridge in Venice with a gondola. Norah always talked about her trip to Italy when she was younger. Gina wondered if perhaps she had run away there with some young man many years ago; or perhaps she had met a romantic Italian while she was on holiday there who had stolen her heart. Norah never discussed her love life, but Gina had seen photos of her when she was in her twenties and Norah Cassidy had been a good-looking young woman. She fixed the throw over her and positioned the cushion on her bed.

'Just a few things for you, Norah. I'll bring you more the next time,' she promised. She'd also got Norah a magazine and a paper. Unfortunately, with her swallowing problem, she was still not able to manage eating cakes or biscuits or sweets.

Sitting down, she filled Norah in on what had happened in the café over the past few days: who was ill, who was away and who had won the local parish Lotto. 'Imagine, eight thousand euro! There's been no winner for a few months and Johnny Lynch goes and wins it. That's a fortune for him!' she laughed. 'Do you know, one of the first things he did was put all the money in the Post Office and then came into the café, sat down in his usual seat and had the full lunch – soup, roast chicken and potatoes and stuffing, then a big slice of apple tart and cream and a pot of tea.'

Norah nodded, taking it all in.

Gina racked her brain for stories of the locals, who were like family to Norah. It was sad the way Norah had ended up, but at least here she was well cared for and near all those who knew her.

'Bridey said to say she'd call in tomorrow after lunch to see you,' Gina said, pulling on her warm jacket. Norah and Bridey had gone to school together and were still friends. Norah held on to her sleeve, getting upset and not wanting her to go.

'Listen, I'll come and see you in another few days,' she promised, giving her a hug.

Walking back out towards the car park a small black cat came across her path and wound around her legs.

'Whose cat is it?' she asked as one of the nurses got into a car beside hers.

'That's Suki. She belongs to the home,' she laughed. 'They all love her.'

'Can I bring her inside to show someone?'

'Of course.'

Gina lifted the little cat up and went back down the corridor to Norah's room.

'Norah – look who I found in the corridor! I have a visitor for you,' she said softly, and gently lowered the black cat on to the old lady's lap. She watched as Norah lifted her hand and very gently began to stroke the cat.

'M-mmy caattt.'

'Yes, Suki is yours, Norah, while you're here,' she explained. 'She lives here at Beech Hill.'

She watched quietly as Norah stroked the cat, which relaxed, settling in on her lap as the old woman kept petting it. She knew that Norah would love this real cat . . .

Driving home from Beech Hill, Gina couldn't help but wonder when a decision about the café was going to be made. It was becoming clear that Norah was not going to be able to return there and things couldn't keep going the way they were with the suppliers. They were being extremely patient and understanding, given the circumstances, but were hinting at being unable to give any further credit unless the payment situation was sorted. Gina was even making some of the payments in cash in order to ensure she was supplied with all the ingredients and food that the business needed.

She'd had a quiet word with the local bank manager, who lived about three miles out along the road. His son James was in Conor's class in school.

'I know the café, and I know about Norah,' he'd said as they stood watching their boys' team play football. 'Keeping a healthy business like the café going is important in these times, and the fact that you are already running the place is a huge factor. I'm sure the credit committee would view a proposal from you very positively, but look, nearer the time come in and see me officially.'

Gina was quietly relieved that he didn't envisage a major problem about her looking for a loan if and when the time or opportunity came for her to try to rent or even buy the café.

Chapter Twenty-three

Molly watched from the bedroom window as the black Audi pulled into the driveway and a tall young man in a suit got out of the car and locked it.

Murphy King, the Dublin auctioneers, had phoned to say that they were coming to value the house and to discuss the possibilities of putting it on the market. Molly had been expecting one of the senior partners to appear to inspect the property, not a junior member of their staff, she thought, as she headed down to open the front door.

'Nice to meet you, Mrs Hennessy,' Niall Devlin said, introducing himself. 'I work in our country-house division. Coming to see beautiful old properties like this is why I like my job so much.'

Molly warmed to him immediately as she began to show him around.

'What a fine Georgian house!' he said, recording detailed notes of every room as he walked around, measuring dimensions. In fact, he was quite an expert, remarking on the ceilings and covings and cornices, on the door frames and shutters, and able to point out to her where work had been done on the house at various times.

'This orangery is a very fine example of the period. Very few of them that have survived are in this good condition and usable; in so many places they have to be demolished as they are unsafe and gone beyond restoration.'

'My husband was determined that this should be carefully returned to its original condition. It cost a fortune sourcing the missing glass panes. We also put in underfloor heating, as in the winter it can be very chilly.'

As they walked around she listened to his comments, which mostly seemed positive. He called Mossbawn a fine example of Georgian elegance. Upstairs he admired the views and said little about the rooms that they barely used. He went up into part of the attic and then returned to the large kitchen, which overlooked the circular herb garden, and looked around the totally restored pantry and the old scullery, which they had turned into a practical utility room.

'The house has been really well updated, keeping the important features intact,' he congratulated her. 'Unfortunately, so many places I see have been irretrievably damaged by the way that people try to modernize them.'

'We loved this house from the minute we saw it,' said Molly. 'It's taken us years, but it was worth spending the time to get it right.'

'It was well worth it,' he said approvingly. 'This is a very fine house, and the fact that it is on the edge of Kilfinn village and is only a short stroll from the shops and pub is a real asset these days.'

'Come on and let me show you the rest of the place,' offered Molly, taking him outside, where he took some photographs.

'Are there any outbuildings?'

'Yes, there's the old courtyard and stables. We just use them mostly for storage of old equipment and junk from the house that we don't want.'

'They must have kept a lot of horses here at one time and had a very busy yard.'

'Yes, it's huge, but we don't really use it. There used to be a laundry area too.'

He took some more photos. 'Any other buildings?'

'Just the old Gardener's Cottage – but it's a bit of a wreck! It's around the other side of the house. Hold on and I'll find the key for it.'

As Niall walked through the rooms in the Gardener's Cottage, Molly thanked heaven that it seemed fairly dry and cosy, though there must be a leak somewhere, as there was a nasty damp patch on the wall and a musty smell pervaded the place. Black mould totally covered the ceiling in the kitchen. It was full of bric-a-brac: old string and seed packets and pots, and worn leather gardening gloves and wellingtons, the dresser covered in cracked mugs and plates, with a trail of mice droppings all over the area around the sink and stove. The windows were small, overlooking a section of the garden where the walls were covered in the thorny growth of old roses.

'Is this cottage part of the sale of Mossbawn, or are you reserving it or intending to sell it separately?' he enquired.

'To be honest, I hadn't even thought about it,' she admitted. 'We never use it.'

'Obviously, given it is in a state of some disrepair and is fairly small, I wouldn't expect it to achieve a huge price, but there is a possibility that a separate buyer could be found for it. Old gate lodges and cottages like this often have an appeal of their own.'

'Do you think so?'

'I know so. Just imagine it tastefully extended, bigger windows to let in more light and heat, with the rooms knocked through and a modern kitchen,' he continued.

Molly smiled to herself; he was very good at his job, because even she began to imagine the old cottage given a new lease of life and being lived in again.

'It's a good bit bigger than most of these types of cottages,' he announced, stepping outside to take some more photographs.

'A gardener used to live here with his wife years ago. He looked after the gardens and farmland and provided vegetables and fruit for the kitchen. But it's been empty for years, as Paddy, our gardener, lives in the village.'

'What a shame,' the auctioneer said, 'as it's got plenty of potential.'

Afterwards she walked him around the grounds, showing him the entire gardens and fields and woods while he recorded the details on to his machine.

'What about the river? Do fishing rights come with the house?'

'Of course. Richard Morton, the previous owner, was a very keen angler, apparently. I remember when we first came to view it there was an enormous stuffed pike in a glass case in the study, and some other strange fish.'

Later they had coffee in the kitchen.

'Do you mind me asking why you are selling?' he enquired.

'My husband died last year and our children are grown up and busy with their own lives,' Molly explained. 'So it's far too big for me now that I'm here most of the time on my own. A fine house like this needs a family, people to upkeep it and live in it and use it to its full, not a lonely soul like me rambling around it.'

'If you sell, where will you move to?'

'Hopefully somewhere pretty close by, near to the village and my friends. I like this part of the country and intend staying here.'

'Well, I have everything I need,' he said, finishing his coffee. 'I will talk to the relevant partner with regard to a current valuation, given the market, and come back to you on that.'

When Molly pressed him, he mentioned a rough figure which was far less than she'd hoped for.

'Molly, I know it's disappointing, because a few years

ago a house like this would have probably gone to auction and achieved far more, but this is the market . . .'

'So what happens next?'

'If you decide that our firm will handle the sale of your property, here's the way it works. Mossbawn would go up on our country-house section of the website and we would inform a number of potential buyers both here and overseas of its availability, then once there is interest we'd come back to you with regard to setting up viewings. But you have to be aware that the market at this time is extremely slow and there are a number of similar properties, some much closer to Dublin, already on our books. However, I personally feel this house has much to offer a potential buyer who wants to live or perhaps have an Irish holiday retreat in this area, given there are fishing rights.'

'Will you be handling the sale?' she asked hopefully.

'Well, Ronan King, one of the senior partners, usually does country houses and castles, but I work directly for him,' he assured her.

'It's just that I'd like the house, if possible, to go to another family; and also I don't want a big For Sale sign up in front, with everyone knowing my business and people coming up the driveway out of curiosity.'

'I'm afraid it's far too early to deduce what kind of interest the sale will bring,' he said, 'though lately two or three large homes like this have been sold to expatriates with families who are returning to live in Ireland after years overseas; they are often cash buyers.

Listen, I will put everything in writing to you with regard to Murphy King handling this sale, to explain our procedures and terms, and I'll make sure there is no signage.'

As she said goodbye to the young auctioneer, Molly was up in a heap wondering if she was making the right decision even to consider selling Mossbawn . . . but maybe she should test the market and see what happened.

Chapter Twenty-four

Emma and Grace were both home for the weekend, and Molly loved hearing them about the place, playing their iPods, singing and laughing, and constantly on their phones. She hadn't realized how quiet the house had become. Emma's boyfriend, Jake, was coming tomorrow for one night. She was keen to have the chance to get to know him properly, as lately he seemed to have become pivotal in her daughter's life.

'Mum, there's something wrong with the shower!' Emma yelled loudly from upstairs.

Molly ran up to see if her usual jiggling and turning buttons would make a difference.

'One minute the water was boiling, nearly scalding me, and then it was like ice!' shouted Emma, clutching a towel, her hair covered in shampoo. 'It's gone crazy and it's spurting at me like a kettle!'

'There!' Molly said, tinkering with it and wetting half her sleeve. 'The water's perfect again!'

'Why is everything in this house broken?' moaned Emma dramatically as she stepped back into the shower.

Molly sighed. The plumber had recommended fitting a totally new shower, but it was going to cost a fortune. She'd been hoping to make do for another while. She was used to making do and managing. David was the one who had always meticulously organized plumbers and electricians and repair work, not her. He had done everything seamlessly, often not even telling her.

Going back downstairs she set the table while Grace went to pull a bit of lettuce from the garden.

With David gone, proper family meals seemed a thing of the past and it was something she really missed, so having the girls here was wonderful.

'Mum, chicken Provençale – my favourite,' grinned Emma as she passed around the plates and put bowls of new potatoes and salad on the table. 'You must show me how to make it so I can do it for Jake.'

'Sounds very serious,' teased Grace.

'He's my boyfriend and I do cook for him sometimes, Grace, believe it or not, and he cooks for me!' retorted Emma firmly.

Molly stifled a grin.

'Well, I'll make it for my boyfriend too – whenever I get one!' Grace joked.

They all chatted easily, Kim filling them in on what she was doing.

'Your friend's art website sounds cool! I must check it out.'

'I'm hoping to design a few more websites,' she grinned, 'but this time hopefully I'll get paid for them, as I need the money.'

'Talking about money and work . . . Kim, I was talking to Frances, Dr Jim's wife, in the supermarket today and she's going in to have a hip replacement in a few weeks. She and Jim are looking for someone to fill in for her on reception while she is off work. She said it will probably be for about eight to ten weeks. They don't really want to have to pay an agency fee and are looking for someone local to help out. I told her that you might be interested.'

'Definitely – I'd definitely be interested!' said Kim, excited.

'I'll talk to Frances then,' Molly offered.

Kim had made chocolate brownies for dessert and Emma got up and made a pot of coffee.

'Hey, I've got to phone Evie,' Kim said, getting up from the table and disappearing upstairs. Molly was glad of her discretion; she needed to talk to her daughters.

'Girls, I have to talk to you about something.' She began by telling them about opening an account for each of them.

'Mum, you need the money more than we do,' protested Emma. 'There's no need to give us money, because once we finish college we'll both get jobs and hopefully have careers.'

'Keep it – you need it for yourself . . . for the house,' added Grace, concerned. 'We know Dad died before he had the time to save a proper pension, so it's for you. You'll need it over the years.'

'Listen, your dad would have wanted you each to have a bit of financial independence, to be able to do things you want when you finish college,' she insisted. 'And don't worry – there's enough for me to manage.'

She could see that the girls were moved.

'Are you sure, Mum?'

'Yes, I'm doing what Dad would have wanted, so that's all there is to it!' she said, brooking no further argument. 'Now, the other big thing I want to talk to you about is selling the house.'

'What?' they both shouted in dismay.

'You want to sell Mossbawn?'

'Why?' asked Grace, perplexed.

'I'm thinking about it,' she admitted. 'Putting Mossbawn up for sale breaks my heart just as much as yours. But living here on my own is so strange! You know how much the house means to me, and the garden, but without your dad . . . it's not the same. I'm rattling around the place here all day and all night. Sometimes I can't sleep with worrying about it and I spend most of the time trying to keep things going, but I don't know how much longer I can keep that up. The mortgage is finally cleared and for the first time ever we owe absolutely nothing on the house, which is one good thing, so maybe it's time to put it up for sale.'

'But we love this house,' protested Emma vehemently. 'It's our home.'

'Mossbawn is ours – we grew up here . . . We love it.' Grace's eyes welled with tears. 'I don't ever want it to be sold!'

'I know that you both love the house, love the place. We all do. It's just that I don't know how much longer I can stay living here on my own. Trying to run a big house like this is a constant worry. With your dad's income we managed just about, but now it's just me trying to do it. I'll be honest, I can't earn enough to keep it properly and I'm not sure what to do.'

'There must be some other way,' pleaded Grace. 'Maybe you could get people to stay here?'

'Grace, I know that we have eight bedrooms, but there are only really four good, presentable bedrooms that people would pay money for,' Molly explained. 'The Kilfinn Inn takes guests, and of course the Woodlands Hotel, judging by the prices, is practically giving rooms away. So I have absolutely no intention of competing with them.'

'But we don't want you to sell Mossbawn!' argued Emma. 'This is our home.'

'You're living in Galway at the moment and Grace is in Dublin,' Molly reminded them gently. 'Only last night you were saying to me that you and Jake are thinking of going travelling for a year when you finish studying – heading to Australia and maybe working there for another year.'

'I'll stay home then if you want.'

'It's not a question of staying home,' Molly tried to explain. 'I want you to go and see the world, travel and have fun. I don't want Mossbawn to be a ball and chain that you have to come home to.'

'It would never be that,' replied Emma angrily. 'It's our home and Dad wouldn't want you to sell it – I know that he wouldn't.'

'If your dad was alive this would not be an issue. We'd both be living here, growing old and crusty together, with you and your husbands and maybe our grandchildren visiting, who knows ... but that's all changed now and it's just me here.'

'Oh Mum!' said Grace, bursting into tears properly now. 'It's so awful – so unfair!'

'We all know that,' said Molly, trying to stay calm. 'But I have to consider selling. I've talked to an auctioneer in Dublin and they have so many old country houses that people can't afford to manage any more on their books ... But he said that doesn't matter: you only need to find one buyer, one person who falls in love with a house, to sell it. The market is still pretty awful, but I just want to see ... there's no rush. There will not be any big For Sale signs or anything like that. They will just have Mossbawn discreetly on their books so if someone does come looking for a house like this, then we can see ...'

'So you mightn't sell it!' said Emma, relieved.

'It might never happen.'

'But if someone did come along and wanted to buy

it,' probed Grace, 'where would we live? Would you move to Dublin?'

'I like Dublin,' she smiled, 'but I'm not sure that I could go back to living there. No, I'm used to Kilfinn, so hopefully that's where I'll stay. We all like it here.'

They all nodded in agreement.

'So it might never happen!' repeated Emma firmly.

'We'll just have to see,' Molly said, getting up to put on the kettle again. 'The Murtaghs' big house on the Kilkenny Road has been for sale for more than two years and apparently no one has even put an offer in on it.'

'It's a dreary-looking house,' said Grace, 'and it's cold. Remember we used to always freeze at Charlie Murtagh's birthday parties?'

As she made more coffee, Molly could see both girls were quiet, thinking about the awful possibility of Mossbawn being sold.

The rest of the weekend flew by. Jake arrived mid-afternoon the next day. With his shoulder-length hair and dark beard he was very different from the guys Emma normally dated, but he was funny and kind and insisted on being given a full tour of the house and garden. Molly was impressed by his knowledge of growing cabbages and potatoes.

'My dad grows them in our garden at home in Limerick.'

Emma had said he was a bit of a science genius and he certainly came across as being intelligent, but not in a nerdy way. Molly was delighted to see the way he treated Emma and how his eyes lit up when she walked into the room. It was clear he adored her older daughter and that the feeling was mutual. David would definitely have approved of the relationship.

After dinner on Saturday Emma was taking him out to meet a few of her friends from the village. Kim and Grace and Molly decided to drive to the cinema in Kilkenny to see the latest Cameron Diaz film. Set in the world of internet dating, it was hilarious. Afterwards, on the way home, Molly dropped the girls off at the Kilfinn Inn for a drink.

Next day, after a family Sunday lunch and a long walk in the woods, Molly was sad to see them pack up and go. Emma and Jake were driving back and Grace was getting the train. She hated them leaving, and grabbing the Sunday papers she went and curled up in the sitting room with Daisy snoozing at her feet.

Chapter Twenty-five

Kim sat behind the desk in Dr Jim McCarthy's reception area. The surgery was busy already and she checked people in as they arrived, adding them to Dr Jim's daily patient list. He would be able to call up their folders on his computer screen in his office. For any new patient, her job was to set up a medical folder with all their details before they went in to see the doctor.

She still couldn't believe that she had managed to get the temping job as his receptionist. Molly had talked to Frances McCarthy and before she knew it Kim was having an interview with the local GP and his wife in the surgery off River Street.

'The last time you were in this surgery you were about thirteen,' Dr Jim recalled. 'You cut your knee and leg badly and needed a few stitches!'

'I fell out of a tree in Molly's, and was scared because

I had to get a tetanus injection too,' she remembered. 'But you were so kind and kept talking to me about your dog Binky.'

'There never was a dog, cat, horse or hamster called Binky!' laughed Frances. 'But Jim always found him a great distraction for nervous patients. We never could have a cat or dog as our middle girl is allergic to cat and dog dander.'

'Well, it worked!' Kim laughed.

They went through the rough daily routine of the surgery.

'I work four and a half days a week,' the doctor explained. 'My Wednesday afternoon off is sacrosanct, as I play golf or get to see my grandchildren. Monday is probably the busiest day in the practice, so I take a long lunch break and do a late surgery.' She listened as he listed the daily surgery times.

'I use the doctor-on-call service mostly at night and weekends, unless I have a special patient I am looking after.'

'I understand,' she smiled.

'Are you squeamish – okay with people being sick?' he quizzed gently.

'Patients come in here with buckets and bowls and kids throwing up, or with tea towels wrapped around their cuts needing help,' Frances said frankly.

'My mother died of cancer twelve years ago,' Kim found herself saying. 'She was very sick, especially after her chemo, so I'm used to being around people when they are unwell.'

She saw a look pass between them.

'The last girl we had temping here while I was away seeing my sister in Canada was a disaster,' explained Frances. 'She nearly threw up if someone was sick and she wouldn't touch the patients.'

They both quizzed her about her experience and how she had found herself in Mossbawn. Kim was totally honest with them. 'I'm not a medical secretary or a receptionist, but I am very good on computers and should be able to manage your system easily enough.'

At the end of the meeting Kim was offered the job. Frances suggested she come in early next week to the surgery and work alongside her for two days to learn the ropes. 'It's simple enough when you know it – and get to know how Jim operates.'

Kim was relieved to find that Dr Jim had a separate medical secretary who worked one afternoon a week for a few hours, dealing with letters and correspondence.

The doctor was well liked in Kilfinn and had a busy practice. He was an old-school type of doctor, who believed the patient always came first. A visit could last ten minutes or twenty, but if a patient needed more time, Dr Jim would make sure they got it, even if it threw the day's appointment schedule into turmoil.

After only a week working in the surgery, Kim was finding the job easy enough. The patients made her welcome and said it was nice to have a new face behind the desk, and Dr Jim was a pleasure to work with. Frances's hip operation had gone really well and in another few days she would be out of hospital and getting used to walking with her crutches.

Kim scanned the waiting room. Two kids with tonsils, two vaccinations, a bad cough, sore toe and a few other things.

She noticed Rita Flanagan wasn't there waiting, so taking up her phone she texted her to remind her of her visit today. Rita was recovering from surgery and needed her bloods checked every few weeks. Rita texted back her thanks and appeared thirty minutes later.

'Thanks, Kim, I'd totally forgotten,' she apologized. 'My brain is like a sieve at the moment.'

Kim smiled. One thing about the job was that she was getting to know so many people in Kilfinn. Now when she walked down the main street people stopped to say hello to her and ask how she was enjoying working with Dr Jim.

Liz and her dad had been delighted to hear that she had finally got a job, while Evie and Lisa kept slagging her off about falling for one of the patients.

'They are mostly elderly or otherwise mothers with babies or toddlers!' she protested. 'And the rest of them are sick and spluttering and coughing, which is hardly attractive!'

But having a job, even if it was only temporary, had finally made Kim feel good about herself, and although the work was a bit of a juggling act it was interesting.

Coming to Mossbawn had certainly started to change things.

Chapter Twenty-six

Niall Devlin from the auctioneers phoned Molly to arrange an appointment for a viewing for a potential buyer who was interested in obtaining a large house with land in her area.

'He's looking at a number of properties, but seems very keen to view Mossbawn. He's been living in England for years,' he confided, 'and has a number of properties and investments already in the UK and over-seas, but is keen to invest and buy here in Ireland.'

Molly didn't know whether to be happy or dismayed about a potential buyer coming to see the house.

'Wait and see what happens,' urged Kim, sensing her panic. 'Just because he's coming to see the house, that doesn't mean that he is going to buy it!'

'I know it's not that easy,' Molly reminded herself over and over again as she and Kim gave the place a massive clean, getting rid of piles of old newspapers and odds and ends and filling the tall vases with arrangements of flowers from the garden. As it was a dull day, she lit a fire in the drawing room so that it felt warmer and more welcoming.

She was so nervous that when a large black Mercedes appeared in the driveway she could feel her heart pounding. What would David think of her showing their home to someone and contemplating selling the house that they had both worked so hard to restore?

'Mrs Hennessy, nice to meet you again,' gushed Ronan King, the tall, grey-haired auctioneer she had first talked to in Dublin. He was impeccably dressed in a grey suit. 'Let me introduce you to Mr Dunne.'

'Frank,' insisted the other man, who was smaller and blockier, reaching to shake Molly's hand. Even though he was well dressed in a tweed jacket and beige cords, there was an air of toughness about him. He was very dark and almost bald, and seemed extremely confident.

'Would you like a tea or coffee after your journey?' she offered.

'We just had some coffee in the hotel, thank you,' replied the auctioneer.

'Well, let me show you around the house then!'

She led them from the hall into the large drawing room, the fire brightly blazing in the grate, the deep mahogany furniture glowing in the light; the dining room, with its massive sideboard and serving table; the library, the study, the orangery; back to the sitting room, then upstairs.

'It's been a wonderful family home,' she enthused. 'My husband and I tried to make it as comfortable as possible while retaining the important classical features.'

'And you have done that extremely well,' agreed Ronan King admiringly.

The other man said very little, but she could see he was taking in everything, studying the windows and fireplaces and architraves.

Back downstairs, she brought them into the kitchen where Kim was engrossed, working on her laptop.

'This place is the heart of the house,' Molly smiled as she showed them the hand-crafted kitchen with its well-stocked pantry, neat utility room and boot room.

'If you don't mind, Mrs Hennessy, I will show Frank the grounds, let him have a bit of a ramble around.'

'Of course,' she said, watching the two men walk out across the terrace and towards the kitchen garden.

'What do you think?' she asked.

'Not sure,' admitted Kim. 'He barely said a word when he saw the kitchen, and most people just love it!'

'I know,' Molly sighed. 'He's hardly spoken as we walked around, but he was definitely checking everything out.'

She tried to keep busy until she saw them returning.

'We just wanted to clarify, Mrs Hennessy, about the back field near the woods – that is yours?'

'Yes. I let my neighbour Pamela use it to graze her horses.'

'And the stables and outbuildings and the cottage are all included in the sale?' added Ronan King.

'Everything is except for the Gardener's Cottage,' she found herself saying. 'I'm afraid the cottage and the garden around it are not part of the sale.'

'It's itemized,' the other man reminded her.

'I'm afraid that's a mistake,' she said slowly. 'I am keeping the cottage for my own use.'

The auctioneer pulled out a small, black, leather-bound notebook and scribbled in it.

'If you would like to have another look around, please do,' she offered.

They went upstairs again before leaving, taking another walk around the house before going out the side door to the old stableyard. The two were deep in discussion from what she could tell when she went out to join them. Frank Dunne was not giving any indication of what he thought of the house.

'I will be in touch,' Ronan King promised as they said their goodbyes.

Standing in the doorway, Molly felt a strange sense of relief as she watched the two men drive away.

Chapter Twenty-seven

Molly had no idea why she had said to Ronan King about keeping the old Gardener's Cottage that they had never used, but suddenly it seemed important. Grabbing the key off the hook in the kitchen, she found herself going down to look at it again. Perhaps it might have some sort of possibility to be renovated and used.

Opening the door, she got that awful, strong, damp, musty smell again and she suspected a cat and her kittens must have found their way into the place. The windows were grimy and covered in cobwebs, and the ancient range looked in a pretty poor state. The fireplace in the sitting room, however, seemed fine. Outside there was a small lean-to with a sink and a disgusting toilet. Up the narrow, rickety stairs there were two small, pokey bedrooms that overlooked the garden, though the tiny windows were so covered in thorny briars that you could hardly see out of them. One wall was black with mould and a hole in the roof could be clearly seen, where the rainwater had poured in.

David had talked about fixing up the cottage sometime in the future, but it had hardly been a priority when there was so much other work to do. An old bed frame took up almost all the space in one room, with a mottled mirror and a plain wardrobe. Whoever had lived here before had lived very simply. Returning to the kitchen, she opened the drawers in the old dresser; they were filled with odds and ends of gardening implements, string and labels and a yellowing notebook full of planting schedules and plans, and a record of vegetables grown in the kitchen garden.

Even though it was smelly and cold and damp, there was something about the place that had an appeal. Going back outside, Molly walked around the small vegetable plot to the side and the simple courtyard-style garden area. It was smaller than she would have liked. A path led towards the house, which was screened by trees. The cottage was closer to the wall of the old rose garden and its rusted entrance gate, and to the large kitchen garden where the gardener would have worked.

It was strange, but there was something about the cottage that she liked. She could imagine it redone – bright and clean and cosy – and her living here. Why would she even consider moving to a small house in the village or a place in Dublin when she could have this cottage to live in if she ended up having to sell the big house? She was excited . . . She'd absolutely no idea how much it would cost to renovate, but the fact that she already owned it was a huge advantage.

Taking out her phone, she searched for Trish's number. Her architect friend would tell her straight out if it was worth putting a bit of money into fixing up the cottage.

Trish McMahon came over the next morning and measured and checked every bit of the cottage, pulling at plaster, kicking at floorboards and scrutinizing the roof.

'Molly, it's a fine cottage. Okay, the roof needs replacing along with the electrics and plumbing, and you would want to put in heating and replace all the windows, but otherwise it's sound.'

'Are you sure?'

'Of course – it's my job to be sure.'

'But that's a huge amount of work!'

'Almost anything you buy will need work,' Trish reminded her. 'If you end up moving out of Mossbawn and getting a cottage or a bungalow near the village, I can guarantee you will be doing a lot of the work you have to do here – and those terraced houses at the end of the village have serious problems. I did work on one of them last year and it all had to be damp-proofed.'

'So what do you think, Trish? Be honest!' she pleaded.

'I think it's a great cottage with huge potential. Even a slight extension would open it up and create more space.' She grinned, walking around the small sitting room. 'A support beam here and a joist and some lovely big glass doors that will help bring in the outside will make a massive difference.'

'That's what I thought,' said Molly, watching Trish scribble on a pad and do some very rough drawings. 'But I wanted to make sure it wouldn't cost a fortune.'

'You will have to spend some money, Molly, but it will be worth it in the long run. You could extend and get a good-sized open living area downstairs, along with a really decent-sized bedroom, and upstairs I'd suggest turning those little rooms into one larger bedroom with an ensuite. You already own the cottage, which is the main thing! I'd certainly advise doing it, whether you live here yourself or rent it out or want to keep it for the girls.'

'I like the cottage – it has a good feel,' Molly said, walking around. 'Even when it's damp and dirty there's something about it.'

'I'll do up some plans for you,' offered Trish. 'Most of the work doesn't need planning permission, but if you extend over a certain limit you will need to apply for planning.'

'But why? There's nobody near – no one to object.'

'It doesn't matter,' insisted Trish. 'I'd advise you to go ahead and get planning now, because who's to say if someone buys Mossbawn that they won't object to you extending the cottage.'

'That wouldn't happen!'

'Believe me, it would!' she warned. 'The Linders sold their house two years ago and kept a site for themselves, but when they went to build on it the new owners of their house objected. It was awful.'

'Trish, do you think it would work, me moving in here?'

'Molly, it's a huge change, but you'd still be living at Mossbawn, still have a garden and lots of open space,' said Trish as she took a few photos with her iPhone. 'This old cottage with a bit of work could look amazing. I love it – I really do.'

'I know, there's something about it . . .'

'Listen, I'll try and get a few drawings to you by the weekend,' promised Trish, who was in a hurry to get to a meeting about a job in Castlecomer.

Standing inside the cottage in the dappled sunshine, Molly got the strongest feeling that she could be happy here.

Chapter Twenty-eight

Kim was out running when she spotted the middle-aged man walking up near the woods, right through to the edge of her aunt's property. He seemed to be taking photos and pacing out the border between Molly's land and the McHughs' farm. What was he up to? she asked herself. She hastened her pace until she was up near him.

'Can I help you?' she asked loudly.

He turned, obviously surprised to see her.

'I'm just getting a better look at the place,' he said gruffly. 'I'm Frank Dunne – I was here last week with the auctioneer.'

'Oh, I remember you! My aunt isn't here, but I can show you around the grounds if you need to see anything,' she offered, but she could tell he'd far prefer to be left on his own.

'Is this the dividing line between the Reynolds' property and your aunt's?' he quizzed, looking around.

'Yes, but Molly lets Pamela graze some of their horses in her field.'

'Generous of her!'

'Here neighbours tend to help each other,' she smiled.

'What about this field? Is this part of the property?'

'Yes, my aunt owns it, but I think the McHughs rent it for their cows. They've a big farm on the other side of the woods.'

'I've seen most of what I wanted,' he said as they turned back towards the house. 'Do you live here with your aunt?'

'No, I'm just visiting.'

She noticed he said nothing about his own family and she tried to draw him out as they walked.

'What do your family think of the house?'

'They haven't seen the house,' he said, looking uncomfortable. 'They are in Manchester with their mother.'

Kim didn't know what to say. Imagine thinking of buying a house like Mossbawn and not having your family even see it. Maybe they were just going to use it as an Irish holiday home in the country.

'My aunt should be back soon if you want to talk to her,' she offered as they neared the house. 'She just went to the local library.'

'No thanks, that won't be necessary,' he said brusquely, before walking down the driveway. 'I can't wait.'

Kim watched him talking loudly on his phone and suspected he must have parked his car somewhere further down the avenue.

She was busy emptying the dishwasher when Molly arrived back.

'I got two wonderful books on roses,' she said proudly, putting them down on the table.

'Frank Dunne was here,' Kim said quickly. 'I found him up near the Blackberry Field.'

'Ronan King should have phoned me to make an appointment for him to view the house.'

'I think he just turned up himself,' Kim shrugged. 'I asked if he wanted to wait for you but he wouldn't. Molly, it's weird, because he never even came inside the house.'

'Maybe he felt it was the wrong thing to do when he hadn't an appointment organized.'

'Do you think he'll buy the place?' Kim asked. There was something about Frank Dunne that she didn't like.

'Well, apparently he put in a very low offer, which I've told Ronan King I wouldn't dream of accepting,' confided Molly. 'It seems he's very wealthy and has made most of his money in the UK, but wants to buy a country house back here in Ireland.'

Kim wasn't sure about someone like Frank Dunne taking over a beautiful house like her aunt's.

'Is there anyone else interested?' she asked.

'The market is terrible at the moment. Mostly it's

people from overseas wanting to move back here or to use an old house as a country getaway.'

'I wish you didn't have to sell!'

'So do I, Kim! So do I . . .'

Kim didn't think she could bear not having Mossbawn to visit and escape to, and to see someone else living here.

'I told the auctioneers that I'm keeping the Gardener's Cottage and a section of the garden around it. It's not part of the sale.'

'Well, that's something!'

'The cottage is so perfect . . . I'm going to do it up and maybe move into it. Trish is drawing up some plans for it, and you know that you would always be welcome, Kim,' said Molly seriously.

Kim knew that her aunt cared deeply about her and was there for her whenever she needed her. Molly was always so supportive and, in a strange way, since her mum's death her aunt had tried to be like a mother to her.

'I know,' she said.

Later, going for a run down by the river and looking back up at the old house with its pillars and its winding creeper around the door, she wished that awful man would never get his hands on it.

Chapter Twenty-nine

Molly was busy digging in Madame Caroline Testout and trying to settle her. She had moved the tall climbing rose from the back of the house, where she was hardly noticed growing near a hedge, and wanted her to take a new central role in the garden. She'd watered her well, prepared the hole with compost, fed her, carefully removed damaged roots and given her a pruning. Now she had to wait to see the results. Rena had offered her a beautiful Charles de Mills rose and she was working out where to plant it. She knew that autumn and winter were better times to move the roses, but she needed to fill the spaces now.

It had taken time, but a lot of the debris and garden tiles and gravel had been moved from the walled garden. The soil had been broken up and enriched by Paddy and herself so that it was workable again. She couldn't believe how much had been done.

Ronan King the auctioneer interrupted the work with a phone call to tell her that Frank Dunne was back in Ireland and wanted to see the house and land again.

'He's very keen, Molly, and I would like to come down tomorrow and show him around myself,' he offered. 'I feel he is ready to increase his offer considerably.'

'Well, that's good.'

She was paying the auctioneer, after all, so next day she let him show Frank around. Kim was working and Molly made herself scarce by taking Daisy for a walk. When she got back, Ronan King had left her a scribbled note on the hall table saying that he would talk to her tomorrow.

She slept badly, tossing and turning all night. When she went down to breakfast Kim was already up and gone to work.

The auctioneer phoned her around mid-morning to say that Frank Dunne had increased his offer. Molly couldn't believe it . . .

'It's under the guideline, but it's probably the best you will get in the current climate. Mr Dunne has no problems with getting a bank loan and is prepared to pay the deposit straight away,' Ronan explained, sounding pleased with himself. 'Buyers like him are few and far between, so I would certainly recommend accepting this offer.'

'I need to think about this and talk to Grace and Emma,' Molly said firmly.

'Certainly, but I will ask your solicitor, Mr Quinn, to go ahead and begin to draw up the sale agreement to send to Mr Dunne's lawyer in England.'

'How long does this all usually take?' she asked.

'Usually we would advise about twelve to twenty weeks for closing,' he replied. 'But Mr Dunne wants a thorough survey done of the house and land.'

Molly was shaking all over. She couldn't believe it – someone was going to buy Mossbawn. She should be feeling elated and happy about it, not this strange sense of guilt, as if she had let the house down.

'I will be in touch over the next few days, Molly, but I must say that I'm very pleased with the outcome.'

She sat at the table for an hour and tried to collect herself before she phoned Grace and Emma. Both of them were incredulous that a buyer had been found for Mossbawn so soon.

'When will we have to move out of the house?' wailed Emma.

'Not for a good few months,' promised Molly, who was absolutely dreading it.

'Well done, Mum.' Grace was trying to be positive. 'I'm sure you're relieved about it all.'

'Grace, you know how much I'm going to really miss the house,' she admitted, 'but at least I have the cottage and will still be living close by.'

She was sitting thinking about it all when Kim returned from work.

'Good news – Frank Dunne increased his offer,' Molly said brightly.

'What!' Kim exclaimed, tossing off her grey cardigan.

'I'm going to have to accept it,' she said. 'David's partner in the firm, Michael Quinn, will draw up the legal documents.'

'So you are really going to go ahead and sell Mossbawn?'

'Yes.'

Kim looked absolutely stricken, as if she were going to burst out crying. She'd relied on Mossbawn so much over the years since Ruth died. Suddenly she ran out of the kitchen and upstairs to her room.

Molly didn't know what to say or do. She was the one who had lived in the house for over twenty years. It was breaking her heart to give it up, but she had to learn to accept that it was perhaps time for another family to live here in Mossbawn.

Chapter Thirty

Cassidy's café was busy at lunchtime on Friday as always, but Gina Sullivan managed to find a seat for the five of them near the back.

'She's got that lovely chicken pie with the crunchy cornflake topping on today,' said Cara, glancing at the blackboard.

'I'm definitely having that,' decided Trish.

'Me too,' added Molly. Gina's food was so good and a change from Norah's regular menu.

A few seconds later Gina had taken their order, everyone going for the chicken except for Brenda, who was a vegetarian and chose the stuffed peppers.

'Any news?' asked Avril as she filled everyone's water glasses.

'Libby is definitely getting married next year,' beamed Trish. 'I know it seems like the longest engagement on record, but they're getting married in early March and everything's booked and arranged. Larry and I are delighted for them.'

'Where's it going to be?' asked Brenda.

'A castle in Tipperary – Foyle Castle. They're renting it for the day. It looks lovely.'

'I've some news too,' said Molly hesitantly. 'I've had an offer on the house.'

'What!'

'I thought you were just testing the market!'

'I was, but Murphy King, believe it or not, seem to have found a buyer for the place.'

'Are you going to leave Kilfinn?' asked Avril, worried.

'Hopefully not. I want to stay living here. But Mossbawn is far too big for me now that David is gone.'

'Who's buying the house?' quizzed Cara. 'Is it someone we know?'

'No. He's Irish, some wealthy property guy, but he's been living in Manchester for years. I think he wants his family to move back here.'

'I can't believe you not living in Mossbawn,' said Brenda slowly. 'Where will you move to, Molly? Will you stay in the village?'

'I'm not sure yet, it's all happened so quickly. But there's an old cottage in the grounds and I am going to do it up. Trish is drawing some plans for it and hopefully I can extend it slightly. If that's not possible, then I'll look for somewhere close by, don't worry. I'm not running back to Dublin – I'm happy here in Kilfinn with all of you lot.'

Gina Sullivan was busy passing round their plates and three bowls of salad.

'Gina, can you believe it? Molly is selling Mossbawn!' said Brenda dramatically.

'I've decided to downsize,' Molly explained, catching the look of sympathy in the other woman's eyes.

'Well, best of luck with it,' said Gina. 'It is a beautiful house. I'm sure you will miss it.'

'Of course I will, but I'm hoping to stay living close by.'

'Well, that's good to hear,' Gina smiled, passing Brenda her roasted peppers.

Over the rest of the meal the girls grilled her about what she was going to do about all her furniture.

'You're not going to fit a dining table that seats twenty or that massive sideboard into a cottage or a small house,' warned Cara. 'What will you do with all your antique furniture? Will you put it in an auction?'

Molly hadn't even thought about the contents of Mossbawn, she had been so preoccupied and worried about selling the house itself.

'Some things like David's family's old grandfather clock and my dad's old cherrywood writing desk I'm definitely keeping,' she insisted, 'but I suppose I'll have to see about the rest. Hopefully Frank Dunne and his wife will be interested in buying some of the bigger pieces, like the dining set, for the house. I must get the auctioneer to ask him.'

179

'Are you okay about all this?' asked Avril softly. 'It's so hard for you!'

'I suppose it's not just about selling the house, but all the things that David and I bought together and collected for it . . . It's like losing another huge part of me.' Molly sighed.

'What do Grace and Emma think?'

'They are sad and upset and are really going to miss it, but they understand how hard it is for me to keep living there without their dad. If he was alive none of this would be happening.'

'It's so unfair!' said Trish angrily. 'Larry might drive me mad half the time but I'd be lost without him!'

'Me too!' added Cara. 'I know that I'd go to pieces without Tim.'

'I did go to pieces,' Molly reminded them, 'but now I'm just trying to get on with things the way David would want me to do.'

Passing through the tall iron gates of Mossbawn, Molly stood looking up at the magnificent old Georgian house, its red-painted front door and fanlight, its tall narrow windows and graceful granite pillars entwined with a mixture of roses and clematis. Maybe she was being fanciful, but it seemed like the house was almost looking back at her and she was overcome with an overwhelming sense of guilt. She felt so sad about the whole thing – the house, the lawns, the kitchen garden, the maze, the pond, the rose garden . . . In a few months' time none of them would belong to her. She hoped that when the new owner took over he would employ a gardener to maintain the garden properly, the way it deserved.

Chapter Thirty-one

Cara had persuaded her to visit Castle Antiques in Kilkenny.

'Molly, you know that you can't possibly keep all the furniture from Mossbawn, so if you want to get an idea how much some of your furniture and antiques will fetch, Myles is the best person to ask. He sold all the stuff from my aunt's house after she died and looked after everything really well.'

'David and I picked up a few nice things from his auctions – a painting, the fire irons . . . '

'There you go. You should only sell through someone you would buy from. Besides, I'm sure he would be glad of the business.'

Molly was looking around the antiques shop, drawn to a pair of silver candelabras.

'You're here to sell!' Cara reminded her. 'Not to buy!'

Molly felt that even coming to talk to someone about putting some of her furniture pieces up for sale was upsetting; it made selling Mossbawn suddenly seem very real.

But Myles Murray was a man with a very good reputation. Tall and grey-haired, with a wiry build, he was dressed in a tweed jacket and beige corduroys. When she and Cara talked to him, he agreed immediately about coming over to Molly's house to take a look at the dining table and sideboard and cabinets and to give her a rough estimate of their value. They arranged for him to visit on the following Monday.

Molly spent the weekend polishing and dusting everything and adding a few more items to the list of things she wanted to show Myles.

'What a lovely house,' he said, his brown eyes enquiring under his grey bushy eyebrows, taking everything in as he walked around from room to room. 'You must be sad about leaving it.'

'It's breaking my heart,' she admitted, 'but as you can see it's far too big for someone living on their own.'

'Most items that find their way to my auction house usually come as the result of a bereavement, or because a large old country house comes on the market. In a way it's my bread and butter, coming to see lovely old places like this and trying to ensure that some of the contents will find their way to a new home where they will still be appreciated and held in value,' he explained enthusiastically. 'I suppose in a manner I am recycling valuable items and making sure that there is a continued

183

appreciation of craftsmanship and silverwork and Irish glassware and art.'

'It sounds like you really enjoy your work, visiting old houses,' she said, relieved that she had asked him.

'I consider myself a very fortunate man,' he laughed. 'I am surrounded by things of beauty every day, and my job is to find a new owner for each and every piece. It's very worthwhile.'

Molly watched as he examined her chairs and table and sideboard, making almost purring sounds as he found the maker's mark.

'The dining table and chairs were made by Gillingtons and were probably commissioned by the original owner.'

'Charles Moore.'

'Then the magnificent hall table, the parlour chairs and library bookcase are by Robert Strahan, a renowned Dublin furniture-maker. There are also side-tables and a serving table by the firm of Mack, Williams and Gibton. You have some very special and valuable pieces here, Molly.'

'Some of them came with the house,' she explained, 'and a few David and I bought at auctions ourselves.'

'Well, you have bought well,' he murmured. 'Obviously the market is not as good as it was a few years back, but still there are always those who are interested in pieces of such fine quality. Is there anything else you'd like me to look at since I'm here?' he offered.

Embarrassed, Molly showed him around the rest of the house. Myles suggested that a few items that were in the spare rooms upstairs also be put into the auction.

'This linen press is magnificent – and what about the writing cabinet?'

'I'm not sure,' she hesitated. 'Obviously I want to keep some of my things around me when I move.'

Myles also picked out some silver pieces.

'This salver and these matching dish rings are beautiful. Would you consider selling them?'

'I really need to think about it,' she admitted, feeling rather overwhelmed.

The grandfather clock in the hall began to strike and Molly realized that poor Myles Murray had spent the past two hours looking all around the house and she hadn't even offered him a cup of tea. He must think her terribly rude.

'Please, Myles, will you have coffee, or a bit of lunch?' she found herself offering.

'I hadn't noticed the time myself,' he smiled, 'but that would be lovely.'

Down in the kitchen she quickly made some toasted cheese-and-ham sandwiches, relieved that she had something in the fridge, and a pot of coffee. He was good company, regaling her with stories of some of the auctions he had held and of magnificent pieces found like buried treasure in all sorts of houses.

'A lot of old convents have been sold recently and they are a virtual treasure trove of furniture and glass and silverware and art. The nuns, God be good to them, seemed to have had no idea what valuable things they were using day by day.'

'But thank heaven they were being used,' insisted Molly, 'instead of being stored in some dusty attic or left in some empty house to rot.'

'You are totally right, Molly. Everything was crafted to be used as well as appreciated. Function was important and still is,' he added seriously.

As she poured him a second coffee she found herself answering his gentle probing about David's death. Myles had lost his wife, Jane, about nine years earlier.

'Colon cancer,' he said calmly. 'We had no children, which was obviously always a big regret. Jane had been sick for years.'

'I'm sorry,' she murmured.

'We had a good, happy marriage, more than most people,' he said proudly, 'but I still miss her terribly.'

'I know what that's like,' she admitted. 'I don't know how I would have got through losing David without the girls.'

'I hate being on my own,' he said vehemently. 'I'm not very good at it.'

'Neither am I,' she said wistfully.

'If you ever need to talk or want a bit of company . . .' he offered.

'Thank you, Myles,' she said, suddenly feeling slightly uncomfortable, which was stupid. She had asked him to the house. He was just being sympathetic, that was all!

'I'd better get going,' he said standing up and carrying his plate and cup over to the sink.

'Myles, thanks for coming over here and for all your good advice. I appreciate it.'

'No problem, Molly! Thanks for the lunch, and I'll draw up a valuation list and email it to you along with the dates of our upcoming auctions.'

Following Myles's visit, Molly made an inventory of all the furniture and paintings, silver and various pieces in the house as he had suggested. Kim helped her by taking photos of some of the larger or more valuable items.

She had asked Ronan King to find out if Frank Dunne was interested in purchasing any of the larger pieces of furniture that had been specifically designed for the house, but got no response.

Grace, her exams over, came home for a few days to flop and relax before heading to Amsterdam to go backpacking around Europe for six weeks with her girlfriends.

'I'd great fun when I did it!' Kim joked. 'But remember, if you are on overnight trains and don't book a sleeper, someone needs to stay awake on guard duty or you will all get robbed! Also, bring lots of knickers! Get paper ones. And don't forget baby wipes and sunblock!'

Molly tried not to think of the antics Grace and her friends would get up to on their travels and just prayed she would return safely.

Trish had drawn up two sets of plans for the cottage: one which just used the existing footprint and the other which included an enlarged kitchen-cum-living area, with ceiling-to-floor windows at the back of the cottage that opened out to the garden, creating almost another room. Molly absolutely loved it. Trish had costed both of them.

'I know it seems expensive, Molly,' she explained, 'but it's nothing compared to you buying a new house in this area or somewhere else.'

Opting for the larger design, Molly went ahead with putting in the planning application for the cottage.

She knew it was crazy, but even though she had found a buyer for Mossbawn she was still engrossed working on the rose garden. Day by day she could see it taking shape, the old roses beginning to bud and flower in the warmth of the summer. The new roses she had planted in the beds, which were edged with lavender and cat-mint, were tentatively pushing out shoots and roots. She loved all her old roses – her French ladies with their wonderful names and some of the newer ones too, like Nathalie Nypels with her pinky flowers that kept com-ing. Imagine having a rose named after you! She wondered about these women, their names captured for ever by a rose . . . She searched her books for their names, puzzled by a sweet rose with a heavy pale-pink head of petals that grew against the south wall. It was a good time to take cuttings and she gently took summer cuttings, as the old-fashioned roses would root easily. She kept them in a propagator, hoping that they would root and she would in time have more roses to plant out in the garden. Some would be used eventually to plant in the new garden at the cottage.

She watched as mauve-pink clematis scrambled to cover the walls, as old climbing roses began to cling and move up through the trellises and up the archways.

The garden was a haven away from the world, and she was determined to enjoy it and to have Mossbawn at its best. Paddy and Tommy were coming weekly to cut the lawns and trim the hedges and shrubs and to keep the place looking well. The large herbaceous borders were in full bloom, filled with tall delphiniums, lupins and foxgloves, and tumbling masses of spreading blue and pink geraniums.

She often worked from early morning till late in the summer evenings, happy to be outside in the garden, working or sitting on a bench reading, her friends welcome to come and enjoy a coffee or a salad lunch on the terrace overlooking the garden. Molly tried not to think of the past or the future, but to enjoy the present.

Chapter Thirty-two

On Tuesday evening Gina was cleaning up the café. She had been kept on the go most of the day. Inga, the new girl she had taken on to help out for a few hours a day, was settling in really well. And the customers liked her. She was chatty and had an interest in cooking. She had worked in a hotel in Poland before she moved to Ireland with her husband, Marek, who worked in the big electronics-payment company near Castlecomer.

Gina sat down and totted up the day's takings; she would lodge the money tomorrow into Norah's business account. Inga had finished at three o'clock, so this evening it was Gina's turn to put all the chairs up on the tables and wash the floor. Bending down, she found a rolled-up menu on the floor, picked it up and flattened it out. She certainly wasn't getting any more of these made. Honestly, someone had scribbled over one side of it, which was annoying. She was about to put it in the bin when something about it attracted her attention.

It was a rough sketch of a house and gardens, but it was definitely familiar . . . Where was it? She recognized the crudely drawn shape of the house and glass orangery. It was a drawing of Molly's house – but someone had put a massive cross through the house, scratching it out, and there were smaller houses added and some kind of roadway around the back near the woods. She had no idea what it meant, but she folded it and put it in her pocket.

Later that night when the kids were gone to bed she showed it to Paul.

'It's a drawing – a rough sketch of Mossbawn House.'

'I know, I recognize it,' he said, studying it. 'Where did you get it?'

'I found it on the floor in the café. I'm not sure about it, but Liam Kelly was having coffee with some other guy this afternoon, and I'm pretty sure they were the ones who must have dropped it, as Molly hasn't been near the place for about ten days.'

'Are they redeveloping the place?' he asked.

'Not as far as I know. Molly was with her friends and they were all talking about some new family from England moving into the big house.'

'Well, this shows a lot of families moving in, not one family . . .' he said grimly.

'Paul, I'm worried that maybe Molly doesn't know about this.'

'If Liam Kelly is involved, heaven knows what's going on!'

Paul Sullivan had absolutely no time for Liam, the local auctioneer, who seemed to have a finger in every pie. He had worked on building an expensive new kitchen for Liam and his wife when they had first moved back to Kilfinn. He'd been glad of the work, but when the time came had only got paid half what he was due. It was still a sore point.

'Do you think I should say something?' she asked, hesitantly. 'Molly's been good to me and I feel she's no husband to look out for her . . . Maybe it's too late . . .'

'Show it to her, Gina, that's all you can do. Maybe she already knows about it, but at least you'll feel that you've done the right thing.'

Paul went into the kitchen to make a quick mug of decaf coffee and get some cheese and crackers for them as she switched over to watch *The Politics Show*. She'd call to see Molly first thing in the morning before she went to work. There was nothing worse than being kept in the dark about something.

Kim and Molly were having breakfast next morning when Daisy started barking.

'It's probably the poor postman at the door!' laughed Kim. 'She hates him.'

Molly put some more bread in the toaster as Kim ran to open the front door.

'I'm sorry for calling so early, Molly, but I'm on my

way to work,' Gina Sullivan apologized as she joined them in the kitchen.

'Will you have a cup of tea?' asked Molly.

'No thanks, I've just had breakfast and dropped the boys to school, but I wanted to give you this before I went to the café,' she said, reaching into her handbag. 'I found it on the floor when I was cleaning up the café last night.'

Molly was puzzled: why was Gina giving her a copy of a menu?

'Turn it over to the other side!'

Molly turned it over, at once recognizing the scribbled drawing of her house and the surrounding land. Someone had scratched out the house and drawn lots more smaller houses around, and the woods were gone . . .

'What is this?' she asked, sitting down at the table.

'I think you should look properly at it. Liam Kelly and some other man were in the café yesterday – I think they were the ones that dropped it,' Gina explained. 'I'm not sure what it means, Molly, but Mossbawn is your house and I thought maybe I should show it to you. I hope you don't think I'm interfering.'

'You did the right thing, Gina, thank you.'

'I'm afraid I have to go and open the café,' Gina said, picking up her handbag.

'Thanks so much for bringing this to show me,' said Molly as she walked her to the back door.

'What is it?' asked Kim, looking at the paper on the table. 'What's on it?'

'It's obviously a plan for Mossbawn,' Molly said, studying it intently. 'Someone has drawn up some kind of development plan which clearly entails knocking down the house and destroying most of the garden.'

'What are you going to do?' demanded Kim, furious.

'I don't know, but it explains a lot: that man Frank Dunne's absolute lack of interest in the house, and when Ronan King mentioned to him two weeks ago about the dining furniture he said I could keep the lot, he didn't need any of it. I presumed he was moving his own furniture, but obviously if the house is going to be knocked down no wonder he doesn't need it!' she said angrily.

'You can't just go knocking down a beautiful old house like Mossbawn, surely?'

'Unfortunately it's not a listed property.'

'What can you do?'

'Well, first off I can talk to Ronan King, find out what he knows about all this and see if he has any connection to Liam Kelly.' She sighed. 'I've already signed the first part of the contract, so I'm not sure what that means. I'll call Michael and talk to him.'

Seething with annoyance, Molly phoned her solicitor, David's partner Michael Quinn, but his secretary told her that he was busy and would phone her back. She then managed to get through to the Dublin auctioneer, who made it very clear that, while he was acting for her in regard to the sale of the property, he had utterly no responsibility for what a buyer might do with a property once they had purchased it.

'Obviously most of us want our homes kept as homes, but with large houses like these, this is often not practical and they may end up as nursing homes or put to some other use. I remember one beautiful house in West Cork was turned into a recording studio by a musician.'

'So you had no idea about Frank Dunne's plans for Mossbawn?'

'We didn't discuss it,' he said defensively. 'I have a large number of properties on my books and could not be expected to follow up what happens to them.'

Fifteen minutes later Michael Quinn phoned her. As she quizzed him about what her legal position was with regard to the sale, he asked if she had signed the contract.

'Yes, I dropped it back into your office last Friday.'

She could hear Michael rustling around searching for something.

'I have it,' he declared.

'A copy?'

'No, the original,' he said slowly. 'I'm sorry, Molly, but Denise has been on sick leave for the past two weeks and we have a new girl filling in for her, so I'm afraid there has been a bit of a backlog with documentation.'

'It's still sitting in your office?' she laughed.

'Exactly!' he apologized. 'I have the contract here in front of me.'

'Tear it up, Michael!' she said and explained to him what had happened.

'Gladly!' he said.

Kim was grinning from ear to ear when Molly told her she would not be proceeding with the sale of the house to Frank Dunne.

'I'm so glad that awful man is not buying the place and getting his hands on Mossbawn.'

'So am I, and hopefully the next time we'll find the perfect buyer,' she said, reminding Kim that the situation with regard to selling Mossbawn had not changed.

'Or maybe you'll find some other way of holding on to the house,' added Kim encouragingly, already texting Emma and Grace with the good news.

Chapter Thirty-three

Kim was walking down by the river when she spotted the pair of swans with their cygnets. Automatically she reached for her iPhone to take some photos of them as they glided along, the baby swans paddling gently between their serene parents. The light was perfect and she did her best to capture the moment without disturbing them.

'Hey, I'd love a copy of that!' said a voice, and she turned to see Luke Ryan sitting on the stone bridge in the sunshine watching her.

'No problem,' she replied. 'Give me your phone number and I'll send it to you.'

He called out his number and she saved it to her contacts.

'Thanks, I left my phone in my jacket pocket in my car.'

'You're welcome,' she said, stopping to watch the swans. 'They are so beautiful.'

'I'm planning on doing a project on legends with my class, so the swans will tie in perfectly.'

'Where do you teach?'

'Kilfinn National School,' he said proudly. 'The village school is small, but the kids are great.'

'It looks cute.'

'It opened over a hundred years ago, so most people in the village went there sometime,' he explained.

'Have you been teaching there long?'

'About two years. I was working in London and one day it hit me that I didn't like what I was doing. I worked crazy hours, and moving figures and numbers on a computer screen just didn't do it for me any more. I didn't give a damn about it, so I applied to teacher training college and was very lucky to get accepted.'

'I worked in banking for years but lost my job last year,' she admitted. 'I guess I'm a bit like you and now I'm ready for a change in direction.'

'Is that why you came to Kilfinn?' he asked.

'Partly. I was in a relationship and that broke up too.' Kim didn't know why she was telling a virtual stranger so much, but she felt that she could trust him. 'It's all been a bit of a disaster and I don't know why, but I just wanted to come and stay with Molly, hang out in Mossbawn, the way I used to when I was a kid.'

'And I bet Molly has you doing plenty of hard physical graft!' he teased. 'Spreading shite and the like!'

198

'Yes, and I smelled to high heaven after!' she said, bursting out laughing.

'Hey, I've got to go,' he said, standing up. 'I've got to see a man about a horse!'

'Me too, I'm due back at Dr Jim's. I'm helping out on reception for a few weeks,' she said.

She watched the swans serenely sail along the river for another few minutes, before heading back to the surgery.

Later on she was cooking pasta for dinner for herself and Molly when she got a text from Luke.

'How about coffee on Saturday morning if you're free?'

She was free . . .

'Sounds good.'

'Pick you up at 11a.m. Luke'

'C u then. Kim'

Kim couldn't believe that she was actually contemplating meeting him. He might be a serial rapist for all she knew, but checking him out in vague conversations with Molly over the following few days she realized he sounded a pretty decent type of guy. Obviously he'd had a few girlfriends over the years, but by the sound of it he seemed to be currently single . . . Besides, Luke was more the kind of guy that you wanted to be friends with rather than get romantically involved with.

They were going to go for coffee, that was all.

Chapter Thirty-four

Luke arrived in the jeep, but this time without the trailer. Kim wondered where they were going as she ran out to meet him.

'How are you?' He grinned admiringly as she slipped in beside him in her jeans and suede jacket.

'Great. I've been kept busy in the surgery and I'm building a website about Mossbawn House.'

'Interesting! What does Molly think?'

'I think at first she was a bit worried about it, but when I showed her how it is going to look and she read some of the content I think that she was actually very pleased.'

'I must look out for it. My brother Justin wants Grangefield to have one, but we haven't got round to it yet. He says it will help promote the stud farm so it won't only be the locals that know about us.'

'It would certainly help.'

'I thought maybe we'd drive over to Rossmore, take a walk around and get a coffee there.'

'Sounds great!'

Rossmore was about a forty-minute drive away, a small seaside village with a cluster of houses and cottages, a few craft shops and a stylish hotel with an award-winning restaurant. A popular tourist spot during the summer, for most of the year it depended on fishing.

They chatted easily and Kim was surprised at how much they had in common. She couldn't believe that in Dublin they had literally worked on the same street for five years, had a few mutual acquaintances and yet had never bumped into each other!

'It's mad!' she giggled.

She discovered that Luke loved Mexican food, had travelled around Australia for a year, owned a horse called Lucky when he was twelve and hated zombie movies.

'They are pathetic! Give me an intelligent vampire any day of the week!'

As it was dry but overcast, Rossmore was quiet as they walked along the steep cliff path, the scenery spectacular.

'I think we deserve a coffee now,' he joked as they found their way to a small café overlooking the seafront.

An hour later they were still sitting there talking, and it had begun to rain heavily.

Coffee turned into lunch and Kim ordered the seafood special plate, while Luke went for a massive bowl of mussels.

'The seafood here is amazing,' she enthused as she tucked into crab, prawns and some spicy chorizo.

As Luke was driving he didn't drink, but she had a glass of white wine.

He was good company, easy to talk to and actually very attractive, with his dark hair and unusual grey-green eyes. And the conversation never flagged as they chatted about when they were kids, their favourite films and places they had both backpacked to when they were younger.

'The next time I go to Melbourne and up to the Barrier Reef I will not be staying in a hostel and sharing a room with ten other sweaty guys,' he vowed. 'I'll be staying in one of those nice fancy hotels sipping cocktails!'

'Me too!' she laughed.

As the weather eased they made a run back to the jeep, Kim flinging herself into the seat. As he reached for her safety belt, his hand brushed hers and Kim had the strangest feeling that she wanted him to put his arms around her. Luke didn't seem to notice as he entertained her with stories about the kids in his school and their ability with iPads, iPhones and all things technical.

'Some of the older teachers in the school haven't a clue as to how tech-savvy most five-, six- and seven-year-olds are!'

'Luke, thanks for the coffee and the lunch,' she said

as he dropped her off at Mossbawn. 'I really had a great time.'

'So did I!' he said as she began to get out. She took her time, deliberately waiting to see if he would arrange to see her again, or even ask her out. But he didn't, and she felt strangely disappointed.

'Bye, Kim!' he called good-naturedly as he turned the jeep and drove off.

She was so stupid, trying to read something into him being nice and polite and asking her for coffee, when that was all it was – coffee! She was the one reading far more into it than there was. Maybe she was kind of desperate after Gareth. Maybe her confidence was so low that if a guy was any way decent to her she presumed it was more. She really liked Luke, but she guessed that he was just being kind and neighbourly. His mum and Molly were friends, for heaven's sake! She just needed to cop on to herself.

Over the next few days she checked her messages, but there was nothing from Luke. She was tempted to text him, but resisted. Kilfinn was a very small place – they were bound to bump into each other again . . . and again . . .

Chapter Thirty-five

Molly had been stressed out for the past few weeks. Frank Dunne had not taken well to her decision not to go ahead with the sale of Mossbawn and had actually been quite threatening. He'd written to her and phoned her three or four times, shouting that they had made a deal and she could not back out of it. But Michael Quinn had been quite firm that she had not returned a signed contract so there was nothing he could do and they had not technically received his deposit from his solicitor.

'I spent time and effort on this project, not to count the costs I've wasted on plans for Mossbawn!' he'd ranted at her. 'You just can't go and change your mind!'

'You own the property!' Michael reminded her. 'And there is nothing he can say or do that will change that.'

She felt so alone and vulnerable, and prayed to David

to give her strength to stand firm and ignore Dunne's bullying tactics.

One day, coming home from the village, she was sure she had spotted his car parked near her driveway and she had panicked, turning around and driving to Rena's.

When Cara phoned to ask her to dinner on Saturday, Molly automatically said no. Over the past few months her friends had regularly asked her along to dinners, meals out, or to join them for a few drinks, but she had refused. She knew they were being kind and trying to include her the way they always had when David was alive, but she just couldn't face it without him. She always found some excuse to back out or cancel arrangements. It was pathetic to isolate herself from their friends, from the other couples they used to hang out with, but she couldn't help herself. How could she pretend to be happy when she saw all those couples and she was the one alone? A widow. She hated that damn word, just hated it!

Of late the invitations were coming less often and she knew that she had no one to blame but herself. She was happy to watch TV or listen to the radio or read a book – was it any wonder her social life had become a great big zero since David's death?

'This time I'm not taking a "no"!' argued Cara fiercely. 'I'm fed up of you saying "no" to Tim and me. We are your friends – remember that. If you were the one who had died, not David, we would still try to be David's friends. You know well, we'd have David here for dinner and drinks, a few meals. Why can't you accept that, Molly, and stop being so bloody difficult?'

'Okay, okay!' she said, giving in. 'I'd love to come to dinner!'

Cara and Tim were such good friends, and Molly knew that Tim really missed David too. They'd been close friends, played golf every week and often went for a coffee or a few pints.

Molly opted for her black satin shift dress, high heels and a soft white wrap. She'd treated herself to a cut and blow-dry in the hair salon in the village. She had been a very infrequent customer over the past few months and Dee, the salon-owner, had tut-tutted about the perils of letting your hair go long at her age. Looking at herself, she could see that Dee had been right and that the shorter cut suited her much better. Her hair felt feathery and lighter and it made her feel younger. A little make-up and a spray of her favourite perfume and she was good to go.

Kim was away, so Molly would drive over to Cara's and get a taxi or a lift home later, then go back there and collect her car tomorrow. With David it had never been a problem, but now being on her own every-thing had to be worked out. Giving a last glance in the mirror as she topped up her lip gloss, Molly grabbed her car keys and jacket before setting the alarm and locking up the house.

Cara and Tim lived about two miles from the village. The evening was still bright as the sun started to go down, and their living room was warm. Cara was big into plush furnishings and luxury, and there were two golden velvet couches, and deep purple armchairs with aubergine and rich purple cushions scattered on all the chairs. It was a bright, welcoming room. Tim hugged her the minute he saw her.

'Molly, it's so good to have you here in the house again for dinner. We've missed you.'

'And I've missed you too,' she said, hugging him back.

Tim got her some wine and she joined the rest of the guests standing around chatting. She was glad to see that Trish and Larry were also invited, and Tim's partner Fergus and his wife, Brigid.

'It's so nice to see you again,' said Fergus warmly, squeezing her hand.

Everyone made such a fuss of her she felt guilty.

'Molly, let me introduce you to Rob Hayes, a client of ours who is setting up a business in the area. His company is building a plant about three miles outside Kilfinn.'

'Oh, I saw it – it's all glass and steel. You can see it from the road.'

'Just about,' laughed the man, 'but I promise we intend screening it with some kind of hedge.'

'Nice to meet you,' Molly smiled, shaking his hand. 'And it's good to hear about some new business coming to Kilfinn.'

'Bio-Cartex make medical devices,' he explained, 'and when we are up and running we should employ at least forty people, possibly more once we get established.' He was a good-looking man, sixtyish, his grey hair shaved tight to his head, his accent a mixture of Irish and American.

'Where are you from?' she asked, curious but unable to place the accent.

'About twenty miles down the road, actually,' he laughed. 'I studied engineering in Cork, but once I qualified I headed to Boston and for the past few years have been working for Bio-Cartex between there and Sweden and Dublin. But it's good to be back on my home patch, as they say. Are you a local too?'

'I live the other side of the village.'

'That's the one thing I can't get over,' he smiled. 'This place has hardly changed over the years. There's still Cassidy's Café, the Kilfinn Inn, O'Donnell's grocery store and Grogan's chemist shop, though I see that Molloy's Drapery has shut down. It was a great old place for everything from pyjamas to shoelaces. There's nowhere like that any more.'

'It was pretty unique,' she agreed. 'Mary Molloy kept everything that you could possibly need. It was such a treasure trove.'

'I got my first Communion suit there,' he said, bursting out laughing, 'along with half the other guys in my class – we looked a right crowd.'

Molly laughed too. Molloy's had never been known for its style and fashion!

'What are you two laughing about?' interrupted Tim, coming to top up their glasses with wine.

'Molloy's!' they said in unison.

'God be good to Mary and Pat, but they were like two old dinosaurs! But we all miss them.' Tim sighed. 'There's a rumour that a bookie's is going to take over the shop.'

'Not in the village!' Molly protested.

'Let's hope it's not true,' agreed Rob.

Two minutes later Andy and Louise arrived, Louise in a pale-pink maternity dress that hung in soft folds, her skin tanned and her shoulder-length dark hair immaculately blow-dried, kissing everyone. Andy worked in David's old law firm. They had always got on well and she knew that Andy was embarrassed by the fact that his promotion to partner had come following her husband's death.

'Sorry we're late, but our babysitter got delayed,' she apologized.

'Harry was having a meltdown, so we were lucky we managed to get away at all,' confessed Andy.

'Well, you're here now and that's all that matters,' Cara soothed them. 'Let me get you both a drink.'

'I'll have a sparkling water and a slice of lemon,' beamed Louise. 'With junior on board I have to be good!'

'And I'll have a beer,' said Andy with a grin. 'It's great that I have a chauffeur to drive me home.'

'My passengers have to behave,' teased Louise.

Fifteen minutes later they were all sitting in the dining room with its formal oak table and high-backed chairs, large silver candelabra in the middle of the table, the soft candlelight casting shadows all around.

Molly was sitting between Tim and Rob, with Louise across from them.

'Cara, do you need a hand?' she offered.

'I'm fine,' she gestured, signalling madly to Molly to make sure that Louise, who was talking about the trouble she had had in her last pregnancy, which had resulted in the need for a dramatic Caesarean, was silenced immediately.

'Do you have children?' she asked Rob.

'Yes, but they're all grown up now,' he explained.

Cara served smoked salmon for starters, then her usual fillet of beef and gratin potatoes. She was a good cook but believed that this was a foolproof menu that always tasted good and appealed to everyone barring vegetarians!

'The beef is amazing!' Andy and Larry congratulated her, tucking in as Tim topped up all the wine glasses with an expensive Bordeaux.

'This is a very good wine,' enthused the visitor.

Molly chatted to Louise as Tim and Rob debated the merits of various wines and regions. She hadn't a clue about grapes or soils or vineyards.

'You must be very pleased about the baby?'

'We are, but it was a shock at first,' Louise admitted. 'Our other three are at school and soon we'll be back to nappies again!'

'It will be wonderful,' said Molly softly. She could see that Louise was tense and tired and probably worried about being older.

'Thanks,' said Louise. 'I'm sure people think that at our age we're crazy.'

'I wouldn't let that bother me,' smiled Molly. 'You obviously feel well and look beautiful, so the baby must be thriving.'

Over dinner the talk went from the global economy to local news and a big argument about various ghost estates around the country.

'Most of them were built where people didn't want to be, miles from the villages and shops and schools, where they would be isolated,' said Trish firmly. 'The local planners and councils got it totally wrong and gave permission for mad schemes that nobody wanted – all they cared about were the development fees and charges that are paid to them.'

'Well, surely the architects are culpable too?' suggested Rob.

'Of course we are,' Trish admitted. 'It will take a long time for our profession to recover from the massive mistakes made. Many architects are struggling and some have even left the profession. Hard lessons have been learned by all involved, I assure you.'

Cara served a melt-in-the-mouth chocolate roulade for dessert and Molly found herself chatting easily to Rob.

'Whereabouts in the village do you live?' he asked, curious.

'Do you know Mossbawn House?'

'The big house?'

'Yes,' she laughed. 'When David and I bought it, the place was a bit of a wreck, pretty run-down, so it's been a real labour of love trying to return it to a family home.'

'I remember Mossbawn – I used to go robbing apples in the orchard there when I was a kid and stuff myself with strawberries and gooseberries. That old codger, the guy who owned it, used to chase us out of it!'

'Richard Morton was a bit of a character,' Molly smiled, 'judging by the stuff around the house and the stories I've heard about him. He used to write books about pirates. Apparently they were very successful and one was made into a film. He was mad into fishing!'

'Eccentric, if you ask me!'

'I suppose,' she said gently. She was rather fond of the previous owner and his family, who had somehow managed to hold on to the house despite a massive downturn in their personal fortunes.

She discovered that Rob was staying in the local hotel for a few days as he was overseeing the construction of the company's new hi-tech plant.

'Bio-Cartex being situated between two big towns and pretty close to a research campus is very useful,' he explained. 'Trish here has done a great job on the designs, and Tim and Fergus are overseeing all the construction and facilities a company like ours will need, while Andy is keeping us all on the financial straight and narrow. So it's a good team!'

'It sounds busy but interesting,' Molly said, slightly puzzled as to why Cara had invited her along to the gathering.

'Busy is the word,' he said ruefully. 'I'm spending a lot of my time back and forth and all over the place.'

The rest of the night flew by and around midnight

Molly found herself accepting a lift from Louise and Andy.

'Cara, it's been a lovely night.' She had actually enjoyed herself and the company. 'The dinner was great and I'm so glad that I came.'

'And I'm so glad you came too,' said Cara, hugging her. 'David wouldn't want you to be hiding away.'

'I know,' she admitted.

Looking out over the fields in the darkness as they drove home, Molly knew in her heart that Cara was right. She had to try to make an effort to rebuild her life.

Chapter Thirty-six

Kim had gone to Dublin, as she'd offered to mind Ava and Finn for the weekend to give Liz and Joe a well-earned break. It was their fifth wedding anniversary and they'd gone to Paris.

Ava and Finn were great kids, but minding them was absolutely exhausting! Her dad had offered to come to the zoo with them on Sunday, which was fun, and she sure had needed the extra pair of hands, as Ava kept running ahead, wanting to see all the animals.

By the time Liz came home on Monday morning she was happy to hand them back, but glad to hear how much her sister and Joe had enjoyed their romantic break.

While she was up in Dublin Kim had decided to do some research on Mossbawn. She was trying to track down Samuel Johnston, a photographer that both the librarian in Kilfinn and also the one in Kilkenny had mentioned to her. Una Swann had told her about him as Kilfinn Library had some prints of photographs he had taken in the locality in the late 1890s and early 1900s.

'He was quite well known and fashionable and might well have visited Mossbawn and taken some photos there,' she suggested. 'The National Library in Dublin has a whole collection of his work that was donated by his daughter a few years ago. It might be worth checking it out.'

Kim spent hours in the National Library's photo archive, going through hundreds and hundreds of photos – Galway, Dublin, Cork, Connemara, Kerry, Kilkenny – when suddenly she recognized the main street in Kilfinn, which to her seemed little changed from when Samuel Johnston had taken his photograph in 1901. Her heart skipped a beat when she discovered black-and-white photos of Mossbawn House and its gardens, the maze and the pond. There were a large number of group photos of members of the family on the steps in front of the house, in the garden, in the drawing room, and a woman in the orangery. There were photographs of staff, of a uniformed nanny with her young charges. Various members of the family were seen dressed for dinner, to go riding, to go to a ball. There were photos of some favourite ponies and the stable buildings. Then of the garden – she recognized the Gardener's Cottage with its hollyhocks and foxgloves growing around the doorway.

One photograph was of an old man squinting in the sunlight, dressed in a shirt and tweed trousers, a hat perched on his head, leaning on his spade. Something about him was familiar. She knew that face – had seen it before . . . Then she read the inscription on the back of the photograph: *Charles Moore – The Gardener. 16th July 1901, Mossbawn House.*

In another photograph he was sitting on a bench in front of the Gardener's Cottage, resting. The door was open, his spade against it, his hat on a peg just inside.

She rechecked a few family group portraits and there he was in the centre, looking far more dapper in a suit. The next three photographs were of the rose garden from various angles. She couldn't wait for Molly to see them. It was incredible, all these photos from long ago . . .

She asked if it was possible to copy the photographs and when she explained about staying at Mossbawn House the librarian helped her to get everything she needed.

Kim had left the library and was walking up Dawson Street heading towards the Luas tram when she saw Gareth in the distance. She wanted to turn the other way and avoid him, but she could clearly see that he had spotted her.

'Kim, wait!' he shouted.

She tried to pretend she didn't hear him and quickened her step, but with his long legs he quickly reached her.

'Didn't you hear me calling you?' he asked, aggrieved.

'No! Sorry.'

She had absolutely no interest in seeing him or talking to him.

'How are you?' he asked, standing beside her. 'I haven't seen you around. Where have you been?'

'Away,' she said, trying to sound mysterious.

'Well, you look well,' he said approvingly.

Kim almost laughed. It was ironic – her hair was longer and, since she couldn't afford highlights, it had returned to its natural colour. She'd lost eight kilos from working in the garden, the weight falling off her better than in any expensive gym or hot yoga workout.

'Thanks,' she said.

'How are things?' he continued. 'Are you okay?'

'Yes,' she said slowly. 'I'm busy. I work in a medical practice, which I really like, and I'm doing a big research project on my aunt's old house. I'm designing a website for it.'

'Kim, don't be annoyed with me,' he begged. 'I'm sorry the way things ended.'

She said nothing.

'Please let me buy you a coffee. We can catch up . . . talk.'

'I don't think we have anything to talk about,' she said wearily, remembering his harsh words when they broke up.

'Don't be like that . . . We were good together – you know we were! Please. Just coffee.'

217

Kim didn't know what to say. She had lived with him, shared her life with him. He'd meant so much to her . . .

'A coffee . . . that's all!' Gareth said, taking her arm as he led her to the coffee shop across the street.

As she sank into the brown leather couch and the waitress took their order, Kim wondered if she was going mad. What was she doing sitting here with her ex, the guy who had broken her heart?

The waitress brought her a large cappuccino.

'I think about you sometimes, about us,' he said. 'I miss you, Kim. Honestly I do!'

She took a sip of the frothy coffee and said nothing. She had missed him so much that she had almost gone crazy. It had broken her . . . But now she was different – she had changed.

'Don't you miss me a little too?' he urged. 'We had something special.'

'I did in the beginning,' she admitted. 'All day, every day all I could think of was us. It was awful. But then I suppose I got used to being alone . . . to not having you around and that's the way it is now . . .'

'I'm sorry,' he said, serious. 'Maybe it doesn't have to be that way . . . Maybe we should go out for dinner, talk, go on a proper date. Give each other another chance.'

She had been waiting for him to say something like this from the minute they split up. Now that he had said it, it felt hollow and empty. She wasn't sure that she wanted to give them another chance.

'I have to think about it,' she said slowly.

She could see that he was surprised. Obviously he had expected her to jump at it.

'Listen, Gareth – I have to go,' she said, standing up and grabbing her jacket.

'I'll phone you, Kim,' he promised, trying to get the waitress's attention as she left him there.

Sitting on the tram a few minutes later, she realized that she was shaking, that old feeling she always had around him of not being clever or pretty or even good enough returning. She couldn't bear it.

Chapter Thirty-seven

Meeting her friends in Ranelagh for pizza and a drink, Kim told them about seeing Gareth earlier.

'Good girl! I can't believe that you left him hanging!' crowed Evie. 'I'm sure Gareth is in utter shock that you didn't come running back to him immediately!'

'It's good to make him wait,' agreed Lisa. 'It's about time he realized that you can do what you want and that everything doesn't just revolve around him.'

'How long will you keep him dangling?' asked Alex, reaching for his beer.

'I'm not keeping him dangling!' she protested. 'You know breaking up with Gareth was the worst thing ever – he totally broke my heart. But now it's weird, because I don't think I could ever go back with him, give him a second chance. Maybe Liz and Molly are right that Gareth isn't meant for me.'

'I can't believe what I'm hearing!' Evie said, serious. 'You've been mad about Gareth for years!'

'I know,' she said, mortified. 'I must have driven you all mad. I guess I realize now that Gareth is not the type of guy I want to spend the rest of my life with.'

'Well, that's a relief!' said Alex. 'He's so up himself!'

Kim burst out laughing. She couldn't believe that she was talking about her ex like this.

'Does this mean that there is some other guy you fancy down the country?' he asked.

'No,' she remonstrated, 'there's absolutely no one. Honestly.'

It was stupid, but it still irked her that she hadn't had as much as a text from Luke Ryan. He had seemed nice, but obviously she was just not his type.

The past few days in Dublin had been great, meeting up with everyone, having time with her family and getting to research in the National Library. Now, as she was still stony broke, she decided another big cull of her clothes was badly needed.

Returning to Chloe's Vintage Room in the Powerscourt Centre, Kim had made the ultimate sacrifice and handed over a gorgeous Missoni wrap-over maxi skirt and her Chloé evening dress, which she could never see herself wearing in Kilfinn, as well as her Lulu Guinness handbag, which had been a present from Gareth. It no longer had sentimental value, but was still worth a pretty penny!

She'd also arranged to meet Piotr, the clever Polish

guy who had been on her web-design course. She wanted his advice about the work she was doing on Mossbawn. Immediately on finishing the course Piotr had landed a job with a big American gaming company that had just set up in Dublin.

'What you've been doing looks very good, Kim!' he praised her, looking at the laptop. 'But what do you need me to do?'

She explained where she was having difficulty technically, the two of them sitting in a huddle in a small coffee shop by the canal.

'Congrats on getting the job! We all knew you'd be the first one on the course to find something!'

'Thanks, Kim. I'm just happy to be working again, especially now with Irina expecting another baby.'

'I hadn't heard the good news!' she laughed. 'When is the baby due?'

'In five months, so it's just as well I got a new job. What about you?'

'I'm still waiting to see if anything comes up,' she admitted. 'I registered on line with some new agency, but you know what it's like.'

'I keep my fingers crossed for you.'

'Piotr, thanks for helping me.'

'No problem, Kim. You phone me if you need any more help, okay?'

As she was working in the surgery again the next morning, she decided to head on back down to Kilfinn. Besides, she was dying to show Molly the photographs from the library and to scan them all in on her computer.

Chapter Thirty-eight

'Kim, you are amazing! I can't believe you found all these photographs of Mossbawn, of the house and the gardens!' Molly said, poring over the copies of the old black-and-white photographs that Kim had found in the National Library. 'Look at the family – that must be his son James and that's his wife and their twin boys. There's dear old Charles . . . He's such a character, isn't he?' she said.

'He's the one started it all!' agreed Kim. 'Yet there he is in his old clothes and with his spade, working and hanging out in the Gardener's Cottage.'

'The mystery of the old gardener solved,' smiled Molly. 'He must have enjoyed living in the cottage and simplifying his life.'

'Yet when he is dressed up he looks the real lord of the manor type!'

'The wonderful thing we can tell from all these old photographs is just how little things have changed,' said Molly proudly. 'I can even recognize bushes and shrubs, and look at the size of that cedar tree compared to now!'

To Molly, the fact that she and David had managed to keep the integrity of the house and grounds was a huge factor. It was what living in an old house entailed, ensuring that it survived to be enjoyed by another generation.

'And look at your rose garden,' teased Kim. 'It was really beautiful back then.'

'And it will be again!' she said defiantly. 'If only these photographs were in colour so I could try and discover which varieties of roses were grown back then . . . I must find my magnifying glass. But at least I can see the layout and design, which is wonderful.'

'I'll scan them in on the computer and then we can blow them up for you to study – but obviously the quality won't be as good.'

'Thanks, Kim . . . I don't know what I'd do without you. I can't wait to show them to Emma and Grace,' she said, engrossed. 'I'm going to get them all copied and frame some of them.'

'And I'm going to put them in the archive and also load them up into our History of the House section.'

It was clear from the photographs that the garden needed far more planting. Molly was determined to try to use as many as possible of the older rose types that would have been available at the time the photographs were taken. She needed some guidance, though, and planned to go and visit Gabriel Boland, the rose expert. His nursery was about an hour from here and he was a fount of knowledge and good advice about everything to do with rose-growing.

Gabriel showed her around his nursery.

'This is the right time to come looking for some of the more unusual roses if you want to plant October–November time,' he explained, leading her to the areas where his older varieties were kept. His own offices and home were covered in a magnificent climber, roses cascading down the wall and scrambling over the porch.

'I'll certainly take two of them,' smiled Molly, hugely impressed.

'It's funny – I don't think anyone has ever come here without ordering Rosa Gabriel!' he laughed.

He showed her some photographs of older varieties.

'There is a beautiful climbing rose that they grow in Mount Congreve; I'll see about ordering you one. What about Bourbon Queen? She loves Irish gardens. And Felicia is a wonderful hybrid musk that will keep flowering,' he said, leading her around. 'And of course I'd highly recommend Ispahan – a truly beautiful pink damask rose.'

Molly was spoiled for choice, but even though in part of the bed she was willing to test out some new varieties that were proving fast and easy to grow, she was determined to keep the rose garden's classic appearance.

'Some will take a few weeks for me to order, but I should have them in plenty of time for you.'

Driving home from Gabriel's, Molly was excited thinking about next year – next summer in the garden . . . roses everywhere.

She was turning into Mossbawn when Avril Flynn texted her to remind her that they would collect her tomorrow to go to the opera at Glengarry Castle. It was something she was really looking forward to and was so glad that she had managed to get a ticket.

'*See you tomorrow,*' Molly texted back. '*Busy day buying lots of lovely roses.*'

Chapter Thirty-nine

Avril and Peter were outside in the car waiting for her as Molly quickly grabbed her warm wrap and handbag. She was really looking forward to tonight's open-air opera performance. Glengarry Castle was only about twelve miles away; Hugh Fitzgerald and his wife Francesca had been clients of David's and they had visited there a few times over the years. Two years ago they'd been to a big garden party to celebrate Hugh's seventieth birthday. He was a great character and was totally devoted to ensuring the survival of the castle and the estate, which comprised about two hundred acres, with a large dairy farm and acres and acres of forestry. 'Apparently they've sold all the tickets,' Peter told them as they drove through the tall iron gates, where their own tickets were checked.

'Let's hope the weather holds,' said Avril as they

turned up the long driveway, which was all lit up.

'Well, there's no rain forecast,' Molly smiled.

Peter managed to find a car park in the back field and, following the crowds, they walked along the gravelled driveway towards the terrace area where lots of tables covered with starched linen tablecloths and tall navy parasols had been set up. People were standing around talking, drinking prosecco and wine as young waitresses passed around the canapés.

'Very civilized,' said Peter approvingly as he accepted a glass.

Everyone was dressed up, with some of the men wearing black tie, and Molly was glad that she had made an effort and opted for her new oyster-coloured silk dress. In the distance she could see that the big field with its ring of tall beech trees, where cows normally grazed, had been transformed into a concert arena. A large protected stage had been constructed and rows of chairs laid out for the audience.

'It looks great,' enthused Avril. 'I'm so glad we've come.'

Molly recognized a few friends from her book club and ran over to say hello to them.

'We've never been to hear opera before,' Miriam Kelly confided, 'but seeing it in a setting like this is wonderful.'

'It's very special,' agreed Molly. 'Katarina Long has such a beautiful voice and to have Marco Reynolds performing with her is amazing.'

Three quarters of an hour later everyone had filed

down along the grassy pathway to take their seats. It was beginning to get darker and the stage lights illuminated the whole area. Cara and Tim arrived in a flurry, coming to sit down beside them.

'God give me patience with that mother of mine! I've been at the hospital with her all afternoon.'

'What's wrong?'

'She's been limping around for days and it turns out she has an infection in her big toe.'

'Poor Margaret! What did they do?' asked Molly, trying not to laugh.

'Bathed it and cut the nail and dressed it and gave her some antibiotics,' Cara sighed dramatically. 'She has a footbath thing we gave her years ago and she won't use it! So from here on in she's going for regular pedicures and looking after her feet.'

'Well, at least you're here now and Margaret is fine.'

'I didn't even get a glass of wine!'

'You can get one afterwards,' Avril soothed her as the orchestra, who were seated towards the back of the stage, began to warm up. The stage darkened and suddenly the lights went up as the large, burly figure of Marco Reynolds, the tenor, appeared and went into the opening aria of *Carmen*.

Molly watched captivated as Katarina Long, the renowned Italian soprano who had grown up in New York, came on stage in a silver fitted gown, her dark hair tumbling around her shoulders, her dark eyes like liquid as she began to sing. Her voice filled the arena, entrancing everyone as she sang from *Aida*. Like Marco, she performed a few arias on her own and then they came back on stage together and duetted, their voices ringing out in the still night across Glengarry's fields. It was almost magical as the late-August night got darker and the stars appeared, forming a perfect backdrop to the performances on stage.

Molly found herself swept up in the emotion of Katarina's voice as the soprano sang about her lost love. Tears welled in her eyes as the singing filled the night.

As the concert came to an end and Marco reappeared on stage with her to sing together once more, Molly was conscious of what a privilege it had been to attend such a performance. The two singers, holding hands, received a standing ovation.

As the stage went dark, everyone crowded along the torchlit path back up to the terraced area. Cara, itching for some wine, managed to get glasses for everyone. It had grown cooler and as they stood around chatting Molly was glad she had brought her warm wrap.

Spotting Hugh and Francesca, she went over to say hello to them. Hugh was looking very handsome in a wine-coloured velvet tuxedo.

'What a wonderful night!' she said, hugging them. 'You must be delighted!'

'We are,' admitted Francesca proudly. 'It was a bit of a worry that it would all work, but thank heaven it did. Ted was the one who came up with the idea of putting on the concert and organizing it all.'

'Well, you must be very proud of him, and Glengarry

looks amazing, as if it was meant for staging things like this.'

'The old place does look good,' chortled Hugh, 'though the cows were very put out not to be in their favourite field for the past few weeks. Teddy's talking about staging two or three events during the year.'

'That would be wonderful.'

Molly knew that their eldest son, Ted, had become more involved with running the castle and the farm over the past few years and was set to take over from Hugh.

'How are you, Molly dear?' asked the older woman. 'I'm so glad that you came along tonight.'

'When I heard about a night of opera here at Glengarry I had to come,' she smiled.

'How are you managing in Mossbawn?' asked Hugh.

'It's hard being there on my own,' she admitted, 'but I'm trying to keep busy. I've started restoring the old rose garden.'

'Oh, I do love roses,' smiled Francesca. 'My mother was mad for them!'

'So am I,' said Molly. 'I'm trying to see if I can get some of the older varieties to regrow.'

'You should talk to our gardener, Seamus – he's the expert here. Why don't you come over next week?' suggested Francesca. 'I'll arrange for you to see him, and Hugh and I always love a bit of company.'

'Thank you, that would be great,' she agreed and they arranged for her to come over on Thursday afternoon.

Seeing that a few people were standing around

waiting to talk to the Fitzgeralds and congratulate them, she returned to her friends.

Rob Hayes had joined them, looking very distinguished in his tuxedo.

'Did you enjoy tonight's performance?' he asked.

'It was wonderful, so moving. And having the concert in the open air makes it so different.'

'It really adds to the experience,' he agreed. 'The last time I was in Verona, we got a lightning storm in the middle of *Aida*. The lightning was all across the night sky and they had to stop the performance for safety reasons. We all had to make a run for the cafés around the piazza, then when the rain and lightning stopped we all went back to our seats and they finished the opera.'

'That's crazy!'

'That's Italy!' he laughed.

Molly would never have taken him for someone who listened to opera, let alone liked it.

'Here, let me get you a glass of wine,' he offered, making his way through a throng of figures to the drinks area.

'Thanks,' she smiled when he passed her a glass of red wine. 'It's a bit of a scrum up there!'

'I'm an old second row, so I'm well able for them.'

'When did you come back to Kilfinn?' she asked, taking a sip of her wine.

'Yesterday. I wasn't going to miss tonight. I'm here for about six days, as there are a few things to finalize with the plant. Some officials from the county council planning department are coming out to check on the place. Tim says they are devils for detail, so it's best that I'm around in case there are any problems to be dealt with.'

'I'd say there must be a lot of work with building the plant.'

'I've never minded work – it never killed anyone. Besides, once it gets up and running it should be fine.'

'Doesn't your family mind you being away so much?'

'My wife and I divorced four years ago,' he explained.

'I'm sorry.' Molly blushed. She hadn't meant to be so personal.

'Don't be. It's all very amicable. Olivia is remarried. Our daughter, Karin, is a teacher and is married to a great guy called Simon; they live just outside Boston and I have a sweetheart of a granddaughter, which is one of the best things about getting a bit older . . . probably the only thing,' he laughed. 'And Kevin, my son, is in New York, working crazy hours as a trainee film editor. Every time I go there we get to hang out. So as you can see there really isn't anyone missing me at all, to be honest!'

'Are you still staying in the hotel?'

'Yeah, for a few days it's fine, but once the plant opens next year I'll get a place of my own. Hotel rooms are a pain to live in. You get so bored with them and of eating on your own. You know what it's like!'

Molly did know – only too well – what being on your own was like.

'Sorry, I didn't mean to be so insensitive,' he

apologized, embarrassed. 'I know you lost your husband last year, so it must be very difficult . . .'

'He died last November and it is difficult. Awful. I know exactly what you are talking about,' she confided. 'Sitting at a table and eating on your own day after day is probably the hardest thing, so I always have to have a book or a magazine or a paper beside me.'

'I usually read the *Financial Times* or the latest John Grisham,' he admitted wryly.

Molly burst out laughing at the absurdity of it, and had a crazy notion of some day inviting him to Mossbawn for a simple dinner and eating in the kitchen. It just showed how sad and lonely she really was . . .

'There you are, Molly!' interjected Cara.

Tim and Cara and the others joined them and they managed to position themselves near a warming brazier as Tim insisted on ordering more wine for everyone.

What a wonderful evening, thought Molly as she looked up at the star-speckled night sky and gave silent thanks for the friends who had all been so kind and good to her since David's death.

As they drove home she thought of David. They had been married almost twenty-four years when he had died. It was so sad that they would never get to celebrate their silver anniversary together, but they'd had a wonderful marriage and she'd been absolutely happy over all those years.

Chapter Forty

Molly could feel the change of seasons. the nights began to get a bit colder, the trees started to change colour and all her plants and flowers were beginning to fade. She kept dead-heading madly, trying to prolong things blooming, but she was fighting a losing battle against nature. Her lupins and delphiniums had both had a second flush but now were gone, cut down as sedum and allium flourished in the beds.

The girls had both come home for two weeks, chilling out before they started new terms in college. Emma and Jake had gone surfing in Biarritz for three weeks with their friends. Both of them were anxiously awaiting their final-year exam and thesis results. Grace had passed her exams, which was all she needed to get into third year. She'd had a brilliant time trekking around Europe and was full of stories of all their adventures as they went from one country to another. Molly's two daughters were both independent and strong, growing up and making lives of their own.

'Grace, what's happening for your twenty-first?' she asked. 'What do you want to do for it?'

'I suppose I'll have a night out, Mum, a bit of a party. I could book a pub somewhere in town, near the nightclubs.'

'Don't you want a proper party?' asked Molly.

'If I have it in a pub or club in Dublin it means we don't have to go spending a fortune and going to lots of trouble . . .' Grace tailed off lamely.

'Grace Mary Hennessy, I don't believe you! Emma had a big summer party – remember the barbecue? We must have had a hundred at it!' she reminded her. 'You're only twenty-one once and it would be lovely to have the party here at home just like your sister did.'

'Mum, are you sure?' she asked hesitantly. 'I don't want you to go spending lots of money on a party.'

Molly knew that Grace was over-conscious of her finances, but she was not going to let that spoil a big family occasion.

'Of course I'm sure. Your dad and I had always planned on having your twenty-first at home here,' she said firmly. 'We can light up the place and roll back the carpet and get some nice food in and lots of drinks.'

'Oh Mum – a twenty-first party at home is exactly what I want! And my friends can bunk in here or stay in the village or the hotel.'

'Good, then we can start planning it!' Molly found herself saying.

The rest of the weekend Grace followed her around with lists and began to make all sorts of plans for her big party. Molly knew that once her daughter started thinking about a proper party she'd be all excited about it.

'I'll talk to Gina Sullivan, find out if she is free to do the catering, and we can hire a barman for the night.'

'Kelly, one of the guys I know, does DJ sometimes, so I'm sure he might do it for less than most other DJs,' suggested Grace. 'And he'd probably do the lights as well.'

Molly smiled. It would be nice to have a big party with all Grace's friends and some of their family and friends along. Who knows, she thought, maybe it would be the last big party held in Mossbawn.

Chapter Forty-one

The café was quiet, Gina studying various shades of paint online, wondering what would be the best colour for painting old pine tables and chairs to give them a fresh look. A soft sage green, a French grey or a creamy-white colour? She was full of plans for the café, what she could do with it: finding ways to attract more customers, changing the menus, even the layout . . .

She looked up as the door opened. It was Molly Hennessy.

'Hello, Gina. How's Norah doing?' Molly asked, sitting down at a table near the window.

'She's getting on fine in Beech Hill. She's made a real pet of the little cat they have there!'

'It's hard to imagine Norah in a nursing home with all those old people . . . '

'I know, but she really needs a lot of nursing care and support,' Gina confided.

'Will you tell her that I was asking for her and I'll try and call in to her next week?' Molly asked, ordering a cappuccino and a muffin as she slipped off her navy jacket. 'I've just come from dropping Daisy to be clipped and I was hoping I'd catch you, as I wanted to ask if you'd be interested in doing the catering for Grace's twenty-first-birthday party. It's at Halloween and we want to have the party at home.'

'Sounds lovely,' said Gina as she brought the cappuccino over to the table. 'What kind of food were you thinking about?'

'Well that's it, Gina – I'm not sure whether we should do a buffet or a sit-down meal.'

'There's quite a bit of a difference in cost terms,' she explained. 'The sit-down would be far more expensive, as I'd have to hire extra help for serving the meal and clearing the courses, so a buffet would work out a lot easier.'

'Good, we'll go for that. I'm not sure of the numbers yet, but I think it should be about eighty guests.'

'Quite a big party then,' she said, passing Molly a caramel muffin.

'Grace has lots of friends and she wants to invite them all,' she laughed. 'Heaven knows how we'll fit everyone.'

'Well, with a big crowd like that the main-course buffet options are things like Thai green chicken curry, beef stroganoff, beef bourguignon, a creamy lemon chicken, lamb tagine, or even a pasta dish. I'll email you a list of menus so you and Grace can choose. There's a big choice of desserts, though usually the girls go for something with chocolate.'

'I know – we are all chocoholics!'

'Me too!' Gina laughed as she took down Molly's email address. 'I'm sure we can sort out a perfect meal for Grace and her friends that won't break the bank.'

'Given the awful year we've had, I really want Grace to have a very special night, the same as if her dad were still alive.'

Gina had helped out with the food after her husband's funeral, Molly and her two daughters distraught and in shock at David Hennessy's sudden death. She remembered coming home from Mossbawn and lying beside Paul in bed and hugging him close, glad of his warmth and comfort and snores beside her.

'Molly, don't worry – she will have a wonderful party,' Gina said gently, full of admiration for Molly Hennessy.

The day had been fairly busy and Gina was just making a fresh batch of scones when Martin Cassidy came in. He wandered into the kitchen as if he owned the place.

'I'll be out to you in a minute,' she said, hoping to get rid of him.

His plump face and beady eyes watched her work as he leant against the presses. His dark hair was receding, and even though he tried to disguise it by wearing an expensive designer sweater and jacket he had a very definite paunch. Gina, conscious of a dab of flour on her cheek, tried to wipe it away with her apron. She continued cutting the scones, set them on the big baking tray and slid them into the oven.

'They look good!' he said. 'How much do you sell them for?'

'One euro and fifty cent,' she said, going over to the sink to wash her hands.

'That's good – a healthy profit . . .'

She coloured. It was none of his business what the café charged for an item.

'Can I help you with something?' she asked, walking deliberately back out to the café.

'I was just wondering how the business is going in the light of Norah's absence?'

She could have throttled him.

'We're lucky, as most of our regulars still come in for their lunches and snacks and to meet for coffee and a cake.'

'Can I see the bank lodgements book or your daily records?' he asked, stepping behind the counter and pulling out one drawer after another.

'I'm sorry, but I've no authority to do that,' she said firmly. 'I report the daily takings to Norah.'

'But I am helping to manage her affairs now.'

Gina knew there was no point antagonizing him and suspected that Martin Cassidy would make a dangerous enemy. She might well have to deal with him about taking over the café.

'I'll ask Norah about it,' she said. 'You know how private she is about things.'

'Very well,' he said grudgingly. He grabbed a menu and perused it. 'Give me a coffee and a slice of the carrot cake.'

She watched as he went and sat at a table against the back wall and took out his phone. He was an obnoxious type of man; no wonder poor Norah didn't want to spend Christmas with him and his family! He didn't even say thank you when she carried his order to the table; and was busy talking loudly to some business associate. Leaving him, she went back to check on the scones. She wondered what he was up to and how much influence he really had over his elderly aunt.

A few more people came in for coffee and she was busy serving them when Martin came and asked her for the key to Norah's place upstairs.

'I know you have the key,' he said. 'I just want to check something and I will drop it back to you.'

She hesitated, but had no option but to give it to him. She was busy clearing the tables when he came in and returned it to her.

'I don't trust him!' she complained to Paul that night.

'Maybe he is looking after Norah's best interest,' he said, playing devil's advocate. 'She is family.'

'The only person's interest he's interested in looking after is his own.'

'That might be, but he's her nephew, her brother's son, and he's flesh and blood,' he reminded her. 'To

242

everyone, you are just someone who works for Norah, a staff member, that's all.'

Gina felt aggrieved, but she had to admit that what Paul was saying was true. She might be fond of Norah, close to her, but to everyone else she was just staff . . .

'I'm going to ask her about the café – find out what she intends.'

'Is Norah well enough to even answer you, Gina love?' asked Paul soothingly, rubbing her shoulders. 'Don't push Norah or her family into a corner. See what happens.'

Lying in bed that night, looking at the ceiling, her brain was racing. She had such dreams for the place, such plans. She liked working there, knew that given the chance to take over the café she could make a success of it . . .

Chapter Forty-two

Molly was up early – she couldn't believe that it was Grace's birthday! Twenty-one years since she and David had held their newborn little daughter in their arms.

Outside it looked cold and rather damp, but thank heaven there was no sign of the heavy rains the weather forecasters had been predicting. Pulling on her dressing gown, she began to get everything sorted: twenty-one presents wrapped and hidden ready to surprise Grace. She'd been buying things for the past few months and hiding them away, big things and little things and quirky things that she knew her younger daughter would love.

'Mum, are you awake?' whispered Emma, padding in in her pink fleece pyjamas.

'Yes,' she laughed, hugging her. 'You can help me carry all this lot into her bedroom.'

'What's in this one?' quizzed Emma, turning a box wrapped in butterfly-design paper. 'It's so heavy.'

'A kettle bell!'

'No wonder I can hardly lift it!' she grinned, helping her.

As they opened Grace's door they began to sing 'Happy Birthday' and Grace sat up in bed as they both hugged her madly while they performed the birthday song.

'Twenty-one presents,' nodded Emma. 'It's a family tradition.'

Molly sat down on the side of the bed as Emma began to take the presents and pass them to Grace to open one by one.

'A new hair straightener! It's exactly what I need.'

'Well, you broke the old one!' Emma reminded her.

'Oh, a glass angel – I love it! My favourite lip gloss – let me put a bit on.'

Soon the bed was covered with wrapping paper and boxes as Grace opened present after present, Emma taking a few photos with the new compact camera they had bought for Grace. There were books, a new top, slippers, pyjamas, hair clips, nail polish and eye shadow, and a big bag of jelly babies, a cuddly dog, her favourite sweets and some chocolate. They were almost down to the last present. Molly took it from her pocket and passed it to Grace.

'Present twenty-one,' she said, hugging her close.

'Oh Mum, what is it?' she asked as she began to unwrap the small, hard box.

'It's a diamond, Grace – your granny's diamond. Put it on and see how it looks!'

'Oh Mum, I love it! It's just like Emma's!' she said, fastening it around her neck where the single diamond on its white-gold chain sparkled against her skin. 'I'm going to wear it for my party tonight.'

'It looks beautiful,' admired Molly, 'and I know that your granny would be very pleased that you are wearing it.'

When her mother, Sally, knew that she was dying fourteen years ago she had divided her jewellery between Ruth, their brother Stephen and herself. 'I want you all to have something of mine for yourselves or my grandchildren,' she had insisted. So Molly had inherited her mother's two-stone diamond engagement ring and had worn it over the years, but once her daughters had got older she and David had decided that the fair thing was to give each of the girls a single diamond in a simple setting on a chain of gold that they could wear, so that it would always remind them of their granny. Today being a special day was the perfect time to give such a present.

'Now you have my present to open,' urged Emma excitedly.

'It's an Eiffel tower and some cheese!' laughed Grace.

'Look again, stupid,' prompted Emma.

'Oh my God – there are two tickets to Paris for the end of March!'

'Yeah, I've already booked the flights and the two of us are going shopping and seeing all the sights, and we can stay in the spare room in my friend Clara's apartment. Springtime is the best time to go,' Emma laughed as Grace hugged her wildly.

'I can't believe it – the two of us going to Paris for a few days!'

'I knew you'd love it!' said Emma proudly.

Downstairs in the kitchen Kim was up making breakfast for everyone, putting on bacon and mixing up pancakes, Grace's favourite.

'Here are my presents!' Kim offered, kissing her.

Molly watched as Grace unwrapped them. There was a beautiful grey-and-green skirt.

'Oh God, it's stunning!' shouted Grace, trying it on over her pyjamas. 'I love it!'

'Good! Now open the other one!' urged her cousin.

Molly couldn't believe it. Kim had taken a wonderful picture of the three of them walking down by the river during the summer, the light catching them all as they laughed at something. It was a most beautiful picture and she had got it framed.

'Oh Kim, thanks!' said Grace. 'I'll take this photo everywhere with me!'

As they ate a long, lazy breakfast, Molly was conscious that they had lots to do. There were eighty people coming to the party and six of Grace's closest friends were staying here in the house. She had made up their beds and had the heating on full tilt in their rooms.

'What time are we booked for the hairdresser's?' Grace asked, pouring maple syrup over her plate of pancakes.

'I told Dee that we would be there for around eleven. I have to be back here around twelve as Gina's husband, Paul, is going to put up the lights in the orangery for us and the extra trestle tables are being delivered.'

'And the girls are all arriving around four o'clock,' Grace added.

'And Jake will be here about six,' Emma reminded them.

'Mum, go on – tell me about the day I was born,' urged Grace.

Molly sipped her coffee. The girls always loved on their birthday to hear the blow-by-blow account of the day they were born.

'I remember we'd only just moved in here and I didn't know a soul. The house was freezing cold as we couldn't get the heating and the old boiler working! You weren't due for another four weeks. I was about to go upstairs to do a bit more unpacking when suddenly I realized that I was in labour. Your dad had already gone to work. He'd only just started working with Michael Quinn, and as a new junior partner he didn't want to be late. They were seeing a client about some upcoming court case. I was getting a bit panicky as the contractions were getting stronger and I couldn't contact your dad because the phone still hadn't been connected. I put Emma in the car, and my hospital bag, and somehow managed to drive to Castlecomer where your dad worked. How I drove was a miracle! I remember hooting the horn madly outside the office until your dad came out and took over. We barely made it to the hospital in Kilkenny and in a few minutes this perfect pixie of a baby was born. It was a bit of a shock! Emma saw you when you were literally only a few minutes old. You were such a beautiful baby.'

'Then what happened?' prompted Emma.

'I remember dreading bringing a new baby home to a cold house full of packing cases and chaos, but when I arrived your granny and grandad were here and the fires were blazing in the hall and the drawing room. Your granny made massive meals in the Aga which kept us all warm. Then Ruth and Bill drove down with Liz and Mike and Kim to have Halloween with us and stay the night. I remember there was a power cut as we had a storm, and we all sat around with candles, talking while I sat in the armchair feeding you in the candlelight and just being so happy . . . It was the best Halloween ever, having everyone here in Mossbawn with us.'

'Let's hope there's no power cuts tonight!' teased Emma.

'Don't even say that!' Molly laughed, glancing at the clock. 'Come on you lot: finish up breakfast! We've a party to organize!'

Chapter Forty-three

Molly studied the house. Everything looked perfect. the driveway was lit up and lights sparkled on the trees that stood near the front of the house. Log fires blazed in the hall, drawing room and dining room; and there were arrangements of pumpkins and candles with autumn leaves and berries everywhere to add to the atmosphere. They had put up fairy lights in the orangery and dozens of sparkling crystal champagne flutes stood on the circular table in the hall to welcome the party guests to Grace's twenty-first birthday. The whole house was in a frenzy of excitement and in the kitchen Gina was busy organizing all the food and canapés for the large crowd.

Grace and Emma were shrieking and laughing as they got changed in their bedrooms. Grace was wearing a stunning pale-pink chiffon dress which made her look so slim and delicate, with her sparkling diamond around her neck. Emma, with her brown hair, looked striking in a figure-hugging, vibrant purple satin dress.

Molly had spent ages trying to decide what to wear for such an occasion, aware of treading a fine line between looking old and dowdy and trying to be trendy and too young. Cara, who was fashion mad and had a real eye for style, had insisted on going shopping with her.

'Molly, this is a big party and whether you like it or not you are going to look good,' she warned. 'You are treating yourself to something new and elegant.'

They had found the most perfect silver-grey knee-length lace dress with a mid-length sleeve in a boutique near the castle in Kilkenny. She absolutely loved it and both girls had given it their immediate approval.

Today was a poignant reminder of David's loss, which always seemed worse on family occasions like this. She was nervous about the party and wished that David was here to organize and run things instead of it all falling on her. She had written a birthday speech and just hoped that her confidence would hold up enough to make it. Grace deserved this party and to have a parent say good things about her.

However, one less worry was that Gina seemed to have everything running smoothly in the kitchen and dining room. There was Inga from the café, along with a barman to help serve the drinks and a young waitress to help with the food. Gina was so calm Molly knew that she could totally trust her to ensure that the food was a success.

Grace's friend, the DJ, had set up in a part of the orangery and there would be dancing there later.

Taking a deep breath, she gathered herself and went downstairs as the doorbell rang and the first guests began to arrive. Grace, in a swirl of chiffon, was being congratulated by a group of old schoolfriends. Molly went to welcome them as Kim helped to take the coats and put them in the study and the barman began pouring them some champagne.

An hour later and the hall, drawing room and orangery were filling with people, the noise level huge as everyone chatted. The orangery looked magical with its fairy lights and flickering candles reflecting and shimmering in the glass. Grace's eyes were sparkling as everyone wished her happy birthday. Her friends were like long, leggy models wearing the most incredible cocktail and evening dresses, while the guys were so handsome in their black tuxes, introducing themselves politely.

Molly had invited some of the family and was delighted to see that Bill and Carole had arrived with Liz and Joe; they had all booked into the hotel for the night, like many of the other guests. Her brother, Stephen, and his wife, Maeve; David's brother, Chris, who was Grace's godfather, and his wife, Penny; David's sister, Jenny, and her husband, Sean, and their son, Rory, who was Grace's age, had all come along too. Grace had insisted that Molly also invite a few of her own closest friends, so Roz, Cara and Tim, Trish and Larry, Avril and Pete, and Rena and Jack were there to join in the celebrations too.

Standing in the orangery, Molly couldn't believe what a wonderful place it was to have a party. You could see out over the lawn and gardens, the high glass ceiling looking up to the starry night sky.

The wine, champagne and beer flowed smoothly, and at ten o'clock Gina served the meal. The guests had a choice of beef stroganoff or chicken in white-wine sauce. They ate in the large dining room, where a number of tables had been set up, each with silver candelabras and a centrepiece of ivy and autumn flowers. For dessert Gina had produced a rich chocolate and caramel tart and a winter-berry-filled Pavlova, both served with cream and ice cream.

'The food is amazing!' beamed Emma, her plate laden with a sample of each.

After the food was served, David's brother, Chris, insisted on standing up and introducing Molly, thanking her for such a wonderful party to celebrate his niece's birthday. Almost shaking with nerves, Molly glanced quickly at the cards that she had written her speech on and then, taking a deep breath, she stood up. Emma squeezed her hand reassuringly.

'I would like to thank everyone for helping us to celebrate our beloved Grace's twenty-first birthday. Twenty-one years ago this beautiful little baby girl with her big blue eyes came into our lives and our hearts. We had just moved into Mossbawn and the house was a wreck, and we found ourselves not only with a new house but a new baby too! Luckily for us, Grace was a happy, good, smiley baby – and if I look back on her childhood years and teenage years, she has never really changed. She is still as beautiful and kind-hearted and smiley as ever.'

Grace's friends from primary school cheered madly in agreement.

'Her childhood was full of dogs, kittens, ponies and all kinds of pets. One time she even had a pet white rat which was kept hidden in her bedroom for weeks so I wouldn't see it, and of course the house was always full of her friends. She climbed trees and built houses and almost every birthday party involved a treasure hunt or a hide-and-seek game of some sort. Now she's in college in UCD, where she's made lots more friends, and I'm so glad you are all here. She and Emma have always been more than just sisters, they've been the best of friends and supported each other, and I know that this will continue all through their lives. As I watch Grace I see a daughter I not only love but am so proud of for all the good things she does and the way she faces life and brings happiness to those lucky enough to be around her. However, there is one person who should be here tonight – someone who loved Grace dearly, and that is her dad, David. We all miss him terribly, but I do feel that he is here in spirit with us tonight as we celebrate Grace's twenty-first birthday.'

Molly took a breath, trying not to let her emotions get the better of her. 'Finally, I'd like to thank everyone who helped with organizing the party: Emma and Kim, and Gina who has made all the lovely food; and of course to thank all of you good friends who have come from all over the place to be here with us as we celebrate Grace's birthday tonight.'

As she finished talking, Gina appeared with the large iced birthday cake with its twenty-one candles and everyone sang, 'Happy birthday to you'. Grace stood up to blow out her candles and then began to say a few words.

'I want to thank my mum for not only having my party but for being the most amazing mum ever, for all her love and support and for not just being my mum but also my friend. Emma and I had the most wonderful childhood, growing up here with the best parents ever. You all know this past year has been a pretty terrible one for my family, but my mum has kept the family together. I miss my dad so much . . . and I wish that he was here tonight with us all,' she said, her eyes welling with tears, 'but I have the most amazing friends, from my Kilfinn primary-school gang to my college crew, and my best friends Ali and Lola and Johnny – you are all the best! Also thanks to my aunties and uncles and cousins, and our family friends who are here with us too. I'm having the best birthday ever! Thank you so much everyone for coming and thanks for all your lovely pressies too! Being twenty-one is great. It's a bit scary to think that now you are an adult and have to be a proper grown-up. Tonight is a night that I will never forget, being here with everyone I love and care about – and the best thing is that the party is only getting started!'

Molly laughed and hugged Grace as the music began

and everyone returned to the orangery where the DJ was in full swing. As she looked around her she couldn't help but wonder if this would be the last big family party held here in the house. It certainly was a night to remember . . . she was glad of that. She lost track of how many times she was up dancing with everyone from Stephen to Chris and Rory and Bill to Emma's boyfriend and Tim and a whole load of Grace's college friends. A few times she retired to the drawing room to have a rest but would be dragged back up again on to the dance floor.

Finally managing to get to the kitchen, she found Gina busy tidying away everything, the dishwasher loaded and the remaining plates and dishes stacked ready to go in later, the place almost immaculate.

'Gina, the food was amazing! Thank you so much. Everything went perfectly!'

'I enjoy doing a big party like this,' Gina admitted. 'It's lovely to see guests happy and enjoying themselves.'

'Well, they sure are. Everyone is dancing like crazy. I was nervous about having it, but I'm so glad we did as Grace is so happy. Will you come and join us for a drink?'

'Thanks, but I'd prefer to finish up here and then pack up some of my cooking things and go home, if that is okay. We're taking the kids to Kilkenny tomorrow as Conor's team have a big football match.'

Back in the drawing room, Molly made an effort to sit down and talk to Carole, who was full of praise for the night.

'The house really lends itself to a big party like this,' Carole enthused. 'It's like something out of a film with the lights and the candles.'

'Times like this, the house comes into its own!' she smiled, glad that Bill and Carole had come along, the two of them getting on really well with Rena and her husband.

At 3 a.m. most of her friends had left, and Grace and Emma were still dancing away with a big gang of friends. She could barely keep her eyes open and, kissing them goodnight, slipped away to bed as the party continued till nearly breakfast time.

Curling up in bed, Molly pulled the pillow near her, pretending, as she did almost every night, that David was lying close to her.

Chapter Forty-four

Gina studied her order book. This Christmas, hopefully, should be a busy one! She'd enjoyed catering for Grace Hennessy's twenty-first and with any luck should have a few more events to cater for in the coming weeks. Dr Jim and his wife, Frances, had already ordered trays of canapés for their annual New Year's Day drinks party. And Bridget Jennings, who was an old friend of Norah's, had approached her about doing a special lunch to celebrate their golden wedding anniversary.

'Donal and I will be married fifty years. The children want us to have a big fancy meal in the hotel, but it would be far too noisy and too busy there. Poor Donal has gone a wee bit deaf, so we'd far prefer to have it at home in our own house. Then everyone can come to us, all the grandchildren and even our new little great-granddaughter, and we can take photos. There'll be no one rushing us off tables or the men disappearing to the hotel bar!'

'That sounds absolutely lovely,' agreed Gina, who knew that Bridget suffered with arthritis and was devoted to her elderly husband and family. 'What about a sit-down three-course lunch and a special golden wedding anniversary cake?' she suggested. 'You won't have to do a thing, as I can come along to serve and then disappear.'

'Oh Gina, that would be grand!' said Bridget. 'Just grand.'

Gina smiled to herself. Kilfinn might be a small village, but thank heaven people still enjoyed family celebrations. She'd put a sign up near the counter in the shop for ordering her mince pies, Christmas puddings and chocolate-and-chestnut Yule logs. Busy in the café all day, she then turned around and baked at night, the smell of Christmas pudding filling the house.

'You're killing yourself!' warned Paul, who was working night and day trying to complete a new kitchen for the O'Donovans, who lived about five miles away.

'You're a fine one to talk!' she teased.

'Gina, I heard something today from one of the electricians. He was talking about the café,' Paul said, sounding worried. 'He seemed to think that it was closing down and was going to be taken over by the pub next door.'

'Norah wouldn't do that!' Gina argued. 'She'd never agree to something like that!'

'It's probably only a rumour,' he said softly, 'but you know how these things spread!'

Gina was worried. What if it was true? Tomorrow she'd go and ask Norah about what was going to happen to the café and talk to her about taking it over ...

Norah was dozing in her chair. She seemed to sleep more and more of the time, like a lot of the residents in Beech Hill.

'Norah, I need to talk to you,' Gina said softly, sitting down beside her.

Over the next twenty minutes she carefully outlined her plans for the café, about doing it up. She explained how she would really like to rent it from Norah, or was even, if necessary, prepared to buy it.

'You've run the café successfully all these years, Norah, but now I want it to continue,' she explained. 'I want to make sure it stays open and that Kilfinn has a place for people to come for their coffees and cakes.'

Norah was listening, but said nothing all the time Gina was talking.

'I have to close my café . . .' she said at last, her eyes welling with tears as she became agitated.

'No, no, Norah – you won't have to close the café,' she soothed, 'because I'll rent or buy the place from you, then I'll keep it open. We can work it out, don't worry!'

Norah held on to her hand.

'But Martin says I have to sell,' she whispered, getting all upset. 'He says that he's looking after it.'

Gina tried to hide her own dismay and comfort Norah. If Norah's nephew was the one going to rent out or sell the premises, then she would have to deal with him. She had his number and when she got home she'd phone him immediately.

Martin Cassidy admitted things were at an advanced stage with regard to the premises.

'But I'm willing to rent it from Norah!' she protested furiously. 'I could easily take it over without any upset.'

'I'm sure you could,' he said smoothly, 'but unfortunately, with Norah's retirement due to her ill-health, the family and Norah have decided it's better to sell the entire premises to pay for her ongoing care and medical expenses.'

'But I can talk to the bank,' Gina offered. 'What kind of figure are you looking for?'

'We have been advised by a local auctioneer that the building, even in the current climate, is worth about one hundred and fifty thousand euro.'

Gina gasped. She had factored in buying the ground floor, but had not even considered buying the whole building. It was far more than she had expected.

'Please, Martin, let me have a chance to talk to my bank manager, see what we can come up with,' she begged.

'Very well, but we are close to making arrangements with another interested party,' he said pompously.

'Martin, for heaven's sake – you know that Norah would want me to have the place, to have the café stay open! I heard that you were talking to the Armstrongs in the pub next door. Please just give me a chance to see about getting a loan first.'

'Very well,' he said. 'Nothing is going to happen for the next few days.'

'Thanks,' she said.

Gina didn't sleep a wink, tossing and turning all night while Paul tried to get her to calm down. All her plans and hopes might come to nothing.

'We'll talk to the bank tomorrow,' Paul promised after they had gone through their figures to see if they could manage such a loan. 'Let's just see what they say . . .'

Billy Wright, their local bank manager, listened to them but they could tell by his demeanour that getting a loan was going to be difficult.

'Your projections are based on an increase in custom,' he pointed out, 'but what happens if this does not materialize?'

Gina tried to explain that she was sure that she could entice more customers to come to the newly done-up café and that she planned to open over the weekends.

'Gina, when you factor in the costs of loan repayments and utilities, as well as local rates and insurance, are you sure this is a business capable of generating profit, let alone a very comfortable income?' he asked, leaning across his mahogany desk.

'It's a good business,' she insisted, 'and I would also be using the café to attract catering business locally, which is something Norah never did, and we would rent out the flat upstairs.'

'Well, that's positive anyway,' he smiled. 'The bank is trying to ensure that businesses within a community stay trading, as there is nothing worse than a street of vacant shops!'

'Kilfinn has enough empty shops,' agreed Gina.

'But there is one thing that I am very concerned about,' Billy said, sounding serious. 'There is a problem showing up on the system with regard to your credit-rating history.'

'That was when we were in Dublin and I lost my job,' Paul explained carefully. 'We fell into arrears with our mortgage, but we moved here and decided to sell the house. All the loans were cleared and paid in full. That was over two and a half years ago, and Gina and I have no loans now. We are home-owners with no mortgage.'

'I'm sure that will all be taken into account by our credit committee,' the bank manager said, shaking their hands as they left his office.

Coming home, Gina felt utterly exhausted with the stress of it all.

'You sit down and relax,' Paul ordered, making her put her feet up on the living-room couch. How could she relax with all that was going on?

'And I'm cooking dinner tonight,' he added. 'My special – spaghetti and mince.'

As they sat at the table with the boys, having big bowls of pasta and salad and garlic bread, Paul opened a bottle of red wine.

'Here's to whatever happens!' he said as he filled her glass.

'But what happens if we don't get the loan and I lose my job?' she worried.

'Ssshhh,' he said calmly. 'We have food on our table, a roof over our heads, two fine sons and each other!'

Gina looked at his kind blue eyes and his still-handsome face. With all Paul had gone through, he still had never lost his sense of optimism and ability to be happy. She knew he was right, that whatever happened would be for the best.

Chapter Forty-five

Gina and Paul were delighted when the bank came back a few days later to say they were prepared to give them a loan; however, it was for twenty-five thousand less than they had expected.

'But what if it's not enough?' worried Gina as they put in their offer for Norah Cassidy's.

They waited on tenterhooks to see if it was accepted. But the local auctioneer came back twenty-four hours later to say that they had received a higher offer from the other party and asked if they wanted to increase their offer.

The bank had been quite clear with regard to the amount that they could borrow.

'We are not going to bankrupt ourselves over this,' warned Paul before phoning the auctioneer to say they would not be making another offer.

Gina tried to keep herself busy, hoping that by some miracle they would be successful. She was just about to close the café on Thursday evening when Martin Cassidy called in.

'I came in to tell you that my aunt has accepted an offer to buy the premises,' he told her. 'Norah has decided the café will close on the twenty-fourth of December. It will not reopen in the New Year.'

Gina couldn't believe it. She took a deep breath, glad that there were no customers around as she grabbed hold of the counter. In a way she had been expecting this . . .

'My aunt is very grateful for your support in running the business in her absence, and of course you will be paid proper redundancy based on the length of time you have worked here,' he said coldly.

'Thank you,' she replied, trying to control her emotions. 'I'm going to really miss working here. What is going to happen to the café?'

'The Armstrongs from the pub next door have bought it,' he told her, 'but I am not sure what their plans are.'

After he was gone Gina locked up, then sat at a table in the window looking out on the village street. It was almost dark and she made herself a large mug of coffee and took a slice of the frosted walnut cake, watching as the shops closed down and their lights went off along the street. She really was going to miss this place and the customers. Taking out her phone, she texted Paul to tell him the news. She'd go and see Norah in a few days when she was less upset. She imagined the older woman would be distressed about seeing her business and home sold.

An hour later, as she was locking up, she saw Bernadette Armstrong getting out of her car outside the Kilfinn Inn.

'Bernadette, I just heard that you and Tom have bought Norah's!' she said, trying to stay calm and composed.

'I'm sorry, Gina. I know that you and Paul were interested in keeping the café, but Tom's had his eye on the place for years,' Bernadette said, stopping to talk. 'He spoke to Norah a few times about it, but she'd always say it was her home and she'd no intention of selling while she was alive.'

'Are you going to keep the café open?'

'No, we're not,' she confided. 'We already do teas and coffees and lunches in the pub, so there's no point. Tom wants to extend the bar – with Mulligan's closed he wants to make a kind of men's snug with a fireplace at the back and add more space for customers in the front. Also, with our own crew, it would be good to have a bit of extra living space upstairs over the pub. The kids kill each other, so it will be great that they can each have a room now that they are getting older and need to study.'

Gina let out a breath. It made sense, as the Kilfinn Inn was a busy village pub with music sessions on a Saturday night and the Armstrongs and their four teenage children lived above it.

'I'm sorry, Gina, about you losing your job,' Bernadette said kindly. 'I'll be sad to see Norah's shut, but I suppose times change, don't they?'

'Yes, times change,' she said, trying not to give in to her tears of disappointment.

Talking to Paul that night, Gina realized that owning the café had been almost a dream, and for someone like her dreams didn't usually come true. But she was determined not to let Norah down, and to ensure that Cassidy's Café said a proper final farewell to all its customers before it closed. She would put on lunch specials and afternoon teas, and the café would do its best to attract all their old customers back for that final coffee or cake or meal. She would put fairy lights up and decorate the window and make it so appealing that no one could pass by without wanting to come inside and sit down . . .

Chapter Forty-six

The twenty-first of November. Molly still couldn't believe that today it was three hundred and sixty-five days, a full year, since David's death. She would never get used to it, or be able to accept that David would never walk into the room, turn his key in the front-door lock, phone her, talk to her, or touch her ever again . . .

Molly would never forget that day – an ordinary day, a Tuesday morning . . . They'd had breakfast together, Molly making coffee, putting the washing in the washing machine, making smalltalk, listening to the morning news on the radio as David grabbed his warm jacket and left for the office where he had an early-morning meeting with a client. It was cold outside, ice on their cars . . .

Why didn't she kiss him? Some mornings they did, automatically brushing their lips together to say goodbye as he left to go to work. But on that day they hadn't . . . She played it over and over again, like a film on a loop, remembering every word, every gesture, wondering whether if the day had gone differently would David still be alive . . .

She was upstairs having a shower. Coming out wrapped in a towel she could see the flashing on her phone. She had missed eight calls and before she could even try to reply the house phone on her bedside table went.

It was the police to say David had been in some sort of car accident and had been taken to the nearby regional hospital.

'Is he okay?' she kept asking again and again.

'You need to come to the hospital immediately, Mrs Hennessy,' advised the Garda officer.

They were sending a car for her. Barry O'Loughlin, a young Guard whose parents lived in the village, would drive her to the hospital. She was shaking as she got dressed, pulled on her boots and raced out to his car, her feet slipping.

'He's going to be fine,' she kept saying, mantra-like, until she got to the hospital.

The A&E department sent her into the main hospital and up to the second floor.

'My husband, David . . . David Hennessy, is here. They said that he was in a car accident.'

A doctor came out to talk to her. A beautiful, dark-eyed young woman from Pakistan, stylish and sympathetic, she made Molly sit down and sat calmly beside her to explain.

270

'I'm afraid it is very bad news . . . the worst news . . . David is dead. He was dead when the ambulance crew came. It was very sudden – he died instantly.'

Molly refused to believe it. 'No! No! No!' she kept saying. 'There's been a mistake.'

The doctor brought her to a room where David lay on a trolley. He was absolutely still, eyes closed, all life gone from him, his skin already cold, and she knew when she kissed him and touched his cheek that the doctor's words were true.

'The car had pulled off the road, hit a hedge,' she explained, 'but you can see that there is only a slight abrasion on his forehead. There is also some bruising on his chest, probably from the safety belt, but otherwise very few injuries.'

'What do you mean?'

'The autopsy will give us a better idea,' the doctor said, 'but we think that there is a good chance that David was already dead when his car came off the road, so he would have felt nothing.'

Molly was so confused, so upset.

Cara and Tim had come to the hospital immediately and Michael Quinn from the office had appeared, also offering to do anything he could to help. Emma and Grace arrived about two hours later, both shocked and hysterical, wanting to see their dad . . .

Molly remembered having to tell David's family. His elderly mother, Maureen, who was in a nursing home, was barely able to take it in; his two brothers and sister were devastated by the news.

The autopsy results two days later showed that David's death was the result of a brain aneurysm which must have suddenly burst, rather than the accident. He would have lost control of the car, which had hit the roadside hedge. The only consolation Molly gained was that nobody else was involved or injured, and from what the doctors said David had died immediately. There had been absolutely no warning and no saving him.

The shock and suddenness had been horrendous. She remembered lying in bed shaking and shivering, covered in blankets, her teeth chattering as she realized that she would never see the man she loved again.

She could barely remember the following days, but she had to be strong for Emma and Grace, who were distraught and overwhelmed by the sudden loss of their dad, and she also had to try to organize his funeral.

Somehow she'd got through the ritual of waking David at home in Mossbawn – their family and friends all equally shocked by his loss – and then the large funeral mass in their parish church and his burial in the nearby graveyard. She remembered being stunned by the fact that David, who had organized everything meticulously in his life, had bought a plot in Kilfinn's cemetery a few years earlier and never said a word to her about it.

The following weeks and months had been a blur as she tried to cope with the massive void in her life that David had left behind, the loneliness of it unbearable. People had been good and kind, supportive, but she still felt so alone, raw with grief and loss. Then as the months went on, she realized that the world kept turning, the seasons came and went, spring, summer, autumn and now another winter . . . She could see it in the garden in Mossbawn.

Losing David had been heartbreaking and there were days when she questioned her will to go on, to continue living without him; but those days were fewer and fewer now as she began to take small step after small step towards building a life without him . . .

Father Darragh was saying an anniversary mass for the family this evening. David's family were all attending and coming back to the house afterwards, but this morning she wanted to go to his grave on her own, have that time with him.

It was strange, but visiting the small graveyard on the other side of the village, which was protected by a grove of elms and overlooked a curving part of the hillside where cattle grazed in the springtime, Molly was comforted. The peace and quiet there, and the stillness, exuded the strong spirituality of a place where generation after generation of Kilfinn's families lay buried. David had chosen well, for he was surrounded by the graves of neighbours and friends.

'Good morning, Molly, 'tis a fierce cold day!'

She nodded to Dan White, the eighty-nine-year-old former postman, who was visiting his wife Lily's grave. He came religiously every day.

Molly turned up to the section where David was buried.

She stood in the silence, listening to the wind and her own breathing, reading the writing on his headstone, leaving a bunch of bright winter pansies and some heather beside it.

Beloved. Beloved – her beloved . . .

Dan was right: it was cold – bloody freezing. She pulled her quilted North Face jacket tighter around her. She had a ham baking in the oven and when she got home would make some brown bread to serve with smoked salmon when everyone arrived back from the church.

Despite the cold it was peaceful here, in this place where her beloved, her David lay.

Chapter Forty-seven

Molly had planned to do a bit of tidying up in the garden, but it had started to rain earlier and it had got heavier and heavier. Giving up the notion, she was engrossed reading *A History of Rose Growing* when Trish's car pulled up outside.

'Come inside out of the wet!' she urged, opening the back door. 'I've just made a pot of coffee. Is there some problem about the planning for the cottage? I've had Paul Sullivan working on repairing the roof all week and I thought that everything had got the go-ahead.'

'It has nothing to do with the cottage, Molly,' Trish said, sitting down.

'Are you okay?'

'No, I'm not . . . I'm stressed out about Libby's wedding!'

Organizing a wedding was a bit of a marathon for

everyone involved, but usually Trish was pretty calm and collected about things.

'How are the plans coming?' she ventured.

'They're not – that's just it. Libby and Brian had put a deposit down on Foyle Castle in Tipperary, but they've just been told that the company that owns it has gone bankrupt and it's had to close down. They have the church booked, the dress, everything practically done for their wedding, but now – nowhere to have a wedding!'

'Oh my God! Trish, I'm so sorry!'

'Larry's going crazy and Brian's parents . . . We are all so upset.'

'What are you going to do?' Molly asked, appalled by their predicament.

'That's the reason I'm here, Molly. I want to ask you something. If the answer is no, that's absolutely fine – I'll totally understand, but I promised Libby that I would at least ask you.'

Molly was intrigued.

'When we were here at Grace's twenty-first, Cara and I were just saying that this house was the perfect place for a big party or a wedding – and the thing is that we really need to find somewhere urgently . . . so we were wondering about here . . .'

'Have Libby's wedding here?' she gasped.

'Yes. I know it might sound a bit crazy, but it could work! Drinks and dancing in the orangery and eating in the dining room, like we all did at the party . . . It was such an amazing night!'

276

'But you'd never fit everyone . . .'

'Libby can scale things down – she'll have to.'

'Haven't you tried the hotels in Kilkenny or the golf club? Or that new wedding barn place in Waterford?'

'Molly – I wouldn't ask you, but we've tried absolutely everywhere and everyone is totally booked out for at least a year.'

Molly didn't know what to say.

'We'd have it at home, but our own house is too small,' she sighed. 'The thing is that you are selling Mossbawn – which I know is awful for you, but maybe we could rent the house out for the day exactly the same as we were going to do with the castle?'

'But Mossbawn is just a house. There are no big kitchens or proper bedrooms or facilities.'

'It's a lovely old country house and it was perfect for Grace's twenty-first party. The food was amazing and with a big crowd it all worked so well,' Trish reminded her. 'We've been at so many lovely parties and dinners here over the years. For a wedding we can hire a caterer and people can stay in the hotel up the road or in some of the local B and Bs.'

Molly was totally flummoxed. This was certainly not what she had expected.

'Libby has always loved this house, and it's only a few minutes from home. Please, Molly, will you think about it? Please?'

Molly took a slow sip of coffee. She'd known Libby since she was a little girl; her brother Rory had started school the same day as Emma. Trish's kids and hers had played here together over the years and visited frequently.

'I don't want to pressure you, Molly, but please will you have a proper think about it? For all you know, the new owners could turn it into a hotel or a restaurant!'

'I will,' she promised as they said goodbye.

Molly was sitting in the kitchen, her mind racing, when Kim came in. She told her about her conversation with Trish.

'I'm in a quandary – I don't know what to say to her,' she sighed.

Kim curled up on the couch in the kitchen, her feet tucked under her.

'Maybe it could work, Auntie Molly, honestly. Nobody wants to get married in the big function room of a hotel any more – they want something different, like that castle Libby had booked. I've been to a few weddings in country houses. Okay, some have been very fancy with golf clubs and spas and bars and restaurants, but my friend Thea got married in a lovely old house in Wicklow last year. They had to hire chairs and tables and plates and glasses and cutlery and lights and everything, but it was a really fun wedding. If I ever get married that's the kind of wedding I'd want – somewhere like here, with the garden and the orangery and the patio terrace.'

'So you think I should say yes?'

'I think you should talk to Grace and Emma first and see how they feel about it.'

Kim offered to make them both some dinner while Molly went and made some phone calls.

Grace had no problem about having the wedding in the house, while Emma worried about what would happen if something went wrong. What if they wrecked the place or there was an accident?

'They are our friends!' Molly laughed. 'I'm sure they would take care of everything.'

Still, what Emma had said did make her think, and if she was to let Libby have her wedding here maybe there should be some kind of extra insurance.

'Well?' asked Kim as she passed her a plate of risotto.

'The girls are okay about it, but Emma suggested I take out extra insurance. She's always so sensible, like her dad! Also, I don't really want Trish and Libby employing any other caterer except Gina. She did Grace's party and the funeral, and she's used to the way this kitchen and the house work. And besides, I can trust her to run things well.'

'Well, maybe you should talk to Gina before you give them your answer,' Kim said, passing her some Parmesan cheese.

'I'll phone her after dinner,' she promised. 'But otherwise it's fine.'

Molly was very glad to have Kim around; she was so easy to talk to and great company. She made living in the house bearable and had even become a bit of a gardener too. They often spent hours talking about the house and the garden, watching programmes about old houses and history on TV. Fascinated by the history of Mossbawn, Kim was enjoying designing its website.

Molly had been telling Bernadette Armstrong about what her niece was doing and they'd asked her to help them create a website for the Kilfinn Inn. Hopefully some more work would turn up for her, as her temping job with Dr Jim had come to an end – though she still worked in the surgery two days a week as Frances had decided it was high time she took things a little bit easier. Dr Jim had asked Kim to put up a very basic website for the surgery and had already implemented some of the changes she had introduced to the practice.

Molly knew that her niece loved village life, but couldn't help but worry secretly about her, at twenty-nine, shutting herself away from all her friends and living down here in the countryside.

Chapter Forty-eight

Gina had been run off her feet all week. Thank heaven she had Inga to give her a hand.

It was as if everyone in Kilfinn and the district wanted to come in and say goodbye to Cassidy's Café. She'd had to take lunch bookings and for the past three days had actually done two sittings, as if it was a fancy restaurant she was running. The Bridge Club, the Book Club, the Anglers, the Kilfinn Walkers Group – even the Kilfinn Traders Group had booked two tables.

'Everyone come here, it's so busy . . . why are you closing down?' puzzled Inga as she carried more plates and bowls into the kitchen and reset the dishwasher again.

'People just want to say goodbye,' Gina tried to explain. 'It's the end of an era.'

The café had never looked so good, all decorated for

Christmas with tea lights on every table, and she had pushed herself on the menu, offering a choice of three different mains. The café was full of chat and people leaving in cards and flowers for her and Norah. She was overwhelmed with their kindness and support, and filled with a huge sense of regret that she'd been unable to save the café.

Bernadette Armstrong had called in last week to say that she was free to take any kitchen equipment or china or cutlery she needed.

'What do I want with mixing bowls and food processors, or that hulking big cooker and water heater?' she said, urging Gina to take them. 'You might use them in your business, Gina; otherwise they'll end up in a skip.'

Gina had talked to Paul, who had agreed they could store the stuff in their large garage.

'Maybe you'll be able to use it,' he said encouragingly.

The last few times Gina had called to see Norah in the nursing home she could tell that, even though she was heartbroken about the café, she'd begun to accept that she would never work there again and would remain living and being cared for at Beech Hill.

'Would you like to come for a coffee and see the place, Norah, before it closes?' she asked gently. 'Everyone has been asking for you.'

'I'd like to see it,' she nodded. So Gina had discussed it with the matron and Dr Jim and it was arranged that Norah would come and say a last farewell on Christmas

Eve. Word must have got out, because Gina couldn't budge a soul from the place as they sat lingering over coffees and cakes and the mince pies that she passed around freely. Every table was full as Margaret Mullen, one of the staff nurses, pulled up at the front door in her car with Norah.

Norah had had her hair washed and set so it was like a fluffy white halo around her head, and she was wearing a new, soft-pink cardigan and her trademark grey skirt. With assistance from the nurse and Kim O'Reilly, who was having lunch with her aunt and cousins, Norah Cassidy was almost lifted into the window seat, where she could hold court and say hello to everyone.

Gina was kept busy, but she could see that Norah was relishing all the attention. She had devoted her life to this place and was an important part of Kilfinn's community and history. Father Darragh, the jovial parish priest, had come along and was giving her a big hug.

'Isn't it grand to see you sitting where you should be, Norah, letting the young ones wait on you for a change?'

Norah held his hand.

'What are we all going to do without her?' he lamented. 'There will never be the like of Norah's apple tart or scones seen again in the village.'

The older woman's eyes were shining as everyone agreed. Gina escaped to the kitchen where she could control her own emotions.

* * *

As it began to get dark outside, the lights flickering on in the street, Margaret decided it was time to bring Norah back to the nursing home as she was beginning to tire. Everyone stood up, clapping and cheering as she was helped out to the car. It was only when she had left that Gina realized that Norah hadn't once asked about the upstairs flat where she had lived all her life.

All the shops were shutting up, closing for the holidays. Gina packed everything away and gave Inga a box full of cakes and biscuits, ham and pudding to take home to her family for Christmas.

She was doing a last check when Paul and the boys arrived.

'We said we'd come down to see how you are getting on,' said Paul, slipping his arms around her in the empty café.

'Just about to lock up,' she said, 'now all the customers are finally gone.'

'We could see from outside how busy it was!' said Conor.

'Mammy, it was even busier than when we had lunch yesterday!' added Aidan.

'Lads, help your mam with those boxes!' ordered Paul. 'Put them out in the car for her.'

'I can't believe that it's finally closing,' Gina said, suddenly overwhelmed and tearful as she began to switch off the lights for the last time.

'It's time to come home, Gina love,' Paul said, taking her hand. 'It seems to me that you've been cooking for the whole of Kilfinn and most of the district. You are coming home now, putting your feet up at the fire and resting. The boys and I are making curry for dinner tonight and tomorrow the men in the family are tackling the turkey!'

'The turkey!' Gina laughed.

'Aye – the turkey!'

'Dad says it's just like cooking a big chicken,' said Aidan knowledgeably.

'And I'm making the stuffing!' insisted Conor.

Gina yawned. She was tired, exhausted, but she was so glad that she had managed to get Norah to come along to say goodbye to her café. For no matter how much she had planned and hoped that she would take it over, she'd accepted today that it would always be Norah's café.

Chapter Forty-nine

Kim had really enjoyed spending Christmas in the country, as Liz and Joe were heading to Belfast to see his family, and her dad and Carole were going to the Canaries for some winter sunshine. Spending Christmas at Mossbawn had made a huge change from the constant rounds of drinking and parties and long lunches back in Dublin, and those crazy days when she had gone mad spending on extravagant gifts and costly clothes and outfits to wear over the festive season. She certainly didn't miss having her credit card and wallet taking a huge hammering as in other years.

Everything here was so relaxed and there had been plenty to do with her cousins and Molly. On Christmas Eve they'd walked to midnight mass in the village and joined in the singing with the Kilfinn choir. On Christmas Day they'd gone to her uncle's grave and then for drinks at Cara and Tim's before coming home to relax and sit around the table eating Christmas dinner.

She had talked to her dad in Gran Canaria and her brother Mike in Canada, and Liz had phoned her on Christmas night. Kim gathered the kids had Joe's mum, dad and family run ragged.

'His mum had to go to bed for a rest after we'd eaten,' whispered Liz, 'and Ava knocked a jug of cream all over the kitchen floor, and his uncle Harry nearly broke his neck when he came in the kitchen to get another mince pie.'

Kim had to stop herself laughing. They were a handful, as she could testify having spent Christmas dinner with them the past three years!

Evie and Alex had phoned her, wondering how she was surviving.

'It's been lovely, really lovely, here in Kilfinn,' she enthused. 'I've had a great Christmas.'

'Kim, tell me you're not staying in the country for New Year!' teased Alex.

'You have to come to Dublin for New Year!' insisted Evie. 'Everyone is meeting up and going to the Chatham for dinner, then we'll all go on to Everleigh, that new nightclub. I've booked a seat for you. The dinner is only sixty-five euro each and it's going to be a brilliant night.'

'I'm not sure I can go.' Kim hesitated.

She'd spent so many New Years in the city in various nightclubs, pretending to enjoy the night, surrounded by strangers, and then with Gareth, frantically pretending despite the crowds and exorbitant costs that they were having one of the best nights ever.

She had always found it a bit of a let-down and really had no intention of putting herself through another evening of that again.

'I'm sorry, but I've already organized to do something else,' she lied. 'But I hope you all have a great night and I'll see you soon.'

Putting down the phone, she could see Grace watching her.

'So you're staying in Kilfinn for New Year?'

'Yeah, looks like it.'

'We usually go to the Kilfinn Inn. Nearly the whole village is there. It's a bit of a mad night, with music and dancing. I know Emma's going to Roundstone with Jake, but it will still be fun.'

'Sounds perfect.'

'Great!' said Grace.

Despite their efforts to persuade her, Molly had refused to join them.

'I'd far prefer to sit here and enjoy my wine and watch *Jools' Annual Hootenanny* on the TV,' she insisted. 'I'm not in the form for a packed noisy pub.'

'Are you sure?' asked Kim, worried. 'I could stay with you.'

'Don't you dare,' Molly ordered. 'I'm perfectly fine here on my own. You lot go off and enjoy yourselves seeing in the New Year!'

Walking down to the main street with her cousin, she could hear the music and there already was a huge crowd gathered outside the village pub.

'Hey, Grace, how are you?' called a tall blonde girl.

'Fine, Melissa! How are you and Ritchie doing?'

'We're just home for the week to see the folks, then we are heading over to London for the weekend. One of Ritchie's friends is getting married!'

Grace introduced them and Kim soon found herself chatting to a huge group of her friends.

'This is my cousin, Kim. She's staying with us for the moment.'

'You used to stay at Mossbawn when you were younger!' exclaimed Roisin, a small, skinny girl with glasses. 'I remember we went fishing in your aunt and uncle's boat on the river and you caught a fish and you got such a shock when you held it that you nearly fell overboard.'

'I could see its gills and eyes and I just wanted to throw it back in the water!' Kim giggled.

'I wanted that fish, but you were the one that caught it,' Roisin explained. 'I wanted to cook it for my dad's supper.'

As Kim went up to the bar to get some drinks, she stopped to listen to the band. They were actually good and soon everyone was getting up dancing. Fifteen minutes later she was up on the floor dancing to 'The Galway Girl' as the crowd swelled and sang along.

Everyone was chatting to everyone and she soon found herself talking to Luke Ryan at the bar as she queued up again to buy drinks for Grace and her friends. She felt momentarily awkward, but as this was the only pub in town she'd better try to appear relaxed and normal. He was wearing a slim-fitting checked shirt, probably a Christmas present, and jeans that showed off how tall and thin he was.

'So you stayed in the country for New Year! I thought that a city girl like you would find Kilfinn a bit boring and quiet.'

She wanted to snap back at him but resisted.

'It's a change . . . but I guess I like change.' She smiled sweetly.

'Come on you two, get up and dance!' urged Melissa.

'Stop telling me what to do!' joked Luke. 'I was going to ask Kim to dance in a few minutes.'

'She's his sister,' laughed Grace, sensing Kim had no idea what was going on.

Luke did ask her to dance a while later and literally swung her around the floor to a few lively reels.

'I feel like I'm in *Riverdance*,' she giggled, trying to keep up, conscious of Luke's strong arms keeping a hold of her.

At midnight everyone in the pub linked arms and sang 'Auld Lang Syne' and Kim couldn't help thinking about her mum and her uncle David as she held Grace's hand, the two of them hugging each other tearfully.

'You okay?' Luke asked, concerned.

'I always find it a sad night – remembering my mum,' she admitted.

Suddenly she was aware of him pulling her into his arms and holding her. He smelled of aftershave and his breath was warm against her skin. For the rest of the night they were together, buying each other drinks, talking, dancing and messing, having fun with everyone.

Last year she and Gareth had gone to some fancy restaurant for dinner with two other couples, Gareth complaining about the service. This year was totally different!

The Kilfinn Inn was packed to the rafters with fiddles and guitars and drums, plates of sausage rolls and cocktail sausages and mini quiches being passed around, old and young, and she knew practically everyone around her, and Luke was . . . Luke was lovely . . .

It was well after three o'clock in the morning when the crowds began to disperse. Grace had already disappeared off to some friend's house.

'I'd better go home,' Kim said, trying to bring herself back to reality as the band began to pack up their equipment and the bar staff collected the glasses.

'I'll walk you home,' he insisted.

As they went he took her hand and she liked it, walking along the roadway in the dark beside him. Molly had left the lights on along the avenue and as she searched her bag for the door key she wondered if she should invite him in.

'Do you want a coffee or a drink?'

'Nah, I'm grand,' he said. 'I'd better get home myself.'

She stood at the back door. It was chilly, but she could feel his eyes staring at her, his hands reaching for her face, touching her. A minute later they were kissing and it felt – perfect, like she was meant to be in his arms, having him kiss her neck and her lips, their mouths and breaths together.

'Wow!' he said, looking at her and grinning.

'Wow!'

He pulled her towards him again. Fireworks – definitely fireworks. She couldn't believe it.

'I'll see you tomorrow,' he said.

'Tomorrow?'

'Aren't you going to Dr Jim's big drinks party with Molly?'

'Oh yes, I think so.'

'Then I'll see you there,' he said, kissing her again. 'Happy New Year!'

As she stepped into the kitchen, Daisy stared up at her from her cosy padded basket. Kim couldn't believe it – she had spent most of the night talking and dancing with Luke Ryan! It had been one of the best nights ever, and the great thing was she was seeing him again tomorrow . . . today!

Up in her bedroom she checked her phone: messages from all her family and from Lisa and Evie, and, to her amazement, one from Gareth – just a group one, which she quickly deleted. She'd no intention of ruining a perfect night by bothering to reply to him.

Chapter Fifty

Lying in bed, Kim couldn't put Luke out of her mind. what if he ignored her when they met later on? Pretended nothing had happened between them? Should she say something? Play it cool? He could well be the type of guy who had lots of girls . . .

'Someone was enjoying themselves last night!' teased Grace as they sat around the kitchen in their pyjamas eating a late breakfast.

'It was a great night,' she grinned. 'Different from most New Years and a lot more fun!'

'You do know that half the girls in Kilfinn are cracked about Luke Ryan,' continued her cousin, 'and you're the one he's dancing with!'

'And walking home . . .' Kim giggled.

'Did Luke walk you home?' quizzed Molly.

'Yes!' she said, helping herself to some more coffee and toast.

'What about the Kelleher girl?'

'He and Alison broke up last year, Mum, you know that!' Grace reminded her.

'Is he seeing someone?' Kim asked, appalled. She had no intention of becoming the talk of a small place like Kilfinn.

'Don't mind Mum! Luke is totally single,' Grace reassured her. 'He and Alison went out for about three years – they were both working in London and when he moved back home they broke up. But lots of girls fancy him.'

'Luke Ryan is a very nice young man from a lovely family,' interjected Molly. 'I have always found him very polite and helpful, and his parents are good neighbours.'

'He seems a nice guy,' admitted Kim, taking her mug of coffee and retreating back upstairs.

The three of them drove to Dr Jim's, the road outside his house and the driveway packed with neighbours' cars as it was raining heavily. Frances and Dr Jim made a big fuss of Kim and began introducing her to everyone the minute she stepped into their living room. The fire was blazing and they had a massive Christmas tree. A waiter was serving champagne and drinks and Gina Sullivan was busy passing around trays of tasty canapés.

Kim glanced around hoping to see Luke, but there was no sign of him. She tried to quash her disappointment and joined Grace chatting to Cara and her family.

'We were at my sister's at a family party in Kildare last night,' Cara yawned, 'and Tim and I are still a bit hungover, but we couldn't miss Jim and Frances's party.'

Kim kept bumping into people from the previous night in the pub. She had moved to the kitchen with a group of friends when Luke walked in with his older brother. She watched as he got a beer and said hello to a few people. It was so embarrassing – everyone seemed to know about last night!

Suddenly he was beside her, kissing her lightly, his arm around her waist, introducing her to his brother, Justin, and then later bringing her into the other room to meet his parents. Kim had to stifle her surprise: he was so like his father, both of them the same height and build, with the same piercing grey-green eyes.

'Nice to meet you, young lady. I believe that you are Molly's niece,' Tom Ryan said politely, shaking her hand.

Luke's mother, Judy, was small and dark with short hair, and Kim could see that she had noticed straight away Luke's arm around her waist.

'I've heard a lot about you,' Judy smiled. 'Molly is enjoying having you staying with her. We're in the same book club, though I'm afraid our tastes are very different. I love a good crime novel!'

'And I hate them,' smiled Molly, coming over to join them. 'I see you've been introduced to Kim already. She's Ruth's daughter.'

A few minutes later the talk turned to the book to read for the next month, by some obscure American author. She and Luke beat a hasty retreat to the kitchen, each grabbing another beer.

'How are you?' he asked.

'Fine,' she giggled. 'I only saw you a few hours ago.'

'I know . . . but I missed you.'

Kim took a breath. He wasn't messing or joking; he was being honest and true.

'And I missed you,' she said softly, realizing it was true.

They hung out together for the rest of the party and when Molly and Grace were ready to go Kim said no.

'I'm going over to Luke's place for a while. I'll see you later.'

Luke lived in a house he was renting with two friends on the outskirts of the village.

'Sinead is teaching in the same school as me and Alan is working in the bank. They're both gone away. Sinead went skiing with her boyfriend and Alan went to Scotland with some friends, so we'll have the place to ourselves.'

The house was pretty basic, but he lit the fire quickly and, getting some drinks, they snuggled in together and talked and talked and talked.

'Why didn't you phone or text me?' she found herself asking, the words out before she could think.

'I liked you, Kim – but you told me you had just broken up with someone and his name seemed to still be coming up a lot. So I waited,' he grinned, kissing her gently.

'You must think I'm kind of screwed up, at my age

staying with my aunt, still trying to figure out what to do with my life.'

'We are all kind of screwed up,' he laughed.

'But you know what you want. You love teaching and you've got the farm.'

'True,' he said, softly kissing her again. 'But it took me a long time to discover what I really want and to realize that it was all here at home.'

'I wish that I—'

'Kim, it's a new year. Wait and see what it brings.'

He made them dinner, a spicy chicken curry with all the trimmings.

'You can cook!'

'Don't be so surprised! My mum has a bee in her bonnet about her kids, especially the male ones, being able to cook. Also, I do a bit of baking with my class, bread and buns and biscuits. They love it!'

Kim thought of Gareth, who hated cooking and refused even to read the Jamie Oliver cookbook she'd bought him.

The hours slipped away and reluctantly she said goodnight to him.

'Stay!' he pleaded.

'No, I'd better get back to Mossbawn or Molly will be worried.'

'You can text her.'

'No, Luke, I need to go home,' she said gently. Everything was happening so fast – maybe too fast. She needed time to think. If she was going to have a relationship with him, she wanted it to work.

'Okay . . . okay,' he grinned, getting his jacket to walk her home.

'I'll see you tomorrow,' he said as they kissed good-night at the kitchen door.

Kim stood looking out of the window, watching as he walked back down the avenue. Luke was everything – everything . . . already.

Chapter Fifty-one

Molly watched from the bedroom window as the snowflakes began to fall. Getting up, she pulled on her heavy pink fleece dressing gown and padded downstairs. Daisy was waiting at the back door to be let out. The garden was already covered in snow, every bush and shrub and tree frosted in white, so it looked magical.

The kitchen was freezing, so she went and switched on the boiler before putting on the kettle. She listened to the news on the radio as she made some porridge. The roads were bad around the countryside, with some of the main routes closed due to ice. The airport was also temporarily shut down and the weather people were predicting more flurries of snow over the next twenty-four to thirty-six hours. She hoped the girls were all okay and sent them a quick text each. Kim had gone to Dublin for a few days.

After breakfast she'd walk to the shops as she was low on milk and bread and needed to get some dog food for Daisy in case the weather got worse. She watched as a robin hopped around near the kitchen window looking for food.

Two hours later she had joined the queue in Donnelly's where everyone was stocking up on groceries as if they were going to be marooned for a week! The snow was falling again and she was glad she had worn her cosy snow boots, as it was treacherous outside. Mary Jennings, the principal of Kilfinn's primary school, had nearly fallen outside the chemist's shop.

'We sent all the kids home as we couldn't risk the school buses not being able to collect them later,' she said, trying to right herself. 'So I'm off home to light the fire and put my feet up and read a good book – enjoy the peace while I can!'

A few people were heading over to the Kilfinn Inn for soup or a coffee now that Cassidy's Café had closed down, but Molly just wanted to get back home. She was worried about the boiler. Thank heaven she'd got Paul to repair the cottage roof, so at least it was protected from the snow. Once the weather improved he was going to lay the foundations for the small extension.

Deirdre Donnelly was flustered and busy at the till, as people stocked up with firelighters and soup and bread and rashers and sausages. Molly grabbed a copy of the newspaper and a few essentials – milk, cheese, eggs, a brown loaf and some ham, and a few tins of Daisy's favourite dog food.

'Everything okay, Molly?' asked Deirdre, concern in her voice as she put her items through.

'I'm fine, Deirdre. There's just me and the dog, but I've got the Aga.'

'They're great yokes. I heard the pipes are frozen down on the new estate and they have no heating or water, God help them! The council are out doing repair work.'

Molly could see a young mother piling her basket with tins of baby food and was glad that at least she only had herself to look after.

Back out on the street the snow was falling more heavily and, grabbing her shopping bags, she began to walk slowly and carefully home.

She had just passed the garage when a black jeep slowed down and pulled in beside her.

'Get in!' yelled the driver.

Molly tried to make out who it was. With the snow falling so heavily she could hardly see.

'For heaven's sake get in, Molly. I'll drop you home,' offered Rob Hayes, opening the door.

Molly hadn't seen him for weeks.

'I was going to walk,' she protested. 'It's really not that far.'

'In this weather?'

'Okay – thanks, a lift would be great,' she laughed, lifting her bags into the back of the jeep and climbing in beside him. 'My car is a disaster in the snow, so I said I'd walk.'

'I was passing this way,' he explained as he turned off

the main road a minute or two later and drove up the driveway, the rhododendrons, like snow-covered sentries, standing guard as he passed them and then came to a halt on the gravel outside the front door.

'Thanks,' she said again, reaching for her bags, unsure if she should invite him in or not.

'I was meant to go to London this morning on business, but all the flights are cancelled. Hopefully they'll be up and running tomorrow.'

'Would you like to come in for a coffee?'

'That would be great,' he said, turning off the engine.

She hadn't really expected him to say yes and she hoped that she had left the kitchen in a decent state and not with clothes drying on the overhead rack.

'Here, I'll get the bags,' he offered as she opened the front door.

She led him through the large hallway and down the steps to the kitchen, flicking on the light switch.

'It's nice and warm in here,' he said, putting the bags down on the kitchen table as Daisy ran around his feet. 'Nice dog!' he added approvingly, patting her.

Molly packed away the groceries quickly and put the kettle on as Rob glanced at the newspaper. She took off her jacket and boots and put them in the cloakroom. Her cheeks were burning hot after coming in from the cold.

'Great kitchen,' he said, sitting at the table and looking around.

'I know – it's the heart of the house and the place to be in this kind of weather,' she said without thinking, then remembered that he was probably still staying in the hotel. 'Listen, I was about to get some lunch – if you want you're welcome to share it,' she offered. 'I've a vegetable soup and some of Donnelly's brown bread and some cheese which comes from a farm about ten miles out the road.'

'Sounds good to me,' he smiled, slipping off his heavy navy jacket.

Molly had a big pot of vegetable soup that she'd made yesterday, cutting up all kinds of vegetables; she had even added the ends off some broccoli and celery and a sweet potato she'd had left in the fridge, to bulk it up. There was plenty and today it would taste even better, she thought, as she put it on the hob to heat.

They talked about Cara and Tim; he had taken them both for dinner recently.

'We went to that fancy French place near the castle in Kilkenny. I think that one of Tim's friends owns it.'

'Marius,' she smiled. 'He's a great guy and the restaurant does really well.'

'Yeah, we had a fantastic meal, then we went to the Riverbank pub after.'

Molly said nothing. The Riverbank had been one of David's favourite spots and the year before last on their anniversary they'd had dinner in Marius's restaurant and gone there afterwards.

She cut up the bread and some cheese and ladled the thick warming soup into two Nicholas Mosse bowls, putting them on the table.

'This looks good and hearty,' he said, taking a

spoon of the soup. 'What kind of vegetable is it?'

'Every kind,' she joked. 'I just cut up whatever I have and throw it in the pot.'

'Well, it tastes great,' he said, helping himself to a few slices of the bread. Molly sat across from him.

'Thanks, Molly – there's nothing like home-cooked food when you can get it,' he said approvingly. 'It beats food in restaurants and hotels every time.'

'It's just a bowl of soup!' she teased, but she knew what he meant.

Rob asked her about the house and she found herself telling him about how she had planned to sell Mossbawn but the sale had fallen through.

'So for now I'm staying put unless I find a buyer. Even though the house is far too big for me, I don't know if I could ever bear to leave the place,' she admitted.

'I can understand that,' he said, looking around. 'This place is full of history and is such a part of the village. I'm sure living here keeps you busy.'

'It does. There always seems to be something to do or to fix, but the thing I love the most is the garden – I spend hours on it. Weather like this is terrible because I can't get out and do anything useful; I can only read gardening books and plan out things for when the weather improves. But at the moment I'm doing research, as I'm trying to restore the old rose garden that was built by the original owner, Charles Moore, for his wife, Constance.'

'That sounds interesting.'

'It is, because they grew some magnificent old Irish country-house roses here. Charles was a keen gardener. It would be lovely to see them growing here again.'

'I remember hearing stories about him and how the house was abandoned for years after his son gambled it away on a racing bet.'

'It's true. Poor Charles was still alive. He was heartbroken after Constance's death and moved to London. His son George took over the house, sold a lot of the land and practically ran it into the ground. It was only about twenty years later, after George's death, that his younger brother James managed to regain the house. He married a Mary Hennessy, who it turned out was a distant relation of my husband's.'

'Old houses and their stories are fascinating,' he smiled.

'I know. My niece Kim is doing all kinds of research about it,' she confided. 'She's always on the internet or off trying to find some photos or information about Charles Moore and his family.'

'Genealogy is such an area of interest these days,' he said. 'Everyone wants to know about their family tree, even if there are skeletons in the closet.'

'That's exactly what Kim says,' she laughed, getting up and asking him if he'd like a coffee.

'I'd love one,' he said, thanking her, 'but I'm due to have a conference call with a few of my associates at three o'clock, so I'd better get back to the hotel where all my notes and work stuff are.'

Molly walked him up to the front door. The snow

had stopped. Rob thanked her again for lunch and she watched as he got in his car and disappeared down her driveway. She'd enjoyed having lunch with him. He's an interesting man, she thought – a very interesting man!

Chapter Fifty-two

The new year had come and gone like the snow, and Gina found it hard, as business was quiet. She missed the café and working, and hated being idle. She wasn't good at sitting around doing nothing.

She was still disappointed about the café, but at least Paul had got the building work on Norah's place, knocking it and the Armstrongs' together and re-decorating the new section of the local pub. It was great that he was busy, and he had more work lined up for the coming months, including Molly's cottage.

She had looked at the old Mulligan's Bar, but Paul had made it clear that it would not work as a café or restaurant as it was too small and too dark, which was fine for a pub but not for a café; besides, it was on a narrow lane overlooking Timoney's, the local car-repair mechanics. Who would want to have a coffee or lunch during the day while someone revved an engine or tried to fix an exhaust or moved cars around?

'Wait and see – something will turn up!' Paul kept assuring her.

She was enjoying spending more time with the boys, seeing friends, going for long walks and pottering around, but long-term she needed to do something else. She was only thirty-six years old, for heaven's sake!

Gina had just come back from visiting Norah when she got a call from Molly Hennessy.

'I was wondering if we could meet up tomorrow, Gina, to talk about Libby's wedding and go through things here in the house?'

When Molly had asked her a few weeks ago about catering for the wedding in Mossbawn, she had said it would be possible as long as the numbers were kept strictly at a manageable level. She had also talked briefly to Trish and the bride, Libby, and done up some wedding menus for them.

'Normally we'd have met up in the café,' smiled Molly, welcoming her and leading her down to the kitchen, 'but now we either go further afield or just stay at home!'

'I know. Everyone seems to really miss the place.'

'Maybe someone else will open up.'

'Actually, I've looked at opening somewhere in the village,' Gina confided, 'but unfortunately I can't find any suitable premises.'

'What a shame! Anyway, the reason I brought you

here, Gina, was to go through the details about this wedding. Trish and Larry are old friends and I've known Libby since she was a little girl, so obviously I want to help. And now that we have agreed to having their wedding here, I want to make sure that it will all work.'

'Listen, Molly, Grace's twenty-first was buffet-style, but guests will expect more at a wedding,' she warned. 'But we can get hot serving trolleys and things like that to keep food warm. That's what I used to do at some of the bigger events we catered in my old job. However, the main thing is that I wouldn't offer a choice of main course. I've told Libby and her mother that it would cause far too much pressure in terms of the kitchen.'

'That's agreed,' nodded Molly. 'How many guests can we fit?'

'A wedding is different from a party, as everyone is expecting to sit down at the same time,' she explained. 'Do you mind if we have a look at the rooms again, Molly?'

Gina paced up and down the dining room, then went into the large connecting living room. She rooted around in her handbag and, taking out a tape measure, she and Molly measured back and forth.

'I think we could get about sixty to sixty-five max between the two rooms. We can take off the doors so it looks almost like one room, and then use the orangery for drinks and dancing.'

'What about the couches and piano and living-room furniture?'

'We'd have to move some of it around – maybe put a couch in the lower hall, and the piano could stay. I'd need to measure properly and look at table sizes. How many does the bride want to invite?'

'I was talking to Trish on Friday and she said the guest list is up over the hundred mark.'

'Molly, that wouldn't be possible!' she said firmly.

'That's what I thought,' Molly agreed. 'I told her that this is just a family home . . .'

'Hold on!' said Gina, getting an idea and walking back into the orangery. 'What about doing it the other way around: the meal in here and the drinks in the living room and dining room?'

'Would we fit more people?'

They measured again.

'We can put long trestle tables here and here and here.' Gina was calculating it in her head. 'I think at a big push we could get around eighty-four people in here. And when the meal and speeches are over, you could take some tables out and use here for dancing like we did at Grace's.'

'So you think it is possible?'

'They are the only two options, as far as I can see, that will work within the confines of the house. There is no problem with extra friends coming on after the meal for drinks and the dancing, but for the formal meal itself we are restricted.'

Gina had always loved weddings: the menus, planning, canapés and creating an overall look for the bride and groom. Organizing a wedding here would obviously present some difficulty and she would need some help, but it was something she knew that she would enjoy doing.

'I'm so glad that I asked you to come over and talk to me about it.' Molly sounded relieved. 'I'll speak to Trish and tell her that if they want to go ahead with hiring Mossbawn the numbers are limited and there is absolutely no budging on that!'

Driving home, Gina hoped that the wedding would happen. Weddings were expensive, but catering one was the opportunity to earn, and earn well, as people didn't skimp on their weddings!

Chapter Fifty-three

The snowdrops were everywhere, gentle heads peeping up from the grass, under the trees, at the edge of each border. Molly was cheered by the sight of them. The garden was beginning to rouse itself, stretch and wake up. She found herself smiling as she walked around checking snow and frost damage. She had lost two or three new roses; perhaps they hadn't been strong enough to withstand the winter's chill and cold. She would find a hardier variety to replace them.

The pipes were rattling ominously every time she switched the 'on' button for the bath. She'd phoned the local plumber to come and check them.

'Have to be replaced, Mrs Hennessy – just all rusted and worn out,' he announced. 'It was a miracle that the immersion water heater didn't burst with the cold.'

She blanched when he told her the cost of the replacement.

'You're a lucky woman,' he said. 'Most people with old pipes like yours, they just burst – terrible damage done.'

More money out . . . Was it ever going to end? she thought, as she wrote him a cheque.

A wealthy American man and his wife had come to view the place. They seemed a nice couple and were looking for a large Irish holiday home. They both loved Mossbawn, the husband, a keen angler, impressed with the river and fishing rights; but apparently when it came down to it they considered it too far from Dublin and the airport.

Molly veered between relief and despair. If someone like that bought the house it would remain empty most of the year, and old houses did not do well being left empty. Mossbawn needed plenty of life and activity . . .

Roz came and stayed for a few days, the two of them going for long bracing walks, and she brought Roz down by the Gardener's Cottage to see her reaction.

'Oh Molly, it's just perfect for you! You've got the garden and all of this, and the cottage is far more manageable than a big pile like Mossbawn,' she enthused as they walked around it and went inside.

'I know it looks run-down and there's a fair bit of work to be done to it, but Roz, there is something about it I really like. It feels like home every time I come through the front door.'

'I could imagine you living here and me coming to stay!'

'If the house gets sold, it's the ideal solution to move here,' Molly confided. 'Given my life now, it feels right.'

'Well, you know if it's all done up and if you change your mind you'd probably have no problem renting it or even selling it.'

'I wouldn't want to sell it,' she said firmly as she told Roz her plans for enlarging the kitchen, for installing glass doors to the garden, for her own sunny bedroom that overlooked the back garden, and for the two pokey attic bedrooms to be converted to one large upstairs bedroom with a small bathroom.

'You put me to shame, Molly,' said Roz. 'I haven't done a tap to my place for years! It's a bit of a time-warp.'

'A new kitchen and some fresh paint in a cottage like this or an old house like yours can do wonders!' Molly encouraged her.

Locking up the cottage, she showed Roz around her rose garden.

'It's a bit bare and I've lost some specimens, but in a few weeks there will be more growth and I'm putting in a proper walkway.'

'No wonder you don't want to come to Dublin,' teased her friend. 'You really are kept busy here.'

Roz loved visiting nearby towns and villages, and trawling around the local craft and antique shops. She couldn't resist buying, no matter where they went:

314

bowls, plates, fine china . . . Was it any wonder her home was so cluttered?

Molly brought her to Myles Murray's antique shop.

'How are you, Molly?' he asked, coming out to greet her warmly.

She introduced him to Roz.

'A friend of Molly's is always very welcome here,' he said gallantly as Roz busied herself searching the shelves and tables of expensive china.

'Look at this wonderful piece of Limoges!' she called, pulling her collector's mini antique handbook from her bag. Myles laughed as she perused it.

'Any more word on Mossbawn?' he asked.

'Not a beep,' Molly admitted. 'I couldn't go ahead with one sale, then two weeks ago these lovely Americans were really interested, but now have decided they need to be nearer Shannon or Dublin airport.'

'Unfortunately the market for things of the past is nothing as good as it used to be,' he said. 'Everyone is struggling, but I always believe that pieces from the past have an intrinsic value far beyond monetary concerns.'

Molly agreed with him. Roz had decided to purchase her pretty blue French chocolate pot and Molly kept out of it as she and Myles argued the price.

'It was a good price!' laughed Roz later, as they ordered soup and a salad in The Weir, the nearby organic restaurant.

A few minutes later Myles came in to have lunch and spotted them.

'Join us, please!' offered Molly.

Myles was good company, full of stories of antique finds and antique cons.

'Oh, Molly, I think that there is a chance I might have someone that's interested in buying the antique linen cabinet you had in the spare bedroom,' he explained. 'A German couple were in the shop last week. They've just bought an old house they are restoring in Castlecomer. It's exactly what they are looking for, and the exact period.'

The linen cabinet had come with Mossbawn, but they had never really used it except for the odd time friends stayed. It didn't have any sentimental value and she couldn't believe the price that Myles felt he could achieve for it.

'I'll get my lads to collect it on Monday,' he offered, 'if that suits you.'

Molly found herself agreeing; she knew exactly what she would spend the money from the cabinet on – the plumber's bill.

'And Molly, I'll treat you to dinner if this all works out,' he promised, getting up to return to the shop. 'Who knows, perhaps we can find a few more pieces that might suit them!'

'Well, he's a lovely man!' said Roz as they watched him head back across the street.

'Roz!'

'I'm just saying Myles is attractive . . . he's into old houses . . . he's a widower . . . has a business of his own . . . You have a lot in common and I think he likes you!'

'Roz Gilmore, don't you dare! He's far too old, he's still obsessed about his wife and I'm definitely not interested. If you are so keen on him, you can have him!' she laughed.

Five days after Roz had gone back to Dublin, Myles phoned her to ask if she was free to attend the Antique Dealers' Dinner with him in Mount Juliet next month. Molly was in a quandary.

She appreciated the invite, but just because she was alone and widowed it didn't make her a candidate for his attentions. She thanked him politely and said no. She'd no intention of encouraging Myles to believe that they could be anything else but friends.

Chapter Fifty-four

As the weather improved, Molly was able to get out in the garden and tackle the nightmare of weeding, taking care that with her boots she didn't step on tender new shoots of green. Bulbs were everywhere as daffodils began to open and pretty primroses gave splashes of colour throughout the garden. She was dividing some shrubs and plants as the soil started to warm up and another season began. She wanted to have the place looking well for Libby's wedding. She was putting in lots of extra bedding to give colour, especially up around the front door and along the avenue. The massive pruning job she had done on the rose garden had left the place looking temporarily decimated, but shortly things would begin to change. The new roses that she had got from Gabriel were settling in as she under-planted them with bright polyanthus for spring, some pink and mauve penstemons for the summer and purple alliums for the autumn.

Ronan King had phoned her personally to arrange for a couple to see the house at the weekend.

'They are very keen!' he warned. 'I think Mossbawn is exactly what they are looking for.'

Molly welcomed the tanned, good-looking couple, who had been busy inspecting the outside of her house for the past few minutes.

'What a beautiful house! Thank you for agreeing for us to see the place at such short notice,' smiled Louise Kelly. 'When Ronan King sent us an email about it, Stuart and I just had to come and see it ourselves.'

'Not at all,' she said, leading them around the upstairs and downstairs of the house, giving them the full tour.

'We were hoping that there would be more bedrooms and bathrooms,' the woman admitted as they chatted in the living room. 'It would require a large amount of renovation to get it to the standard that we require for our clients.'

'My husband and I have done a lot of work on the structure of the house,' Molly assured them, 'but to be honest we didn't need eight bedrooms, and managed very well with the two bathrooms upstairs.'

'We would have to have en-suites in every room and would probably have to extend the house to get more bedroom space,' added her husband.

'Perhaps we could knock down that old glass

extension and build there. But I do like the privacy and the garden and the feel of the place.'

'Knock down the orangery! Are you going to run it as a country-house hotel?' Molly ventured, unable to disguise her dismay.

'Something like that,' nodded the husband.

'Actually, we run a cosmetic-surgery business,' explained Louise. 'We are looking for somewhere in this part of the country to cater for those that want to avail themselves of our services. They would come and stay here, have their procedure done, then rest and relax afterwards with good care while they recover. This house is very private and discreet and yet has great charm.'

'It's a big business and we already have a centre in Dublin and one outside Belfast,' Stuart Kelly added, 'but for something like that here we would need to add on consulting rooms and a theatre and recovery area.'

'But I do like this house,' Louise smiled, her skin and teeth absolutely flawless, 'and there is plenty of space in the garden for us to extend into and also put in a lot more car parking for staff and clients.'

Molly didn't know what to say. She couldn't imagine Mossbawn being used for plastic surgery, tummy tucks, boob jobs and face lifts!

'Molly, we'll talk to your auctioneer,' they promised as they said their goodbyes.

Over the following days she couldn't get the handsome couple and their plans for the house out of her mind. Is that what she wanted for Mossbawn? She thought of Charles Moore and his wife, Constance, and how they had built this house and garden for their family, and how much effort and work and love she and David had put into this place . . .

A few days later Ronan King phoned with an offer on the house. It was far less than she was hoping for.

'This is the Kellys' offer,' he said wearily. 'They know it's a buyer's market, especially for people like themselves with easy access to finance and cash. What do you want me to do? I can try to get them to come up a bit.'

To Molly it was clear that they were trying to take advantage of her situation. They had such big plans for the place, but she'd no intention of letting her beautiful old house be knocked and altered beyond recognition, the garden she loved destroyed. Her disappointment at their offer was tinged with a massive relief as she told the auctioneer to refuse it and make it quite clear that Molly Hennessy had no intention of selling to them.

Busy with getting the house ready for Libby's wedding, Molly put further thoughts of selling Mossbawn from her mind as she concentrated on getting the house and garden looking well.

Trish and Larry and Libby were paying a very generous amount for the use of the house for the day; she couldn't believe it and felt guilty about taking money from her friends.

'Don't be guilty!' warned Cara. 'That big castle in

Tipperary was costing them an absolute fortune and then everybody was shelling out for travel and very expensive accommodation. Now half the guests are near home and the rest are getting a great rate at the Woodlands Hotel.'

A week after the wedding, Molly was heading off to Italy with Roz and the girls for a few days' break.

'You are coming, Molly, even if I have to drag you there myself!' Roz had told her dramatically.

'You badly need a holiday,' insisted Emma and Grace. 'Dad would want you to go – you know that!'

In her heart she did know that. She knew that David would want her to be happy, to enjoy things, to accept that the world kept turning no matter how bad or sad she was feeling, and that her life would have to go on without him.

Chapter Fifty-five

Gina had meticulously checked and re-checked all her preparations for Libby and Brian's wedding. She wanted the young couple to have the perfect day in the perfect place. The tables and chairs and table linen and plates and cutlery and glasses had all been delivered in good time to Mossbawn House, and Kim and Inga had helped her to set the room up. Libby had brought along some wonderful tall white lanterns and candles, and, taking Molly's good advice, the bride had chosen swathes of spring flowers which looked wonderful on all the tables but were also scattered in tall vases and jugs and containers all around the house.

Gina had done as much preparation beforehand as possible and the dessert was in the chill cabinet of her spare fridge. She was so glad that she had taken Norah's kitchen equipment, as she certainly needed it now. For starters there was a large platter of tasty antipasti for each table, followed by slow-roasted fillet of beef with herb-tossed potatoes and a variety of vegetables, then a rich chocolate-and-hazelnut torte with home-made praline ice cream for dessert. Inga would help her in the kitchen and she had hired two Polish friends of hers and Brendan, a cousin of Paul's who was strapped for cash and had worked in a hotel, to help with serving the food and drink.

She prayed that everything would run smoothly and could feel her adrenalin surging as she raced around trying to get everything done.

'It will all be fine,' said Paul reassuringly. 'You are used to running things like this. Think of some of the massive events you catered back in Dublin.'

'I know, I know – but here is different because if I mess up everyone will know about it!'

'You won't mess up!' he declared loyally. She wished that she had his belief in her ability. She went to bed early, as she planned to be up in Mossbawn by eight, she had so much to do and organize.

It was drizzly and wet when she woke up, the day grey and dull as she loaded things into her car and Paul and herself drove to the house. Molly and Kim were already busy and the tables set with their candles and flowers looked amazing.

Libby had given them her guest list yesterday and Molly and Kim were going around placing the individual hand-written name cards on each table, meticulously following the table plan. Brides and grooms spent hours trying to get their tables organized, so it was really important to get it right.

Gina disappeared off to the kitchen, saying a silent prayer that all would go smoothly and calmly. There were bags of vegetables and potatoes to prepare. She discovered that they were missing some water jugs, but a quick call to Andrew Lynch, the manager of the hotel, and it was sorted; Paul offered to drive over to collect them. She kept an eye on the clock and suddenly noticed that it was almost lunchtime and that soon the bride would be driving to the church.

'Is everything going okay?' asked Molly, who had changed into a beautiful aquamarine silk suit. 'I can stay and help if you need me.'

'Thanks, but we're fine. Kim is setting up the glasses in the living room for the champagne when everyone arrives back from the church. We are leaving the French doors unlocked, so if it dries up people can spill out on to the patio and chat out there.'

'Don't forget to get someone to dry the chairs and tables and throw out the cushions if it does clear,' Molly reminded her. 'Well then, I'd better hurry. I don't want to be late for the church,' she said, grabbing her clutch bag. 'Everything looks beautiful, Gina. Well done! Anyone would want to get married here.'

'Molly, thanks, but it's your house! It's the perfect place for a wedding.'

Once Molly had left, the serious countdown began. Everyone changed into their black-and-white uniforms.

Kim, in a simple black dress, was helping out too and Gina noticed her taking lots of photos of the tables and flowers and the lanterns and things. She and Brendan would serve the drinks while the girls helped her with the food.

An hour and a half later, the first of the guests had begun to arrive and the champagne flowed. The bride and groom and the wedding party were getting their photos taken in different parts of the garden.

'Is everything okay?' worried Molly, coming into the kitchen to her.

'Everything is fine. Relax and enjoy your friends' wedding!' she urged. 'Go and have some champagne!'

The drizzle had finally cleared up by the time the bride and groom arrived to join their guests in the drawing room. Kim partially opened the doors and put flowers on the outside tables as some people went out into the open air.

Libby looked absolutely beautiful in a fitted cream lace dress, her dark hair partly up in an antique jewelled tiara. Her eyes sparkled with happiness as she and Brian made a point of talking to everyone. Trish and Larry were pleased as punch and went around introducing everyone and catching up with all the relations and the new in-laws.

'It's all going so well!' Kim grinned, coming in to get some more champagne. 'You can tell they are all really enjoying themselves.'

An hour later everyone had moved to the candlelit orangery. The combination of flowers, glass and lights with Molly's statues, ornaments and plants had certainly created the necessary surprise element. Father Darragh said the grace before the meal, then the dinner service began.

Once the dessert plates were served, Gina allowed herself a cup of coffee as the speeches began. She remembered her own wedding in the small hotel near where she and Paul had grown up and lived all their lives. They'd had about seventy-five people to the reception in the hotel's bar and dining room. It was all gold and red, with big roses on the table and velvet curtains, and they'd had chicken as they couldn't afford the beef. Paul's brother Billy and his band had played afterwards. It had been a great night, up dancing with all their family and friends. They'd gone to Majorca on their honeymoon for two weeks and when they came home had moved into their little house on Fairdale Crescent, near both sets of families. Every wedding was special and theirs had been such a great family day.

An hour later some of the tables and chairs had been cleared away, the music had started and everyone was up and dancing. She began loading and reloading the dishwasher with glasses and plates, and stacking things into the back of her car. At midnight there would be cocktail sausages and mini quiches for those that were hungry.

'Gina, everyone is raving about the food!' Molly said, coming into the kitchen. 'It's all working so well, and Trish and Larry are over the moon.'

'I'm glad to hear that.'

'You should be very proud of yourself!' Molly continued. 'This has worked better than any castle or hotel, and Libby's having a wedding to remember!'

It was nearly 2 a.m. before Gina finally finished. Brendan and Inga and Kim were still serving drinks and collecting glasses, but things were beginning to wind down. In an hour maybe she would slip away. Her feet were killing her, but otherwise she felt ecstatic about how the day had gone. She hadn't lost it, the ability to cater a big event and run it well!

Chapter Fifty-six

Molly had gone off to Italy for a week with her friends, leaving Kim to mind Daisy. Gina called over the next afternoon to collect the remainder of her equipment, which had been left in the utility room.

'The wedding was brilliant, Gina. Everyone was saying how well you organized it.'

'Thanks for all your help,' she smiled. 'You and Molly made having it here easy.'

'Weddings are always wonderful,' replied Kim, 'no matter if they are big or small, because it's all about two people being in love and committing to each other for life.'

She wondered if she would ever find someone to love and commit to. She was seeing Luke, and even though it was early days their relationship felt right. They both just wanted to be together all the time.

'Also, when you cater a wedding,' Gina confided, 'people don't want to scrimp and scrape on the big day. So for once their hearts overrule their heads and they spend, whether it's a family dinner for thirty people or a big bash for two hundred.'

'Are you doing lots of weddings?'

'Unfortunately things are pretty quiet since the café shut down,' Gina admitted. 'I used to get a lot of my work through our customers, but now that's gone I desperately need to find a way to attract more business.'

'Maybe if you had a website people could go on to that and find out about what you do,' Kim suggested.

'Do you think that would work?'

'Yes, definitely. Brides spend half their time on the internet searching out venues and flowers and dresses and all kinds of things. The girls in my office used to spend hours just looking at locations and churches and invitations and menu packages!'

Before she knew it, Kim was discussing helping to create a website to promote Gina's business.

'I'd keep the site very simple,' she advised, 'with menus and photos, and information about you and what kind of events you do and how to contact you. I'm working on a website for Mossbawn, but I've done one for my friend Evie. You should check it out. She's an artist. Her stuff is great, but the galleries take so much commission if you manage to sell a painting that it's crazy! And even getting to show at a gallery is really hard. The website is getting lots of hits and already she's sold a few more paintings and sketches and has got a few commissions. One guy

330

in California has even bought a painting and wants another for his sister. She's having a big exhibition in a few weeks, so the website will help promote that too.'

'I'd love to have a website, but I'm afraid I'm not very techie,' Gina admitted. 'I'm far better on the cooker than the computer.'

'That's fine, because I could set everything up and then you can just update it. It's very simple, or otherwise if you need me to I can do it. Do you know the lovely vintage fashion shop in Kilkenny?'

'Yes, some of their stuff is gorgeous. I got a lovely lace blouse there last year.'

'I sold them some of my clothes and handbags. Sylvia, the girl who owns it, wanted to put some of their stock up online to reach a much bigger customer base, so I've just done a website for them.'

'By the sounds of it, a website is something I should think about . . . Let me talk to Paul and see what he thinks,' agreed Gina, arranging to meet up later on in the week to have a chat about it.

Kim couldn't believe it – she was finding herself work where she hadn't expected to. She was also able to take some of the photographs needed for a site and knew that if there were any big techie issues, Piotr was on hand to help her sort them out.

Having Mossbawn to herself for the few days was weird, but in a nice way. She'd invited Luke over for dinner. He was always cooking them meals in his house, so it was definitely her turn.

She lit the fire in the drawing room and they would eat in the kitchen. There were candles everywhere and it looked really romantic. They saw each other all the time and the more time they spent together, the more she began to care about him. He was old-fashioned and good and kind, and had that rare gift of being happy and content. Walking down the street in the village, the kids from school and their parents would say hello to him; everyone liked Mr Ryan. The truth was, she really liked him too. Their relationship was so different from the one she had had with Gareth; she was far more relaxed and she had fun hanging out with him.

Her balsamic chicken was in the oven, and she was making a prawn pil pil for starters, as guys loved that. Earlier she had made a chocolate cake for dessert. Wine and beer were chilling in the fridge, and she ran upstairs and changed out of her usual jeans and jumper into a black dress that she hadn't worn for ages. Her hair was longer and she had lost some weight; all that garden work and dog-walking sure beat sitting at an office desk all day! As she tipped her eyelashes with mascara, she realized that she had changed so much from what she was – obsessed with make-up and clothes and looking good and going to the right places . . . It all seemed so long ago.

Daisy began to bark and she tore down the stairs to let Luke in. He pulled her into his arms and as she kissed him she knew tonight would be perfect, because she was with him.

They had a drink first, curled up on the couch in the living room.

'Let me help you,' he offered in the kitchen when the food was ready.

'You open the wine!' she giggled as she carried the piping-hot prawns to the table.

'Wow!'

She burst out laughing and as they ate the hot spicy shellfish they chatted easily. Luke always had so much to talk about.

She told him about Gina.

'That would be great for her and for you!' he said.

'Well, hopefully it works out,' she replied cautiously. 'But I still need to get a job.'

'Kim, I know it must be so different for you living here compared to working in the city, but you'll get used to it – believe me, you will!'

'I know. But Luke, I need to earn. I'm staying here with Molly at the moment, which is great, but I need to have a proper income.'

'Maybe the website business will grow and you'll find something else as well,' he said encouragingly.

'I hope so.'

'I'd take my class of seven-year-olds in school and the farm any day over a bloody office in London!' He took her hand, curving her fingers into his. 'Kim, I want you to stay here. I guess I worry that if you go back to life in Dublin I'll end up losing you.'

'You won't,' she said slowly. 'I promise you won't.'

After they'd eaten they went back and snuggled up in

333

front of the fire, taking turns telling each other about when they were kids.

'I wanted to be a jockey.'

'A jockey?' She laughed.

'I know – I'm far too tall! By the time I was twelve I was towering over most jockeys, so my dreams were dashed.'

'I wanted to be a ballerina. Mum used to bring my sister Liz and me to ballet classes every week. I was obsessed with it. But then, like you, I began to grow and realized that I was never going to dance in *Swan Lake* on some big stage . . . so I changed to Irish dancing with loads of the girls in my class instead, which was a lot more fun.'

'Funny how dreams change,' he said, suddenly serious.

Kim looked at him, his grey-green eyes and long nose with the bump in it from the bang of a football. And the little scar on his chin where a horse had kicked him and his mass of thick, wavy dark hair; and she knew that he was part of her dreams. She thought about him all the time . . . she couldn't help herself.

Later, lying in his arms in bed, she watched him breathe, his eyes closed, sleeping. They might only have known each other a short while, but already Kim knew that she loved Luke and wanted to be a part of his life for ever.

Chapter Fifty-seven

To Molly it felt strange going away on a week's holiday without David. But Roz and her friends wouldn't countenance her dropping out of the few days in Italy.

'It will do you good,' Anna assured her. When Anna had got divorced six years ago it had been a massive adjustment for her friend to make to being alone after years of marriage, but she had got used to it.

'Dad wouldn't want you to just sit moping around the place!' encouraged Grace and Emma. Molly certainly wouldn't consider herself the sitting-around-moping type, but she understood what her two daughters meant.

They were flying in to Venice, staying there for two nights, then going on to Verona and staying four nights at Lake Garda. She and David had been to Venice years before on a day trip when the children were small, but she was looking forward to having the time to explore it properly. She was sharing a room with Roz, which would be fun.

Venice was beautifully warm and sunny, and on the first day Molly and the girls joined a tour with a guide to show them around, taking in all the sights. Every step you took, you were conscious of the city's unique history and of all those that had walked its narrow cobbled streets and bridges for centuries before.

They were staying in a small boutique hotel only a few minutes from St Mark's Square. Dinner at night was great fun, the five of them all choosing different items on the menu so they could taste them all, washed down with lots of lovely Chianti. Anna had turned fifty only two days before the holiday, so they got the waiters to bring her a birthday cake and wish her *Tanti Auguri*. David had treated her to a long romantic weekend in a beautiful hotel in Kerry for her fiftieth – time with her husband she would never forget.

She'd known the girls for years and though they all tried to persuade her to think about moving back to Dublin and she knew that they meant well, when she explained her plans for the cottage they were happy for her. She couldn't imagine ever leaving a lovely place like Kilfinn and moving back to the city.

Molly loved to explore the little streets between the canals, discovering some beautiful old houses full of history, owned by generations of the same family, the fabric of each building almost a work of art. St Mark's was busy and noisy, full of tourists with their guides, but in the dark silence of a small church on a narrow side-street she asked for the strength to learn to carry on without David. So many had mourned their dead, marking the passing of loved ones with tombs and statues and paintings, century after century, ensuring their dead would never be forgotten.

They travelled on to Verona, exploring the town where Shakespeare's Juliet had lived, and went to a wonderful outdoor performance of *Carmen* in the ancient open-air amphitheatre. Sitting under the stars listening to such music was an incredible and emotional experience.

The next day they journeyed up to Lake Garda, where they were staying in the old town of Riva, built between the mountains and the lake. Their hotel, a former private villa, was set in lush gardens full of such colour and vigour that Molly couldn't resist talking to the gardener and finding out about their plants and what helped make them flourish. Silvio told her about two spectacular gardens nearby.

While the others went shopping and sightseeing, she and Maeve went to Villa Ragusa, with its tiered gardens and statues of some of its former owners, and a kitchen garden full of herbs, peppers, fruit and tomatoes – all the ingredients for a perfect Italian meal. There was a rose-covered loggia and from the top of the garden a spectacular view of the lake.

'This house has stayed in the one family for centuries,' the pretty young guide explained. 'In good times and of course in bad, the house and its family somehow survived. One of Mussolini's generals wanted it for himself, but the family somehow tricked him into believing that it was unlucky and brought misfortune to those who owned it. He was a very superstitious man so he went and got a villa further down the lake, near Limone.'

'It's such a perfect place, no wonder he wanted it,' laughed Maeve.

'Who lives here now?' wondered Molly.

'The family,' the girl smiled. 'My grandmother and my parents.'

'This is your home?' exclaimed Maeve.

'Yes. I love this villa, and the garden, and to tell people about it and the plants and the history. We open only four days a week, but the rest of the time it is ours, which is what I like!' admitted Giulianna.

'You must get lots of visitors.'

'Yes, we do, but visitors are important,' she smiled. 'They make it so we can keep this villa – keep it well.'

'The gardens are so beautiful,' enthused Molly.

'We get the sun, but we also get the rain sometimes,' she replied. 'It is good for our plants.'

'My friend is mad on gardens,' explained Maeve. 'She has a beautiful old house and garden in Ireland.'

'You have visitors come to your garden?' asked Giulianna with a smile.

'No,' she laughed, 'just my friends and family.'

'It's a beautiful garden, and visitors would love it!' added Maeve loyally.

* * *

Anna and Helen just wanted to shop, so the next day Molly, Roz and Maeve went further afield, taking the ferry across to Isola del Garda, the magnificent Venetian Gothic villa on an island in the lake, with its terraced gardens and woods. Molly was immediately drawn to the classic Italian-style garden with its fine selection of roses, recognizing one or two varieties which were the same as in her own garden.

Afterwards, sitting in the loggia surrounded by bougainvillea, Molly had to admit that she was enjoying this holiday far more than she'd expected. The girls were fun, and everyone was able to do what they wanted. She had actually relaxed and enjoyed seeing so many places. The Italians had learned the importance of history and keeping their buildings and churches and gardens, preserving them for future generations.

Standing in the garden, Molly thought of Mossbawn . . . How could she ever let her old house and its beautiful garden go?

Chapter Fifty-eight

Checking out Facebook and Flickr, Kim noticed lots of comments about the photos she'd put up of Libby and Brian's wedding.

'Great-looking venue . . . where is it? We've just got engaged, Kim, and are looking for somewhere to have our wedding!'

'Kim, where is this place? My brother and his girl-friend are looking for a country house like this!'

'Hi Kim, it's Steve, your old American college buddy. I'm living in Washington but my girlfriend's family are Irish so we want an Irish country house or castle for our wedding next summer. Where is Mossbawn House?'

'Love the dress, love the flowers, and love this house! I want to get married there!'

'Where is this venue? How do we contact them?'

Kim couldn't believe the interest her few photos had

generated. Wait till she told Molly – she wouldn't believe it!

She replied quickly, giving them her email and phone number. If they were seriously interested, they could contact her. Molly had agreed to let Libby get married here because she knew the family, but whether her aunt would be interested in letting it be used as a wedding venue by other people was a totally different matter.

Kim decided to do a bit of research and looked at some of the better-known country-house venues. From what she could see, with most of them you had to rent out the house for a night or two nights. The catering and food and wine were all added on separately. They cost a fortune – an absolute fortune.

She'd gone to lots of weddings, but had no idea how expensive they were. She should have listened more when her married friends were talking about it. She'd phone Rhona. She had got married only two years ago. Her wedding had been absolutely perfect, on a bright autumn day in Carlingford House, overlooking the river, with fireworks that night. Rhona and Will were always going to weddings, so her old friend was a bit of a wedding expert.

'Talk to you about weddings?' laughed Rhona. 'Do you know how many weddings I've been to over the past seven or eight years? Some have been amazing and great fun, others too fussy and formal even though they cost a fortune.'

'What makes it work?' she quizzed.

'Well, everyone wants their day to be pretty unique,

special to them and their friends and family,' Rhona said seriously. 'I guess that's what we all want. Couples are veering away from the big hotel with its huge function room.'

'So what's happening now?'

'Everyone is madly trying to find somewhere different – old houses, restaurants, places their friends haven't been – old stables and barns apparently are big. Obviously if you have a garden or field big enough to put a marquee in, you're flying. Last summer we went to a wedding on a canal boat, which was really cool.'

'And what about cost?' she pressed.

'Well, usually you have to rent the place, or hire it for a day or two, or if they have a load of bedrooms you have to fill them. Sometimes you just literally get the shell of the house or rooms and you then organize caterers, drink, even your tables and chairs. That's what we did.'

Kim had loved Rhona and Will's wedding.

'You had to do it all?'

'Well, they recommended caterers and bar staff and stuff for us to use,' Rhona explained. 'Why the sudden interest? Are you and Gareth back together again?'

'No!' she protested, explaining about her aunt's house and the interest the photos she'd uploaded had generated.

'If you do a big trawl on the net you will see there are actually not that many places for people to have their wedding. Check them out, Kim, and you'll see what I mean. Most of their websites will give you an idea of the costs or post you a wedding-package brochure so you can get an idea.'

Kim checked out the websites Rhona had mentioned, and some wedding ones, which were incredible and showed a photographic record of various weddings in all kinds of places – Georgian townhouses, castles, an old farmhouse, an old mill, a barn and some really lovely country houses scattered around Ireland. There was a restaurant on a marina, golf clubhouses with stunning views, a converted schoolhouse and even a Martello tower.

From what she could see, Mossbawn House was ideal and it had the added benefits of being so close to the village with its church and pub, and the Woodlands Hotel only down the road.

Kim decided to talk to Molly about it. Her aunt wanted to sell the place, but it was proving difficult. Maybe she would be better to consider using the house to make an income if that was possible. That way she could keep the home she loved and still live here.

Chasing upstairs, Kim got changed quickly into a skirt and wrap-over top as Luke was collecting her in a few minutes and they were going for dinner to Justin's house. It was Luke's nephew Aaron's second birthday, so it was a bit of a family affair, with all the Ryans going. She'd got some Disney cars and a dinosaur book for Aaron. Luke was his godfather and had got him an enormous big garage with a lift to put all his cars in.

'I know it's almost as big as he is, but I couldn't resist it,' he admitted.

The more she saw of Luke's family, the more she liked them. His mum and dad were old-fashioned, but they were a great pair, both obsessed with horses and riding and the farm. His sister Melissa and brother Sam were friendly too and made a point of including her in things. Little by little, she found she was becoming more involved, her old life back in Dublin seeming miles and miles away . . .

Chapter Fifty-nine

The sun slanting in through the tall bedroom window woke her. She should have guessed that Molly would be out in the garden already. On days like this it was impossible to keep her in the house, and she was most likely busy working somewhere outside.

Washing and dressing quickly, she had her own breakfast and went out to join her aunt.

'Perfect timing, Kim. I need you to hold this ladder while I fix some extra trellising for this beauty of a rose.'

Kim took a firm hold of the ladder as her aunt went up a few rungs and began to attach the trellising to hooks that she'd already drilled into the walls.

'Pass me that taller piece with the lovely ornamented top section, please!'

'Molly, why don't you let me do that?'

'Because I know what I'm doing and you don't,' her aunt replied briskly. 'Madame Isaac Pereire is looking for a bit more height and support, and this lovely wooden arch will help.'

Kim had to stop herself laughing. Her aunt treated her plants like they were children, to be cosseted and pampered and encouraged, but, looking around her, clearly whatever Molly did, it was working. Roses, along with clematis, had begun to grow everywhere, Albertine scrambling over arches and walls and stone pillars. The rose garden was losing its bare look, and cottage-garden plants were beginning to fill one of the borders.

'Molly, everything is beginning to grow!' she said, amazed. 'It's going to be glorious by the summer!'

'That's the plan,' agreed Molly. 'There's been a few casualties, but most of the roses seem to be settling in well and I can't believe that ancient pink Louise Odier seems to have got a second lease of life. I think she just needed attention – being ignored doesn't suit my French ladies.'

'Is the gazebo finished?'

'Nearly. Paul is coming back to give it another coat of paint next week.'

'It looks just like the one in the old photographs we found.'

'I know, he's done a great job and made it look like the one that Charles originally built here for Constance. I want this to be a lovely, peaceful rose-covered spot to day-dream in.'

For the next few hours Kim helped as her aunt directed her to get this, put that in the compost heap, fetch this from the shed.

'Molly, can you take a break? I need to talk to you about something.'

'Okay, ten minutes and a cup of tea in the kitchen,' agreed her aunt. 'Run ahead and put the kettle on. I'll be there in a minute.'

Kim had her laptop set up in the kitchen, a pot of tea ready on the table. Molly, in her green knitted jumper and old cord trousers, padded across the kitchen floor in her slippers and sat down.

'Is everything okay, Kim?'

'Oh yes – it's not about me. It's about Mossbawn and you.'

'What do you mean?'

'Well, it's just that I put some of those lovely wedding photos of Libby's and Brian's up on Facebook and Flickr – and you won't believe it, but a few people have contacted me to find out about having a wedding here.'

'And what did you do?'

'Well, nothing yet really, because it's your house . . . But I did check out other wedding venues to get an idea of how it all works and the costs. Molly, I know you plan to sell the house, but maybe having a few weddings here every year might help you to cover the cost of running and keeping the place.'

She could see Molly staring at her. Shit – she'd been far too presumptuous, overstepped the mark . . . She was Molly's guest, for heaven's sake! Her aunt had let her stay here for nothing for the past few months and must think she was being incredibly rude and interfering.

'Hold more weddings here?'

'Yes,' Kim said, taking a deep breath. 'But only if you want to . . . It's just that it could make some money.'

Molly began to laugh and laugh.

'Kim, you won't believe it, but I've had three people ask me about weddings in the last few weeks. Roz has me pestered, as her niece Susan is getting married. She's thirty-six and apparently he's been married before, so she wants something discreet and out of Dublin for close family and a few friends – only fifty or sixty people. Then Dr Jim mentioned their daughter Jenny is getting married next year. And Trish says lots of people keep asking her and Libby how they managed to hire here!'

'I don't believe you!' she said, taken aback.

'Great minds think alike!' said Molly firmly. 'But you know, it was one thing to help out by having Libby's wedding here, but having more . . . I just don't know. How would I go about even organizing such things?'

'Well, if you were considering it – you would need a website, a really good one, and to get someone like Gina on board in terms of running the whole food end of it.'

'It has crossed my mind,' Molly admitted, 'but if you look at some of these places they have twenty and thirty bedrooms and cottages and that – it would all be too much. Far too much work!'

'Molly, Mossbawn is different. Only the bride and

groom get to stay here and maybe the parents, otherwise all the guests go and stay in the Woodlands. You are not running a hotel or guest house, just a one-off venue.'

'I know the house is lovely, but it's not very big . . .'

'You don't want really big weddings. Mossbawn would be more exclusive and you have the most amazing garden for photos and the drinks reception. Honestly, Molly, I think it might work.'

'Do you really think so?' she asked.

'Yes. The wedding here was great and you know Gina loves catering for that kind of an event.'

'Listen, let me think about it over the next few days,' she said slowly. 'It might be too complicated.'

'Promise me you will think about it,' Kim urged. 'It could help solve your problems and mean that you could stay living here.'

'To tell the truth, I've been worried sick about selling the place. I feel I'm letting David down,' admitted Molly. 'I know it sounds crazy, but I've been trying to work out all kinds of ways of keeping Mossbawn without bankrupting myself. Pamela Reynolds offered to buy the back field months ago when we thought that dreadful Dunne man was buying the place. I think she was worried he wouldn't let her use it the way I do, and of course it's true – he wouldn't have let her. But after all the years of grazing the land, she's made a good offer and I decided to accept it.'

'Well done!'

'It's two acres we won't miss, and I'd prefer to see

their animals on it and not some new development.'

'Molly, honestly, you need to think about this idea. Go online and check country-house weddings.'

Kim showed her how to search the wedding sites to see what people were offering and the enormous costs involved. Molly was absolutely stunned at the possibility of not having to sell Mossbawn and that her lovely old country house would be able to pay for itself.

Chapter Sixty

Molly was all excited, dying to talk to the girls about her plans for Mossbawn. She collected them from the train station. Emma had just handed in an important science research paper which would go towards her college finals marks and looked absolutely wrecked.

'Mum, I'm just going to crash for the next few days,' she said as they drove home in pouring rain. 'I'm exhausted.'

Putting on the kettle, she got them to sit down. 'I want to talk to you both about the house,' she said.

'What's happening?' quizzed Emma warily.

'Oh, Mum – don't tell us someone is going to buy it?' pleaded Grace nervously. 'I can't bear it.'

'No! No one is going to buy Mossbawn,' she said firmly, 'because I've decided to take our house off the market. I told the auctioneer a few days ago.'

'You're not going to sell the house? We're staying here?' Grace sounded so relieved. 'So nothing's going to change!'

'But how are you going to manage, Mum?' worried Emma, serious.

'Well that's just it – things are going to change. First of all, I've sold two acres – the back field – to Pamela for her horses. She's been using it for years and only paying a little bit of rent, but she was really worried about what would happen if someone else had the house, so she made me an offer – a fairly good offer too,' she laughed, 'so I've decided to accept it.'

'That's brilliant, Mum!'

'I know your dad wouldn't want me to sell it, but it seems an ideal solution. Nothing will really change except that that field will officially become Pamela's and I have a few acres less to worry about. And even though I'm not selling Mossbawn, I still plan to move out of here and into the cottage. This house really is too big for me most of the time, so the cottage will be far easier to run and will do me fine.'

'Then what will happen to here?' worried Grace.

'Are you going to rent it to someone, is that it?'

'Well, in a way.' Molly hesitated. 'You won't believe it, but since Libby's wedding people have been contacting me and Gina and Kim, enquiring about having their weddings here. And some of Libby's photos went up on some big wedding site and have attracted people to contact us. Someone else wants to hold a big family reunion! Kim thinks that I should let people hire the house to hold a wedding or function. The money is quite generous, but I need to know: what do the two of you think?'

'You'd rent it out for weddings and special parties, but you'd still own it?'

'And we'd still be able to stay living here?'

'Yes, that's the beauty of it. Mossbawn is ours and I intend to keep it that way,' she explained. 'But having a few weddings and events here during the year would more than cover our costs, and Kim thinks it could become a profitable, good business. Gina will look after the catering end, I'll do the house and the garden, and Kim will do the website and social media stuff so people will know about us.'

'Mum, it sounds great!' Grace exclaimed, all excited. 'I'll help out too when I'm on holidays or home at weekends.'

'It sounds perfect!' Emma grinned. 'And the main thing is that we are able to keep our house. I couldn't bear to have seen it sold!'

'Well, don't worry, because it's not going to be sold. I lost your dad and I don't think that I could bear to lose this house too. But for me, moving into the cottage will make day-to-day life a bit easier.'

'Are you sure you will manage it all?'

'Look, Kim was already working on a website about the house and its history, but says she can make a really great site for people to see what Mossbawn is like if they want to hire it for a wedding or big event. The photos she took look amazing. Ever since the café closed, Gina's been looking for something to do and she is a very experienced caterer. It's what she did before she moved here. And I'll run the house and the garden like I've always done and try to keep the place looking well.'

'Oh Mum, it's a wonderful idea,' enthused Grace. 'And best of all, it means Mossbawn will still be ours.'

'I know that Jake and I are heading off travelling for the year,' said Emma, 'but I was so worried that Mossbawn would belong to someone else by the time we got back – I was so upset about it!'

'But you never said anything!'

'Because we knew you needed money,' Emma said gently. 'We weren't going to stand in your way if you needed to sell the house. But now it's great because say if Jake and I get married, we could have my wedding here!'

'Well, I've talked to Bill and to Michael Quinn about the legal end of things. Obviously I will have to set up a company and do things properly and take out extra insurance, but it looks like I'm going to have my own business! Can you believe it?'

'Dad would be very proud of you, Mum.'

'You've been amazing,' added Emma, 'coping without Dad and managing to keep everything going, and now this!'

Molly was overwhelmed with utter relief and the certainty that she was doing the right thing. She just somehow had to make it all work!

* * *

Over the next few days she and the girls came up with lots of ideas and both of them were interested in everything they could do to help. Grace promised she would help out during the holidays and in the summer when things were busy.

They were both dying to see how work was coming along in the cottage, where Paul and the builders were busy with the new extension.

'There's going to be ceiling-to-floor glass windows at the back overlooking the courtyard garden,' Molly explained. 'But from the front the cottage won't really change. My bedroom is downstairs, but upstairs in the attic space Trish has designed lovely skylight windows and there'll be a big bedroom with two beds and a small bathroom.'

'Mum, it's going to be gorgeous!' Emma enthused as they stood in the middle of the enlarged room with its steel-beam support.

'I love the way it's old and yet it's modern too,' added Grace.

'Don't you think the cottage is perfect for me?'

'Perfect!' they agreed.

The weekend went far too fast. Molly felt encouraged by her daughters' enthusiasm and support for all her plans for Mossbawn. Already this week she had a few people coming to talk to her about holding their weddings here and possible dates during the summer. It was all so exciting.

Chapter Sixty-one

Kim checked her emails.

'Have the perfect job for you. When can we meet up to discuss it? Joanne'

Joanne was a recruiter from Citi Careers. A phone call later and Kim couldn't believe it. Her old boss in the bank, Mark, had moved to Allemana Finance, a big German funds company, and apparently was now involved in setting up a new team there. Their offices were down on the docks and they were looking for staff. Her name had come up.

'I'm putting you forward for an interview, Kim,' said Joanne. 'You have the experience, and the fact you have worked with Mark should hopefully be a bonus.'

Kim remembered Mark as being utterly driven, working crazy hours, obsessed with his job and expecting a huge amount from everyone around him. He'd been married, but his marriage had broken up. She hadn't worked that closely with him, but they had always got along with each other.

'Great!' she said, as Joanne promised she would confirm the interview details. She was going to be in Dublin for the next few days anyway, as she was helping Evie get organized for the opening of her big exhibition in the Peppercanister Gallery on Friday.

There was a hell of a lot to do, as Evie was already panicking about her work and being ready. Kim was dying for Luke to meet Evie and the rest of her friends, and the exhibition was the perfect opportunity.

'Please say you'll come, Luke! You'll get to meet everyone, and Liz and Joe are going and even my dad and Carole might turn up. Evie's dad, Kevin, and my dad are good friends.'

'So you want to throw me into the lions' den!'

'Something like that!' she teased. 'It's about time you met them.'

If Luke was going to be part of her life, she wanted him to get to know her close friends and her family.

She was staying with Liz, who was excited about her sister's interview, telling her she needed to get back into business mode.

'You look great in that black suit,' said Liz, making her turn around.

'It feels weird after my jeans and wellies!'

'Well, you look amazing, Kim. You've lost weight and got so trim – it's not fair!'

Kim didn't like to say anything, but Liz had put on a few pounds and with trying to manage the kids and work looked pretty wrecked. Finn was going through a nightmare stage, waking every night and ending up in their bed.

'What shoes?'

'Those black Italian ones look perfect – not too high, and classy and businesslike.'

'I'm so bloody nervous about this,' she admitted.

'Why?' asked Liz. 'It's just the opportunity you've been waiting and hoping for!'

'I know, but . . . things have changed. I've changed, and there's Luke.'

'I'm dying to meet him,' her sister laughed. 'But Kim, this is about you, your career, and your job – that's the thing to focus on.'

'I know . . . I know!'

She had driven into town early and got a parking space down near the docks, in the heart of Dublin's International Financial Services Centre. She found her way to the fifth floor, where Allemana's offices were located.

A young secretary led her into a conference room where Mark Hogan and two other people were sitting at a big table with a chair opposite them for her. She felt shaky already as she was introduced to an older German man, who was obviously in charge, and an elegant dark-haired woman in a killer black suit and heels.

'This is Erik and Carla,' said Mark, smiling and welcoming her, trying to put her at her ease. He got her to detail her previous experience and her functions in her former role.

'You would be doing something very similar here,' explained Carla, 'but obviously here it is a smaller, more focused team, with everyone having to play their part. The funds we manage are active and because we are new to the market here we need to prove ourselves.'

'We put in long days here, much as you did in the old job, Kim,' smiled Mark, 'but here things are a bit more frantic and we have to be flexible with our hours. So there wouldn't be much time for other commitments during busy periods.'

'Naturally,' she smiled, trying not to flush. She had noticed Carla discreetly checking out her ring finger.

'Have you any questions?' the handsome middle-aged German asked her.

She knew not to ask about pay or conditions – it was too soon for that – and instead asked about the size of the team and the types of funds that they were managing, and how long the company had been set up and where its offices were based.

'Do you mind me asking what you have been working at over the past year almost?' enquired Erik. Kim could feel herself flush. Here it was – the nightmare question which she had rehearsed and rehearsed.

'Well, jobs are scarce, so I decided to up-skill and have done a website-design course and photography course, as they have always been two of my interests,' she said calmly. 'Since then I've been working on developing a number of websites for clients and have been busy doing a research and photography project on an old Georgian house outside Dublin.'

'That sounds interesting,' said Erik encouragingly. 'Very interesting.'

'But now you are back ready to do what you do best!' urged Mark, as if trying to refocus her.

'Of course,' she beamed, meeting their gaze.

'Kim, you seem to be very much the type of person we are looking for on our team,' the other woman smiled. 'From your CV and what you have told us, your experience is excellent.'

Kim could feel her heart beating, knowing that deep inside she wasn't that person any more . . . not at all.

'It's been lovely to have you come along this morning, Kim,' said Mark smoothly. 'Obviously, given the role there will be a second-interview stage, but Joanne will fill you in on that.'

She stood up and politely thanked them.

Outside, she gazed at the river below and the city sprawled out before her. She had got a very definite feeling they might offer her the job, or at least the next-round interview. She felt shaky and quickly took the lift downstairs. She was dying for a coffee, so she made her way to one of her favourite coffee places. It was already busy, everyone in suits, some looking for a seat, others wanting a cappuccino or latte to go. She slid into one of the brown leather chairs, ordering her regular special with its double hit of Colombian coffee. These things had kept her going for years. She got herself a cherry muffin. She'd been too nervous to eat before the interview and had just had a glass of orange juice in Liz's.

Kim picked up her phone. She'd just got a text.

'*Well done you aced it! They want you back for second interview to go through terms and conditions and other details. Joanne.*'

She sipped her coffee slowly. She should be exhilarated, over the moon: the first proper chance of a job that had come her way, a job with great prospects, back where she had lived, in the city, working in funds again . . .

She watched a seagull outside pull at a piece of food someone had dropped. She still felt shaky. This wasn't what she had imagined. She wasn't even sure this was what she wanted any more . . .

Chapter Sixty-two

Evie O'Connor stood surrounded by her canvases and artwork.

'Where is my *Mayfly* canvas?' she wailed.

Kim knew that Evie was stressed out about the exhibition, but she was having an utter meltdown.

'We'll find it,' she promised calmly, trying to make sense of the piles of canvases stacked everywhere. Earlier she had very nearly put her foot through a beautiful seascape of Evie's.

'They've got to be to the gallery by three o'clock, as Valerie said that Hugh can only give me a few hours today for hanging.'

'Listen, Evie, why don't I take this group here and put them in my car and then drop them over to the gallery while you can be sorting the rest of your paintings and be ready when I come back?'

Getting rid of some of the artwork from the cluttered flat was the only way Evie could hope to get organized.

Together they carried and dragged the larger canvases to the lift and out to her hatchback car. Fully loaded, she had some difficulty finding the gallery, but eventually spotted the sign, 'The Peppercanister Gallery'.

Two hours later, all Evie's work for the exhibition had been delivered safely and Evie herself was prowling around the gallery, which was in the basement of a large Georgian house off Fitzwilliam Street. Hugh, the painting hanger, had arrived and Kim was studying every wall carefully as she and Valerie tried to position each piece of work to its best advantage.

'I think we need to group things,' said Valerie intently. 'Buyers like to make sense of what they are looking at.'

Evie wanted things scattered all over the place to make an impact, but Kim could see that, where there were two or three paintings that were very similar in terms of themes, it worked well placing them near each other and even attracted you more to them. A massive sea painting and an incredible one of a wood each deservingly got a space of its own. If she had the money, she would have bought them. Evie's work was getting better and better.

They worked there until almost nine o'clock. Hugh was gone, but they had decided where most of the rest of her pieces were to go.

'He'll finish it off tomorrow,' Valerie promised as they said goodnight and she locked up.

'What do you think?' Evie yawned.

'I think your work is amazing and that the show is going to be a great success! But we need to get some food into you.'

Every time she was working on a big project or an exhibition it took so much out of her friend. Evie would barely sleep or eat for weeks and usually radically changed her hair. At the moment it was bleached an almost white-blonde colour, as against her natural brown, and had been cut into a cropped pixie style which showed off her face and amazing green eyes.

Passing Caruso's, Kim decided this would do the trick and soon they were sitting at a table having big plates of creamy lasagne. Evie wolfed it down and Kim topped up her wine glass with more Chianti. Her friend needed to sleep and unwind, otherwise she would be too uptight to enjoy the exhibition.

'What will I do if no one shows up tomorrow?'

'Lots of people are coming, don't worry.'

'But what about if people only come to see Fergus's work?'

'Fergus?'

'Fergus McGuinness, the sculptor – you must have heard of him?'

Kim shook her head; she really was hopeless.

'He's a friend of mine, but he's brilliant. He does these amazing bronzes, they cost a fortune. He's showing about twelve of his pieces at the exhibition.'

'Well then, both of you will bring a crowd,' Kim assured her, 'so there is no need to worry, Evie, honestly.'

Back in the flat, Evie fell into bed almost immediately and began to snore. Kim, who was sleeping on the futon again, was tempted to catch her nose but resisted.

Outside she could hear the traffic and the noise of the odd ambulance siren as she tried to sleep. She closed her eyes, thinking of the peace and quiet of Mossbawn, a gentle breeze blowing through the leaves, the sound of the river . . . birdsong . . . as she too finally slept.

Chapter Sixty-three

The gallery was packed and, looking around, Kim could see Evie in the midst of it all, her shock of blonde hair, dangling silver pyramid earrings and her trademark black skirt and biker boots ensuring that she stood out from the crowd. Valerie and Hugh had done an amazing job and her work looked incredible. Kim noticed that three pieces already had red stickers placed on them. Also dotted around the two rooms were a number of striking bronzes on white plinths and on the window-sills: crows, swans, a single seagull and a bronze of a group in flight. They were so powerful and raw and imaginative. These Fergus McGuinness pieces were getting lots of attention – but they were very expensive.

Alex and Vicky and most of their crowd had turned up and she was anxiously waiting for Luke to arrive.

He'd texted her to say he'd been slightly delayed on the farm but would be here soon.

'Well, it's lovely to see you,' said Alex, hugging her. 'There must be some very big draw in the country to keep you there so long! When are you moving back up to Dublin?'

'Who says I'm moving back up?' she teased him.

'We miss you,' pouted Vicky. 'Really miss you!'

'I miss you too!'

Rhona and some of her friends arrived and she found herself frantically trying to catch up with everyone as Liz and Joe appeared.

'We managed to get a babysitter for the night, so we said we'd pop in here and then find somewhere for dinner,' Liz smiled, before heading off to congratulate Evie.

'It's like getting out of prison for a few hours, escaping on our own somewhere,' added Joe, grabbing a glass of red wine.

Kim had made Evie get some cards printed with her contact details and the website address, and she passed them around to people and left some near the long wine table and on the table with the gallery catalogues.

Suddenly she spotted her dad and went over to join him and Carole. She hadn't had a chance to see him since she'd come up from Kilfinn. He was chatting to Evie's parents.

'Hello, darling. Has that young man of yours appeared yet?' he asked, hugging her.

'Dad, he'll be here soon!' she promised, glancing quickly around the room.

The speeches were about to start. Valerie had asked Neil Shaw, the renowned art critic from the *Irish Times*, to open the exhibition.

'Let's hope that stops him saying anything really bad about my work!' Evie said, worriedly.

The critic had just started talking to the large crowd when Kim spotted Luke coming down the steps. He caught her glance and moved silently towards her.

'Hi,' she whispered as he took her hand.

Neil Shaw had done his homework; he knew almost every detail of both Evie's and Fergus's background and a huge amount about each of their work. Across the room she could see Evie visibly relax as he talked about her style and vision and the collectability of her work. He cited a few paintings that he believed were important, mentioning *The Woods* as his own favourite. He was equally generous about the young sculptor and urged those buying for serious collections to consider one of his bronzes.

Evie thanked him and said a few words about her own work and inspiration. She thanked her mum and dad and friends and family, and Kim for her unceasing support since the day they first sat beside each other in school.

'And that includes helping me lift every painting you see on these walls!'

Fergus was skinny and wiry with long black hair, his brown eyes nervous as he stepped forward and said as few words as possible.

'Words are not my thing,' he admitted. 'Metal and bronze are!'

Everyone cheered and clapped as wine was passed around again once the speeches were finished. Kim could see Evie and Fergus deep in conversation. She knew that look. Evie fancied him – definitely fancied him.

'Luke, I was getting worried,' she said as they were handed some wine.

'I'm here now,' he replied calmly.

'Come on, I want to introduce you to everyone,' she said, leading him around from group to group. Alex and Lisa both gave him the thumbs-up.

'He's really handsome – you never mentioned that!' whispered Aisling accusingly. 'And really tall!'

'I know,' Kim laughed, noticing suddenly how he was so much taller than everyone else in the room.

Luke and her dad got on really well and she could hear her dad asking him about the stud farm and how they were surviving the downturn.

Luke seemed totally at ease with everyone. He loved Evie's work and chatted to her about it. Liz and Joe were very impressed when he asked them about Ava and Finn.

'Most guys never remember anything like that!' remarked Liz.

'It's because he's a teacher, he's kind of into kids and has to remember all their names.'

As the crowds began to disperse, Evie announced that they were all moving to Searson's pub. Liz and Joe had sloped off, but most people, including her dad and Carole, were going on to the pub.

Luke pulled her into his arms as they walked along the street.

'I parked the car up at the Fitzwilliam,' he said. 'The hotel is only a few minutes from the pub.'

Searson's was busy, but Evie had reserved an area down the back for all of them and plenty of finger food was being served. Fergus and Evie were still engrossed, chatting together. Carole and Luke seemed to be getting on great and she was telling him about her daughter, Lara, who had trained in the same college as Luke but was now working as a teacher in London.

'It's an inner-city school with a lot of problems, but she loves it!'

Evie's dad made a bit of a speech about how proud he was of Evie and her work, and that she was getting the recognition she so well deserved. Kim could tell Evie was happy, as her ears had gone a pinky colour – they always did when she got excited!

It was around two o'clock before the crowd broke up and they finally made it back to the hotel Luke had booked into.

On Saturday they had a late lunch in town with some of Luke's friends, who worked in London but were home in Dublin for the weekend.

'Bet you don't miss it!' said Annabel.

'Not at all,' answered Luke. 'I'm doing what I want to do, and I'm living where I want to live, and now I've found Kim!'

Kim had booked a table in Harry's for that evening, and most of her gang came along. Evie appeared with Fergus in tow, which was no surprise! Luke got on with everyone. He and Alex had a similar sense of humour and taste in music, and he enthralled Aisling and Pete with his stories of growing up on the farm and travelling in Asia and Australia. Fergus had travelled much of the same route and they soon discovered they had stayed in some of the same hostels and both got food poisoning in the same restaurant, which created a weird bond!

'I was really nervous about meeting your friends, but they are great,' Luke admitted as they walked back to the hotel arm in arm. 'Just like you.'

On Sunday they took it easy, strolling through St Stephen's Green, sitting on a park bench watching young families with babies and children in buggies, and older couples hand in hand.

'Are you coming back to Kilfinn tonight?'

'No, I'll stay on for a few more days,' she said slowly. She hadn't got around to telling him about her job interview; she hadn't wanted to say anything in case it didn't work out.

'Why?' he persisted.

'I have an interview for a job,' she answered reluctantly.

'A job back here in Dublin?'

'I met the company a few days ago and they want me back for a second interview.'

She could see he was not only surprised but hurt by her not telling him.

'Luke – I didn't want to say anything because I've had lots of interviews before and they all went nowhere.'

'But this time it's different.'

'Maybe. I might get the job . . .'

'Then you will move back up here . . . take up your old life . . .'

'Not necessarily.' She fumbled, searching for the right words.

'When were you going to tell me? Didn't you think it was something we should talk about?'

'I know,' she sighed. 'I was scared of saying it to you, because it mightn't have mattered to you if I did move back.'

'Well it does!' he said firmly.

She could see in his eyes that it did matter to him, she did really matter to him.

'Why?' she pushed.

'Because . . .' He hesitated. 'Because I've fallen in love with you. You know that!'

Kim took his face in her hands.

'Now I know,' she teased him. 'And you know I love you too!'

They sat for an hour talking, then went and got some food before he drove back to Kilfinn. She hated him leaving, being apart from him. They had discussed commuting, trying to manage living in two places like lots of couples juggling careers. Everything was so up in the air . . . But the important thing was that Luke Ryan loved her. Nothing else really mattered.

Chapter Sixty-four

Kim O'Reilly's second interview with Allemana Finance was on Tuesday. This time Erik and Mark were the ones she had to impress. She felt very nervous about it and had barely slept the previous night.

Mark was businesslike as he laid out the terms of the job, the hours and salary and what was expected of someone in the role. She tried to disguise her disappointment, as the salary was less than in her previous job.

'I'm afraid the market has changed, Kim, and it has affected everyone in this industry too.'

'We start early, as you will be dealing with our offices in Berlin and Frankfurt and Zurich most days,' Erik explained.

It was a numbers job, what she was used to: making sure and checking that numbers and figures and payments were correct and that transactions happened on time, and that funds were monitored and managed correctly. She would start work at 8.30 in the morning and work through till six or seven most days.

'Once a month or so you might have to go to Germany,' said Erik with a smile. 'And sometimes Zurich. Mark and I are over there tomorrow at a meeting.'

Kim asked a few small, pertinent questions, discovering that everyone worked from a hot-desk system, with no desk of their own.

'That's why we all have to come in early!' Erik joked. 'So we have somewhere to sit and work!'

The annual holidays were four days less than in the bank, and there was no car parking and a lot fewer perks.

'Miss O'Reilly, we are happy today to offer you the role of Fund Manager, and obviously we would see you becoming very much part of the Allemana Dublin team,' Erik said warmly. 'Naturally, we will get our HR department to send you the official job offer and copies of the job contract and forms that we would need you to sign and return to us. You will also need to have a medical examination which we can organize for you.'

She sat stunned for a few moments.

'How soon can you start, Kim?' continued Mark. 'We would need you on board as soon as possible.'

'I need to think about it.'

'Think about it?' queried Mark, staring at her. 'Think about what?'

'It's just that I wasn't expecting this,' she said slowly, trying to gather her thoughts. 'Thank you so much for your job offer. I'll read the contract, sign things . . .'

She smiled at the two of them as they finished the meeting, trying to mask the growing sense of turmoil she felt. Erik disappeared off to another meeting and Mark walked her to the elevator.

'Is everything okay, Kim?' he quizzed. 'There isn't a problem, is there?'

'No!' she lied. 'No problem!'

Back in her car she felt shaky. She had got a job – a really good job. She should be over the moon. What the hell was wrong with her!

She drove to Evie's.

Evie was in her pyjamas painting. Kim made herself a big mug of coffee.

'Are you okay?'

'Not really!'

'You're all dressed up.'

'I had an interview and they've just offered me the job!'

'That's good news!' Evie, excited, put down her paintbrush to hug her. 'Where's the job?'

'A finance company in the docks. I'd be doing what I did before.'

'But I thought you didn't like it,' Evie mused, sitting on the couch beside her.

'I didn't.'

375

'What are you going to do?' asked Evie, suddenly serious.

'That's it. I just don't know. Financially, I really need the job. I need money but I'm not sure it's what I want any more.'

'Is this to do with Luke?'

'Yes, in some ways, but even before I met him I'd changed. I want to do something different, rather than move money around and monitor funds for some unknown faceless conglomerates and clients in God knows where!'

'Then don't do it!' urged Evie. 'You'll find something else!'

'Like what?'

'Well, you did an amazing job on my website.'

'That's because you're my friend.'

'Okay, it was a freebie, but you can charge other people.'

'I do!' Kim laughed.

'I know that Valerie wants to totally update the crappy one the gallery has. I'll get her to contact you.'

'Thanks.'

'Listen, I can't tell you what to do,' Evie admitted. 'My career is hardly rock-solid and financially sound. But being an artist is all I've ever wanted and since I started giving more time to it, my work is getting better. I can see it myself. I enjoy my job teaching art, but when I worked full-time I was too exhausted to come home and paint, so now working part-time suits me much better. I've got some income that I can rely on and the rest is up to me. But my long-term goal is to work full-time as an artist with a proper studio where I can paint all day.'

'That will happen,' said Kim, 'I know it will.'

'Dad always worried about me giving up a secure, full-time, pensionable teaching job,' Evie sighed. 'He begged me to stay on, to see my painting as a hobby.'

'And now he's telling everyone about his daughter "the artist",' Kim teased.

'I know it's all crazy, but I'm happy.'

'I'm happy too,' she admitted. 'I thought I'd miss the money and the clothes and the social life and having someone like Gareth in my life, but now I don't give a rat's ass about things like that. Everything is less complicated and simpler in Kilfinn with Luke.'

'Maybe you have your answer,' nodded Evie. 'What will you do?'

'Talk to Luke, talk to Liz . . . I don't know!' she worried. 'You know me. I absolutely hate making decisions.'

'But it's *your* decision,' Evie reminded her. '*Your* life.'

Liz met her for soup and a sandwich in the coffee shop across from the offices where she worked.

'I can't make your decision for you, Kim,' she said seriously. 'It's like there are two paths and you have to choose which one to take.'

'But I don't know,' she fretted.

'I think you do know,' her sister said softly as they paid the bill and Kim walked her back to her department. 'What are you doing now? Are you staying tonight?'

'No, thanks. I'll head back down to Kilfinn. I need to talk to Luke.'

'You're getting wise!' Liz said, hugging her. 'Very wise.'

Chapter Sixty-five

Driving back down the country to Kilfinn, Kim's mind was churning over and over as she thought about the new job offer. Working in a growing company with someone like Mark would be interesting. In one way, accepting Allemana's job offer and moving back to town, having a good salary, taking up where she had left off with all her old friends was really appealing. But then she thought about her old job. She was a good worker and diligent, but had felt bored and trapped in a day-to-day routine and never felt she was accomplishing much. The last few months, however, had been totally different . . .

Okay, financially they had been a disaster, but in terms of enjoying what she was doing, they had absolutely been a total turnaround. She loved staying in Mossbawn and helping Molly. Designing websites and getting them up and running and managing them was a challenge, something she really enjoyed, and she would love to try to develop more and set up a proper business, as every client and every day was different. Then there was Luke.

When she thought of Luke, she couldn't help but smile. He made her feel happy, made her feel special in a way that Gareth never had. She couldn't imagine her life without him, but she knew that he would not move back to the city. He had turned away from his job in finance in London to come back to Kilfinn and to build the kind of life he wanted. And in her heart she knew that wasn't going to change.

As she passed hedgerows and fields and farms, she felt herself automatically beginning to unwind, relax and slow down. Luke had texted her and called her a few times earlier, but his phone was on silent when she tried to return the call, which meant he was in class.

Arriving in the village, she parked her car across from the school. One class was singing, their voices floating from the open window, others were kicking a football in the school yard. Fifteen minutes later the bell rang and she watched as the kids began to stream out, some climbing on to the school buses, some being collected by their parents, and others laughing and chatting as they walked home. A few minutes later she saw him coming across the yard with another teacher, talking and saying hello to kids and mothers as he came through the school gate. She stood up and he saw her, his eyes immediately lighting up. She could feel her heart jump as he came nearer.

'Hey, Kim, I wasn't expecting you,' he said, hugging her. 'How did your interview go?'

'Fine,' she smiled. 'Do you want to go for a walk?'

'That sounds ominous!' he teased.

Luke put his bag of books and copybooks in the car and the two of them decided to take a walk down by the river where it was peaceful and quiet.

'Well, how did it go in Dublin? You're moving back – is that it?' he asked, grabbing her hand and looking into her face.

She swallowed hard. She loved him, couldn't bear to be apart from him. Luke Ryan was the best thing that had happened to her in such a long time. She couldn't – she wouldn't – jeopardize it!

'The interview was awful. Mark was trying to pull me apart and as for that German man, the questions he asked were totally out of order. Anyway, whatever I said about salary and holidays, it didn't go down well. They were obviously very polite, but it was clear that they had no interest in continuing on,' she lied.

'Maybe you've got it wrong,' he consoled her.

'No. Mark talked to me afterwards on the way to the elevator. He told me that they had already interviewed a more suitable candidate. He's such a shit!'

'I'm sorry, Kim, really sorry. I know that you had your hopes up about this job,' he said, pulling her into his arms. It felt so good there . . .

'So, there's no new job!' she said trying to sound disappointed. 'So unfortunately you're still stuck with me here in Kilfinn.'

'Kim, that stupid company has no idea what they are missing!' he said vehemently. 'But their loss is our gain. I'll take you to dinner tonight to cheer you up. What about going over to the Mill House in Glengarry for an early-bird special?'

'Sounds lovely,' she smiled, trying to hide her relief.

Looking into his eyes, Kim knew that she had definitely made the right decision. She would contact Joanne, talk to Mark, tell them that she was sorry but unfortunately she was turning down their job offer.

Chapter Sixty-six

Kim stared nervously at the computer screen. She had worked so hard at this that she couldn't bear for it to go wrong. She had tested out various templates for the site before finding the right one and had also decided with Molly on the right font to use. For the background she had tried so many options and then one day, looking at the old, soft, flower-patterned wallpaper in her bedroom, it had come to her that that might work, combined with an illustration of the house that she had discovered hanging in her uncle's study. Molly really liked it and now everything was uploaded and it looked exactly as she had intended.

'There will always be hitches and gremlins!' Piotr had advised her as she showed him everything in detail and he checked it during a trial run.

She had uploaded photos of Mossbawn House and

the garden through the seasons, the history of the old Georgian house with the family tree and portraits, as well as old photographs of Charles Moore and his wife, Constance. There were details from his sketchbooks and original designs for the garden, and pictures of his tools and even of pages from his garden diary. There were photos of the borders and lawn, the maze and the walled kitchen garden, and one section was devoted to the rose garden. Then, in a separate section, she had put up events at Mossbawn, with a few photos of Libby's wedding and the orangery lit up at night, tables set, flower arrangements, Daisy with a pink bow tied to her collar, champagne and wedding cake. It all looked cool and inviting.

She knew that Molly was worried about it and what people's reactions would be, but Kim was so pleased that Mossbawn and its history would now finally have the web presence it deserved. She would add more pages in time. There was also a Facebook page about Mossbawn House, which she promised Molly that she would manage closely.

A few minutes later, at midday, it went live.

Kim web-texted everyone to tell them and prayed that Mossbawn would interest people the same way the old house and gardens had always fascinated her.

When Molly Hennessy looked at the screen, she couldn't believe it. Most old houses were just a dusty mention in a parish history, or had a small brochure or leaflet printed about them. Yet here was Mossbawn House – their house – preserved for ever, standing proudly surrounded by the garden, the lawn, the avenue of rhododendrons. She felt overcome.

'Kim, I can never thank you enough for what you've done!' Molly felt so emotional. 'It's amazing, truly amazing. If David were here he would love it. He was such a techie compared to me! Mossbawn will live for ever. We have to celebrate!' she insisted. 'I have a bottle of champagne in the fridge that I have been saving for a special occasion – for something good!'

'Molly – it's just a website!'

Molly fixed her with a look she knew well. 'Really?'

'It does look really good, doesn't it!' Kim laughed. 'I can't believe how well some of my photos turned out, and we were so lucky to be able to find so much about Charles and his family.'

'Champagne!' Molly grabbed the bottle and opened it, filling their two glasses to overflowing. 'You putting Mossbawn up on the web like this certainly calls for a celebration!'

Kim could see she was getting lots of texts and emails and messages for the site already. Emma and Grace were as delighted as Molly at the results, and even her dad was chuffed!

'Kim I'm very proud of you! Dad'

'Hey Kim, great place! If I ever find a guy to marry will have my wedding there! Lisa'

'Love it, Love you, Luke'

'Well done Kim! Gareth'

She laughed. She must have sent the message to everyone, even Gareth!

385

Chapter Sixty-seven

Molly did a last quick check around the house. There were flowers everywhere, and in the orangery Gina had put up a few tables set with crisp white linen, flowers and glasses, as Mary and Sean Kennedy, a couple who were planning to celebrate their fiftieth wedding anniversary with a big family dinner, were coming to see the house along with a son and a daughter.

Saturday was busy, as later in the afternoon two couples who had only just got engaged were also coming to see the place, as well as an older couple who wanted to hold a small post-civil-wedding meal. The website was certainly attracting lots of people and Mossbawn House had got very positive reviews on two of the big wedding sites.

She had lit lots of tea lights and candles everywhere, and the fire was warm and aglow, with soft classical music playing in the background. She had just taken a plate of biscuits from the oven when she heard the first people arrive and she ran to the front door to let them in.

'Come in out of the rain,' she said, leading them inside. She hoped that it would clear up so that at least they would get a chance to see the garden properly. 'You are very welcome to Mossbawn House.'

As she walked them around, she discovered that the older couple wanted to celebrate their golden wedding anniversary in style.

'We were poor as church mice when we got married and had sixteen to a meal in the Metropole Hotel, worried how we were going to even pay for it!' confided Mary, a sprightly seventy-two-year-old.

'We went to Killarney for our honeymoon and it rained every day,' added Sean, laughing. 'Not that we noticed it that much!'

'Life has been good to us, so now we want to celebrate the anniversary properly, with all the children and our grandchildren and family and friends around us. But do it properly!'

'Do it in style!'

Molly smiled as she led them from room to room. They were such a lovely couple. She opened the door into the orangery.

'Sean, this is exactly what we are looking for!' Mary was excited as she walked around it, looking at the tables and at the fabulous view of the garden.

'There's plenty of space,' remarked her daughter, Jane.

'What I like about it,' added Sean, 'is that it's not at all like a hotel.'

Molly showed them around the house, suggesting they have arrival drinks in the drawing room and, if the weather permitted, on the terrace with its view of the pond and garden. Then the meal would be served in the orangery. She went through things with them for the next half-hour, teasing out exactly what they wanted for their family party.

'Flowers on the tables are freshly cut from our garden and we would also try to use as many seasonal vegetables and herbs and salads from our kitchen garden as possible for the meal,' Molly smiled. She could see that had impressed them. 'I see it's just started to dry up outside. Why don't I give you all a bit of a tour of the garden? There are some lovely places for family photographs.'

Outside, she brought them around the pond and the walled garden, the lawn, and finished up in the rose garden.

'Mary's a great rose woman,' teased Sean. 'We grow them at home. This is a perfect spot for photographs of the two of us.'

Molly could see that Mary was quite knowledgeable about roses.

'This is a special garden,' Mary said, impressed, 'with real old-world style! It's lovely here and it's exactly what we want.'

'Then let's just go ahead and book it!' said Sean decisively as they went back inside.

Kim had made Molly buy a large, expensive, leather-bound desk diary to impress people, and she pulled the book from the drawer in the hall and took down all the Kennedys' personal details and contact numbers as she booked in their golden anniversary party for three weeks' time.

Just as they were about to leave, Sean and Mary asked if they could take another look at the orangery. Standing there hand in hand, it was clear that they were still mad about each other.

'What a lovely couple!' she thought, pleased to be having their anniversary party here in Mossbawn.

When Kim came over on Monday, she couldn't believe that Molly had three bookings already: a wedding in late August, a wedding in mid-October and the golden wedding anniversary party on the very last Saturday in June.

Chapter Sixty-eight

Kim lay in Luke's arms. She loved watching him sleep. He was so calm and reassuring. Last night they had gone for dinner with a few of his friends and to a gig with The Coronas playing afterwards. They'd had a great time and hadn't got home till all hours. Spending most of Sunday in bed was very tempting.

She looked at him. She was mad about him in a way that she had never ever been before. She really, really liked him as a friend and not just a boyfriend. She could talk to Luke about anything and he wouldn't be fazed. He was kind and good-hearted and old-fashioned, mad on animals; he'd punch anyone who hurt a horse or a dog. Luke was obsessed with history and Celtic legends, a big follower of the local hurling team. He'd taken her to a few of their matches and she had struggled to understand what was happening, which had made him laugh instead of getting annoyed. He loved curry, hated bananas, had a thing about yellow and wore these weird Dennis the Menace slippers around his house. And already she loved him.

'Are you awake?' he asked, yawning heavily.

'Yes.'

'What are you doing?'

'Watching you,' she teased, snuggling in beside him. 'Sometimes you say a word or two.'

'What?'

'Honestly you do!' she persisted. 'Like . . . "banana"!'

'Never!' he laughed, pulling her under the bedclothes.

A long time later, as they lay listening to traffic and kids playing out in the street, Kim began to get up.

'We should eat, get some breakfast.'

'I want you to stay,' he said softly, running his finger along her spine.

'We should get up – it's really late . . .'

'I want you to stay here,' he said, serious. 'I don't mean just now, today. I want you to move in with me, for us to live together.'

Kim stopped for a few seconds, considering.

'What's brought this on?' she teased, looking at him.

'Well, you know Sinead and her boyfriend are moving in together.'

'I know they were talking about it.'

'Well, they're leaving in three weeks' time,' he continued. 'They've bought a place in Castlecomer. It needs a bit of doing up, but they want to move in once they get the keys.'

'So you want another housemate to move in and help pay the rent, is that it?'

'No!' he protested. 'That's not it! The fact that they are leaving just makes it easier.'

'What about Alan? You want me to move in here with the two of you?'

'No, I already told Alan that if you agree to move in he needs to find somewhere else to live. He's chilled about it.'

Kim didn't know what to say.

'We are both crazy about each other,' he said softly, 'so I think it is high time we gave living together a chance.'

'You're sure?' she hesitated.

'Yes, I mean it.'

'I've already lived with Gareth.'

'And I lived with Alison,' he replied. 'But this time it will be different, because we are different together. We both know it's what we want – to be together all the time. It's the next step, and we both want to take it.'

Kim laughed. She was moving in with Luke! She'd see him first thing every morning, last thing every night. Living with him was definitely what she wanted. She knew that saying yes meant committing to staying here, to staying with him. This time was so different, nothing like before – because she truly loved him.

Chapter Sixty-nine

With the summer days, Molly was working at full tilt in the garden. The herbaceous borders around the house and along the walkway were glorious and bursting with colour, the kitchen garden flourishing with the first crops of summer vegetables. In her rose garden the climbing roses she was training up the walls and frames, arches and gazebo had all suddenly put on a stretch and were beginning to cover them. The smaller shrub roses of Gertrude Jekyll, which she had repeated through the beds, were beginning to flourish too in the warm weather, as the first buds began to appear. She had twenty-eight varieties growing in the rose garden, something she was very proud of, each chosen with great care. The beds were edged with box or bay or lavender, and along with feeding her roses she was keeping an obsessive eye out for any signs of black spot or rust or mildew.

'Molly!'

She looked up. It was Cara. She'd totally forgotten the time. She'd invited her over for lunch last week.

'I rang the bell a few times and tried your phone,' Cara laughed, 'but I guessed you'd be out here somewhere working!'

Molly had intended changing out of her gardening clothes before Cara arrived but here she was in an old T-shirt and baggy jeans, her hair scrunched up in a hairband and with dirt under her fingernails.

'Sorry, I didn't realize the time!'

'It's fine Molly, honestly – it's only me! I love this new garden of yours!' she said, walking around looking at the beds and the painted gazebo, and the archways of tumbling pink roses. She sat down on one of the benches.

'It's been a lot of hard work trying to recreate the original rose garden that Charles Moore planted, but I think I've succeeded,' she said proudly. 'Later in the summer, with all the roses blooming, it will be wonderful. And next summer even better. The one thing roses need is time.'

'It's beautiful! And you've so many roses.'

'It's been a bit of an obsession, trying to get it right, but I'm glad you like it. Here, let me give you a nice bunch to take home,' she said, going to her bed of roses for cutting and getting a bunch of varied colours for Cara. 'Now, let's get that lunch I promised you.'

'How's the work going on the cottage?' Cara asked as they walked back to the house.

'Great! Paul says it should be finished in a few weeks.'

Molly changed out of her gardening boots and washed her hands.

'I've made stuffed peppers and salad.'

'Sounds delicious!' replied Cara with a smile, setting the table.

Over lunch Molly showed Cara some photos of her holiday in Italy.

'That holiday did you a lot of good!'

'I know! Poor Roz had to practically drag me away, but the break was great because it made me realize that selling Mossbawn would have been a huge mistake,' Molly admitted. 'I'm so much happier now with getting the cottage and house sorted.'

'I heard that you've a few weddings booked in already!'

'Who told you?'

'I bumped into Kim and Luke the other night in the Kilfinn Inn.'

'Kim's done an amazing job on the website and she's already put up a gallery of some of our events in the house and garden.'

'She and Luke Ryan make a lovely couple.'

'I know. They seem to be crazy about each other.'

'God, I wish I could find some nice girl for Danny. Remember that awful anorexic girl he went out with last year, with her hot yoga and weird faddy-food diet? Tim and I were at our wits' end.'

'He's only young!' Molly laughed as she put on the kettle for coffee. 'Give him a chance.'

'Molly, the golf club barbecue is on next week. We were wondering if you wanted to come?'

Molly hesitated. She and David had gone to the club's summer barbecue almost every year. Kilfinn was only a small local golf club and it was their annual shindig with most members and their partners going. The club had sent her a lovely letter following David's death, saying how much he would be missed.

Cara and Tim and all her friends had been so good to her this past eighteen months. She'd have been lost without them.

'Of course I'm coming,' she promised. 'David would want me to go.'

Grace had driven her to the golf club.

'Are you going to be okay, Mum?' she asked anxiously. 'If you need me, phone and I'll come and get you.'

'I'll be fine,' Molly said, trying to compose herself, remembering all the times she had dropped David here or collected him, nights they had popped into the small clubhouse for a drink, or for a Sunday lunch with the girls. David had loved the old wooden clubhouse with its eighteen-hole golf course and the bar overlooking the river.

'Hey, Molly! We're here!' shouted Cara.

The smell of the barbecue filled the air and everyone was outside, standing around having a few drinks. Half the town was here, so it really was very much a local affair. Molly was relieved as everyone welcomed her.

'Trish and Larry are slightly delayed,' said Tim, getting her a glass of wine, 'but they're on the way.'

Molly was surprised to find Rob Hayes there, chatting to Peter and Avril.

'Molly, nice to see you again,' he said politely. 'I was playing golf with Tim this afternoon. I've joined the club. So when he heard that I had no plans for tonight he insisted that I join you all.'

'Well, I'm glad you came along,' she replied, with a smile.

'How's your house sale going?' he asked.

'It's not!' she laughed. 'I took Mossbawn off the market. The house means far too much to me to sell it, but it's going to have to help pay for itself. So we're going to hold a few weddings and special events in the house every year, which should help financially.'

'That sounds like a very good idea!' he said admiringly.

'I hope so. I'm a bit nervous about it – well, about doing it all on my own,' she admitted.

'You seem to be doing fine, Molly – really fine . . .'

As the barbecue was ready, they all took plates and queued for chicken and sausages and burgers before helping themselves to baked potato and side salads then grabbing a table. Sitting between Larry and Rob, Molly was well looked after as they both made sure her glass was topped up with Rioja.

Rob filled her in on the upcoming opening of the plant. 'A few people will come from Boston and our

Swedish office, and there'll be an official opening with a fancy dinner after.'

'It sounds fun!'

'Hopefully – that's the plan,' he said, smiling as he passed her the barbecue sauce.

After dessert Molly changed places so that the girls were sitting at one end of the table and the guys at the other, the conversations running in two totally different directions. It was after midnight when they finally left the clubhouse. Molly shared a taxi with Cara and Tim, who insisted on giving her a lift home and dropping her right at her doorstep.

'Thanks so much,' she said, hugging them both. 'I'm so lucky to have such good friends!'

'Same here,' replied Cara, watching her go inside and lock the door.

Molly was busy making up the floral table arrangements for tomorrow's golden wedding anniversary party. Sean and Mary Kennedy were a wonderful pair with five children, sixteen grandchildren and three great-grandchildren. Their daughters were organizing it all and there was family coming from Canada, Brussels, Dubai and London to celebrate at Mossbawn House.

Suddenly Daisy began to bark like crazy and, putting down the flowers, Molly went to see who was at the door.

It was Rob Hayes.

'Hello!' he said. 'I hope I haven't got you at a bad time.'

'Not at all! Come inside. I'm just down in the kitchen doing some flowers.'

'I hope I'm not disturbing you, but I wanted to call to ask you about using Mossbawn, if it's available, for having a meal after the opening drinks reception for the plant.'

'What date is it, Rob?' she asked, reaching for the bookings diary.

'In less than three weeks. The opening is in the plant itself but, as I was saying to you the other night, we need to go on somewhere close by afterwards for dinner and drinks. Kilkenny's a bit far. We were considering the Woodlands, but having a dinner here in an old Irish country house would be far more impressive.'

'We've nothing booked in for then,' Molly agreed. 'Why don't I show you the rooms?'

'There must have been some great dinners held here!' he said, admiring the dining room.

Rob was an interesting man, intelligent and bright. She was surprised by the way he recognized the makers of the table and chairs and sideboard.

'You have an interest in the furniture of the period?'

'My dad was a carpenter. He spent most of his time building wardrobes and kitchens and putting in floors and stairs, but at heart he was a craftsman. He made some beautiful pieces of furniture and had a huge respect for the craftsmen of old and their work.'

'He sounds a nice man.'

'He was old-fashioned and decent. Never earned that much, but he was proud of his work and of us, his family. He hoped I'd follow him into the trade, but my passion was engineering. I was all fingers and thumbs when it came to woodwork. I nearly chopped off my finger one time!' Rob laughed, showing her his middle finger, which was scarred and rather swollen.

Molly led him into the orangery.

'This is some room!' he exclaimed, amazed. 'It feels like you are outside although you are inside. It's perfect for what we want. Maybe there could be a little music to welcome everyone?'

'A harp or violin playing?'

'Nah – I was thinking more along the lines of a bit of light jazz or something.'

Molly loved jazz. It was her secret passion.

'I know a good local jazz trio,' she offered, 'so leave that with me.'

A few minutes later Molly was giving him the details and costs for hiring the house and handing him a copy of Gina's menus.

'I'll talk to her about the food,' he promised, 'but can you book us in for having the post-launch dinner here?'

She smiled. He certainly was decisive.

After tea Molly was curled up in the chair in the kitchen reading her copy of James Joyce's *Dubliners*, her book club's latest choice. Soon she was lost in the short stories of a master. The next meeting of their book club was here in Mossbawn on Tuesday. She looked forward to these meetings, where people of all ages got together to talk about books. She had already picked out her choice for next month: *The Secret Garden,* a classic and so well loved.

There was a text message on her phone and she checked it.

'Thanks for showing me around your beautiful home, Rob.'

He really was a nice man, she thought – really nice.

Chapter Seventy

Gina checked the table layouts. The church service should be finishing, with guests arriving in about fifteen to twenty minutes. Everything looked perfect. Inga had the champagne flutes set up and tall mojito glasses prepared; Brendan was ready to make up jugs of the cocktail for the guests on arrival. The weather was glorious and the drinks would be served out on the lawn, where they had set up tables and chairs and parasols. Kim had told her it would be a fun and rather stylish wedding, as the bride worked designing film and theatre costumes and her partner was a film editor. The garden looked amazing. Molly had had Paddy and Tommy cut the grass the day before and the flowerbeds were bursting with colour. The lamb was roasting in the oven and everything was running smoothly, with plans to serve in about two hours. This week had been busy, with the dinner for the launch of that new bio-engineering company on Thursday night. There had been a big crowd attending that, but it had all gone perfectly.

Looking at the diary, they seemed to have a good range of bookings for the months ahead. She enjoyed the fact that she knew where she was and what she was doing and that prices were pretty much set by people's menu choice.

'I think at the moment one wedding a week or at the weekend is plenty for us to manage,' Molly had insisted. 'I have no intention of letting Mossbawn become one of these places that has one couple going out the door when another is coming in. We have something very special here and we need to hold on to the fact that visiting Mossbawn is a unique and rare experience.'

Gina totally agreed and felt if they held another, smaller event or celebration during the week that would be ideal. The diary gave her a very good picture of planning the coming months and deciding if she needed to hire serving or bar staff. She still missed the café and working with Norah and meeting all the customers. Now her job was very different and involved working evenings and late on a Friday or Saturday. Kim's website certainly had done the trick: it was getting attention and attracting people to Mossbawn House and Gardens.

The three of them worked well together. Molly and Kim dealt with all the initial enquiries about the house and then later Gina was the one who met people to discuss the function they were planning with detailed menus, costings and wine lists. That was something she really enjoyed – tailoring the event to what they wanted.

Andrew Lynch, the manager of the Woodlands Hotel, had arranged to meet Molly, Kim and herself about Mossbawn's new plans.

'We don't intend to compete with you,' Molly assured him. 'The kind of weddings and functions we are doing are first of all limited by the size of the house itself, and also we have no intention of taking on large functions.'

'I know that. The kind of person who wants to hold a gathering or meal or wedding in Mossbawn is not interested in the kind of function space we offer,' he ruefully admitted, 'but what we would hope is that the Woodlands could offer guests attending here a special room rate and even a family meal the night before the wedding. Attracting visitors to a country hotel is tough, as we all know, in this climate! I think having Mossbawn House so close to us is a positive.'

'That's nice to hear,' said Molly with a smile, 'and it should be no problem. We all need to pull together, help each other out. Gina and I are doing our best to source most of our meat and fish and vegetables and cheese locally.'

Gina smiled. Andrew Lynch might only be young, but he had a very good business brain and recognized an opportunity when he saw it.

In three weeks' time they were hosting a big family reunion over two days. A sit-down meal, drinks reception and a barbecue and family picnic for young and old in the garden. It was the O'Flynn clan family gathering, with O'Flynns returning from Chicago and New York to meet up with all the Irish side of the family who lived in the Kilfinn and Glengarry area. Gina was trying to create a menu that would suit everyone and yet was firmly traditional. Andrew had organized rooms and car hire for all those that needed them.

'Gina, you're busier than ever!' teased Paul. 'At this rate I'll have to book a Saturday night to take you out.'

'We can go out on a Thursday or maybe a Friday!' she joked. 'But if we have a function, Saturday is my busy night. I have to make sure everything is right. It's my responsibility.'

'I know you do, love,' he said. 'You are the best organizer I know, but that doesn't mean we can't have some time for ourselves.'

Gina knew he was right. There had to be more than just work and the kids. Paul was getting a lot more work lately and was doing a great job on the renovation of Molly's cottage.

'So I've booked for us to go away to Kinsale for two nights,' he said, brooking no arguments. 'Your sister will mind the kids while we have a break. God knows you deserve it. I've booked a few fancy restaurants and our hotel is the big one overlooking the water.'

'Can we afford it?' she asked, worried.

'I got a great deal because we are going mid-week.' He laughed. 'And I checked with Molly to make sure that you were free!'

Gina hugged him. Paul was the best husband ever. He was so kind and thoughtful. Even if he hadn't a penny he would treat her to something. Two nights away was paradise. She loved Kinsale with all its restaurants and cafés and bars. The Cork fishing village was a renowned foodie paradise, with some great fish restaurants and chefs. She couldn't wait for their romantic break.

Ellie Gould, the bride, looked stunning in a bejewelled, floor-length, thirties-style dress which showed off her tall, slim figure and striking red hair. The wedding meal had gone smoothly and the speeches had been hilarious, everyone relaxed and at ease as the bride and groom's three children ran around the place. They cleared away some tables from the orangery for dancing; there would be a DJ later, but as three members of one of the country's well-known rock bands were guests, they would perform a few numbers first. Just before twelve there would be fireworks in the garden, followed by midnight snacks. The night was warm, so many of the guests were drifting in and out of the orangery to chat and smoke.

Gina finished clearing up and checked her phone, which she had put on silent for the past few hours. There was a message from her sister and one from a number she didn't recognize an hour ago. She phoned it back.

'Oh Gina, it's Marian from Beech Hill nursing home. I'm sorry it's so late, but I was just phoning to let you know that Norah Cassidy passed away very peacefully a few hours ago. I know you were a friend of hers and I thought you should know.'

'Oh Marian, thanks. What happened to her?'

'Nothing dramatic, really. She'd had her tea and was sitting in the chair in her room watching the TV. One of our nurses went in to help her get changed and ready for bed and she thought at first Norah had dozed off, but then realized that she had passed away peacefully in the chair . . .'

'Oh, I'm sorry to hear she's gone! I saw her last week, but to be honest I don't think she had a clue who I was, though she enjoyed having a bit of company.'

'She was a nice woman. I've informed her family, but I know you were very good to her, Gina.'

'Marian, thanks for letting me know – I appreciate it.'

Gina walked outside to gather herself.

The fireworks had already started, crowds everywhere on the lawn as the explosions of noise and colours and shooting flames lit up the night sky. As she looked up in the darkness she thought of Norah. She would miss the old woman, but was so glad she was finally free of old age and illness.

Chapter Seventy-one

Gina Sullivan couldn't believe it when Michael Quinn, the solicitor, asked her to come to a meeting with the other beneficiaries of Norah's will in his office two days after Norah's funeral.

The funeral had been a big one, attended by all the people of Kilfinn who had enjoyed the hospitality of Norah's café over the years. Father Darragh said the mass and spoke some lovely words about Norah and her life lived in the heart of Kilfinn village and parish.

'Norah never needed to travel, as her life was enriched by those around her. And there were many whose lives she touched, whether it was a cup of coffee for a poor man, an apple tart for a friend, or a birthday cake for a family that were struggling. Norah could always be relied on to help those who were in need.'

Norah was buried simply and without fuss in the

local graveyard beside her parents, with a roast-beef lunch held in the Kilfinn Inn afterwards.

Paul came to the meeting with Gina. Norah's nephew and cousin were there, sitting in front of them, and Father Darragh was also present as Michael read out the will, which had been written almost two years ago. There was a generous donation to the parish-church restoration fund and to the local Vincent de Paul Society, which Father Darragh helped to run. There was also a donation to the County Cats Rescue Society, and money for an overseas charity working with women in Africa.

Gina couldn't believe it when she was named as the next beneficiary, with the remainder of Norah's estate to be divided equally between her remaining family.

'As you all know, even though Norah's business and home had been sold prior to her death, there were certain costs with regard to her nursing and medical care and other expenses, but I have prepared a letter detailing the amount each of you will receive once probate has been granted,' Michael said, distributing copies to everyone.

From the sharp intake of breath when he opened his letter, Gina could tell that Norah's nephew, Martin Cassidy, was disappointed. Father Darragh's eyes were shining as he read his letter. Gina was nervous opening hers.

First off she had been left all Norah's collection of cookery books. She smiled. They were classics, all currently stored in various boxes in their garage. The next part she could hardly believe. Norah had also left her money, a very large amount: twenty thousand euro! It was so generous. Norah knew how much she and Paul had struggled financially when she first came to work for her. Paul took the letter from her hands to read it.

'She was very fond of you, Gina. You know that.'

She nodded, so glad that she had made the effort to keep up their special friendship till the end, but still she couldn't believe it. Thanks to Norah she was going to have money in the bank – money she intended to use well, and in a way of which Norah Cassidy would approve.

'What the hell has my aunt done?' protested Martin, standing up. 'Leaving money to a cats' home, to the parish, to a girl who worked in the café for her . . . Norah was gone soft in the head and people were taking advantage of her. She was senile – this isn't right. I am objecting legally to whatever has gone on here. Norah's own flesh and blood have been almost cut out of her will!'

'Your aunt has been quite generous in her bequest to family members,' the solicitor pointed out.

'I object to your tone,' said Father Darragh coldly. 'Your aunt was a parishioner in St Patrick's in Kilfinn all her life. It is not unusual for our parishioners to remember us in their wills.'

'And she loved cats,' added Gina. 'You ask anyone in Beech Hill!'

'You influenced her. I'm surprised she didn't leave

you everything! You were the one around her . . . You tricked her, Gina, when she was gone into that home and got her to sign the will.'

Gina swallowed hard. She'd had absolutely nothing to do with Norah's will.

'I had no idea Norah would leave me anything,' she protested. 'Honestly, Martin, I didn't expect anything from her except her friendship.'

'Mr Cassidy, these kinds of accusations do no good,' said the solicitor. 'As a matter of fact, your aunt wrote this will here in my office about fifteen months before her illness. She was totally of sound mind and very competently running her own business at the time.'

Martin Cassidy suddenly looked deflated.

'My duty is to carry out your aunt's wishes and that is what I intend doing,' Michael Quinn continued, brooking no further argument as Martin and his wife got up angrily and left his office.

Chapter Seventy-two

Molly had been surprised when Rob Hayes phoned to ask her to come to a jazz night in the Store House on Saturday.

'I wanted to say thank you for letting us use Mossbawn. It was the perfect venue and our chairman and my colleagues were most impressed.'

'That's good to hear.'

'Johnny Kershaw and Drew Fox are playing there and Dianne Rubin is singing. It's a great line-up,' he said excitedly. 'It's totally sold out, but I managed to nab two tickets because I know you are a bit of a fan, like me.'

'Rob, it's so nice of you to ask me,' she said, without even thinking. 'I'd love to come. I saw Dianne a few years ago at the Cork Jazz Festival and she was amazing.'

'Well, I'm looking forward to it.' He sounded pleased. 'I'll pick you up about seven thirty.'

Afterwards she sat staring at her phone, asking, 'What the hell have I done? I've agreed to go out with Rob Hayes. What if he thinks it's a date or something like that?'

She phoned Cara immediately as she was in such a quandary about accepting.

'Molly Hennessy, don't you dare say no to Rob. He's a lovely man – you know that!' declared Cara dramatically. 'If he'd have asked me, I'd go with him!'

'And what would Tim say?'

'I mean if Tim was not around, or if Tim was away, of course I'd go,' she replied. 'Rob's good company, intelligent and actually quite good-looking too. And it's not like he's asking you to go away for a dirty weekend with him or something like that. It's just a bloody concert!'

'I suppose you're right.'

'Of course I'm right. It's just tickets to a concert, Molly, and Rob is trying to be nice.'

'You're right, Cara . . . I'm just over-thinking it,' she agreed as they finished the call.

She spent most of Saturday in the garden, directing Paddy and young Tommy as they edged all the pathways and cut and trimmed the hedges beside them so that they looked neat and structured. Then she showered quickly, washed her hair and slipped into a pair of taupe linen trousers with a linen-mix top. It was a warm night, but she decided to bring her warm cream wrap just in case she needed it later. Lip gloss, perfume and she was good to go.

Rob was very prompt and chatted easily as they drove to Kilkenny.

'I'll collect the car tomorrow,' he said as they pulled up into one of the town's car parks.

The Store House was already busy but they managed to find a table for two quite near the stage.

'Molly, I'm so glad that you could make it,' beamed Rob, 'otherwise I'd be sitting here on my own.'

'I'm sure there would be lots of takers for tonight!' she replied with a smile.

'People have their own things on at the weekend. Don't you find that?' he asked.

Molly hadn't really thought about it. She was happy at the moment to be on her own.

'Don't get me wrong – I'm not complaining,' he continued as the waitress served their drinks. 'It's just that it's nice to have company sometimes, someone to talk to, go to a movie or concert with . . . have a meal with rather than always eating alone.'

'I know what you mean.' She sighed in recognition of his sentiments. 'David and I loved going to dinner on Friday night – just the two of us, somewhere local, no big deal. It was kind of a routine since the kids grew up. It's funny, but I miss those Fridays more than anything.'

Rob was easy to talk to and she soon found herself telling him all about her cottage and the rose garden.

'Obviously I still have Mossbawn, but now with the

414

house getting busier at the weekends it will be nice to escape to the peace and quiet in my cottage. I hope to move in there in a few days' time.'

'You certainly are a busy lady,' he said approvingly. 'I must come and visit this garden of yours.'

'I'll give you a tour,' she promised.

'I've moved too,' he confided. 'With the plant open, I decided to rent an apartment in that development in Riverside. At least I have a bit of space for when my kids or friends come to visit.'

After the food was finished and the tables cleared, the lights went down and Johnny came on to introduce the band and straight away kicked into a Miles Davis classic. The band held the crowd as they worked interpretations of Coltrane and Brubeck and Dizzy Gillespie, Drew using his saxophone to captivate the soul of everyone present. Dianne sang everything from Gershwin's 'Summertime' to 'My Funny Valentine' and Billie Holiday's 'Good Morning Heartache', then swung into the mellow *bossa nova* sound of 'Girl from Ipanema'. Johnny launched into the 'Jelly Roll Blues' and they performed a few of their own songs before finishing with their rendition of 'Fever'.

'What an amazing night!' said Molly as she thanked him. 'I'm so glad that you asked me along.'

'It was pretty special all right,' he smiled, delighted. 'How about one last drink before we head for the hills?'

An hour later they were still chatting. Molly thought again what good, easy company he was.

'I hope that we can do this again sometime?' he

asked, as they went outside to pick up a taxi on the main street.

'I'd like that,' she said, realizing that she genuinely meant it. She really had enjoyed the night – not just the music and concert, but being with him, feeling relaxed and able to talk together. It was as if Rob understood what it was like for her to be alone . . .

The perfect gentleman, he dropped her home to Mossbawn first before going on in the taxi to his own place. Daisy was sitting in her bed in the kitchen, waiting patiently for her. She opened the back door for the dog to go out and made herself a cup of decaf tea. She smiled at a text message from Cara:

'*Hope u are home safe and sound and enjoyed the concert!*'

She laughed at Cara checking up on her and immediately phoned her back.

'You were right – I had a great time,' she said, sitting down on the couch for a chat.

Chapter Seventy-three

Moving day, and the weather was bright, sunny and dry. All the building work was done and the Gardener's Cottage was finally ready. Paul Sullivan had gone through a complete building snag list with Trish and herself to ensure everything was functioning perfectly and that nothing had been overlooked. He was a very thorough type of man, reliable and trustworthy, and had done an amazing job converting the empty old cottage for modern living.

Molly still couldn't believe how well it had all turned out. The small, poky cottage was now airy and bright, the painting finished, the colour scheme of soft whites and buttery creams making it seem more spacious, the new modern kitchen fitted, with its oven and hob and fridge-freezer and washing machine all working properly. She knew that she was taking the right step by downsizing and moving in here.

She was taking a few favourite pieces of furniture from Mossbawn – a cherrywood desk, a coffee table, a bookcase and some ornaments, but otherwise most things were brand new. She'd had such fun shopping for her new home with Grace and Emma over the past few weeks. A couch and armchairs, a circular painted dining table, plates, towels, bed linen – everything was new. She had also treated herself to a new king-size bed and fitted wardrobes for her sunny bedroom and two new beds that could be made into a double bed for the other bedroom.

She was nervous about the move, but standing in the cottage gave her an immense sense of peace, calm and independence – something she had yearned for since David's death.

'What a lovely day for moving!' remarked Grace as they ate breakfast together.

'Paddy and Tommy are coming at eleven to move the bookcase and the desk and some of my heavier things.' Molly smiled, realizing that today's move really was happening.

'And I'll help you with all your clothes and shoes and the things you need.'

'I'm leaving some of my very heavy winter clothes and boots in the wardrobe in the Willow Room,' she explained. 'I don't want the place to be cluttered and to be squashed out the door on day one!'

'Mum, leave whatever you want here!' chided Grace. 'This is still your home. You know that.'

'Of course, love, but I'm really looking forward to moving into the cottage.'

Molly got dressed into her jeans and a T-shirt quickly, ready to supervise Paddy and Tommy moving the furniture, and to direct them where to put everything in the cottage.

'The desk is going in my bedroom – there, near the window. The bookcase is for the living room on the far side of the fireplace. The coffee table – try it there near the armchair.'

She and Grace did a number of trips back and forth in the car, moving clothes from one set of wardrobes to the next, knitwear and underwear and shoes. She had carefully packed her books and some family photographs and albums. She wanted to have some familiar things around her in her new home, pride of place given to the photograph she and David had had taken with the girls five years ago, all of them wearing white shirts and tops, all smiling, relaxed and happy, into the camera.

'Mum, do you need any more things?' asked Grace, in her cut-off shorts and checked shirt, flopping down on the couch.

'I think that's it for today,' she agreed, exhausted, as she threw her feet up on the comfy ottoman with Daisy lying down beside her.

She was aching all over and there were still boxes everywhere.

'Maybe we should do the boxes.'

'Not yet!' pleaded Grace. 'We need a break.'

'I've some beer in the fridge. Do you want one?'

A few minutes later they were both stretched out in her new garden chairs in the sunshine, sipping chilled beer and eating bread with pesto and cheese as Daisy rambled around.

'I never imagined this being my first meal in the house!' she laughed.

'I'm sure there will be lots of fancy dinners here, Mum, but this cottage is the perfect place to chill. I really like it. It's so relaxed.'

Later they unpacked some of the boxes and made the beds. Molly felt delighted at the way it was all shaping up. Everything around her looked clean and fresh and totally different from Mossbawn. Tonight she and Grace would just relax and settle in.

They were taking another break from unpacking some of her books when Kim and Luke arrived. Kim had brought her a present of three off-white and pale-blue ceramic bowls, with two serving plates and some matching napkins.

'Kim, they're gorgeous!' she said, appreciatively. 'They go perfectly with the kitchen.'

'That's what I hoped when I saw them in the Design Yard!' her niece beamed, hugging her.

Molly was giving them a quick tour of the place when she spotted Gina and Paul's car pulling up outside.

'I thought maybe you didn't want to cook your first night here,' explained Gina, laughing, as she carried a big pot of chicken casserole and an apple tart into the kitchen, 'so I brought you dinner. There's enough here for two nights.'

'Gina, how thoughtful you are,' Molly said, thanking her.

'You can just pop it in your new oven to heat it up.'

Paul was wandering around each room, taking in how the cottage worked with furniture and beds.

'It looks great, Molly,' he said, approvingly. 'Really great!'

'I'm so pleased with it, Paul. Thank you for all your hard work.'

'Hey, more visitors!' called Grace, opening the door for Cara and Tim.

'Molly, we just had to come over to wish you luck,' Cara said, hugging them both. Tim, following behind her, carried in two boxes of wine, red and white.

'Just a small house-warming gift,' he said, kissing her.

'We are both dying to see the place now that it's all finished,' Cara urged her, looking around.

Molly laughed. Cara always had to be the first with news and to go places.

Cara admired everything. 'It's just so perfect for you! I love all the prints of flowers you've hung around the place. And your bedcover is gorgeous.'

'It's called white rose.'

Tim was fascinated by the way they had managed to create so much space.

'Paul, you've done a great job on the place,' he acknowledged. 'It's far better than most renovations I've seen.'

'It's a very special house,' said Paul softly. 'It just needed some tender loving care to restore it to what it should be, but also to ensure that it was in keeping with the traditions of Mossbawn.'

'Well, you certainly have achieved that.'

'What about a glass of wine, everyone?' Molly offered. 'Let's open some of these bottles! We should celebrate. I was planning on having a house-warming party in a few weeks, but we can have a mini one now.'

'Are you sure?' asked Gina.

'Yes, I'd love a bit of company for my first night here.'

Molly got Grace to root out some more glasses and plates as they spilled out on to the patio.

'I'll put the chicken in the oven and there's lots of French bread, and we've one of Gina's amazing desserts, some beer and, thanks to Tim and Cara, plenty of wine. Please stay!'

Molly couldn't believe it – everyone did stay! They moved between the courtyard garden and the kitchen, eating and drinking and chatting.

'Mum, I know what I'm getting you for here!' Grace teased her. 'A bigger garden table and more chairs!'

In the middle of it all, Emma phoned from Galway.

'Grace just sent me some photos. It looks so gorgeous! I can't believe you've moved in and are already having a bit of a party!' she teased.

'You'll see it all properly next weekend,' Molly promised. 'Everyone's so good, calling in to say hello and check that I am okay.'

*　*　*

A few hours later the last of the visitors had gone, with Jimmy Mac, the local taxi driver, taking everyone home. Molly yawned as she loaded the dishwasher, realizing just how tired she was. Grace had gone upstairs to bed and Daisy was dozing in the kitchen as she locked up, turned off the lights and went to bed.

Climbing into her new bed, she pulled the quilt around her and lay against the pillows. She loved the atmosphere of this new bedroom, with its simplicity and uncluttered feel. The calm and stillness of the cottage seemed to wrap around her, making her relaxed and at home here. As she closed her eyes ready to sleep, she thought of a gardener, alone in this room, surrounded by his books and drawings and plans, finding contentment and acceptance here in this cottage.

Chapter Seventy-four

Kim looked at the screen. She was uploading some more photos of Mossbawn House on to the gallery: the firework display and more wedding photos with quirky details; a photo of Daisy chasing a butterfly and some kids playing in the maze. It all looked great. She had put up a few photos she had taken in the rose garden two weeks ago and had got a huge response on the blog. Two gardening clubs had contacted her, asking her if it was possible to arrange to come and see the garden over the next few weeks. Lots of people were constantly asking about coming to see it and it was something her aunt should consider – opening the gardens for a few weeks or months of the year . . .

Kim was very proud of this site and it was proving very popular. The event calendar for Mossbawn was filling up bit by bit. She kept busy, dealing with enquiries and helping Gina and Molly with the day-to-day running of 'the house'. She was also designing a site for Jenny Costello, a young florist whose work was pretty amazing, as she used a lot of wild flowers and Irish-grown flowers and leaves. She had contacted Kim after seeing the site for Mossbawn House. The business was growing in a way she hadn't expected; for once, work seemed to be finding her!

Her thirtieth birthday was in ten days' time and she was dreading it. How had she gone from celebrating being twenty-one to now being almost a decade older? She had wasted so much time over those years! At least now she was happy and had found Luke, her life turned around so unexpectedly.

Alex and Evie begged her to come to Dublin for the weekend to party with all the old gang, but she wasn't sure that's what she wanted any more.

'Let's have a party here in the house,' suggested Luke. 'All our friends here and your friends from Dublin too. It would be fun! You have to celebrate it!'

'Why don't we just go away somewhere quiet and romantic for the weekend?' she asked, trying to persuade him to change his mind. She really didn't want to think of getting older.

'We can do that another weekend – but this is your birthday!'

Somehow, between Luke and her friends and family, it all snowballed. There would be a barbecue in the house they rented on the Saturday night, with Molly insisting

425

on hosting a big family lunch for her the next day in Mossbawn.

'Kim, if you hadn't come along to stay here, heaven knows what would have happened. The house would be sold or I would be run ragged trying to keep it. You're the one who has given me such encouragement and support and helped to put Mossbawn House on the map,' her aunt said gratefully. 'So the very least I can do is to hold a birthday lunch for you.'

Beginning to get in the party mood, Kim organized accommodation for all her friends in the Woodlands Hotel. Andrew gave them a good rate.

'Am I invited too?' he asked.

'Of course!' she laughed.

The party was shaping up to be really good and she was beginning to look forward to it.

'I told you that you would!' said Luke smugly.

Kim had been busy talking to a locations person from one of the Irish film companies who had spotted Mossbawn on the website and was now interested in hiring the house and gardens for a full month in the winter for shooting a new three-part historical drama. She tried to remain calm and composed at the amount of money being offered.

She would need to check if they had events already booked in during that period, and also it would mean closing the house for events, but the money was incredible! She couldn't wait to tell Molly about it.

Driving home to Kilfinn, she couldn't believe that

somehow she had created a job of her own that was fun, rewarding and, best of all, interesting. Her party was shaping up well too, with most of her friends coming down from Dublin for the weekend. Liz and Joe would stay with them.

'I think we should have our own private little celebration on your actual birthday day,' insisted Luke.

'Can we afford it?' she asked, worried. They were already spending a lot on wine and beer and food for the barbecue and the next day's lunch. 'Maybe we could just get a takeaway and a bottle of wine or something?'

'No, I'm taking you to dinner,' he insisted.

When she woke on Friday morning, Luke had cooked her breakfast and gave her a birthday present of a beautiful silver chain with a circle of gold and silver. She had admired it in the designer workshop in Kilkenny one day when they were wandering around the town.

'Luke, it's stunning thank you so much!' she said, hugging him.

'I'll see you tonight for dinner,' he told her, kissing her again.

All through the day she was getting text messages and calls to wish her happy birthday. Her dad got emotional on the phone when they talked.

'I wish your mum was here at times like this,' he said.

'So do I, Dad,' she said, conscious of the enormous lump in her throat. 'But listen, I'll see you on Sunday.'

Molly had given her a beautiful antique photo frame,

427

some perfume and a massive bunch of flowers from the garden.

'This frame was in the house; we found it in the sideboard when we moved here. I thought it might be nice for you to have it – a little piece of Mossbawn.'

'Oh Molly, I love it,' she said. 'The perfume's my favourite and the flowers will look wonderful in the house for my party.'

'Emma and Grace picked the perfume out,' admitted her aunt as they had soup in the kitchen.

Gina arrived with some special birthday cupcakes.

'I'm making a big batch of them for your birthday lunch here on Sunday!'

Back at home, Kim put her feet up for an hour. It had been a busy day. Realizing the time, she wondered where Luke was. They were going for dinner at eight o'clock, but where was he? She texted him and called him a few times. He must be gone to the farm.

She got changed into her favourite cream lace dress and her nude-coloured heels. Her hair was longer than ever, but Luke liked it that way. She added a little vintage clip to one side as she glanced at the phone.

There was a message from Luke:

'*I can't pick you up so Jimmy Mac will collect you.*'

How strange, she thought. Why would he go and book the local taxi?

A few minutes later Jimmy McCarthy collected her, but he wouldn't give her any idea of where they were going.

'Which restaurant did Luke say?' she quizzed him.

'I'm saying nothing,' he grinned. 'My job is to drive you.'

She looked around. Well, they weren't eating in Kilfinn. Jimmy took the turn outside the village to the road that ran along by the river. A mile or so later, he pulled up at a small jetty with a boat moored to it.

'Why are we stopping?'

'Because we're here!' he said, getting out of the car and opening her door for her.

Suddenly she saw Luke standing on the boat waving at her.

'Be careful!' he warned as she stepped on to the boat – these heels were definitely not a good idea.

Up on the deck a table was set for dinner and fairy lights, strung around the edge of the boat and over the mast and cabin, sparkled in the evening light.

'It's beautiful.' Kim was almost overcome.

'Sit down a minute while I cast off and we get going,' he told her, laughing and hugging her close.

Sitting on the side, she watched as they left the jetty and moved into the middle of the river.

'Whose boat is it?'

'Justin's.'

She stood beside him as they moved along the waterway until they reached a part where the river widened and he turned the boat left, stopping a few minutes later. They were totally alone, the bridge and roadway far in the distance, a group of swans dabbling in the reeds nearby. Luke dropped the anchor and poured her a glass of her favourite wine.

'The day I fell totally in love with you was the day you were down by the river taking photos. Do you remember?'

'Yes.'

'That day I said to myself, this is the girl that I want to . . .' Suddenly he was holding her hand, kneeling down on the wooden deck '. . . ask to marry me. Will you marry me, Kim?'

She felt the breath tight in her throat as he held her hand, his gaze on her.

'Yes. Yes!' she said, beginning to cry.

The ring in the palm of his hand was beautiful, white gold with a simple single diamond. It fitted her finger perfectly.

'Why are you crying?' he teased her, pulling her into his arms.

'I'm so happy, Luke. I'm just so happy.'

She couldn't believe it. She was going to marry Luke, be his wife . . .

'Now we need to really celebrate!' he laughed, making her sit down at the table and pouring her more wine as he served dinner – rosemary chicken with salad and her favourite dessert, ice cream with a hot fudge sauce.

'How did you do all this?' she asked, incredulous. 'I can't believe it!'

'I wanted it all to be a surprise for you,' he said. 'I've been planning it for ages. I've cooked on Justin's boat before – mostly burgers and sausages, but a simple meal wasn't too much of a problem. I knew you liked Killian

Fields designs, so I commissioned him to design the ring for you and I went to Dublin three weeks ago and had lunch with your dad and asked him about marrying you.'

'You are incredible!' Kim burst out laughing. 'I never guessed a thing!'

They sat watching the sun go down, the darkness falling around them, the water slapping against the side of the boat.

'Wait till our friends hear! I can't wait to tell everyone.'

'Can't we wait tonight?' he pleaded, taking her hands in his. 'Just enjoy it.'

Kim knew he was right. This was their time.

'We'll see everyone at the party – let's wait till then,' she agreed.

They stayed on the river for another two hours, planning the future, then Luke turned on the engine and brought the boat back to the jetty to moor. The night was warm and starry as they walked hand in hand along the river path towards home.

Chapter Seventy-five

The small house on Mill Street was crowded. Kim and Luke were in the middle of it all, welcoming their guests, everyone absolutely delighted to hear that not only was Kim celebrating her thirtieth birthday but that she and Luke had just got engaged.

The night was warm and everyone moved outside to the garden where they had put up a few tables with candles and lanterns and tea lights. There was chilled prosecco and beer and lots of wine for everyone. Burgers and sausages were cooking on the barbecue, with big bowls of salad, baby potatoes and plates of crusty French bread.

'Let me see your ring!' screamed Evie the minute she heard the good news. 'I can't believe you're getting married!'

'Neither can I!' laughed Kim. 'It's all happened so

fast, but maybe that is the best way. We are mad about each other and just want to get married and be together for ever.'

She was glad to see that Evie and Fergus seemed to be a real pair. Two artists together!

Alex and Vicky and Lisa and Mel and the gang, all her friends had come.

'I can't believe I dragged you all away from Dublin!' she joked.

'We wouldn't miss it for the world,' Alex said, serious, hugging her and shaking Luke's hand.

Liz and Joe were so delighted for them.

'I can't believe my baby sister is getting married!' Liz cried, her eyes welling with tears.

'I want you to be my bridesmaid and Ava to be my flower girl.'

'Of course,' sniffed Liz, wrapping her in her arms.

Molly was so delighted for her. 'Your mum would be so happy for you, Kim. Luke is one of the good guys, and they are a pretty rare commodity these days.'

'I know. Molly, imagine if I hadn't come to stay with you – I would never have met Luke!'

'I'm glad to have had a little hand in this romance,' her aunt laughed. 'And you know, if you need a nice place for a wedding, Mossbawn is there for you.'

'Oh thank you, Molly. We haven't got around to even thinking that far yet, but you know how much Mossbawn means to me.'

Emma and Grace were delighted that she was going to be staying and living in Kilfinn.

'We'll have our favourite cousin living here! Brilliant!'

'Luke is such a cool guy to marry!' said Grace, slightly enviously.

More and more friends kept arriving, all surprised to find it had become a double celebration.

'When he asked me for the loan of the boat, I guessed something big was brewing!' Justin teased them.

'And you never said a word,' joked his wife, Claire.

'I was under orders!'

'He's not usually good at secrets,' laughed Luke's sister, Melissa.

His parents arrived a little later and came over to them straight away.

'We are both very pleased for you and Luke,' his mother said, smiling as she took Kim's hand and admired her ring. 'Such a beautiful ring. I love the simple design.'

'Thanks!'

'You know that you have made our son very happy,' added his dad. 'And we are both very much looking forward to meeting your family.'

Kim introduced them to Liz and Joe and was delighted to see her dad and Carole suddenly appear. Bill O'Reilly, wearing a blazer and tie, looked so handsome. She could see the emotion in his eyes when he came over towards her.

'Well, my little Kim – celebrating a special birthday and now engaged! I can't believe it. Where have all the years gone?'

'Dad, you never said a word to me about meeting Luke!' she teased.

'He swore me to secrecy. I remember when I had to go and ask your grandfather about marrying your mother . . . My knees were shaking, I was so scared of him!'

'Pops was a bit of a tyrant and a grump, I have to admit,' she laughed.

'But thank heaven he said yes, otherwise Ruth and I would have had to elope!'

'And at least when we came to marry, Bill, we were two middle-aged birds who'd been through it all before!' said Carole softly, squeezing his hand.

'I'm a lucky man,' added her dad, 'to have found love again.'

'Two is so much better than one,' Carole agreed. 'Kim, I'm so glad that you and Luke have found each other.'

'Thank you, Carole,' Kim said, understanding exactly what she meant. She was so glad that her dad had found Carole and that they made each other happy.

Her dad and Luke's dad got on like a house on fire. Molly came over to join them all as they chatted together over plates of food.

Gina and Paul arrived with a big chocolate birthday cake.

'My contribution to the party,' she said, placing it carefully in the kitchen before they got some beers and headed out to the garden.

'Enjoying yourself?' asked Luke.

'It's the best night ever!' she said, kissing him to huge cheers from all around.

'It's okay! We're engaged!'

Everyone sang 'Happy Birthday' loudly as Kim blew out the candles on her cake. The party went on for hours and they stayed outside, as it was such a warm, still night. Luke's friend Alan had brought along his guitar and soon everyone was singing Dubliners and Beatles and Thin Lizzy and Frames songs. It was nearly morning before she and Luke eventually got to bed.

On Sunday Molly had organized a late lunch for Kim's family and her friends from Dublin before they went back, but now Luke's family were invited too.

'They have all got to get used to each other,' remarked Luke as he shaved and pulled on his pale-blue shirt.

Molly had set out two long tables on the terrace, the large canvas parasols open as the sun streamed down on them all. Kim was delighted actually to get time to talk to everyone properly. Emma and Jake were leaving for Australia in two weeks' time and she would miss her cousin.

'We'll be back,' Emma promised. 'We just want to see a bit of the world before we settle down to our careers.'

'Go and enjoy Sydney and Melbourne and the Barrier Reef and New Zealand and Fiji for the year,' Kim urged. 'I had a wonderful time there and still think about it.'

'I'm going to really miss her,' admitted Molly, getting a bit tearful.

'I promise to bring her back home safely,' Jake reassured her.

'Tell us about the wedding plans,' urged Evie and Lisa, coming over to sit beside Kim.

'For heaven's sake – give us a bit of time! We've only just got engaged!'

'So it won't be till next year or so?'

'No,' she said firmly. 'The one thing Luke and I have decided is that we are definitely not waiting a whole year to get married. We just want to get on with our lives.'

Later that night they collapsed on the sofa together, exhausted.

'Why does everyone keep asking about the wedding?' she yawned.

'It could drive you mad!' complained Luke.

'I know. At the party Jenny was talking to me about themes and flowers for a wedding.'

'Don't mind her!'

'She's a florist – it's her business,' she reminded him. 'My job is to try and help her sell them! But maybe she's right – we do need to start thinking about what kind of wedding we both want.'

She looked up and realized that Luke was fast asleep and snoring.

Chapter Seventy-six

Gina still found it hard to believe that Norah Cassidy had been so generous to her. She and Paul debated long and hard over what to spend the money on, torn between setting up a college fund for the boys, taking a big family holiday of a lifetime, or just putting the money in a high-earning interest account. With her inheritance from Norah there was a very real chance that she would be able to rent or put a down-payment on a small café or restaurant of her own. It was something she still really wanted and dreamed of.

She had found the perfect place but was unsure how to approach it. Molly had been so good to her and given her so much business already over the past few months, but Gina had no idea how she would react to this proposal.

'You have to say it!' urged Paul. 'She will understand – I'm sure she will.'

Mossbawn was busy with the O'Flynn family gathering, Molly and Kim trying to make sure everything ran smoothly.

'Gina, did you see the plans of the maze anywhere?' asked Kim. 'It's time for the big treasure hunt now!'

'I think I saw them on top of the piano in the drawing room,' Gina replied, laughing and going to look for them.

Molly was outside cutting flowers for the hall and the tables for tomorrow's welcome dinner.

'Here, Gina – please take these blue delphiniums and some roses. I just need to get some more gyp to add to the vase.'

Gina filled her arms with the flowers, bringing them back into the kitchen as Molly followed after her.

'They all look lovely! The garden is really at its best. You won't believe it, but two gardening clubs wanted to come to visit. Kim set it up for next Saturday morning. She thinks I should consider opening the gardens next month and for a few months of the year. I know gardeners – they just love to ramble around places like this and compare them to their own gardens and get ideas, and of course we have the kitchen garden, and the rose garden and the lavender walk and the borders to explore. The club asked if we could give them morning coffee or a lunch. Did you ever?' she laughed. 'Where would we put them? In the drawing room?'

'Actually, Molly, Kim mentioned it to me and that is something I wanted to talk to you about.' Gina hesitated.

'The garden?'

'No,' she explained. 'I mean, maybe it is something we should consider – opening a café here in Mossbawn and serving afternoon teas, and lunches, and probably morning coffees.'

'A café! Where would we put it?' Molly laughed.

'There are the old stables and outbuildings. They are totally separate from the house and yet overlook part of the garden,' Gina said calmly. 'I'm sure they could be converted to tea rooms or a café.'

'But they haven't been used for anything except storage for years.'

'I know – I store some of the tables and chairs, and wine and all kinds of things there, but everything is bone dry and I'm sure you could convert a part of them the way you have done with your cottage.'

'But why? Why bother?' asked Molly, flummoxed.

'I believe a café here could do very well. There's a big gap for people living locally since Norah's café closed, as there's nowhere to go for a lunch or a scone or afternoon tea, or to just meet for a coffee, and I'm sure if you open the garden to visitors they would also enjoy it. I certainly would be interested in opening and running a place like that.'

'Gina, do you mean it?' asked Molly, sitting down at the table. 'But we're not even in the village.'

'There is the Maids' Gate – the pedestrian entrance that practically opens next to the lane beside the chemist. People could use that if they are walking, otherwise there is plenty of parking.'

440

'You've obviously been thinking about this!'

'Ever since Norah's closed, I've been thinking about it and trying to find somewhere to rent.'

'But what about catering for our weddings and events here?' asked Molly.

'That wouldn't change at all, I promise. With only a function or so a week I can easily manage to do both,' she reassured her. 'If anything, it could be useful, as we could put in a larger kitchen and also do some smaller events within the café.'

'I understand what you are saying, Gina, but Mossbawn is not some big stately pile. It's just an old Irish country house.'

'Molly, please think about it. There is nowhere decent to go for a nice coffee or a lunch close by – you know that.'

'That's true, and it's such a nuisance,' agreed Molly. 'You either end up having lunch in the hotel or the Kilfinn Inn, or staying at home having coffee.'

'A café set here in a courtyard garden, only a few minutes' walk from the village, would do well. I know it would,' she insisted.

'Let me have a think about it,' said Molly, seriously. 'I don't know if I can afford to take on something like that, or if I even want to.'

'I'm willing to invest or rent from you – whatever you want,' Gina found herself offering.

That night, as she lay in Paul's arms, she told him what had happened.

'I know that I said far too much. I should have done

it slowly, taken my time approaching her. I've probably blown it.'

'Molly Hennessy is a good woman, kind as they come, but remember she's smart too and wants only the best for Mossbawn,' he counselled. 'Don't rush her. Just see what happens after those visitors turn up next week.'

Gina knew he was right. She just had to be patient.

Chapter Seventy-seven

So Gina had taken Paul's advice and been patient, and as the summer days turned to autumn Molly finally made her decision.

'Gina, I think you are right about the café. Having somewhere to have a cup of tea or light lunch here in the gardens would be a great addition to Mossbawn House and to the village,' she said decisively. 'I think we should both put on our thinking caps and talk to Trish. She's the architect and will know what she can do with the old stables in terms of design and costs. And of course Paul would do all the building work.'

Gina was so happy she felt like jumping up and down like a little kid. She couldn't wait to phone Paul to tell him the good news.

'We want the café to be a place people really want to come to,' Molly continued, serious. 'Not just in the summer, but all year round. They need to feel relaxed meeting their friends or comfortable to just have a bowl of soup on their own.'

'Molly, I've been thinking of nothing else for months,' Gina admitted, 'and I've lots of ideas for what we can do with the stables and a new kitchen that I'll talk to Trish about. However, the most important thing is to keep the garden element as much as possible.'

The following few months were hectic, with everyone trying to agree a design with Trish and waiting for planning permission to come through.

The house itself had been hired by the film company for six weeks' shooting and Gina found herself catering for the crew and cast, doing everything from early breakfasts to late dinners and a huge number of warming tasty meals twice a day.

Mossbawn's calendar of events for the rest of the year was also beginning to fill up and Gina was working harder than ever, but loving every minute of it. The fact that she would now have a business of her own was exciting. She was taking a ten-year lease on the new café premises. Both she and Molly were investing in the business, and Molly would take a percentage of the profit once the café began to make one.

As March turned to April, the days brightened and Molly had decided to open Mossbawn's gardens for a few months of the year, closing them early if they were hosting a function.

The old stables were now transformed into a bright

café area. The original stone walls had all been preserved and Trish had designed an inner courtyard with a glass roof which connected the old tack and harness room to the rest of the buildings. Molly was delighted to be able to start planting all around it.

'That courtyard is small, I know,' the architect explained, 'but on wet Irish days it will ensure the café still feels open air.'

The back of the stables opened up by simple drop-down windows and garden doors that gave out on to a large new terraced area that Molly was planting with pretty cottage-garden plants and year-round cover.

The old wash-house was now a modern kitchen. Gina stood there, wishing that Norah Cassidy could see the place. She had sunk practically every penny of her inheritance from Norah into the new venture. They had talked about a big family holiday to Disney World, but had settled instead on a weekend trip to Eurodisney in Paris. The boys, Paul and herself had had a great time!

For the new café she was re-using as many of Norah's old tables and chairs as possible. They had been sanded down and repainted in soft Farrow & Ball colours, which worked well with the old stone walls. She had worked out a simple menu and would use as much produce from the kitchen garden as possible.

As the opening of the Garden Café neared, Gina was nervous as hell that people mightn't turn up, or that she had got it wrong and it would all be a disaster.

'It will all be fine!' said Paul soothingly. 'The café is lovely.' But the night before the café opened she tossed and turned, unable to sleep, worried that things would go disastrously wrong . . .

She and Inga were there bright and early to bake fresh scones and cakes to welcome visitors. They chopped up vegetables for the soup of the day, rolled out pastry for the goats' cheese tarts and cut up chicken for the chicken-and-leek bake. The place looked wonderful and she thanked heaven that the day was dry and fairly bright. Molly had put little glass vases of fresh flowers on each table and Gina had hung a framed photograph of Norah Cassidy behind the counter.

They opened at eleven and Gina could hardly believe it when Johnny Lynch walked through the door and took a seat near the window. He ordered his usual: a scone and a pot of tea.

'It's on the house this morning, Johnny!' she laughed, giving him a welcome hug.

The old man was like a good-luck charm, she thought, as a load of her regulars came along to wish her well too. The café was kept busy all morning and was packed out at lunchtime. Everyone wanted a table and a chance to eat at the Garden Café.

Chapter Seventy-eight

Molly sat in the rose garden. This garden, which had possessed and obsessed her, was finally finished. When she had begun this garden she had been so sad, so full of grief and loneliness. She had buried herself in the task of restoring it. Now there were roses everywhere, old roses and new roses covering the stone walls and the frames and the painted gazebo with the archways, creating a rose bower just like she had imagined, pink and peach and blush-coloured roses in bloom everywhere, and the garden bringing her immense joy.

Here the roses were protected from damage by wind and bad weather; the garden was sunny and warm even in winter. She watched the buds and leaves of each rose bush protectively, ready to deal with black spot or aphids or fungus. Each one needed care, and they rewarded her well for the attention they received. She was especially proud of the old roses, planted long before her time, that had suddenly rallied, returned to vigour and begun to grow again, sending their new shoots and tendrils skyward as they reached for the sun and light, producing buds and blooming in their heavy, blowsy fashion like old film stars and divas attracting the attention.

It was peaceful and quiet here, away from everything, and Molly loved to sit and read or just relax, the way the gardener who had first marked out this patch must have done. Roses filled the herbaceous borders and she had created separate beds for cutting, with rows of coloured red and yellow and cream and pink roses that bloomed again and again.

One rose in particular intrigued her. Neither Paddy nor she could find a name for it. She searched David Austin and numerous other rose catalogues. Gabriel, the rose expert, had visited and was equally miffed, declaring he'd never seen a rose like it with its perfect bowl of a flowerhead and rich pink colour, tinged almost purple as it turned. Gabriel had taken photos of it and was testing growing it. She had managed to propagate it and planted another one near the gate and also one beside her cottage. Gabriel was certain that it was a new, unregistered variety and she had secretly named it Rosa Constance Moore, convinced that Charles Moore must have developed and bred this special rose for his beloved wife. It was a Mossbawn rose – something very special.

The roses were wonderful this year, but she knew that

with hard work and care and attention every year they would get better. She was so glad to be still living here, part of it all.

Mossbawn House was building up a good reputation and each event they held was different. Molly was surprised by how much money a wedding or launch or anniversary celebration could earn. Gina was an absolute star at providing the type of meal or buffet that their clients wanted, and Molly was delighted to see the drawing and dining rooms busy again the way they should be. She enjoyed showing people around the house and the garden, telling them stories of the previous owners and their families. Kim's research had been meticulous and there were family trees, portraits and photographs all on display now in the library.

When she had opened the gardens a few months ago she had been filled with trepidation, but to her delight twenty-six members of her local gardening club had arrived to support her. And it had been a success. Now gardeners and enthusiasts were discovering Mossbawn and visiting it along with their families, or those just interested in having a stroll around the lawn and beds and walled gardens.

At first when Gina Sullivan had suggested opening the Garden Café, Molly had been very sceptical about it, but Gina had been really determined to make the new venture work. Even in the few short weeks since it had opened it had become not only a great attraction for visitors to the garden but, more importantly, had become a café used by all the locals in Kilfinn.

'I told you it would work!' Gina had declared proudly. 'People need to have some place close by to go for coffees and cakes, or soup and a sandwich, or to have a tasty lunch with their friends.'

Sitting in the garden with the sun warm on her skin, Molly closed her eyes. She wondered what David would have made of it all. Of all the changes she'd made, moving out of the house and into the cottage. Of her running a business that was making a profit. She hoped that he would be proud of her, proud of what she'd done . . .

'Molly – Molly!'

She stirred, realizing that someone was standing in front of her.

'I guessed that I'd find you here,' Rob said, sitting down beside her on the garden bench.

Over the past few months Rob had become part of her life. He was easy company and they got on really well. She liked having him around; he was a good man, kind and loving. They were two lonely people who had somehow had the good fortune to find each other.

She had been surprised when Rob had confessed to her that he had spoken to David on the phone and had kept in touch regularly with him by email.

'I was his early-morning meeting that day . . . the day he died. I was the client he was meant to see. David was handling the legal work on the Irish end for the project,' he had told her miserably. 'I was looking forward to meeting him, this guy I'd been chatting to and emailing so much. When he didn't turn up and I heard what had happened . . .'

She had sat taking it in. Rob hadn't been to blame for David's death – nobody was to blame. But in a strange way it had comforted her that Rob and David had actually spoken.

She would never ever get over losing David. He would always be her husband, the father of her daughters, her very best friend. But Rob was different, very different from him – which she suspected was a good thing. With Rob she felt young again, ready to try out new things. She liked being romanced and told how beautiful she was. Their relationship was new and fresh, but she suspected it was one that would last.

At first she had told him it was far too soon for her even to consider a relationship, but Rob had been tenacious, bit by bit seeing her and working his way into her heart. He was full of plans. He wanted to bring her to see the Grand Canyon, to watch the Northern Lights, to swim in the Barrier Reef . . .

Now he took her hand in his, his grip strong and warm as they sat together in the sunshine, talking and laughing.

Chapter Seventy-nine

Kim looked in the mirror. She loved her dress. She had found the fitted off-white lace wedding gown with its satin-ribbon trim in a designer's small studio. With its old-fashioned vintage look it made her feel like a princess. Her simple veil was held in place with her mother's antique diamante-studded tiara. Her long hair had been blow-dried, with part of it pinned up, her make-up was classic and natural, and she carried a beautiful hand-tied bouquet of roses from her aunt Molly's garden.

'You look beautiful! Truly beautiful!' said her father, standing behind her. 'So like your mum!'

'And you look very handsome, Dad!' she said, hugging him.

Liz and Evie, her two bridesmaids, wore matching dusky-pink chiffon dresses and high heels. Three months ago she had discovered that both her brides-maids were pregnant and expecting within a few weeks of each other! A dress disaster threatened, except for the handiwork of Mary Cummings, the local seamstress, who had managed to alter both dresses to fit.

'Time to put your shoes on, Ava!' ordered Liz, as she slipped the satin ballet pumps on to the little flower girl, who was running around pretending to be a fairy.

'I'm a princess like Auntie Kim,' she boasted, grabbing her posy of flowers.

'The car is outside,' called Molly, running in to make sure the bride was okay. 'You don't want to keep Luke waiting!'

Standing at the door of Kilfinn's church, Kim took a deep, wobbly breath and held her dad's arm. The church was packed with people she loved – her family and friends and Luke's family. Liz and Evie and little Ava walked slowly ahead of her as the choir sang and the organ played. She smiled, her dad steadying her as, overwhelmed with emotion and happiness, they began to walk slowly up the centre aisle of the church. She felt an immense wave of love and support and goodwill welcoming her as she took one step after another.

Luke was there at the top of the church, standing waiting for her, his eyes lighting up when he saw her, his gaze holding hers. She was tempted to run up into his arms, but she kept her eyes steady on him as she walked nearer and nearer, her dad hugging her at the top as she let go of him and took Luke's hand.

Father Darragh welcomed them to the church and

began the wedding ceremony as they lit the candles that would symbolize each of them and their marriage. Kim's eyes filled with tears as they pledged their love and commitment to each other and Luke slipped the simple wedding band on her finger. She knew as he kissed her and took her hand that they would never ever let each other go.

Standing at the door of the church afterwards, they talked to everyone, all their guests congratulating them, everyone taking photos and hugging and laughing in the sunshine before they headed back to Mossbawn for their reception.

As they drove up the avenue to the old house, Kim felt as if all her dreams had come true. Ever since she was a little girl Mossbawn had symbolized happiness to her. Even when she was lost and scared and sad, the old house had comforted her, made her feel safe. Now here she was with Luke, her handsome husband, beside her, celebrating their marriage in the place she loved.

Molly, Gina and Grace had all gone to immense trouble for her wedding and she smiled, seeing that there were flowers everywhere. Pink roses cascaded down the front of the house along with full-headed creeping hydrangeas. The garden and grounds were immaculate – Paddy and Tommy had been on duty all week. Their photographer, Leo, made sure they got lots of photos around her favourite spots, including the woods where she had climbed the tall beech trees and down by the fountain in the pond.

Molly had insisted they use the rose garden for the

drinks reception, as it was enclosed and sheltered, and a sun-trap. There were the painted benches, and tables and chairs had been set up so everyone could relax. There was champagne and prosecco and chilled beers, and Inga and Brendan carried around trays of canapés as guests chatted and everyone enjoyed the party.

Molly herself, in an expensive beige lace dress and jacket, moved around the garden ensuring that everyone had a drink, introducing people and welcoming them to Mossbawn. Rob Hayes was there too, relaxed and at ease, chatting to everyone. Kim was so glad to see her aunt happy again. In his own quiet way, Rob was becoming a part of her life.

Kim couldn't believe that she was actually married now. She kept touching the band on her finger to remind herself. It was as if she was in a perfect dream.

'You are such a beautiful bride,' said Liz, teary-eyed. 'I can't believe it – my little sister married and to the nicest guy ever!'

'I can hardly believe it myself,' she admitted. 'If someone had said to me two years ago that I would have met Luke and found love, and be standing here in my wedding dress with all the people I care about around me, I would have thought they were mad!'

'Life's funny, isn't it?' agreed Liz. 'We thought we were a two-child family. We were happy with that, and now there is going to be a new little person in our lives. We'll probably move – Joe's always been dying to buy an old house, a doer-upper, outside Dublin. Then crèche fees will be enormous, so it makes no sense for me to keep working full-time. Maybe I'll just work part-time, or try something else – work from home if we have the space. Can you imagine that?'

'It sounds good,' Kim encouraged her, relieved, as Liz had been looking so tired and stressed lately.

Looking around, she could see that Luke's mum and dad were chatting away with her dad and Carole. It was great that both families got on really well together. She looked over at her cousin. Grace had asked her if she could bring Andrew Lynch from the hotel to the wedding. He was a friend of Luke's, and even though he was a few years older than Grace they seemed pretty keen on each other.

'He's a hundred times nicer than all the guys I know from college,' Grace had confided, 'and he always makes me feel I'm special!'

'Hey, Mrs Ryan!' called Evie, sipping a glass of sparkling water and ice. 'How does it feel to be a married lady?'

'I recommend it totally,' she giggled. 'It feels wonderful!'

'Fergus and I might try it once this little pumpkin is born.'

'I can't believe you're going to be a mum in a few months!'

'Scary thought!'

'No, you'll be a brilliant mum. Really cool, doing art and finger-painting and making puppets and sand stuff.'

'I know it's going to be mega fun, and Fergus wants us to do this big bed thing where we all sleep together.'

'Maybe you should talk to Liz about that!' she teased.

The party moved inside to the orangery, the room lit up by candles, with vases filled with roses and garden flowers everywhere. Everyone stood and cheered as she and Luke entered to walk to their places at the top table.

The meal went perfectly. Gina had outdone herself with a fabulous menu that everyone was raving about. Then it was time for the speeches. Kim's dad said how he wished her mum had been here today to see their beautiful daughter marry and told everyone how proud he was of her, adding how glad he was that she had found the man to love her and care for her the way she deserved. Luke's dad, Tom, recalled a few tales about Luke's antics and warmly welcomed Kim to their enlarging family. Luke, clear and strong, stood up beside her, telling the world how much he had loved her from practically the first day they met.

'I fell headlong, hook, line and sinker for Kim the minute I saw those amazing blue eyes!' he admitted. 'I knew then that I couldn't let this girl ever get away.'

Slightly nervous, Kim stood up, Luke holding her hand, as she said a few words about how happy she was and that she had felt when she met Luke that the missing piece of her heart had been found. She thanked her family and his. 'And I specially want to thank Molly for not only being the best aunt ever, but for being like a second mum to me over the past few years. She has always made me feel welcome here and there is no other place in the world I would want to get married except in Mossbawn.'

Everyone clapped madly and then it was Luke's brother Justin's turn to give his best-man speech. He had everyone rolling around laughing as he told them about the misdeeds of his younger brother and the night he had borrowed his boat to propose.

As the sun went down and darkness fell, the party got into full swing, everyone up dancing as the lamps were lit and fairy lights twinkled everywhere. Luke held Kim in his arms as they danced together.

The sun was coming up as the wedding party finally ended, Kim and Luke, arm in arm, saying goodnight to all their friends.

'I love you,' said Luke.

'And I love you,' replied Kim.

She was bursting with happiness, more fulfilled and contented and happier than she could ever have imagined. She wasn't even tired, for today had been the most perfect day ever – and today was only the beginning . . .

Acknowledgements

Thanks to my husband, James, for being my rock and support.

Thanks to my children, Mandy, Laura, Fiona and James, my sons-in-law Michael Hearty and Michael Fahy, and my two pets, Holly and Sam Hearty. You all make my life a joy.

Special thanks to my wonderful editor, Linda Evans, for her enthusiasm, dedication and work on my books.

My sincere gratitude to Joanne Williamson, Vivien Garrett, Brenda Updegraff, and everyone at Transworld London for all their work and input on this book and their support and encouragement. And thanks to Sarah Whittaker for the lovely cover.

Grateful thanks also for my agent Caroline Sheldon for her constant belief in my writing and the excitement that working together on every new book brings!

For Eoin McHugh in Transworld Ireland's Dublin office.

For Simon and Gill Hess, Declan Heaney and Helen Gleed O'Connor and everyone at Gill Hess, Dublin, for making it all seem easy and looking after me and my books so well!

For booksellers everywhere . . . thanks for bringing my books and readers together.

For bookshops . . . what would we do without you?

For Sarah Conroy . . . for all her patience and kindness.

To all the gardeners and gardening writers and columnists that have inspired me over the years . . . thank you so much.

Arianne Menut . . . thanks for helping to keep my own garden in shape.

For Sarah Webb, Martina Devlin, Larry O'Loughlin and Don Conroy and all my fellow writers . . . thanks for just being there!

For my readers . . . thanks for making writing such a pleasure.

A Taste for Love
Marita Conlon-McKenna

Alice loves to cook. She believes the secret of good food is to cook with passion.

Her love affair with cookery began in her parent's seaside hotel, followed by her training in Paris and her years working in one of Dublin's finest restaurants. But when she marries Liam she is happy to hang up her chef's hat and cook for her family and friends instead.

But now she's cooking for one!

Her marriage to Liam over, Alice finds herself struggling not only emotionally but also financially. It is high time she learns to stand on her own two feet and begin again . . . urged on by her friends Alice decides to open a cookery school in her Monkstown home.

'The School for Cooks' opens its doors and Alice begins to teach a group of total strangers to create food that is tasty and delicious . . . And in the comfort of the kitchen these strangers find that there is much to learn, not just about baking and sautéing but about recipes for life.

Three Women
Marita Conlon-McKenna

Love and its consequences last a lifetime . . .

Kate Cassidy is celebrating twenty-five years of marriage to Paddy. But the secret she has kept all this time is about to be discovered.

Erin Harris has always known that she is different from the rest of her family. Over the years she has put the pieces together and now is determined to find out who she really is and where she comes from.

Nina Harris has put her marriage and family before everything else. But now she must learn to accept her daughter's decision to go and search for a woman she doesn't know.

There is no escaping the past. As Kate, Erin and Nina face the truth about what happened so many years before, each is given a second chance for love and happiness.

Mother of the Bride

Marita Conlon-McKenna

A SUMMER WEDDING – WHAT COULD
BE MORE PERFECT?

Everyone knows that **Amy** and **Dan** are made for each other.
So when they announce their engagement their families are
over the moon, especially Amy's mother **Helen**.

What could be more exciting than planning a daughter's
wedding?

But as the countdown to the Big Day begins, and mother and
daughter throw themselves into creating the wedding of their
dreams, not everyone's prepared for the commotion this
involves.

Bride-to-be Amy sees her best laid wedding plans start to
unravel and things go from bad to worse, as Helen struggles
to pick up the pieces and get her family back on track.

Amy and Helen each discover what love and marriage is all
about . . . but is it too late?

It's not easy being a mother, let alone the *Mother of the Bride*!